ᒫᑯᓯ ᑲᓗᐊᒃ

ᐅᓂᑉᑳᖅᑐᐊᑦ ᐊᕐᕕᐊᓂᑦ

Mark Kalluak's TRADITIONAL STORIES FROM ARVIAT

ᒫᑯᓯ ᑲᓗᐊᒃ

MARK KALLUAK

Inhabit Media Inc.

Iqaluit • Toronto

Published by Inhabit Media Inc.
www.inhabitmedia.com

Inhabit Media Inc. (Iqaluit) 2434 Paurngaq Cres., Iqaluit, NU, X0A 2H0
(Toronto) 612 Mount Pleasant Rd., Toronto, Ontario, M4S 2M8

Editors: Neil Christopher, Jaypeetee Arnakak, and Anne Fullerton
Art Directors: Danny Christopher and Astrid Arijanto
Designer: Fabiana Marino

We acknowledge the support of the Canada Council for the Arts for our publishing program.

This project was made possible in part by the Government of Canada.

ISBN: 978-1-77227-511-7

Printed in Canada

Library and Archives Canada Cataloguing in Publication
Title: Maakusi Kaluaq Maakusi Kaluaq unipkaaqtuat Arvianit / Maakusi Qaluaq = Mark Kalluak's traditional stories from Arviat / Mark Kalluak.
Other titles: Mark Kalluak's traditional stories from Arviat | Uunipkaaqtuat Arvianit | Traditional stories from Arviat
Names: Kalluak, Mark, 1942-2011, author.
Description: Text in Inuktitut and in English.
Identifiers: Canadiana 20230474527 | ISBN 9781772275117 (hardcover)
Subjects: LCSH: Inuit—Nunavut—Arviat—Folklore. | LCSH: Inuit—Nunavut—Arviat—Social life and customs. | LCSH: Folklore—Nunavut—Arviat. | LCSH: Tales—Nunavut—Arviat.
Classification: LCC E99.E7 K35 2023 | DDC 398.2089/9712071958—dc23

NBES
Nunavut
Canada
Canada Council for the Arts Conseil des Arts du Canada
Canadian Heritage Patrimoine canadien

ᒫᑯ ᑲᓗᐊᕐᒃ ᐅᓂᑉᑳᖅᑐᐊᑦ ᐊᕐᕕᐊᓂᑦ

Mark Kalluak's TRADITIONAL STORIES FROM ARVIAT

ᒫᑯ ᑲᓗᐊᕐᒃ

MARK KALLUAK

ᐃᓗᓕᖏᑦ
TABLE OF CONTENTS

ᓇᓗᓇᐃᖅᓯᔾᔪᑦ
FOREWORD

ᒫᑯᓯ ᑲᓗᐊᖅ ᐃᓅᓚᐅᖅᐳᖅ ᐱᓪᓚᑦᑖᖅᑐᓂ ᓱᓕᓪᓗᓂᓗ ᐃᓄᐃᑦ ᖃᐅᔨᒪᔭᑐᖃᖕᖏᓐᓂᒃ; ᐱᒃᑯᓕᕆᓚᐅᙱᑦᑐᖅ, ᐃᓅᖃᑎᒥᓂᒃ ᐃᑉᐱᒍᓱᑦᑎᐊᓚᐅᖅᑐᖅ, ᐱᓐᓇᕆᔭᖃᑦᑎᐊᖅᑐᓂᓗ ᓇᒻᒥᓂᒥᓂᒃ, ᓄᓇᖅᑲᑎᒥᓂᒃ, ᐅᖃᐅᓯᕐᒥᓂᒃ, ᐊᒻᒪᓗ ᐱᖅᑯᓯᒥᓂᒃ. ᔪᓚᐃ 18, 1942-ᒥ ᐃᓅᔪᕕᓂᖅ ᖁᕕᐅᔭᕐᒥ, ᐊᕐᕕᐊᑦ ᐅᐊᖕᓇᖅᐸᓯᐊᓂ, ᐊᖓᔪᖅᑳᖏᓐᓄᑦ ᔫᓐ ᑰᒐᖅ ᐊᒻᒪᓗ Hᐃᐊᓚᓐ ᐸᐅᕐᖓᑦ ᑰᒐᖅ.

Mark Kalluak lived and personified the *Inuit Qaujimajatuqangit* (IQ; traditional Inuit knowledge) principles authentically and genuinely: he was humble, thoughtful, and very caring towards his family, his community, his language, and his culture. He was born on July 18, 1942, in Qurviujat, north of Arviat, Nunavut, to parents John Kuugaq and Helen Paurngat Kuugaq.

ᓱᕈᓯᐅᓪᓗᓂ ᐋᓐᓂᐊᑖᕐᓂᕐᒥ ᐋᓐᓂᐊᕕᓕᐊᖅᑎᑕᐅᔭᕕᓂᖅ ᖃᓪᓗᓈᑦ ᓄᓇᖓᓐᓄᑦ. ᒫᑯᓯ ᑕᐃᑉᓯᒪᓂ ᐃᖅᑲᐅᒪᔪᖅ ᐃᓕᑉᐸᓪᓕᐊᓂᐅᓪᓗᓂ ᐃᒻᒥᓂᒡᓗ ᑲᒪᒋᔭᓐᓇᖅᓯᓂᐅᓪᓗ ᖁᒪᐃᑳᓪᓚᖕᒪᑦ ᐊᖏᔪᖅᑳᒃᑯᖏᓐᓂᒃ ᐊᖏᕐᕋᕐᒥᓂᓗ. ᖃᐅᔨᑦᑕᐅᑎᒋᓚᐅᖅᐳᖅ ᐃᒻᒥᓂᒃ ᐸᖅᑭᔭᓇᐊᖅᑲᕐᓂᐊᓕᖅᑐᖅ. ᐱᖅᑯᓯᖅᑲᑎᒋᙱᑕᖏᓐᓄᑐᐊᖑᙱᑦᑐᖅ ᐃᓕᔭᐅᓚᐅᖅᐳᖅ, ᑭᓯᐊᓂᓕᑦᑕᐅᖅ ᐅᖃᐅᓯᕐᒥᒃ ᓄᑖᕐᒥᒃ ᐃᓕᑦᑕᕆᐊᖃᓕᓚᐅᖅᐳᖅ. ᑕᒪᓐᓇ ᐅᖃᐅᑎᒋᓚᐅᖅᐹ “ᓵᕐᓗ ᐃᓅᓯᕐᒧᑦ ᓄᑖᕐᒧᑦ ᐅᐸᒃᑑᔫᕐᓚᐅᖅᐳᖅ.”

As a child, he was stricken with polio and sent to a hospital in the south. Mark remembered this experience as a time of learning and becoming stronger as a person because he was suddenly separated from his parents and home. He realized almost immediately that he had to learn how to take care of himself. Not only was he placed in an entirely different culture, but he also had to learn a new language. He said that it was like “stepping into a different life.”

ᒫᑯᓯ ᐊᑯᓂᐊᓗᒃ ᐋᓐᓂᐊᕕᖕᒦᓚᐅᖅᐳᖅ, ᐃᓘᓐᓂᒃᑯᓪᓗ ᐃᓯᒪᓕᖅᐸᓚᐅᖅᐳᖅ ᐊᖏᖅᓚᐅᖅᓯᒪᔾᔭᕈᓐᓃᖅᑐᒋᑦᓗᓂ. ᐋᓐᓂᐊᕕᓕᐊᖅᑎᑕᐅᒐᒥ ᖃᓪᓗᓈᑎᑐᑦ

ᐅᖃᓪᓚᒍᓐᓇᓚᐅᙱᑦᑎᐊᖅᑐᖅ, ᑭᓯᐊᓂᓕ ᖃᐅᔨᒪᓚᐅᖅᐳᖅ ᐅᖃᕈᓐᓇᕋᓗᐊᖅᐸᑦ ᐋᓐᓂᐊᓯᐅᖅᑎᓄᑦ ᓘᒃᑖᓄᓪᓗ ᐊᖏᕋᕈᒪᓂᕋᓗᓂ, ᐊᖏᕋᖅᑎᑕᐅᔾᔮᙱᑦᑐᖅ.

Mark was in the hospital for a very long time, and he often thought that he would never see home again. He did not speak a word of English when he was sent away, but he realized that even if he could tell the nurses and doctors that he wanted to go home, they would not let him.

ᑭᓯᐊᓂᓕ, ᓈᓚᑦᑎᐊᕐᓂᖅ ᕿᓄᐃᓵᕈᓐᓇᕐᓂᕐᓗ ᑭᓇᐅᓂᖓᓄᑦ ᑐᙵᕝᕙᓚᐅᖅᐳᖅ. ᐃᓱᒪᓇᖅᐳᖅ ᕿᓄᖅᑲᓚᐅᙱᓐᓂᖓᓂᒃ ᐋᓐᓂᐊᕝᕕᖕᒥᑦᑐᓂ. ᒫᑯᓯ ᐅᐃᒻᒪᑐᐃᓐᓇᖅᑲᓚᐅᙱᑦᑐᖅ; ᐃᓱᒪᑦᑎᐊᖅᑲᓚᐅᖅᑐᖅ, ᑕᐃᒫᒃ ᐃᓕᓐᓂᐊᖅᑎᑕᐅᓯᒪᒐᒥ ᐊᖓᔪᖅᑳᖏᓐᓄᑦ, ᐊᒻᒪᓗ ᐸᓇᓱᒍᒪᓕᓚᐅᖅᐳᖅ ᑕᒪᑐᒥᖓ ᐃᓕᓐᓂᐊᕈᑎᖃᕈᒪᓪᓗᓂ. ᑕᐃᒫᒃ ᐃᓱᒪᓕᐅᓚᐅᖅᓯᒪᓂᖓ ᐱᑦᑎᐊᕈᑎᒋᓕᓚᐅᖅᐹ ᐋᓐᓂᐊᕝᕕᖕᒥᑦ ᐊᓂᓯᒪᓕᖅᑐᓂ. ᖃᓪᓗᓈᐅᔭᕈᓐᓇᖅᓯᓐᓂᕐᒥ ᐋᓐᓂᐊᕝᕕᒥᑦᑐᓂ, ᐃᑲᔪᕈᓐᓇᖅᓯᓚᐅᖅᐳᖅ ᐃᓄᐃᑦ ᖃᓪᓗᓈᓪᓗ ᑐᑭᓯᐅᒪᖃᑎᒌᒍᓐᓇᖁᓪᓗᒋᑦ.

However, humility and patience were part of his foundation. It is doubtful that he would have complained. Mark did not react; he responded, as he was taught by his parents, and he decided that he would learn from this experience. This response would serve him well when he got out of the hospital. Because he had learned English while away, he felt he was now able to help both Inuit and *qallunaat* (white people) to communicate with each other.

ᒫᑯᓯ ᐅᖃᐅᓯᓕᕆᔨᐅᓚᐅᖅᐳᖅ ᐱᖁᓯᓕᕆᔨᐅᓪᓗᓂᓗ ᑐᑭᓯᐅᒪᑦᑎᐊᖅᑐᒥ ᐃᓄᐃᑦ ᖃᓪᓗᓈᓪᓗ ᐱᖁᓯᖏᓐᓂᒃ ᐅᖃᐅᓯᖏᓐᓂᓪᓗ. ᐊᓯᒐᓗᐊᖏᓐᓂᒃᑕᐅᖅ ᐃᖅᑲᓇᐃᔭᖅᐸᓚᐅᖅᑐᖅ, ᒫᑯᓯ ᑐᑭᓕᐅᖅᑎᐅᓚᐅᖅᑐᖅ ᑐᓵᔨᐅᓪᓗᓂᓗ, ᐊᒻᒪᓗ ᐃᓕᓭᐃᔨᐅᓪᓗᓂ. ᐃᓄᐃᑦ ᐱᖁᓯᓕᕆᔾᑯᖓᓂ (ICI), ᐃᖅᑲᓇᐃᔭᖅᑎᖅᑲᓚᐅᖅᐳᖅ ᐃᓄᒃᑐᑦ ᐅᖃᐅᓯᓕᕆᔨᒪᕆᐊᓗᖕᒥᒃ ᖃᐅᔨᒪᔭᐅᑦᑎᐊᖅᑐᒥᒃ ᔫᓯ ᑯᓱᒐᖅ ᖃᓂᐅᔫᖅᐸᐃᓂᒃ ᖃᓕᐅᔫᖅᐸᐃᓂᓪᓗ ᐱᓕᕆᑦᑐᒋᑦ.

Mark was an Inuit language and cultural specialist with a keen awareness of both Inuit and qallunaat languages and ways. Among other things, Mark worked as an interpreter, translator, and teacher.

At the Inuit Cultural Institute (ICI), he worked with the famed Inuk linguist Jose Kusugaq on the reformation of the dual ICI writing system (*qanniujaaqpait,* or syllabics, and *qaliujaaqpait,* or roman orthography).

ᑎᑎᕋᖅᐸᓚᐅᖅᑐᖅ ᑐᓴᐅᒪᔾᐅᓯᓇᐊᖅᑲᖅᑐᓂᒃ ᑐᑭᓯᒋᐊᖅᑎᑦᑎᔾᔪᑎᓂᒡᓗ, ᐅᖃᓕᒫᒐᓕᐅᖅᐸᓚᐅᖅᑐᖅ, ᐊᒻᒪᓗ ᐅᖃᑦᓚᒃᑎᐅᖃᑦᑕᓚᐅᖅᑐᖅ ᓈᓚᐅᑎᒃᑯᑦ ᐃᓄᐃᑦ ᐱᖅᑯᓯᖏᓐᓂᒃ, ᐅᖃᐅᓯᓯᖏᓐᓂᒃ, ᐃᓕᓐᓂᐊᕐᓂᖏᓐᓂᒡᓗ ᑐᓴᐅᒪᔾᐅᑦᑎᐊᕐᑯᓰᑦᑐᓂ. ᐃᓚᖓᑕ ᐱᖅᑲᓐᓇᓇᓚᐅᖅᑕᖓᑕ ᐱᓕᕆᖅᑲᑎᒋᑦᑐᓂᐅᒡᓗ, ᑖᓄᑦ ᐅᑐᐊᑦᑐᐊᖅ, ᐅᖃᓚᐅᓯᒪᒍᖅ ᐃᓐᓇᐃᑦ ᑲᑎᒪᑎᑦᑐᒋᑦ ᒫᑯᓯᒎᖅ ᖃᐅᔨᒪᓂᓕᐊᓗᒃ ᑐᑭᓯᐅᒪᑦᑎᐊᖅᑐᓂᓗ ᐅᒃᐱᕐᓂᓕᓇᓂᕐᒥᒃ, ᐊᒻᒪᓗᒎ ᕐᑯᕕᐊᒋᕙᒃᐸᐃᑦ ᑕᒪᒃᑯᓂᖓ ᐅᖃᑦᓚᖅᑲᑎᒋᔭᓇᐊᖓ. ᑕᒪᔾᔭᒐᓚᐅᕗᑦ ᓇᓄᓇᐃᖅᓯᕙᑦ ᒫᑯᓯᐅᑉ ᖃᐅᔨᒪᓂᖓᑕ ᐃᑎᓂᐊᓗᐊᓂᒃ ᐱᕕᑐᓂᐊᓗᐊᓂᒡᓗ, ᑐᑭᓯᒋᐊᕋᔅᓯᒪᔭᓕᒫᖏᓂᒃ, ᓴᖅᑭᑎᑦᑎᖖᒋᑦᑑᒐᓗᐊᑦ ᐃᓄᖅᑭᑦᑎᐊᓚᐅᕐᓂᖓᓂᒃ, ᑯᖓᓴᕋᐃᓚᐅᕐᓂᖓᓂᒃ, ᑐᖖᒐᓇᑦᑎᐊᓚᐅᕐᓂᖓᓂᒡᓗ.

He wrote articles and essays for newsletters, he wrote books, and he spoke on local and regional radio shows to promote and talk about Inuit culture, language, and education. One of his close friends and colleagues, Donald Uluadluak, said that Mark had deep spiritual and religious knowledge and insight, and that he loved his private chats with Mark on these matters. All of this speaks of the depth and breadth of Mark's knowledge and insight into all that he examined and reflected upon, if not of his warmth, good humour, and approachability.

ᐃᓕᓐᓂᐊᖅᓂᓕᕆᔩᒃᑯᑦ ᐱᒋᐊᖅᑎᑦᑎᖕᒪᑕ ᐃᓕᓐᓂᐊᒐᒃᓴᓕᐅᕐᕕᖕᒥᒃ ᐊᕐᕕᐊᓂ ᐊᕐᕌᒎᑦ 2000 ᐱᒋᐊᓕᖅᑎᓪᓗᒋᑦ, ᒫᑯᓯ ᓂᕈᐊᖅᑕᐅᖅᑲᑕᐅᓚᐅᖅᐳᖅ ᐃᓄᐃᑦ ᐃᓐᓇᕐᓂᒃ ᐊᑦᓚᒡᕕᖕᒥ ᐃᖅᑲᓇᐃᔭᕐᓂᐊᖅᑐᓂᒃ ᑲᑎᒪᔨᐅᓂᐊᖅᑐᓂᒡᓗ ᐅᖃᐅᔾᔨᒋᐊᖅᑎᓄᑦ. ᑖᒃᑯᐊ ᑲᑎᒪᑎᓪᓗᒋᑦ ᐱᖅᑕᐅᔭᕆᐊᖅᑐᖓ ᖃᐅᔨᓚᐅᖅᓯᒪᕙᕋ ᒫᑯᓯ, ᐅᔾᔨᕆᑦᓗᐊᓚᐅᖅᓯᒪᕙᕋᓗ ᐃᓄᖅᑭᑦᑎᐊᕐᓂᖓ. ᖁᕕᐊᓱᓚᐅᖅᑐᖅ ᐃᓄᐃᑦ ᖃᐅᔨᒪᔭᑐᖅᑲᖏᓐᓂᒃ ᐅᖃᑦᓚᐅᑎᖅᑲᕐᓂᐊᓕᕐᒥᒐᑦᑕ, ᐃᓕᕝᕕᕆᖅᑲᑎᒌᒡᓗᑕᓗ. ᑭᓯᐊᓂᓕ—ᑕᐃᒫ ᐃᓕᖅᑯᓯᖅᑲᕋᒥ—ᓯᓚᑐᓂᖅᑲᓚᐅᖅᐳᖅ ᑭᓯᓕᒫᑦ ᓇᑦᓕᐅᓐᓂᖅᑲᕐᒪᑕ, ᐊᒻᒪᓗ ᐅᑎᓚᐅᖅᐳᖅ ᑲᑎᒪᓂᕐᒧᑦ ᐸᕐᓇᖅᑕᐅᒐᒥ.

When the Department of Education established a curriculum development office in Arviat in the early 2000s, Mark was selected and hired as part of a group of Inuit Elders who would be both support staff and members of an Elders Advisory Committee. I first met him in one of the committee meetings, and I was immediately struck by his dignified, soft-spoken way of interacting. He was eager to discuss the IQ principles and values with me, and for all of us to learn from each other in the meetings. But he—by the way he carried himself—personified the ancient wisdom that everything has its season, and he politely went back to preparing for the meeting.

ᕿᓚᒥᒃᑯᑦ ᑐᑭᓯᓇᖅᓯᖅᑕᐅᑎᒋᓚᐅᖅᐳᖅ ᒫᑯᓯ, ᐃᓛᒃᑯ ᔩ ᖃᕆᑕᖅ, ᐃᑲᔪᑕᐅᓂᖓᓂᒃ ᐃᓐᓇᕐᓄᑦ, ᐊᐅᓚᑦᑎᔨᓄᑦ ᐅᖃᐅᓯᓕᕆᔨᓄᑦ, ᐊᒻᒪᓗ ᐃᓕᓴᐃᔨᓄᑦ. ᐅᓪᓗᒍᓕᒫᖅ ᑕᑎᒋᖃᑦᑕᓚᐅᖅᑕᕗᑦ ᑲᑎᒪᓃᑦ ᐊᐅᓚᓂᖃᑦᑎᐊᖁᑦᑐᒋᑦ. ᐃᓕᑉᐹᑦᓘᓐᓇᖃᑦᑕᓚᐅᖅᑐᖓ ᑳᒃᑯᓂᖓ ᑲᑎᒪᖅᑲᑕᐅᑦᑐᖓ ᒪᑭᑉᐹᑦᑎᖅᐸᒃᑐᖓᓗ ᐱᔪᒪᑎᖅᐹᑦᑎᖅᑐᖓᓗ ᐱᑎᓇᐊᓇᔭᑦᑎᓐᒃ, ᐱᔅᔪᑎᒋᑦᑐᒋᑦ ᐃᓐᓇᐃᑦ ᓄᓇᕗᒻᒦᖕᒎᖅᓯᒪᔪᑦ, ᑳᒃᑯᐊᑦᑕᐅᖅ ᑕᑎᒍᓱᖅᑲᑦᑕᐅᕆᔪᑦ ᒫᑯᓯᒥᒃ. ᒫᑯᓯ ᐃᑳᕈᑎᑦᑎᐊᕙᐅᓚᐅᖅᑐᖅ ᐱᓕᕆᖃᑎᒌᖕᓂᕐᒧᑦ/ᐃᑲᔪᖃᑎᒌᖕᓂᕐᒧᑦ.

I quickly figured out that Mark, along with Joe Karetak, acted as a bridge between the Elders, the senior staff, the language specialists, and the educators. All of us relied on him in part for these meetings to go smoothly. I always learned new things in these sessions and invariably felt revitalized and reinspired in my commitment to what we were doing, in large part because of the Elders from all over Nunavut, who were similarly served by Mark. He was a vital nexus in this *piliriqatigiingniq/ikajuqatigiingniq* (working together) endeavour.

ᒫᑯᓯ ᐅᕙᑦᑎᓐᓂᒃ ᕿᒪᐃᓚᐅᐳᖅ ᒪᐃ 12, 2011-ᒥ, ᐃᓅᓯᓕᒫᕐᒥᓂ ᐱᔨᑦᓯᕋᓂᖅᑲᓚᐅᖅᑐᓂ ᐃᓄᐃᑦ ᐊᓯᖕᒋᓪᓗ ᐃᓕᖅᑯᓯᖅᑎᒌᖕᒋᑦᑐᑦ ᑐᑭᓯᐅᒪᖅᑲᑦᑕᐅᑎᑦᑎᐊᕈᓐᓇᕐᑯᑦᑐᒋᑦ.

Mark left this world on May 12, 2011, after *pijitsirarniq* (a life of service) in the interest of deeper, more equitable understanding between Inuit and the rest of the world.

ᔭᐃᐱᑎ ᐊᕐᓇᑲᒃ

Jaypeetee Arnakak

ᐃᓄᐃᑦ ᐅᓂᒃᑳᖅᑐᐊᖕᒋᑦ
Traditional Inuit Stories

ᕿᓴᕈᐊ'ᓈᖅ ᐊᐃᕕᕐᓗ
QISARUA'NAAQ AND THE WALRUS

ᕿᓴᕈᐊ'ᓈᕉᖅ ᑕᐃᒻᓇ ᓴᐅᓂᖅᑰᕐᒥᐅᑕᕕᓂᖅ ᐱᑦᓗᐊᕕᖕᓂᑯ ᐅᓂᑉᑳᖑᕙᒃᑐᖅ.

Qisarua'naaq was a descendent of the *Hauniqtuurmiut* (the people who live in big bone place), and this true story about him is often told.

ᑕᐃᑉᑯᐊᑑᖅ ᕿᓴᕈᐊ'ᓈᕐᓗ, ᓂᒡᕕᒡᓗ, ᐊᓕᖅᑎᒃᓴᕐᓗ, ᑭᓇᓘᒐᓗᐊᑭᐊᖅ, ᐅᐱᕐᖕᒑᒃᑯᖖᑑᖅ ᐃᓄᐃᑦ. ᖃᔭᐃᓂᒃ ᐊᑐᖅᐸᒃᑎᑦᓗᒥᑦ. ᐊᐃᕕᖅᓯᐅᕐᒪᑕᑑᖅ ᐊᐃᕝᕙᖕᒪᑕᑑᖅ ᕿᓴᕈᐊ'ᓈᖅ ᐊᐃᕕᐅᑉ ᑑᒑᖕᒐᓂᒃ. ᒥᒃᑕᐅᒐᒥ ᐊᓐᓄᑦᑕᓕᖅᐳᖅ ᑑᒑᕐᑯᑎᑖᖅᑲᑕᐅᓯᐊᖅᓱᓂ. ᐊᐃᕕᓕᓇᒃᑲᓐᓂᕈᐊᖅᓱᓂᑑᖅ ᐃᓚᒥᓂᒃ. ᐃᓇᕐᓯᓕᖅᐳᖅ. ᐱᖅᑖᐃᑕᑑᖅ ᑲᒪᒋᑦᑕᐃᓕᓖᑦ ᐅᖃᐅᑎᕚᒃᓱᒍ, "ᐊᐃᕖᑦ ᐊᒥᓱᕘ'ᒪᑕ ᑲᑉᐱᐊᓇᖅᑐᖃᖅᓯᓐᓇᓇᐊᖃᕐᒪᑦ."

The story begins with Qisarua'naaq, Nigvik, Aliqtiksaq, and another person out hunting in the spring, at a time when Inuit were still using *qajait* (kayaks). They came upon walruses, and Qisarua'naaq was angered when the others did not spare him a pair of tusks after a few walruses were captured and butchered. He became aggressive and tried to coax his hunting partners to capture more walruses. His hunting partners refused to give in to his strange behaviour and advised him, "The number of walruses are such that one of them can be dangerous."

ᐃᓂᖅᑎᖅᑕᖅᓗᐊᒑᑦ ᐊᐃᕕᒥᐊᖑᒻᒪᑕᑑᖅ ᐳᒃᑖᓂ. ᕿᓴᕈᐊ'ᓈᕉᖅ ᑐᖅᓱᑖᖅᓱᓂ ᐊᒡᓛᑦ ᑎᐊ'ᓇᐃᓕᐅᖅᑐᖅᑲᒡᓛᑦ ᐊᐃᕖᑦ ᓇᓛᓄᑦ, "ᑑᒐᔾᔭᓂᒃ, ᑑᒐᔾᔭᓂᒃ!"

They kept on discouraging him, as there were walruses everywhere hauled out on ice pans. Qisarua'naaq broke into a hollering fit, yelling at the walruses, "A pair of tusks, give me a pair of tusks!"

ᐃᓚᐃᑕᑑᖅ ᐃᓂᖅᑎᖅᓗᐊᓇᕖᑦ ᑎᐊ'ᓇᓗᐊ'ᔪᐊᖅ ᐃᓕᐅᖅᑯᖖᒥᔅᓱᒍ. ᐊᐃᕝᕕᐊᑭᐊᖅᓱᓂᑑᖅ ᓴᖕᖑᓐᓂᐊᖅᒪᑦ ᑲᒪᒋᒥᐊᓕᖅᐹᑦ. ᖃᔭᖅᑲᐅᖅᒥᑑᖅ

ᖃᔭᖅᑐᖅᓱᑎᒃ ᐊᐃᕝᕕᐊᓕᖅᐳᑦ. ᐊᐃᕕᕐᓄᖖᒎᖅ ᖃᒡᓕᖕᒪᑕ ᕿᓴᕈᐊ'ᓈᕉᖅ ᓯᕗᓪᓕᐅᔪᖅ ᐱᑕᓇᓯᐊᒃᑲᒥᓂᒃ ᓂᕈᐊᖅᓵᕐᓂᐊᖅᓱᓂ.

His hunting partners again tried to calm him down. Since he was so intent on going after the walruses again, the rest finally agreed to go along with his plan. Each had his own *qajaq* (kayak), so they began to chase in their qajait. When they came within striking range of the walruses, Qisarua'naaq took the lead to pick his walrus kill.

ᐊᓯᐃᓛᒎᖅ ᐊᐃᕕᕐᓅᓕᕐᒪᑕ ᕿᓂᖕᒐᕙᖅᑕᖅᑲᕐᓂᕐᒪᑦ ᒥ'ᖕᕆᓚᐅᓕᕐᒪᑦ ᐳᒃᑖᕐᒧᖖᒎᖅ ᖃᓂᑦᑐᒥᐊᕐᒧᑦ ᕿᒪᑎᐊᕐᒪᑕ. ᑖᒻᓇᒎᖅ ᕿᓴᕈᐊ'ᓈᖅ ᑭᖑᕙᕐᒥ ᐊᐃᕕᕐᒧᑦ ᐊᖑᔭᐅᔾᔨᐊᖅᐳᖅ. ᐊᐃᕕᐅᒻᖕᒎᖅ ᐊᖑᒐᒥᐅᒃ ᖃᔮᑕᒎᖅ ᑭᖑᓂᐊᓂᑦ ᐱᒋᐊᖅᓱᒍ ᐊᔭᑉᐹᒃᓱᒍ, ᖃᔮᒎᖅ ᑑᓚᑦᑐᐊᖅᐸᒃᓱᒍ ᐃᓄᖕᒧᓕᐊᕐᒥ. ᕿᓴᕈᐊ'ᓈᕉᖅ ᑎᑭᓐᓇᒥᐅᒃ, ᐃᑎᕐᕕᐊᖅᓱᒍ ᑑᓕᔪᐊᕐᒪᒍ. ᑑᓕᖕᒋᒎᖅ ᐊᒧᖕᒪᑭᒃ ᐊᐅᐸᓪᓚᐅᒥᓪᓗᐊᖅᑐᖕᓘᕐᒪᓂᒎᖅ.

Sure enough, one of the walruses was a dominant aggressive bull and wasted no time in charging after him. The other hunters scrambled for the closest ice pan to escape the attack. Qisarua'naaq fell behind, naturally, when the walrus caught up to him. It bumped the qajaq from the rear, punctured the qajaq with its tusks, and climbed over the qajaq towards the man.

ᐊᒻᒪᔫᖅ ᕿᓴᕈᐊ'ᓈᑉ
ᐃᔨᒋᒃ ᐊᐅ'ᕗᐊᕐᒥᒃ
ᑎᒃᓴᓗᒃᑲᐅᒻᒥᒋᐊᕐᓗᐊᑐᖕᒎᕐᒪᓂᒃ.
ᐊᒻᒪᔫᖅ ᑖᒪ ᐃᓄᒃ
ᐃᕐᑭᕐᔪᑐ ᑑᒎᒃᑲᓐᓂᒻᒫᖅᔪᑐ
ᖃᔮᓂᑦ ᐊᒧᑉᓗᑐ ᐊᖅᑲᐅᑎᕖ.
ᖃᔮᔫᖅ ᐃᓄᕐᑲᕈᓐᓃᕐᒥ
ᐳᒃᑖᒥᐊᓕᖅᓱᓂ. ᕿᓴᕈᐊ'ᓈᑰᖅ
ᐊᐃᕚᕐᔪᑦ ᐊᖅᑲᐅᑎᔭᐅᒐᒥ
ᓄᐃᓐᓇᓲᑦᓯᐊᒥᐊᓕᖅᓱᓂ.

When the walrus reached him, it sunk its tusks between his neck and chest. When it pulled its tusks out, they were totally seeped in red. Also, blood was squirting through Qisarua'naaq's eyes. The bull walrus put its front flippers around the man for another attack with its tusks, pulled him out of his qajaq, and dove under the sea with him. The wrecked qajaq was now just floating around with no occupant. The walrus pulled Qisarua'naaq under the water, and he did not resurface.

ᑖᑉᑯᐊᔫᖅ ᐱᕐᑲᑎᓚᐅᖕᒋᑦ ᐳᒃᑖᕐᒦᕐᓱᑎᒃ ᐅᑕᖅᑭᖅᑲᑦᑖᖅᑐ'ᕗᑖᑦ ᕿᓴᕈᐊ'ᓈᖅ ᐳᒃᑕᕐᓚᓐᓂᐊᙱᒪᖕᒎᑦ. ᓇᐅᔫᓂᓈ. ᖁᓚᓕᕐᓇᖅᓯᑦᑐᐊᖅᓯᓐᓇᕐᒪᙳᖅ, ᐃᓚᖕᒋᙳᖅ ᑖᑉᑯᐊ ᑎᓕᐅᕆᓕᖅᐳᑦ ᓂᒡᕕᖕᒥᒃ ᓴᑐᕐᓂᐊᕐᑯᔭᐅᑉᓗᓂ. ᓂᒡᕕᔫᖅ ᐊᖕᒐᒃᑯᔾᕗᖕᒪᑦ ᐊᐃᕕᕐᒥᔫᖅ ᑑᕐᖕᒐᕐᑲᒻᒫᕐᓂᖅᓱᓂ ᐊᖕᒐᒃᑯᐊᕐᑭᕐᑯᔭᐅᕗᖅ ᐃᓚᒥᓄᑦ.

His former hunting companions sat around on a pan of ice for a long time waiting for Qisarua'naaq to resurface. There was no sign at all. When it seemed all hope was lost, some of them began to persuade Nigvik to perform a retrieval ritual. Apparently, Nigvik was a great shaman who possessed a walrus helping spirit, so the rest begged him to perform the shamanistic ritual.

ᓂᒡᕕᐅᒻᖕᔫᖅ ᐱᕐᑲᑎᓂ ᐅᕐᑲᐅᑎᓕᖅᐹ, "ᐊᐲᐊᐃ ᐆᒃᑐᕐᓂᐊᕐᒪ ᐸᑦᓗᕐᓗᑎᒃ ᓯᑭᖕᒐᓚᐅᓇᑦᑎᒃ ᓯᑯᙱᒻᒫᕐᓗᑎᒃ. ᒪᑭᕐᑯᐃᓕᕈ'ᒪ ᑭᓯᐊᓂ ᐅᐃᑦᓲᒫᖅᐳᑎᒃ, ᐅᐃᑦᑕᐃᓕᒋᑦᑎᒃ."

Nigvik said to his partners, "Now, as I attempt to perform the ritual, I want you to fall face down with your eyes closed. You will open your eyes only as I give the command. Do not open your eyes!"

ᑖᑉᑯᐊᒨᖅ ᓂᒃᕖᐅᑉ ᐱᖅᑲᑎᒥᒃ, ᐊᓕᖅᑎᒃᓴᖅᓗ, ᑭᓇᑭᐊᖅ ᐱᖅᑲᑖ ᓯᑭᖕᒐᖅᑲᑦᑖᖅᑐᑦ. ᓂᒃᕖᖕᒥᒃ ᐅᑕᖅᑭᖅᑲᑦᑖᓕᖅᑐᒃ ᒪᑭᖅᑯᔩᓕᖅᐸᑦ ᑭᓯᐊᓂ ᒪᑭᓐᓂᐊᖁᒥᒃ. ᐅᑉᓛᖅᐸᑐᐃᓐᓇᒃᑯᙳᖅ ᐅᐃᑦᑕᐃᓕᒋᐊᖅᑐᒃ. ᓯᖅᑭᓂᕉᖅ ᑭᕗᑕᖕᒋᐅᑎᓐᓂᖅᓱᓂ ᐊᒡᒑᑦ. ᐅᐸᓗᒃᑖᖅᑲᔫᖅ ᐳᒃᑖᖅᒥ ᓯᑭᖕᒐᔪᒃ ᐅᐃᑦᑕᖕᒥᒫᖅᓱᑎᒃ.

The people with Nigvik were Aliqtiksaq and another unknown person who kept their faces to the ground for a long time. They were waiting for a long time, as they would only lift their faces off the ground at Nigvik's command. By the time he instructed them to open their eyes, it was the early morning. The sun in fact had made a big swing around the south while their eyes were closed. They had been on the ice practically the entire day with their faces to the ground.

ᐊᓱᑦᑐᐊᑕᐃᓐᓇᕉᖅ ᓂᐸᓕᖅᑐᖅᑲᑦᑐᐊᑐᐃᓐᓇᖅᐳᖅ ᑎᐊ'ᓇ ᐅᖅᑲᖅᐸᓪᓚᒃᓱᓂ, "ᑭᕕᓕᖁᒪ!"

Finally, a voice was heard calling out in distress, "Help! I'm sinking!"

ᑖᒻᓇᒎᖅ ᓂᒡᕕᒃ ᓂᑉᓕᖅᓯᐊᓇᕐᑲᑦᑖᒑᑦ
ᓂᑉᓕᕐᖕᒐᑦᓚᕐᒥᓗ ᑐᐊᕕᐅᖅᓵᓇᑉᓗᓂ
ᐅᖅᑲᖅᓗᓂ: "ᑕᑲᓐᓇ, ᑐᐊᕕ!"

Nigvik, for whom the rest had waited for ever so long, uttered an urgent call: "Down there, quickly!"

ᑖᑉᑯᐊᒎᖅ ᓯᑭᖕᒐᕐᑲᑦᑖᓚᐅᖅᑐᒃ
ᑐᐊᕕᐅᖅᓵᒐᐅᒐᒥᒃ ᒪᑭᐊᑦᓚᒃᓗᑎᒃ ᑕᑲᓐᓇᒎᖅ
ᕿᓴᕈᐊ'ᓈᖅ ᐳᒃᑕᓛᕋᐅᔭᖅᑐᖅ ᑕᑯᐸᓗᓂᒃᑯ.
ᖃᔭᖅᑐᖅᓗᑎᒎᖅ ᑖᑉᑯᐊ ᓯᑭᖕᒐᕐᑲᑦᑖᓚᐅᖅᑐᒃ
ᐊᐃᖕᒪᒃᑯ, ᓱᓇᐅᕝᕙᒎᖅ ᐊᐃᕕᐅᑉ ᐊᒫᖅᓗᓂᐅᒃ ᐳᒃᑕᑦᓚᖅᑎᓐᓂᕐᒪᒍ,
ᑎᒍᖕᒪᒃᑯᒎᖅ ᐊᐃᕕᖅ ᐊᖅᑲᓇᐊᕐᔫᒥᕗᖅ.

The people who had their faces to the ground stood up when they heard this urgent call to see Qisarua'naaq casually floating on the water. They went in their qajait to fetch him, discovering that a walrus had put him on its back to bring him to the surface. When they grabbed Qisarua'naaq, the walrus slowly dove under the water.

ᕿᓴᕈᐊ'ᓈᖀᖅ ᓴᑐᕋᒥᔾᔪᒃ ᐊᐃᖅᑲᑎᒥᑕᓇᑉᓗᓂᔾᔪᒃ.

When they retrieved Qisarua'naaq, they took him home.

ᑕᒡᕚᒡᓛᖖᒎᖅ ᕿᓴᕈᐊ'ᓈᑉ ᐱᓯᐊ:

Here then is Qisarua'naaq's *pihiq* (song):

ᓴᒧᖕᒐ ᐃᔭᔭᐃᔮ ᑕᒡᕙᖄ ᐅᕙᖕᒐ
ᐳᒃᑕᑦᓚᕐᓂᐊᖖᒋᓚᖕᒑ ᐊᒪᒡᒐᕐᑲᖖᒋᓐᓇᒪᓕ
ᓴᒧᖕᒐᐃᔮ ᐃᔭᔨᔭ ᐊᔨ
ᐊᖅᑲᖅᑎᕈᑎᓕᕐᒪᖕᒐ ᓂᕐᔪᑎᑦᓕ ᐃᓛᑕ
ᐳᒃᑕᓚᕐᓂᐊᖖᒋᓚᖕᒐ ᐊᒪᒡᒐᕐᑲᖖᒋᓐᓇᒪᓕ
ᓴᒧᖕᒐᐃᔮ ᐃᔭᔨᔭ ᐊᔨ

Samungaa (way down there) ajajaija
Will I resurface as I'm denied protection of being carried in my mother's *amauti* (woman's parka with a pouch for carrying a child)
Samungaa ajajaija
When one of the animals pulled me under water
Will I resurface as I'm denied protection of being carried on a person's back
Samungaa ajajaija

ᐊᒻᒪᒨᖅ ᑭᖑᓂᒐᒍᑦ ᐊᒪᕈᕐᒧᑦ ᐋᖕᒐᔮᖅᑐᒧᑦ ᕿᖕᒑᒍᑦ ᑮᔭᐅᓚᐅᖅᓯᒪᓯᑉᐳᓂ. ᐅᓐᓄᐊᒃᑯᖖᒨᖅ ᐊᒪᕈᕐᒧᑦ ᐋᖕᒐᔮᖅᑐᒧᑦ ᑎᑭᑕᐅᖕᒪᑕ ᐅᓚᒪᐅᒻᒥᒃ ᑎᒍᓯᑉᐳᓂ ᐊᓂᕆᐊᖅᑑᒐᓗᐊᖅ. ᐊᒪᕈᕐᒥᒨᖅ ᐹᒥ ᐊᑕᐅᑦᓯᒃᑰᖅᑲᑎᖅᑲᑦᑎᐊᖅᐳᓂ ᐊᐳᖅᓯᒐᒥ ᕿᖕᒑᒍᖖᒨᖅ ᐊᒪᕈᕐᒧᑦ ᑮᔭᐅᔪᖅ. ᕿᖕᒑᒍᒨᖅ ᒪᒃᐱᖅᐳᓂ ᐊᓚᖕᒪᑦ ᐊᑕᑉᖅᑲᓕᖅᐳᓂᒨᖅ ᕿᖕᒑᒍᒨᖅ ᓂᕕᖕᒐᒥᐊᓕᖅᑐᖅ. ᑎᐊ'ᓇᐃᑐᐃᓐᓇᖅᐳᓂᒨᖅ ᒪᒥᒻᒪᑦ ᓂᕕᖕᒐᔪᒥᐊᒥᒨᖅ ᕿᖕᒐᖅᑲᓚᐅᖅᑐᖅ.

Some time later after this, he was also attacked and bitten by a rabid wolf. One night a rabid wolf stumbled upon their winter camp. Qisarua'naaq grabbed an axe and rushed out of the entrance. As he stepped out he met the wolf, and it bit him on the nose. His nose was torn up and left to dangle. It healed up that way, so he ended up with a dangling nose.

ᕿᓴᕈᐊ'ᓈᕉᖅ ᐊᔪᙱᑦᑐᕐᔪᐊᖑᓚᐅᕐᒪᑦ ᐊᖑᓯᖅᐳᓂᓗᒨᖅ ᐱᓚᐅᕐᒪᑦ, ᓄᓕᐊᕐᑲᓚᐅᖅᑐᕉᖅ ᐊᒡᒐᐃᑦᑐᒥᒃ ᐊᑎᓕᖕᒥᒃ, ᐃᕐᓂᕐᑲᓚᐅᖅᑐᖅ ᐅᑐᓂᒥᒃ, ᐸᓂᕐᑲᓚᐅᖅᐳᓂ ᖁᐃᓇᒃᓴᐅᒥᒃ.

Qisarua'naaq was a brave man and a great hunter. He was married to Aggaittuq, and had a son called Utuni and a daughter called Quinaksaut.

ᐊᔪᙱᑦᑐᕐᔪᐊᕕᓂᖅ ᑖᒪᓇ ᐊᖑᑦ.

He was a great man.

ᑕᖅᑭᕐᒧᑦ ᐃᔨᒋᖅᑲᑦᑖᖅᑕᐃᓕᓂᖅ
AVOID PROLONGED GAZING AT THE MOON

ᐅᓂᑉᑳᕐᓂᐊᖅᑐᖓ ᐃᓄᐃᑦ ᐅᒃᐱᕈᓯᖏᑕ ᐃᓚᖓᓐᓂᒃ ᑕᖅᑭᕐᒥᒃ ᐃᔨᒋᖅᑲᑦᑖᖅᑕᐃᓕᓂᕐᒥᒃ ᐃᐊ'ᓇ ᐅᓂᑉᑳᒐᐅᕙᓚᐅᖅᑐᒥᒃ.

I am going to tell, based on traditional Inuit beliefs, about why you should avoid prolonged gazing at the moon.

ᓄᑕᕋᐅᑉᓗᑕ ᐊᖓᔪᖅᑳᑉᑎᖕᓂᑦ ᒥᐊᓂᕆᔭᐅᕐᔪᐊᕐᓂᑰᒐᑉᑕ ᐅᒃᐱᕆᓪᓗᐊᕕᒃᖢᒋᓪᓗ ᓈᓚᒍᐊᔭᓚᐅᕋᑉᑎᒍ ᓯᓇᓗᒃᑖᓂᒃ ᖃᐅᔨᒪᔪᕐᔪᐊᕐᑯᑎᒋᒐᑉᑎᒋᒃ, ᐊᔪᙱᑦᑐᕐᔪᐊᕐᑯᑎᒋᑉᓗᒋᑦᓗ. ᓯᓇᒥᐊᒥᒃ ᐅᖃᐅᑎᒃᐸᑎᒍᑦ ᐊᐱᖅᓱᕐᓇᕆᑦᓘᖕᓃᑦ ᓈᓚᔪᓚᐅᖅᐸᕗᑦ ᐅᒃᐱᕆᑉᓗᒋᑦ ᓯᓚᑐᓂᖏᑦ.

A lot of our childhood days are surrounded by overwhelming love and protection. This creates a strong trust and desire for children to obey their Elders' words. As children, we consider them to be most knowledgeable and skilled in everything. When they tell us to do anything, we don't ask questions but follow their instructions because we respect their wisdom.

ᑕᐃᑉᓱᒪᓂ ᓯᓇᒥᐊᓂᒃ ᐱᑦᑕᐃᓕᔭᖅᑲᕋᖢᒃᖢᑎᒃ ᐃᓕᖅᑯᓯᖅᑲᓚᐅᖅᑎᑦᓗᒋᑦ ᐅᖃᐅᑎᔭᐅᕙᓚᐅᖅᐳᒍᑦ ᑕᖅᑭᕐᒥᒃ ᑕᐅᑐᖅᑲᑦᑖᖅᑕᕐᑯᔭᐅᓇᑕ, ᑕᐅᑐᖅᑲᑦᑖᓕᕈᑉᑎᒍᒎᖅ ᐱᑎᒐᐅᓇᕗᒍᑦ. ᑲᑉᐱᐊᓱᒃᖢᑕᓕ ᑕᐃᒪ ᐱᑎᒐᐅᓯᐊᙱᔅᖢᑕᑐ ᐃᔨᒋᖅᑲᑦᑖᖅᑕᐃᓕᕙᓚᐅᖅᐳᒍᑦ ᑕᖅᑭᕐᒥᒃ.

Long ago, Inuit were forbidden to do certain things. One was that we were told to never gaze too long at the moon; otherwise we would be hit with an arrow from it. So because we were afraid, we avoided staring at the moon too long.

ᐱᑎᒐᐅᔭᒥᒃ ᑐᓴᕐᓇᖏᑕᐃᓐᓇᕐᒪᑦ, ᐃᒻᒪᕐᑳ ᓈᓚᑦᓯᐊᔭᓐᓂᕐᒪᑕ ᓄᑕᖅᑲᑦ.

And, since we have never heard of anyone being shot at with an arrow from the moon, we assume our children are very well-behaved.

ᐃᓱᐊ
The end

ᖃᖓᓯᕐᔪᐊᖅ ᑖᖖᒐᐃᓐᓇᔪᓚᐅᖅᑎᓪᓗᒍ
WHEN DARKNESS STAYED CONSTANTLY

ᐅᓂᑉᑳᖅᑐᐊᕐᓂᐊᖅᑐᖓ ᖃᖓᓯᕐᔪᐊᕉᖅ ᑖᖖᒐᐃᓐᓇᔪᓚᐅᖅᑎᓪᓗᒍ ᓄᓇᒥ ᖃᓄᖅ ᖃᐅᓱᖅᓯᒋᐊᕐᓂᕐᒪᖔᑦ. ᐊᐅᓚᔨᓂᕋ ᐊᑐᕐᓯᐊᓇᐊᕐᓗᒍ ᐅᓂᑉᑳᕐᓂᐊᖅᐸᕋ ᐅᓂᑉᑳᒐᐅᑎᓪᓗᒍ ᐅᓂᑉᑳᖅᑐᐊᖅᑎᓂᑦ. ᖃᐅᔨᒪᓂᐊᖅᐳᓯ ᐅᑭᐅᖅᑕᖅᑐᒥ ᐃᓄᐃᑦ ᓄᓇᖅᑲᑎᒌᖕᒋᑦᑐᑦ ᐃᖕᒥᒃᑯᑕᐅᖅ ᐅᓂᑉᑳᖅᑐᐊᕐᑯᑎᖃᕐᒥᖕᒪᑕ ᓄᓇᖅᑲᑎᒥᖕᓂᑦ ᐱᔪᓂᒃ, ᑖᒻᓇᓕ ᐅᓂᑉᑳᕐᓂᐊᒐᕋ ᓴᐅᓂᖅᑰᕐᒥᐅᓂᑦ ᐅᓂᑉᑳᒐᐅᑎᓪᓗᒍ ᑐᓵᑦᑕᕐᓂᑯᒐ ᐃᐊ'ᓇᐃᓕᐅᖅᑐᖅ.

I'm going to tell a story about a time when there was constant darkness on Earth and how daylight began. I will tell it in the best way I remember it being told by storytellers. Please note, though, people in different regions and communities have their own unique version. This version is one told by Hauniqtuurmiut.

ᖃᖓᓯᕐᔪᐊᑦᓯᐊᒥᐊᕉᖅ ᓄᓇ ᑖᖖᒐᐃᓐᓇᒥᐊᓚᐅᖅᓯᒪᔪᖅ ᖃᐅᒻᒪᔪᐃᑦᑐᒥᐊᖑᑉᓗᓂ. ᐊᖑᑎᑦ ᐊᒃᓛᖖᒎᖅ ᑎᑭᕐᒥᖕᓂᒃ ᐃᑭᑦᓯᐊᓪᓚᒃᕗᑎᒃ, ᑎᑭᕐᒥᖕᓂᒃ ᓇᓂᕈᐊᖅᑲᕐᓂᓗᒃᕗᑎᒃ ᒪᖃᐃᓐᓂᓗᒃᐸᓚᐅᖅᑐᑦ.

It is said that a very long time ago, the world was always in the dark and there was no daylight at all. In fact, men would light their first finger and use it to find their way around during their hunting trips. Imagine living constantly in the dark with no days to tell time!

ᓂᕐᔪᑎᖖᒎᖅ ᑕᐃᑉᓱᒪᓂ ᐅᓐᓄᐊᒥ ᑖᖖᒐᐃᓐᓇᔪᓚᐅ'ᑐᐊᕐᒪᑦ ᐃᑖᓐᓇᓲᖅᑕᑦᑐᐊᔪᓚᐅᖅᓯᒪᖕᒪᑕ ᑕᒡᒐᒥ, ᖃᐅᓱᖅᓯᓂᐊᓕᕐᓂᖅᑎᓪᓗᒍᒎᖅ ᑕᐃᑯᐊᒃ ᐊᒪᕈ'ᑐᐊᕐᓗ ᑎᓇᒐᓂᐊ'ᓈᕐᓗ ᖃᓈᓗᒃᐸᓗᒃᑐᓗᐊᑯᓘᒃ. ᑎᓇᒐᓂᐊ'ᓈᕈᖅ ᐊᖖᒍᑎᓯᐃᑦᑑᒐᒥ, ᐱᓐᓂᑯᐃᓐᓇᐅᓕᖅᑎᑦᓗᒥᑦ ᑎᑭᐅᑎᕚᒃᑲᒥ ᐅᖅᑲᖅᓗᓂ: "ᐅᑉᓗᕈᖅᐳᖅᓕ, ᐅᑉᓗᕈᖅᐳᖅᓕ!"

Long ago, when it was always dark, animals would eat food that Inuit had cached on the land. But there came a time (on what was to become the beginning of the first day) that a bitter brawl occurred between a big wolf and a little fox. The little fox was always eating leftover scraps of food, and this time he called out, "It is day. It is day!"

ᓱᓇᐅᕝᕙᒎᖅ ᖃᐅᓱᖅᓯᕐᑯᔨᓚᖅᑐᖅ ᑕᐅᑦᓯᐊᖅᑕᕈᐊᖅᖢᓂ ᒪᓂᖅᑲᒥ ᓂᕆᔭᒃᓴᖅᓯᐅᓗᒃᖢᓂ ᐱᓱᓗᓚᕌᖕᒐᒥ.

You see, the fox was wishing hard for daylight to begin so he could have a better view of the land while he scurried about in search of food people had hidden.

ᐊᒪᕈᕉᖅ ᖃᐅᓱᐃᑦᑑᑐᐃᓐᓇᒥᐊᕐᑯᔨᒐᓗᐊᒧᑦᓚ ᐅᓐᓄᐊᒥ ᑕᒡᒐᒥ ᓂᕆᑦᑕᕈᐊᒧᑦ ᑭᐅᑉᓗᓂ, “ᓈᒡᒐ, ᐅᓐᓄᒃᐳᕐᓚ, ᐅᓐᓄᒃᐳᕐᓚ!"

But the wolf was wishing for constant darkness, because he could eat easily in the dark. So the wolf said, “No, no! It is night. It is night!”

ᑎᓇᒐᓂᐊ'ᓈᕉᖅ ᐅᑉᓗᕈᕐᑯᓯᑉᓗᓂ ᓴᖕᒍᓐᓂᐊᖅᑐᐃᓐᓇᖅᑐᐱ'ᑑᖕᒪᑦ ᖃᐅᒻᒪᖅᓴᓯᑦᑐᐊᖅᐳᖅ ᐅᑉᓗᕈᑦᑐᐊᑦᓚᕐᒥᓗ ᖃᐅᒻᒪᑦᑐᐊᖅᐳᖅ. ᑕᐃᒪᙵᒐᑦᓚᒨᖅ ᑕᐃᒪ ᐊᓱᐃᓛ ᖃᐅᑦᑕᔭᓯᒐᒥ, ᐅᑉᓗᕐᓗ ᐅᓐᓄᐊᕐᓗ ᐊᑉᓯᒪᐅᓚᖅᐳᒃ ᐅᑉᓗᒥᒧᑦ ᑎᑭᕐᖢᒍ, ᓴᖕᒍᑦᓯᐅᒪᓐᓂᕐᒪᓂᒃ ᐊᒪᕈᕐᓗ ᑎᓇᒐᓂᐊᕐᓗ.

But the little fox kept insisting for daylight to begin. Then, sure enough, it began to dawn a bright daylight. So from the time of the beginning of the first daylight, day and night were equally divided. It has been this way ever since—all because of an argument between a wolf and a fox!

ᐃᓱᐊ

The end

ᓄᑲᓖᒃ ᓵᑉᑕᐅᓐᓂᑯᒃ ᑕᕆᐅᒥ
BROTHERS ADRIFT AT SEA

ᐅᓂᑉᑳᖅᑐᐊᕐᓂᐊᖅᑐᖓ ᓄᑲᓖᖕᓂᒎᖅ ᓵᑉᑕᐅᓐᓂᑯᖕᓂᒃ ᒪᐅᓕᖅᑑᒐᓘᓐᓃᖕᓂᒃ ᐆᒃᑲᕈᑎᓐᓂᖏᒥᒃ ᓵᑉᑕᐅᔫᓐᓃᒃ ᐊᒻᒪ ᐊᒃᓯᕈᕐᓇᖅᑐᒃᑰᕐᓂᑯᒥᒃ ᐅᑎᕐᓂᓗᒃᔪᑎᒃ ᐊᖏᕐᕋᒥᖕᓄᑦ. ᐃᐊ'ᓇ ᐅᓂᑉᑳᒐᐅᑦᑕᖅᑎᓪᓗᒍ ᐊᐅᓚᔨᕙᕋ:

I am going to tell a story about two brothers who drifted out to sea while they were out hunting, and how they experienced a difficult ordeal trying to return to their family at home. This is how I remember it being told:

ᑕᐃᑉᓱᒪᓂᒎᖅ ᐊᖑᑎᑦ ᒪᐅᓕᑦᑐᐊᔪᓚᐅᕐᒪᑕ ᐅᑭᐅᒥ ᑕᕆᐅᒥ ᑐᕝᕙᒥ ᐊᒡᓗᓂᑦ ᓇᑦᓯᕐᓂᓗᒃᔪᑎᒃ. ᑕᐃᑯᐊᒎᖅ ᓄᑲᓖᒃ ᑲᑎᒪ'ᓈᖅᔪᑎᒃ ᒪᐅᓕᖅᑑᒐᓗᐊᒃ ᑎᑭᙱᑕᐃᓐᓇᓕᕐᒪᓂᒃ ᐅᑎᓚᐃᖅᑐᒃ ᖃᐅᔨᒪᔭᐅᓕᖅᐳᒃ ᐃᓅᙱᓕᕐᒪᓂᒃ.

Long ago, men would go out on the sea ice to hunt for seals at their breathing holes. This story is about two brothers who were out hunting seals as partners. Unfortunately, they didn't return home when they were supposed to. One eventually returned, but when he did, he was no longer living.

ᓱᓇᐅᕝᕙᒎᖅ ᓵᑉᑕᐅᓐᓂᕋᒥᒃ ᐅᖕᒪᕙᑦᑐᐊᕋᓗᐊᖅᑐᑎᒃ ᑐᕙᕕᓂᖅ ᓇᔪᒫᒃ ᑐᕙᓇᖕᓂᕐᒧᑦ ᑐᓗᕐᒪᑦ ᖃᑭᓐᓂᖅᑐᑎᒃ ᐊᖕᒥᑦᕋᒧᑦ ᐱᓱᖕᓂᓗᕐᑲᑦᑖᓕᖅᑐᓐᓃᒃ.

Now, the story begins when the sea ice the brothers were on broke away, and the brothers drifted out to sea until the floating ice bumped into the solid ice of a distant shore. The two brothers set foot on the shore ice and started the long trek back home.

ᑕᐃᒫᒎᓇᓛᒃ ᐱᓱᕐᑲᑦᑖᖅᐸᒃᑲᒥᒃ ᒥᕐᖑᐃᖅᓯᓚᐅᖅᐸᒃᑐᑎᒃ ᑖᖅᓯᓚᓯᔭᕐᒑᖕᒪᑦ ᑕᖕᒫᖅᐸᒃᑐᑎᒃ. ᐅᖕᒪᕙ'ᑐᐊᕐᓂᕋᒥᒎᖅ ᐱᓱᑦᑐᐊᖅᐸᓕᕋᓗᐊᕋᒥᒃ ᐊᖕᒥᑦᕋᒧᑦ ᑎᑭᑦᓴᓇᐊᒃᓴᖅ ᓇᑐᓇᖅᓯᑉᐳᓂ. ᕐᑯᓚᕐᓇᖅᓯᓕᕋᓗᐊᖅᑎᑦᑐᒍ ᐅᓐᓄᒃᓴᕆᐊᒻᒫᕐᒥᖕᒪᑦ ᐃᒡᓗᓂᒃ ᑕᑯᓱᖕᒪᔭᒃᑲᒥᒃ ᐅᕐᓂᕆᐊᕐᓂᓗᙵᕆᕐᑐᓂᒃᑯᒃ. ᐅᓐᓄᒃᓴᕆᐊᒻᒫᕐᒪᖖᒎᖅ ᑕᖕᒫᖕᒥᓕᖅᑐᑎᒃ ᐃᒡᓗᓄᑦ ᑎᑭᓐᓂᓗᕆᐊᑦᑐᐊᖅᐳᒃ.

It was going to be a long trek back, so the brothers took care to rest once in a while. Just before dusk came, the pair decided to stop for the night. The brothers had walked for a very long time, and they began to doubt they would ever reach home. But just as their doubts were growing, they spotted *igluit* (snow houses) in the distance. So they pressed on with renewed energy.

ᑕᖅᓯᑦᑐᐊᖅᑐᒥᓗᒎᖅ ᐃᒡᓗᓄᓕᑦᑐᐊᑕᐃᓐᓇᕋᒥᒃ ᐊᓪᓚᔪᒍᓯᒃᑲᓗᐊᖅᐳᒃ ᖃᒧᑎᕈᓈ'ᑐᐊᕐᓂᒃ ᖃᓕᓃᒃᑐᑦᑐᐊᕐᓂᒃ. ᐃᒡᓗᖖᒎᖅ ᐃᑯᒪᓇᒃᓴᖅᑐᑲᑕᐅᓴᒪᑕ ᖃᒡᒋ'ᔫᓐᓂᕐᒧᑦ ᐃᑦᓱᐊᕐᒪᓂᒃ, ᑕᖅᑲᑉᑯᐊᒎᖅ ᒧᒥᖅᑐ'ᔪᐃᑦ ᐊᑯᕋᐅᔮᓐᓇᒥᐊ'ᔪᐃᑦ, ᓱᓇᐅᕝᕙᒎᖅ ᑲ'ᑕ'ᑑᓐᓃᑦ, ᐃᓄᕉᒻᒥᔪ'ᔪᐃᑦ.

Darkness had settled in by the time they finally reached the igluit, but the brothers noticed there was something strange about the encampment when they saw dogsleds neatly stacked on top of each other. Each iglu was lit and shining brightly. The brothers decided to peak inside a *qaggiq* (a large iglu made for celebration purposes) where drum dances were being held. When they looked in, they

noticed a drum dance was being held where all the men had long back flaps on their parkas. That is when they realized these beings were really wolves that could make themselves look like humans.

ᖃᐅᔨᒐᒥᔫᖅ ᐃᓄᑦᑐᐊᕕᐅᙱᑦᑐᓂᒃ ᐃᓯᒪᓕᖅᐳᒃ ᐊᕕᑦᑐᑎᒃ ᐃᑎᒐᖅᑲᐅᕈᐊᖅᑐᑎᒃ. ᑖᒻᓇᔫᖅ ᓄᑲᖅᑲᓚᖅ ᑳ'ᑕᓄᑦ ᐃᓐᓇᖕᒐᓕᖅᑑᓐᓂᕐᓄᑦ ᐃᑎᕋᒥ ᐅᖃᖅᐳᖅ, "ᐊᓂᖕᒐᒐᐃᒻᓇ ᐃᒥᖅᓯᐅᕋᑐᐊᕋᑉᑯ."

When they realized that these were not real human beings, the brothers decided to each enter a different *iglu* (snow house). The younger brother entered an iglu where part of the wolf pack was already in bed and said, "I'm here to fetch water for my older brother, if I may."

ᐅᖃᐅᑎᔭᐅᕗᕉᖅ, "ᑕᑲᓇᖖᒐᑦ ᒪᑦᑕᖅᑐᑎᑦ ᖃᓗᓰᑦ."

The wolves replied, "Well then, remove your *atigi* (coat) and fill your cup."

ᒪᑦᑕ'ᓈᖅᔪᓂᔫᖅ ᖅᑲᔪᓯᒋᐊᓕᕋᔪᐊᕐᒪ, ᑲ'ᑕ'ᑐᐃᖕᖑᔫᖅ ᐱᒡᒐᔪᐊᓪᓚᒃᔪᑎᒃ ᒥ'ᖕᒋᐊᓪᓚᒥᐊᖅᐹᑦ ᐃᓂᖕᒐᓂ.

The younger brother removed his atigi and started to fill his cup, but the wolves instantly jumped out of their beds, attacked him, and killed him.

ᐊᖕᒐᔪᒃᑖᕉᖅ ᐃᒡᓗᑦ ᐃᓚᖕᒐᓐᓄᑦ ᐃᑎ'ᔪᐊᕆᒥᑉᑕᐅᖅ, ᓯᓇᐅᐤᕚᔫᖅ ᐊᒪᕈᖅ ᐸᐃᔾᔪᖅ ᒧᒥᖅᑐ'ᔫᖕᒪᑕ ᐅᐃᖕᒐ ᒧᒥᖅᑐᓂᓯᐅᕐᓂᕐᒪᑦ. ᐃᓄᔫᖅ ᑖᒻᓇ ᐃᑎᖅᑎᓕᕆᒥ ᐸᓇᓂ ᑐᓂᒻᒥᔮᕆᐊᓪᓛᓪᓗ ᐅᕐᑲᖅᐳᖅ ᐊᓚᓂᕐᑭᑉᔪᓂ.

The older brother had decided to go into another iglu. Inside was a lone lady wolf whose husband was at the drum dance. As the young Inuk entered, he stretched out his hand and offered a *pana* (snow knife) to the lady wolf. He then asked her to sew new soles onto the bottom of his *kamiik* (two skin boots).

ᐊᒪᖅᑯᒻᖕᒎᖅ ᐱᒪᑐᓇᐊᐱᑦᑐᐊᓪᓛᓪᓗ ᐅᖃᐅᑎᕚ ᑲ’ᔭ’ᑐᐊᕐᓂᒃ ᓄᓇᖅᑲᑎᖃᕐᓂᕋᖅᓱᓂ. ᖃᐅᔨ’ᓈᑐᐊᕈᒥᒃᑯᒎᖅ ᐱᓇᕖᑦ ᑭᓗᒥᓄᑦ ᐃᔨᖁᕖ ᐅᓕᒃᑐᕐᓂᐊᕐᒥᐅᒃ. ᐅᖃᐅᑎᒻᒫᖅᓱᒍ ᒍᒥᖅᑐ’ᑑᖕᒪᑕᒎᖅ ᐅᐃᖓ ᑲ’ᑕ’ᑐᐃᑦ ᐃᓚᖓᑦ ᐊᐃᒍᒥ ᖃᐅᔨ’ᑐᐊᕐᓂᐊᕐᒪᒍ ᐅᐊᔅᓴᒃᑕᐃᓕᖁᑉᓗᒍ.

The lady wolf immediately offered to help him. She told the man that the neighbours were all wolves, and she said if he didn’t want to be captured by them right away he should hide under the covers on the bed. She also told him that her husband was part of the wolf pack holding the drum dance. She told the man it would be easy for her husband to find him when he came home, so she advised the man to hold very still when her husband returned.

ᐊᒪᖅᑯᒻᖕᒎᖅ ᐃᓄᒃ ᐊᓚᓂᒃᓵᓚᓴᓇᐊ’ᕙᐊᕐᒪᒍ ᒥᖅᓱᖅᑎᑦᑐᒍᒎᖅ ᓯᓚ ᐅᐃᖓ ᐃᑎᓱᖕᒐᔭᖕᒪᑦ ᓂᕿ’ᓈᒥᒃ ᒥᓇᖅᑕᒥᓂᒃ ᑐᓕᒫᖅᒧᑦ ᑲᐸᑎᓯᒪᐸᓗᒍ ᓇᒃᓴᒌᔭᒃᓱᓂ. ᐅᔭᖕᖏ’ᓈᑐᐊᖅᒥ ᐅᖃᑦᑐᐊᖅᐳᖅ, “ᑕᐅᓂᒦᒃ.”

The man hid under the covers, and the lady wolf began sewing new soles onto his kamiik. Soon, though, her husband came home. He was holding a small piece of human flesh on the end of a rib bone. As soon as his head appeared in the iglu, the half-human wolf said, "*Taunimiik*. (Oh, a human scent in the air.)"

ᐊᒪᖅᑯᒪᖑᖅ ᐸᓇ ᐃᓐᓂᑕᕐᒥᓂᑦ ᑎᒍᓯᐊᓪᓛᓪᓗᒃ ᐃᓕᐅᓇᐊᐱᑦᑐᐊᖅᐳᖅ, "ᐄᖅ, ᓱᓪᓗᖅᐱᑦ, ᐃᓅᓄᓇ ᐸᓇᓂ ᖃᐃᑳ ᐊᓚᓂᓱᙱᕈᑉᓗᓂ."

The female wolf immediately picked up the pana she had carefully placed on her drying rack and said, "Oh, please hold your peace. This human gave me his pana to have his kamiik soles mended."

ᐊᒪᕈ'ᔪᐊᕈᖅ ᐃᓕᐅᓇᐊᑦᑐᐊᖅᐳᖅ ᐸᓇᒥᒃ ᐃᓴᒫᖅᕗᓂ. "ᐊᓚᓂᒍᒃ, ᐊᓚᓂᒍᒃ, ᐊᓚᓂᒍᒃ."

The pack wolf stretched out his hand, accepted the gift, and said, "Then mend, mend, mend his boots."

ᒧᒥᐊᓂᖓᒪᑕᔫᖅ ᑲ'ᔾᑦ ᐃᓚᖕᒐᓐᓂᒃ ᐅᒡᓚᖑᒃᑐᖅᑲᖅᒪᑦ ᑕᒡᕙᖓ ᐃᓄᖕᒥᒃ ᑭᓗᒥᖕᓂ
ᐃᐳᖅᑐᐊᓕᖕᓄᑦ. ᐃᑎᓇᐊᖅᒥᔫᖅ ᐅᖄᑦᓚᓱᖕᒐᔾᖕᒥᖕᒪᑦ, “ᑕᐅᓂᒦᒃ.”

When the drum dance was over, one of the wolf pack came for a visit to the ones who were hiding the man. As he stepped inside, the wolf said, “Taunimiik.”

ᐊᒪᕈᕉᖅ ᐅᖅᑲᖅᑐᓂ, “ᓇᑭᑦᑭᐊᖅ ᑕᒡᕙ ᑕᐅᓂᒥᒃ ᓇᐃᒪᐅᕙ?”

But the wolf who was hiding the man simply said, “Now, where could this one be smelling human scent?”

ᐃᓄᔫᖅ ᐊᑕᐅᖅᑳ, ᑐᓵ'ᔭᐊᖅᒥ ᐅᖅᑲᓐᓂᔭᓂᒃ ᐅᐊᔾᔭᒃᑕᐃᓕᑦᓯᐊᓇᐊᓗᐊᒃᑲᓐᓂᖅᑐᓂ
ᖅᑲᐅᐳᔭᐅᑦᑐᐊᖅᓂᐊᓕᕈᒐᓗᓂᔫᖅ, ᖅᑲᐅᐳᖅᑳᖅᑎᓐᓇᔪ ᐊᓂ'ᔭᐊᖅᒪᑦ.
ᐊᓂᑦᓯᖅᓯᓐᓇᖅᑐᔪᔫᖅ ᐊᓪᓚᒥᒃᑕᐅᖅ ᐃᑎᖅᑐᖅᑲᑦᑐᐊᓕᓇᕗᖅ ᐃᓕᒪᓱ'ᔭᐊᓕᖅᒥᒃ.
ᑲᑕᖕᒥᔫᖅ ᓄᐃᑎᓪᓚᖅᒥᓗ ᐅᖅᑲᖅᒥᖕᒪᑦ, “ᑕᐅᓂᒦᒃ.”

Under the covers, the man could hear their conversation, and he kept as still as possible—he was terrified to be discovered! But the visiting wolf left without discovering the man. Soon after, though, an entire group of wolves came in. Before the first wolf had even put his head inside the iglu, he said, "Taunimiik."

ᐊᒪᕈᕉᖅ ᕿᐸᕿᑦᑐᐊᖅᖢᓂ ᐅᖃᖅᖢᓂ. "ᐋ, ᓇᑭᑦᑭᐊᕈᑯᐊ ᑕᐅᓂᑦᖁᑉᓗᒍ ᑕᐅᓂᒥᒃ ᑕᐅᓂᒥᒃ!"

By this time, the lady wolf was pretty upset and said, "Oh my, where on Earth do they think they can smell human scent?"

ᐊᒪᕈᕉᖅ ᑲᒻᒪᖕᓂᒃ ᐳᑦᑐᐃᔭᒐᐅᔪᖕᓂᒃ ᑕᑯᒐᒥ ᐊᐱᓚᑉᓗᓂ, "ᑭᐊᑕ, ᐅᑯᐊᒃ ᑲᒪᒃ?"

Then, one of the wolf pack noticed the pair of strange kamiik the lady wolf was repairing, and he said, "Well, then, whose kamiik are those?"

"ᐊᒥ ᑭᐊ, ᐅᐃᒪ."

"Well, who else's?" she answered. "My husband's, of course!"

ᐊᒪᕈ'ᔦᐊᕉᖅ ᑲᒻᒪᖕᓂᒃ ᐊᓪᓚᔦᐊᖅᑐᐃᓐᓇᕐᒥ ᐊᐱᓚᕆᑉᓗᓂ, "ᓲᕐᑕᐅᑯᐊᒃ ᑎᒍᔭᖃᖅᐸᒃ?"

The wolves were still quite suspicious, and one of them asked, "Well then, why do the stitches have gatherings?"

ᐊᒪᖅᑯᒪᖕᔫᖅ ᕿᐸᐱᑦᑐᐊᖅᖢᓂ ᑭᐅᓗᑲᕐᓗᖅᐹ, "ᐊᒥ ᓲᖅ, ᑎᒍᔭᔪᒐᒪ."

The lady wolf was utterly upset, and she replied, "Why, I can sew gathered stitches!"

ᐊᓂᖕᒪᖖᔫᖅ ᖃᐃᔪᖅᑲᕐᓇᓵᓚᕐᒪᑦ ᐊᒪᕈᖅ ᐅᖃᓚᖅᖢᓂ ᐊᒃᓗᓈᒥᒎᖅ ᓂᖕᒋᑦᓯᔦᒫᕐᓇᓪᓂᐊᕐᒪᑕ ᐃᓄᒎᖅ ᑎᒍᑦᑕᐃᓕ'ᔦᐊᓂᓕ ᐊᒃᓗᓈᕐᒧᑦ, ᑎᒍ'ᓈᑐᐊᖅᐸᒍᒎᖅ ᐊᒧᓗᒋᑦ ᐅᒋᐊᖅᑕᓂᓗᒍ ᓂᓂᔭᐅ'ᔦᐊᕈᒫᕐᒪᑦ.

The wolves left. But the wolf man said they would come back again. He warned the man that the next time they came, the wolves would throw a leather thong into the iglu. The wolf told the man that when this happened, he shouldn't grab it because, if he did, they would all be pulled out, and the other wolves would attack the man and eat him up.

ᐊᒃᖢᓈᒥᒎᖅ ᐊᓯᐃᓛ ᓂᖏᑦᓯ'ᖤᐊᕐᒪᑕ, ᐊᒪᕉᒎᖅ ᓄᓕᐊᓈᒃ ᑎᒍᒪᒥᒃ ᑲᑕᐅᑉ ᐃᓱᒃᑭᖕᓄᑦ ᑐᑭ'ᓈᖅᖢᑎᒃ ᐱᓇᐃᒻᒥᓗᐊᕆᐊᑯᓗᖕᒪᓂᒃ, ᒪᑦᕉ'ᓈᖖᒍᒪᒥᒎᖅ ᐊᑕᐅᖅᑲ ᓄᓯᒐᐅᖅᑲᔭᑦᑐᐊᖅᐸᒃᑲᓗᐊᖅᖢᑎᒃ ᒥᖖᒍᖅᑐᖅᑳᖅᑎᓐᓇᒥᒃ ᓄᑦᓰᖅᑲᑕᐃᑦ ᐊᓰᖅᒪᑕ ᓄᖅᑲᖅᖢᑎᒃ.

Sure enough, the other wolves soon returned and threw a long leather thong into the iglu. The wolf couple grabbed the thong and set their feet firm on each side of the entrance, locking themselves in place. Naturally, being only two against many, the couple was almost pulled out. But they held their ground, and the wolves outside gave up before the couple was exhausted.

ᐊᒪᖅᑯᙳᖅ ᖃᐃᑦᑕᕈᖕᓇᐃᕐᒪᑕ ᐊᖑᑦ ᐊᐃᓂᓗᓯᐊᒃᑲᓐᓂᕈᒫᓕᕐᒥᖕᒪᑦ ᐊᒪᖅᑯᒪᖕᖑᖅ ᐅᖃᐅᑎᕚ ᑲ’ᑕᑦ ᖃᒧᑕᐃᑕ ᓇᐳᑕᐅᑕᐃᓂᒃ ᑭᐸᓗᐃᔭᖅᑐᕐᑯᐸᓗᒍ ᑭᐱᙵᑎᑕᖅᑲᙵᑎᑦᓯᐊᓇᐊᒥᐊᕐᓗᓂ, ᐳᐃᒍᐃᓐᓂᖅᐸᙳᖅ ᐊᑕᐅᓯ’ᓈᒥᒃ ᓘᓐᓂᑦ ᒪᓕᒃᓴᒐᐅ’ᑐᐊᓇᐊᕈᒫᕐᒪᑦ. ᐊᒪᕈᕉᖅ ᐅᖃᖅᖢᓂ ᓯᓂᓕᖅᓰᓂᐊᕐᒥᒃ ᓯᓂᓕᖅᐸᑕ ᐅᖃᐅᑎᔪᒫᕐᒪᒍ.

Eventually, no more curious wolves came by to snoop, and the man decided to try again for home. The wolf man told him that if he wanted to escape, he should go out and cut all the ropes that held the crosspieces on the wolf pack's *qamutiit* (sleds) in place. The wolf man warned him that he shouldn't miss cutting even a single one, because if he forgot, the pack would be sure to go after him. The wolf man then told the man he would watch to see when all the wolf pack fell asleep.

ᐊᒪᕈᕉᖅ ᐃᑦᓯᖅᑕᖅᖢᓂ ᓯᓂᓕᖖᒥᒻᒪᖕᒑᑖ ᖃᐅᔨᓴ’ᔪᐊᓕᕐᒪᑦ, ᖃᐸᑎᓗᒃᑖᖅᑑᔭᕐᒪᑕᑰᖅ ᐃᓄᒃ ᑭᐸᓗᐃᔭᖅᑐᓇᐊᑐᐊᕐᒪᑦ ᑕᖅᑭᖅᑐ’ᑑᖕᒪᙳᖅ ᑲ’ᑕᓐᖑᖅ ᑕᒪᒃᑯᐊ ᖃᒍᑎ’ᑐᐊᖕᒥᑦ ᖃᓚᓈᒃᑐᐊᖅᑐᐃᑦ ᑭᐸᓗᕐᓂᐊᒐᐃᑦ ᐊᒥᓰᑯᓂ.

The wolf man kept going out to see if the other wolves were all asleep. Finally, when all of them had extinguished their lamps, he let the man out to cut the ropes that held all the crosspieces of the wolves' qamutiit. The moon was shining brightly, and the man saw the wolf pack's qamutiit neatly stacked on top of each other. The sheer number of crosspieces he was supposed to cut loose gave him chills of apprehension.

ᐱᐊᓂᕐᑐᐊᑕᐃᓐᓇᕋᒥᒎᖅ ᐃᑎ'ᔪᐊᕐᒪᑦ ᑐᔪᕐᒥᕝᕕᖕᒥᓄᑦ ᐊᒪᖅᑯᒻᖕᒎᖅ ᓴᕝᒍᑎᒥᓂᒃ ᑐᓂᒻᒫᖅᓗᒍ ᐅᕐᑲᐅᑎᓕᓇᕚ, ᐅᖕᒐᓯᒃᑐ'ᑑᖕᒪᑕᒎᖅ ᑖᒻᓇ ᓴᕝᒍᑦ ᓇᓗᓕᕌᖕᒐᒥ ᓇᑉᐸᖅᑖᕈᒫᖅᐹ ᐅᕿᒍᐊᑕᒎᖅ ᓇᑖᓄᑦ ᐅᕕᖅᑕᕈᒫᕐᒪᑦ. ᐊᒻᒪᒎᖅ ᑭᐱᐊᓂᖖᒋᑕᕐᑲᕐᓂᖅᐸᑦ ᒪᓕᒃᓴᒐᐅ'ᑐᐊᕈᒫᕐᒪᑦ ᑲ'ᑕᓂᑦ ᒪᓕᒃᓴᒐᐅᑦᑐᐊᕐᓂᕈᒥᒎᖅ ᑲ'ᑕᑦ ᓯᕗᓪᓕᖅᐹᑐᐊᖕᒐᑦ ᐊᑯᓕᐊᕈᑦᓯᐊᓇᐊ'ᑐᐊᕐᓗᒍ ᐱᑎᒍᒫᖅᐹ ᐊᖕᒍᔭᐅᑦᑐᐊᓕᕐᓂᕈᒥ. ᐊᒻᒪᒎᖅ ᒪᓕᒃᓴᒐᐅᒃᑲᓐᓂᑦᑐᐊᕐᓂᕈᒥ ᐃᓄᒃᓲᒻᖕᒎᖅ ᑭᓪᓕᖕᒐᓄᑦ ᐊᕐᑯᕕᒥᐊᓂᓕ.

When he finally finished his chore, the man went back into the iglu. The wolf man then handed the man his *savgut* (snow depth tester). The wolf reminded the man that his home was very far, and he told him that if he ever felt uncertain about where he was, he should stick the savgut in the snow. The savgut would always lean towards the man's home. The wolf man then warned the man again that if he had missed cutting a single crosspiece rope, the pack would be sure to follow him. He told the man that if this happened, and the pack caught up with him, he should shoot an arrow right between the eyes of the wolf pack's leader. And if the wolf pack came after him a second time, he should crouch against an *inuksuk* (stone marker).

ᑐᐸᙵᕆᓚᐅᖅᑐᓂᒎᖅ ᑕᖅᑭᓇᒃᑐ'ᑑᒐᒥ ᖃᐅᒪᓇᐅᖕᒪᑦ ᐅᓐᓄᐊ'ᓈᒥ ᐊᐅᓪᓚᒥᐊᐱᑦᑐᐊᖅᐳᖅ ᐊᖕᑭᓪᖁᒥ ᓇᓚᑭᔪᓇᒫᓄᑦ ᐃᓄᑑᓕᖅᓱᓂ ᓄᒃᑲᓂ ᑲ'ᑕᓂᑦ ᐱᔭᐅᓚᐅ'ᑐᐊᕐᒪᑦ. ᖃᐅᒪᕐᒪᙳᖅ ᐱᓯᓕᖅᑲᒥᙵᕆᑐᐊᖅᑎᓪᓗᒍ ᑖᕋᒎᓇᑖᒃ ᑲ'ᑕ'ᑐᐃᑦ ᑭᖑᖕᒐᓂ ᐳᓯᐅᑎᑦᑐᐊᖅᐳᑦ ᓇᐳᓕᐅᒪᒥᒃ ᑭᐱᐊᓂᖕᕆᑕᕐᑲ'ᑐᐊᕐᓂᕐᒪᑦ. ᕿᒪᖕᓂᐊᓚᐅ'ᑐᐊᕋᓗᐊᕐᒪᙳᖅ ᐅᕿᓚ'ᑐᐊᕋᒥᒃ ᖃᐃᕋᓚ'ᑐᐊᕐᒪᑕ ᐅᖅᑲᐅᑎᔭᐅᓂᓚᐅᓂᒎᖅ ᒪᓕᒥᐊᖅᓗᒍ ᑎᑭᑦᑐᐊᓕᖅᓯᓐᓇᕐᒪᑕ ᓯᕗᓪᓕᖅᐹᑐᐊᖕᒐᑦ ᐊᑯᓕᐊᕈᑦᓯᐊᓇᐊᖅᓗᒍ ᐱᑎᒃᓴᑦᑐᐊᖅᐹ. ᐊᑯᓕᐊᕈᖅᓗᒍᒎᖅ ᐱᑎᓗᒃᑲᕐᓗᕐᒪᒍ ᐃᓚ'ᑐᐊᖕᕆᒎᖅ ᐅᑎᒧᑦ ᕿᑉᓴᐅᑎᓱᖕᒐᔭᓕᕋᒥᒃ ᑕᓕᐊᓂᑲᑐᖕᒐᓕᓇᕗᑦ ᐳᑦᓯᐅᑎᑉᓗᑎᒃ.

The full moon was shining brightly, and the man set out in the middle of the night towards his home. But this time he was all alone because his younger brother had died when he was attacked by the wolf pack. By daybreak the man had travelled quite far, since he had been walking for a long while. But sure enough, he spotted the wolf pack in a cloud of smoke in the distance, and he knew he had forgotten to cut loose

one crosspiece rope. Naturally, the man tried to escape as best he could. But the wolves were fast runners, and they caught up with him in no time. Remembering the advice he was given, the man pulled out his bow and arrow and aimed between the eyes of the leader. He hit him right between the eyes, and the rest of the pack turned back and disappeared instantly in the cloud of smoke.

ᐊᐃᓱᐊ'ᑐᐊᕐᒥᒨᖅ ᐱᓱᒥᐊ'ᑐᐊᓕᕐᒥᖕᒪᑦ ᓇᓗᓕᕐᒥᒨᖅ ᐊᔭᐅᑉᐱᐊᖅ ᓇᑉᐸᕋᓗᐊᕐᒪᒍ ᓇᓗᓇᐃᑉᑳᖅᖁᓂᒨᖅ ᐅᕙᒍᐊᑕ ᓇᓛᓄᑦ ᐅᕕᒐᔫ'ᓈᓱᖕᒐᔭᖕᒪᑦ ᓇᓛᓄᑦ ᐱᓱᒋᐊᒃᑲᓐᓂᑦᑐᐊᓕᓇᑉᑐᓂ. ᐅᖕᒐᕙᑦᑐᐊᕋᓗᐊᖅᑎᑦᓗᒍᒨᖅ ᒪᓕᒃᓴᒐᐅᒃᑲᓐᓂᓱᖕᒐᔭᖕᒥᒐᒥ ᑲ'ᔭ'ᔪᐊᕐᓂᑦ. ᒥᕐᖑᓯᓪᓛᑦᑐᐊᓕᕋᓗᐊᕐᒥᒨᖅ ᑎᑭᐊᓕ'ᑐᐊᖅᐸᖕᒪᑕ ᐅᔭᖕᒋᓱᖕᒐᕌᖕᒐᒥᒃ, ᐊᒪᖅᑯᒧᖖᒨᖅ ᐅᖅᑲᐅᓯᓕᐅᖕᒐ ᒪᓕᒥᐊᓇᑉᓗᒍ ᖅᑲᑦᖅᑲᒥ ᐃᓅᒃᓱᖅᑲᖅᒪᑦ ᐅᖅᓂᒃᓗᒍ ᑭᒡᓕᖕᒐᓅᑦ ᐊᖅᑯᕕᖅᓗᓂ ᐅᑕᖅᑭᒥᐊᒥᐊᓕᓇᕗᖅ ᑎᑭᐊᓕ'ᔪᐊᕐᒪᑕ.

Since he was filled with longing to be home, the man continued on, and whenever he wasn't sure where he was, he put the savgut in the snow, and it would tilt ever so slightly towards his home. He had travelled quite far when he spotted the pack coming towards him a second time. He was exhausted by this time and the wolves were swift, so remembering the advice he had received from one of the wolves, he approached an inuksuk up on a hill. He crouched beside it and waited for the pack to come closer.

ᑎᑭᐊᓪᓚᒥᐊ'ᑐᐊᕐᒥᒐᒥᒨᖅ ᑳ'ᑕ'ᑐᐃᑦ ᐊᕙᑎᓗᒃᑖᒥᐊᖕᒐᓃᓗᕐᑭᒥᐊᓯᖕᒐᔭᓕᕐᒪᑕᒨᖅ ᑯᓂᐅᖅᓴᓗᕐᑭᑦᑐᐊᓪᓚᕐᒥᒡᓗ, ᐃᓄᖕᒥᒃ ᑕᐅᑐᑉᓚᖕᒋᑦᑐᑦ ᐃᒻᓈᒐᓗᕐᑭᒥᐊᑦᑐᐊᓪᓚᕐᒥᒃᑯᓗ ᐃᓄᒃ ᒪᓕᒃᑲᓗᐊᒃᑲᑎᒃ. ᕐᑯᓕᒑᔭᕆᓗᒥᐊᖕᒐᓂᒨᖅ ᐃᑦᑕᕆᓗᐊᕐᒪᑕ ᐅᕐᑲᓐᓂᖅᐸᓗᑦᑐᐊᓪᓚᕐᒥᒡᓗ, “ᑕᒪᐅᖕᒐᐃᒻᓇ ᑐᒪᖕᒋᕆᓗᐊᕐᓂᕐᒪᑦ.”

The wolves ran up fast and stood all around the man, sniffing the area. They could not see the man but somehow urinated all over him—the very person they were chasing! They even stood right above him and he could hear them mumbling. “This is puzzling because his tracks end right here,” they said.

ᑎᑭᓯᒪᓚᐅᑦᑐᐊᖅᓱᓇᖅᔪᑎᒎᖅ ᐃᓄᒃᓯᖕᒋᓐᓇᒥᒃ ᐊᐅᓪᓚᑦᑐᐊᓂᕗᑦ ᐅᑎᒃᑲᓐᓂᓚᐃᖅᓂᖅᔪᑎᒃ. ᑕᓕᓪᒪᑕᒎᖅ ᐱᓱᒋᐊᒃᑲᓐᓂᑦᑐᐊᓂᕗᖅ ᓇᓕᒋᔭᓇᒃᑲᒥᖕᓄᑦ. ᓇᓗᓕᖑᖕᒐᒥᒎᖅ ᓴᕝᒍᑦ ᓇᑉᐸᖅᐸᖕᒪᒍ ᖃᓪᓕᓴᓕᖅᓂᖅᒪᖔᒎᖅ ᐅᕕᖅᑐᐊᖅᑕᓕᒪᒋᓐᓇᖅᔪᓂ.

The wolves stayed around the man for a while, but when they couldn’t find him they all departed, never to return again. When they disappeared into the distance, the man again started the long trek towards where he thought his home might be. Whenever he became confused, the man would set the savgut in the snow, and each time it tilted a little more, indicating that he was getting closer to home.

ᐱᓱᖅᑲᑦᑖᑦᑐᐊᒐᓂᖕᒥᒐᒥᒎᖅ ᓴᕝᒍᑎᓂ ᓇᑉᐸᖅᑎᒃᑲᓗᐊᖅᒥᖕᒪᒍ ᐅᕕᖅᔭᐊᑦᓯᐊᒥᐊᖅᒪᑦ ᒪᓂᖅᑲᓘᑦ ᐃᓐᓇᖅᑲᔭᖅᑐᐊᕕᒃᔪᓂ, ᐱᓱᒋᐊᓚᐅᑉᖅᑲᖅᔪᓂᓗ ᐃᓪᓗᑦ ᑕᓕᓯᒪᒐᔫᒃᓱᓐᓇᓕᖅᓂᖅᒪᑕ ᑕᑲᓐᓇᒎᑎᓈᒃ ᖃᑦᖃᑉ ᐊᑎᒐᔫᖕᒐᓂ ᐃᓪᓗ’ᑐᐃᑦ. ᖁᕕᐊᓇᖁᓂᒎᖅ, ᑎᑭᓱᓐᓇᖅᔪᓂᒎᖅ ᖃᑦᖃᒥ ᐃᒥᐊᓕᖅᒪᑦ, ᓄᑕᖅ’ᓈᖕᖓᒎᖅ ᑕᑯᒐᒥᔾᔭᒃ ᖃᑦᖃᒥ ᐃᒃᓯᕚᔭ’ᑐᐊᖅ ᐅᐸᔭᐊᖏᓪᓚᒃᑐᐱ’ᔮᖕᒪᑕ ᐅᖅᓂ’ᔭᐊᖅᒪᔾᔭᒃ ᓄᓚᐊᖕᒐᑕ ᐃᓕᑕᓇ’ᔭᐊᖁᒥᐅᒃ ᐊᒡᒋᑎᑉᐳᓂᐅᒃ.

After a very long walk, the man stuck his savgut in the snow again, and it tilted so far that it was almost flat on the ground. He took a few more steps and there, just below a hill, he spotted a lot of igluit side by side. The man was really happy to be home, but he just sat there on top of the hill. Finally, some children who were playing outdoors saw him sitting alone, and they rushed home to report what they saw. Then everyone came out and, of course, his wife recognized him and took him home.

ᐅᔾᔨᓇᒐᓗᐊᖅᐸᔫᒎᖅ ᐃᓪᓚᐃᔭᐃᑦᑐᒥᐊᖕᒍᖕᒪᑦ, ᓯᓂᓪᓚᖅᒥᐊᓪᓛᖖᒎᖅ ᐃᓪᒋᔭᐃᓐᓇᒥᐊᔭᖕᒪᑦ. ᓱᓗᐊᑦᑐᐊᖅᒪᖕᒑᖖᒎᖅ ᐃᓱᒪᒋᑦᑕᓕᖅᒥᐅᒃ ᐊᐱᓇᑦᑐᐊᑕᐃᓐᓇᖅᒪᒍ ᓲᖅ ᐃᓪᓚᐃᔭᐃᑦᑑᖕᒪᖕᒑᑦ ᑭᐅᑦᑕᖅᓱᓇᖅᔪᓂᒎᖅ, “ᐃᑖ ᐃᓪᓚᐃᖁᓗᐊᕈᒪ ᑲᑉᐱᐊᒋᓕᖁᔭᖅᑰᖁᖕᒪ, ᐃᓪᓚᐃᔭᐃᑦᑑᔭᖕᒐ.”

Once home, though, the wife found it strange that her husband would never take his eye goggles off—even in his sleep he wore them. She began to wonder about this unusual behaviour, and finally she asked why he never took his goggles off. He simply answered, "Well, I think you would become frightened of me if I took them off. So that is why I always wear them."

ᐅᓐᓄᒃᑯᓐᖕᒎᖅ ᓯᓂᓚᓯᑎᓪᓗᑎᑦ ᐅᐃᓂ ᐃᓪᓚᖅᒥ ᓂᖅᖃᓚᐅᔪᖅᖢᓂ ᓯᓂᓪᓚᒃᓴᐅᔪᖅᑐᖅ ᖅᑭᑉᐸᑎᑉᑐᒍᒎᖅ ᐃᓪᒐᒥᒃ ᒪᒃᐱᖏᐊᓪᓛᖕᓂᓪᓗ ᐅᖅᑲᐅᑎᕚ, "ᒪᐃ, ᓱᒐᕕᑦᑭᐊᖅ ᐃᓪᕆᔭᐃᓐᓇᒥᐊᓗᐊᑦᑐᐊᔭᕕᑦ?"

Then, one night, as her husband lay on his back in bed trying to sleep, she rudely grabbed his goggles, lifted them up, and said, "For goodness' sake, why are you always wearing these goggles?"

ᐃᓪᒪᒋᒎᖅ ᐃᑭᖁᑦᓯᒪᔫᖕᒪᕆᒃ ᑕᖅᑲᑉᑯᐊᒎᖅ ᑭᖑᑦᑐᐃᑦ. ᑕᑯᐊᓪᓚᑦᑐᐊᖅᒥᕆᓐᖕᒎᖅ ᐅᐊᔪᑦ ᐃᓪᒪᒋᒃ ᐸᑎᒃᑎᐊᓂᑲᓗᐊᑦᑐᐊᖅᐸᒃ. ᓱᓇᐅᕝᕙᒎᖅ ᐃᓪᒪᐃᔭᐃᑦᑑᓗᐊᑐᖕᓖᖅᑐᖅ ᐊᖏᓂᐅᓐᓂᖅᒥ, ᑕᑦᑖᕐᓯᐊᖖᒋᔅᖢᓂ ᐅᖅᑲᐅᑎᔅᓯᐊᖅᑕᓚᐅᖅᑐᐊᖅᓂᖅᒪᒍ ᓄᓕᐊᓂ ᖅᑲᐅᔾᒍᒥ ᑲᑉᐱᐊᓱᒍᒫᖅᑰᖅᒫᓚᑦᑕᖅᖢᓂᐅᒃ.

As soon as she had lifted the goggles a wee bit, the woman saw that her husband's eye sockets were filled with live shrimp. As soon as she discovered something alive in his eye sockets, she put the goggles back in their place right away. She realized then why her husband had insisted on always wearing his goggles: he was someone who had come back from the dead. No wonder he had told his wife that she would become afraid of him! He had only tried to protect her from being frightened.

ᖅᑲᖕᒐᓴᖅ ᐃᓛ ᐃᓄᐃᑦ ᐊᖏᑦᓱᕋᓱᒋᖕᓈᕙᓚᐅᖅᓯᒪᖕᒪᑕ ᐃᓄᖕᓂᒃ. ᑖᒪᓇ ᐊᖏᓐᓂᖅ ᑐᑭᖅᑲᖅᑐᖅ ᑐᖅᑯᓚᐅᖅᑳᖅᖢᓂ ᐆᒻᒪᒃᑲᓐᓂᖅᓂᖅᒥᒃ. ᑎᐊ'ᓇ ᐱᑦᑕᓪᓗᐊᕕᔭᓚᐅᖅᒪᖕᒫᑖ ᖅᑲᐅᔾᒪᓐᓇᖖᒋᑦᑐᖅ ᑖᒪᓇ ᐅᓂᑉᑳᖅᑐᐊᒥᐊᖕᖑᖕᒪᑦ ᐱᓪᓗᐊᕕᖕᓂᑰᓐᖏᔅᖢᓂ.

Well, you know, long ago, Inuit had a belief that people could come back to life after they were dead. It is called *anginniq*. It literally means "becoming alive again after he was dead." Now, it's not known whether this actually happened, because this is just a story and not necessarily something that literally happened.

ᐃᓱᐊ
The end

ᖃᓄᖅ ᑕᒃᓯᔭᓯᖕᒪᖕᒑᑦ
HOW FOG CAME TO BE

ᓱᓇᓗᒃᑖᑦ ᐱᒋᐊᕐᓂᖅᑲᔪᖕᒪᑕ ᐅᓂᑉᑲᐅᓯᖅᑲᖅᖢᑎᒡᓗ ᐱᒋᐊᕐᓂᕕᓂᖕᒋᑦ ᑕᒃᓯᕐᓂᐅᑉᑕᐅᖅ ᐱᒋᐊᕐᓂᕕᓂᖕᒐ ᐅᓂᒃᑲᐅᓯᖅᑯᑎᖅᑲᖅᐳᖅ ᐃᒪᓐᓇᐃᑦᑐᒥᒃ:

Everything has its own beginning, and each beginning has a story of how it came to be. Even the fog has its own origin, and the story that goes with it goes like this:

ᖃᖕᒐᓴᖅ ᐱᓱᓗᒃᖢᑎᒃ ᑭᓯᐊᓂ ᓂᖅᑭᒃᓴᖅᓯᐅᖅᐸᓪᓚᐅᖅᒪᑕ ᑭᖖᒐᐃᑦ ᐳᖅᑐᓃᑦᑐ ᐅᕐᓂᒃᐸᒃᖢᑎᑦ ᓇᓯᐹᕆᐊᖅᔭᓚᐅᖅᒪᑕ ᖃᓂᑦᑐᒥ ᐅᖕᒐᕙᓂᓘᓐᓃᑦ ᐱᑕᒃᓴᖅᑲᖖᒋᒪᖕᒑᑦ ᓂᕐᔪᒻᒥᒃ ᑐᒃᑐᓂᓪᓘᓐᓃᑦ.

Long ago, hunting for subsistence was commonly done on foot. Hunters would climb mounds and hills in search of any game or caribou they might see close by or in the distance.

ᑕᐃᒻᓇᒎᖅ ᐊᖑᑦ ᒪᕐᑲᐃᑦᑐᖅ ᓇᓯᑦᓴᖅᑐᖅᑐᖅ ᑭᙵᒐᐅᑉ ᖄᖕᒐᓄᑦ.
ᓇᓯᐹᓗᕐᑭᑎᑦᓗᒍᒎᖅ ᐅᐱᙵᒐᖅᓯᑎᖅᑑᓐᓂᖅ ᐊᒃᔭ'ᑐᐊᕐᒧᑦ ᑎᑭᖄᒐᐅᑎᕐᒥ.
ᐊᕙᒻᒧᖖᒎᖅ ᕿᓇᕗᔾᔨᓇᐊᖅᓗᐊᖅᒥ, ᑖᒻᓇᒎᖅ ᐊᒃᔭ'ᑐᐊᖅ ᑎᑭᑎᖅᑐᐊᑕᖅᑲᓛᑦ.
ᓱᖅᑯᓯᒃᓴᖅᑕᐃᒪᓂᐅᖕᒪᙱᒎᖅ, ᕿᒪᒋᐊᖅᓗᐊᖅᐸᑦᓗ ᐊᖑᑦᓗᒃᑐᖅᓯᓐᓇᓯᒋᐊᕐᒪᒍ
ᒪᓂᖅᑲᒧᖖᒎᖅ ᐊᓯᐃᓛ ᓇᑦᑕᒥᐊᖅᑕᖅᐳᖅ ᒪᓂᒻᒥᒋᐊᒥᐊᑎᖅᓗᓂ,
ᑐᖁᖓᓯᖅᑐᓇᐊᑦᑐᐊᑦᑕᕐᒥᓗ.

One time, a man was out hunting, and he climbed a hill to search the surrounding area. While he was on top of the hill, a big brown bear came up behind him. The man turned around to get a different view and there, right in front him, was the brown bear. Totally surprised, there was nothing the man could do—even if he tried to run away, the bear would attack him before he could escape. So the man did the next best thing: he lay down on the ground in submission and played dead.

ᐊᒃᔪᐅᒻᖑᒎᖅ ᑎᑭᓐᓇᒥᐅᒃ ᐃᓄᒃ ᓈᑕᓯᑦᑐᐊᖅᐹ, ᐅᐊᔾᔭᖅᓯᐊᓇᑦᑐᐊᑎᖅᐸᒃᓗᒍ.
ᓂᐊᖁᐊᑕᒎᖅ ᓇᓛᓂᑦ ᐊᓂᖅᑎᓇᙱᒪᖑᓖᑦ ᓈᑕᖅᑲᑦᑖᑦᑐᐊᓚᓂᒃᑳᖑᒥᐅᒃ
ᐃᑎᓚᐃᑕᒎᖅ ᓇᓛᓅᖅᓗᓂ ᐅᐊᔾᔭᒃᓯᐊᓇᖅᑲᑦᑖᑦᑐᐊᑎᖅᐸᒃᑭᕚ. ᓂᐊᖁᐊᑕᒎᖅ
ᓇᓛᓅᑎᖄᖑᓚᒥ ᐃᓄᒎᖅ ᓱᖅᑐᖖᒍᑎᖅᓯᐊᓇᐊᑕᒻᒦᓚ'ᑐᐊᓇᖅᑰᖃᒥᐅᒃ

ᓴᓂᕗᕐᓇᓵᑦᓯᐊᒥᐊᖅᑕᕐᒪᑦ, ᓯᖅᑐᑉᕐᑲᓪᖅᑎᓪᓗᒎᖅ ᑭᓯᐊᓂ ᐃᑎᒐᐃᑕ ᓇᓛᓄᓇᐊ'ᓈᑦᑐᐊᖀᖕᒐᑦ ᖁᕕᐊᓇᖅᐸᑯᓂ.

When the bear approached, it began to listen to the man, and it examined him to see if he would move. The bear first listened near the man's head for breathing, then it looked at the man's feet for movement. The bear dwelled in the head area the longest. It seemed to wait and wait for the man to breathe, but just when the man was about to gasp for breath, the bear moved away to the man's feet. Oh, the man was so happy when the bear moved to his feet!

ᐃᓄᒎᖅ ᐊᓂᖅᑎᓇᔮᖖᒋᒻᒪᑦ ᐅᐊᔾᔭᒃᐸᑦᑕᐊᖕᒥᓇᓂᓗ ᑐᖁᖕᒐᓱᒋ'ᑐᐊᓕᕐᒥᐅᒃ ᐃᖅᓯᐅᑎᓱᖕᒐᔭᖕᒪᒍ, ᐅᖕᒐᒻᒎᑎᐅᔭᓇᐊᑦᑐᐊᓪᓛᓪᓗ.

Finally, seeing the man did not appear to have any breath, the bear took him for dead, lifted him off the ground onto his back, and started to walk away.

ᐃᖅᓱᒃᕈᒍᒎᖅ ᓄᒃᓯᒥᐊ’ᑐᐊᓕᖅᒪᒍ ᐅᖅᐱᒃᑲᑎᒎᓕᖅᒪᖖᒎᖅ ᐃᓄᒃ ᐃᓱᒪᓱᖕᒐᔭᓕᖅᒪᑦ ᐅᖅᐱᒃᑲᓄᑦ ᑎᒍᕝᓗᓂ ᑲᓕᕝᔭᕋᖅᑎᑦᑐᐊᕿᐊᖅᕈᓂᐅᒃ ᖃᓄᖅ ᐱᑦᑐᐊᕐᓂᐊᕐᒪᖕᒑᑦ. ᐊᓯᐃᓛᒎᖅ ᐅᖅᐱᒃᑲᓄᑦ ᑎᒍᖕᒪᑦ ᑲᓕᕕᓯᑦᑐᐊᖅᐳᖅ. ᑲᓕᕕᖅᑲᑦᑖᑦᑐᐊᒐᓂᒃᑲᒥᒎᖅ ᐃᓄᒃ ᑲᑖᓪᓚᒃᕈᓂᐅᒃ ᓅᓚᓯᑦᑐᐊᓇᕚ ᐊᕐᖕᒐᔪᕐᑯᓂᒃᑐᐊᓪᓚᕐᒥᓗ.

As the bear walked, it went through a thick-shrubbed valley. The man decided he would grab hold of the twigs to make it hard for the bear to move forward. So the man grabbed on to the twigs, making the bear tug away. After a particularly long tug, the bear let the man down to see if he was breathing.

ᐃᖅᓯᐅᑎᒃᑲᓐᓂᓇᑉᓗᒍᒎᖅ ᐅᖅᐱᒃᑲᑎᒎᓇᐊᕐᒥᖕᒪᑦ ᑎᐊ’ᓄ ᑎᒍᕝᕈᓂ ᐅᖅᐱᒃᑲᓄᑦ ᐅᑉᓗᓗᒃᑖ’ᓅᖅ ᑲᓕᕝᔪᕋᖅᑎᖅᑲᑦᑖᖅᒪᒍ ᐃᓇᕕᓴᖅᕈᒍ. ᑎᐊ’ᓄᒎᖅ ᓴᑉᑯᓚᐅᖅᐸᒃᕈᓂ ᐅᑉᓗᓗᒃᑖ’ᓅᖅ ᐱᖕᒪᒍ ᐊᓯᐃᓛ ᐅᓐᓄᒃᓯᒥᐊᓕᖅᕈᓂ ᐊᒡᓛᑦ.

The bear noticed nothing, and so it put the man on its back again and walked some more across the valley through the thicket. All the while, the man would grab on to the twigs and make the bear pull and pull to exhaust it. He did this all day long, even until the evening's approach.

ᐅᖅᐱᒃᑲᓐᖒᖅ ᐊᓂᒍᕐᒪᑕ ᐊᒃᔭ’ᑑᑉ ᑎᑭᐅᑎᑉᓗᓂᐅᒃ ᐃᓄᒃ ᓯᑎᒐᓇᓐᓂᒃᑲᒥᓄᑦ. ᐃᑎᖅᑎᕈᑎᓕᕐᒪᒍᒎᖅ ᑕᑯᐊᓪᓚᓚᐅᓱᖕᒐᔭᖕᒪᑦ ᑐᖅᓲᖕᒥ ᐅᖅᓲᒻᒥᒃ ᑎᓐᖓᐅᓚᓯᒪᒥᐊᑐᐃᓐᓇᕐᒥᒃ ᑕᑕᓗᐊᒧᑦ. ᐃᒡᓗᑕᕐᒧᓐᖒᖅ ᐃᑎᕐᒪᑕ ᑕᒪᒃᑯᐊᒎᖅ ᓇᑉᐸᖅᑎᑕ’ᑐᐃᑦ ᐊᑭᒥ ᐃᓄᕋᓗᒥᐊᑦ ᑐᒃᑐᕋᓗᒥᐊᑦ. ᐃᓚᖏᒎᖅ ᐃᓄᐃᑦ ᓄᑕᐅᒥᐊᐱᑐᐃᓐᓇᐃᑦ. ᐊᒃᓚᐅᒻᖒᖅ ᐃᑎ’ᓈᓪᓚᕐᒥᓗ ᐃᓄᒃ ᓇᑉᐸᖅᑎᑦᑕᓄᑦ ᓇᑉᐸᖅᑎᐊᓪᓚᑦᑐᐊᖅᓯᓐᓇᖅᓱᒍ, ᑭᓗᒧᑦ ᓵ’ᓈᖅᓱᓂ ᐃᓐᓇᖅᓱᓂ.

Finally, the pair passed through the thicket and arrived at the bear's den. As they passed through the entrance, the man spotted a skin container of oil so full it was ready to burst open. When they entered the sleeping area, the man saw some stiff figures that had been stood up against the wall. They were a mixture of caribou and human

carcasses—some of which hadn't been there long. The bear placed the man beside the rest of the bodies, then jumped on the bed platform to rest, putting its head against the bed's far end.

ᐊᒃᓴᒎᖅ ᐃᓐᓇᖕᒐᓚᕐᒪᑦ ᐃᓄᒃ ᐅᐃ'ᑐᐊᕐᒪᑦ, ᑖᒪᓇᒎᖅ ᐊᒃᓵᑎᓇᓂᖅ ᓇᑎᕐᒥ ᐱᙳᐊᖅᑐ'ᓈᖅ, ᑕᐅᑲᓂᓗᒎᖅ ᐃᒐᒥ ᐊᓈᓇ'ᑐᐊᖕᑲ ᐃᒐᕙᓗᐊᑯᓗᒃ. ᖃᓄᑮᖅ ᐱᑦᑐᐊᕐᓂᐊᓕᕐᒪᖔᕐᒥ ᐃᓱᒪ'ᑐᐊᓕᕐᒥᒐᒥ, ᐅᐃᓐᒥᒐᒥᒎᖅ ᑕᑯᓱᖕᒐᔭᖕᒪᑦ ᐊᑭᒥ ᐅᓚᒪᐅᒻᒥᒃ ᓇᑉᐸᖕᒐᕙᒥᒃ. ᐃᓱᒪᓱᖕᒐᔭᓕᖅᐳᑮᖅ ᐅᓚᒪᐅᑦ ᑎᒡᒍᐊᓪᓚᒡᓗᒍ ᐊᓂᐊᓪᓚᒋᐊᑦᑐᐊᕈᐊᖅᓯᓗᓂ, ᑕᐃᒻᓇᓗ ᑐᖅᓲᖕᓂ ᐅᖅᓲᑦ ᐅᓚᒪᑦᑐᐊᖅᓯᓐᓇᖅᓗᒍ ᐊᓂᑦᑐᐊᕈᐊᖅᓯᓗᓂ, ᖅᑭᒪᒋᐊᑦᑐᐊᓪᓚᖅᒥᓗ.

When the bear lay on the bed, the man opened his eyes and spotted a little bear cub playing on the floor. A mother bear was busy cooking at her hearth. The man then closed his eyes and began to design his way of escape. When he opened his eyes again, he noticed an axe near the entrance against the wall. He decided he would quickly grab the axe, put a big slit in the skin oil-container that he had seen at the entrance, and run away as fast as he could.

ᑕᐃᒻᓇᒎᖅ ᐊᒃᓵᑎᑎᓂᖅ ᓇᑎᕐᒥ ᐱᙳᐊᖅᑐᖅ ᐃᓅᖕᒧᑦ ᕿᕕᐊᖅᐸᒃᑲᒥ ᐅᐃᑕᑎᓪᓗᒍᒎᖅ ᐊᖑᐊᓪᓚᒐᑦᑐᐊᓂᒐᒥᐅᒃ ᐅᖅᑲᐱᔪᖕᒐᔭᖕᒪᑦ, “ᐊᑖᑖᒃ, ᐊᑖᑖᒃ, ᐋᑉᐹᑉ ᐃᔨᖕᓂ ᐅᐃᑦᑭᒃ.”

But the little bear cub playing on the floor kept turning its head towards the man, and suddenly it caught him with his eyes open. The bear cub cried, “Papa! Papa! The creepy one opened its eyes!”

ᐊᑖᑖᒎᖅ ᒥᖅᖑᓯ’ᑐᐊᕐᒥ ᑭᐅᙱᕐᕗᑐᓂ, ᓇᓚᑐᐃᓐᓇᐅᔭᒥᐊᖅᕗᑐᓂ.

The bear answered angrily, “Oh, let him open them! Let him open them! It was he who exhausted me silly by holding on to shrubs all day!”

ᐅᐃᑉᐸᓕᕐᒥᒎᖅ ᐊᓂᐊᓪᓚᒋᐊᑦᑐᐊᕈᐊᖅᕗᑐᓂ ᐃᓯᒪᑦᑕᓕᕐᒥ, ᐊᓯᐃᑖᒎᖅ ᐅᐊᔅᔭᒋᐊ’ᓈᓪᓚᕐᒥᓗ ᐅᓕᒪᐅᑦ ᐊᑭᒥ ᑎᒡᒍᐊᓪᓚᑦᑐᐊᖅᓱᓐᓇᖅᕗᒍ ᑐᖅᓲᖕᒥ ᐅᖅᓲᑎ’ᑐᐊᖅ ᐅᓕᒪᑦᑐᐊᖅᐹ. ᓇᑎᕐᒨᙴᖅ ᖁᕕᓗᕐᑭᒋᐊᒥᐊᑦᑐᐊᕐᒪᑦ

ᐊᒃᓴᐅᑉ ᐊᕐᓇᓪᓗ’ᑑᑉ ᐱᓗᕐᑭᕆᐊᑦᑐᐊᕐᒃᐹ. ᑖᒻᓇᑑᕐᒃ ᐊᖑᑦ ᓯᑕᒧᑦ ᑲᔪᑦᓴᐃᓐᓇᕐᓂᕐᓗᙱᒻᒪᑦ ᕐᑭᒪᕆᐊᐱᑦᑐᐊᓪᓚᕐᒥᓗ, ᑭᖑᒻᒧᑦ ᕐᑭᖄᐊᓚᐅᐱᑦᑐᐊᕐᒃᐸᒃᓱᓂ ᐊᒃᓴᒃ ᒪᓕᙱᒻᒪᖕᒎᑦ ᐊᕐᒃᐸᒥᐊᓯᑦᑐᐊᕐᒃᐳᕐᒃ.

So the man kept opening his eyes from time to time, wondering when he could make a quick dash for the entrance. Then, on an impulse, he grabbed the axe from the side wall and struck the skin oil-container with it. Of course, the contents spilled all over the floor, and the big female bear rushed to clean it up. But the man kept right on running to escape capture, only looking back occasionally to see if the bear was following him. The man ran as fast as he could.

ᐊᒃᓱ’ᑐᐊᑮᕐᒃ ᐅᔭᖕᑭᓐᓇᓵᓚᐅᑦᑐᐊᕆᓗᐊᕐᒃᐳᕐᒃ ᐅᕐᒃᓰᑎᒥᖕᓂᒃ ᐱᓗᕐᑭᕐᑲᑕᐅᓯᓐᓇᓕᕆᒥ. ᐃᓄᑑᕐᒃ ᐅᖕᒐᕙᑦᑐᐊᕆᓗᐊᕐᒃᑎᓪᓗᒍ, ᐊᓯᐃᑖ ᑕᐃᑲ ᐅᔭᖕᑭᑦᑐᐊᕐᒃᐳᕐᒃ. ᒪᓕᖕᓂᓗᙱᓴᕐᒃᑐᐱ’ᑐᐊᑮᕐᒃ ᐳᑦᓰᒥᕗᕐᒃ ᒥᒃᓯᒧᐊᒃᓱᓂ. ᐅᕐᒃᐱᒃᑲᑎᒍᙲᕐᒃ ᐊᓂᒍᕆᓗᐊᕐᒃᑎᓪᓗᒍ ᐊᖑᑦᑐᐊᓕᕐᒃᓯᓐᓇᕐᒪᒍ ᒥᙳᕐᒃᑐᒫᑦᑐᐊᕆᒥ, ᑕᒪᓐᓇᑑᕐᒃ ᒪᓂᕆᕐᒃ ᐃᕐᑭᑦᕐᑯ’ᓈᒥᓄᑦ ᑎᑎᑦᑐᐊᕐᒃᐹ ᐅᕐᑲᕐᒃᓱᓂ; "ᑰᓕᓇᕐ!" ᑎᑎᐊᓂᖕᒪᒍᓗᑑᕐᒃ ᑰᕆᐊᑦᑐᐊᓪᓚᕐᒥ ᐊᒃᓴᒡᓗ ᐊᑭᓕᓅᓯᐊᓪᓚᒥᐊᕐᒃᓱᑎᒃ.

The big bear did not appear for a long time, as it was busy tending to the spilled oil. But after the man had covered considerable distance, sure enough, it came running. With all its eagerness to chase the man, the bear appeared in a cloud of dust heading in the man's direction. When the man had just passed safely through the thicket of shrubs, he saw the bear within range of catching him. The man was exhausted and could run no farther. So he made a mark on the ground with his little finger and said, "Flow as a river!" No sooner had he made the mark then a river appeared—instantly separating the two.

ᐃᓄᒎᖅ ᑰᑉ ᐃᒡᓗᐊᓂᖅᓱᖅ ᐃᑕᕿᒥ ᒥᖅᖑᐃᖅᓯᐅᔭᑦᑕᕐᒥᑐ ᐊᒃᓴᒃ ᐅᑕᖅᑭᐅᔭᒥᐊᑕᕐᒪᒍ, ᑰᒻᒎᖅ ᓱᓈᓄᑕᓐᓇᒥ ᐊᒃᓴ'ᑐᐊᖅ ᑐᖅᓴᑕᓯᖕᒋᔭᖕᒪᑦ, "ᖃᓄᕐᑕ ᒪᓐᓇ ᐃᑳᖅᐱᐅᒃ?" ᐃᓅᒻᒎᖅ ᓴᓂᒃᑎᓇᖖᒋᑲᑕᖅᓱᓂ ᑭᐅᑉᓗᓂᐅᒃ, "ᐊᓗᒃᓱᒍ!"

The man, who was now on the other side of the river, sat confidently catching his breath and waited for the bear to arrive. When the big

bear appeared at the river's edge, it called out, "How did you cross this obstruction?"

ᐃᓅᒻᖕᒎᖅ ᓴᓂᒃᑎᓇᙵᕆᑲᑕᖅᕈᓂ ᑭᐅᑉᓗᓂᐅᒃ, “ᐊᓗᒃᕈᒍ!”

The man casually replied, "Oh, I slurped it empty."

ᐊᒃᓴᐅᒻᖕᒎᖅ ᑰᒃ ᐊᓗᑦᖅᕈᓂᐅᒃ. ᑎᐊ’ᓇᒎᖅ ᐊᓘᔭᖅᑲᑦᑖᒥᐊᖅᑐ’ᑑᑕᖅᒪᑦ ᓄᖅᑲᓚᐅᖅᐸᒃᕈᓂ ᑰᖕᒥᒃ ᐊᓗᒡᓗᒍ ᐃᒪᐃᖅᓂᖕᓂᓗᒃᑐᖅ. ᐊᒃᓴᒎᖅ ᓱᓕ ᐊᓗᒃᑎᑦᓗᒍ ᐃᓄᒃ ᒥᖕᒍᐃᖅᒥ ᐊᐃᖅᐅᔭᓇᐊᒥᐊᖅᕈᓂ ᑯ’ᑐᐊᖅ ᐊᓗᒡᓗᒍ ᐃᒪᐃᓚᙵᕆᒻᒪᒍ ᖃᐅᔨᒪ’ᑐᐊᖅᒥ.

So the bear began to slurp the river. It slurped and slurped for a long time, only stopping once in a while in its attempt to drink the river dry. Then the man, having rested all he needed, started home. But the bear kept trying to slurp the entire river empty—a task the man knew was totally impossible.

ᐊᒃᖤᒎᕐᒃ ᐃᒥᕐᒥᒃ ᐊᕐᑭᐊᑦᑐᓱᓗᐊᒧᑦ ᐋᖕᒪᓘᖕᒥᖕᒪᕐ, ᐊᓗᒋᐊᕋᓗᐊᕐᒥᖕᒪᖖᒎᕐᒃ ᕐᑳᕐᒃᑐ'ᑑᖕᒪᑦ ᑕᒃᓯᓕᒥᐊᓱᖕᒐᔾᔭᖕᒪᕐ, ᑕᓪᖁᖕᒐᒐᔫᕐᒃ ᓄᐃᑕᔪᐃᕈᑎᑉᓗᓂ. ᑕᐃᒻᓇᒎᕐᒃ ᐃᓄᒃ ᑕᒃᑐᕐᒃᓯᐅᓗᐊᑯᓗᒃᖢᓂ ᐊᐃᖕᒪᑦ ᕐᑲᐅᔾᔨᑕᐅᓕᕐᒃᑐᕐᒃ ᐊᒃᖤᐅᑉ ᓈ'ᑐᐊᕆᒃᑕ ᕐᑳᕐᓂᖕᒐᓄᑦ ᑕᒃᓯᓕᕐᒃᑐ'ᑑᖕᒪᕐ, ᑕᐃᒪᖖᒐᑦᓗᒎᕐᒃ ᑕᐃᒪ ᑕᒃᓯᔪᓯᒐᒥ ᐅᑉᓗᒥᒧᑦ ᑎᑭᕐᖢᒍ ᑕᒃᓯᕐᒃᐸᓕᕐᒃᐳᕐᒃ.

The bear became so full of water that it bulged into a ball. As it took one last slurp, it exploded and created a thick fog—so thick that not even something close could be seen. The man then made it home under thick fog, and he became the source of information on how fog originated from the bursting of a bear's belly. From then on, it is believed that is where fog came from.

ᐃᓱᐊ
The end

ᑭᕕᐅᖅ
KIVIUQ

ᐅᓂᑉᑳᖅᑐᐊᕐᓂᐊᖅᑐᖓ ᑭᕕᐅᕐᒥᒃ ᐋᓈᓇᓚᐅᒻᓂᑦ H ᐊᓛ ᐸᐅᖕᒐᕐᒥᑦ ᑑᓵᑦᑕᕐᓂᑯᒻᓂᒃ ᒪᓕᒡᓗᖓ. ᖃᐅᔨᒪᓂᐊᖅᐳᔪ ᐅᑭᐅᖅᑕᖅᑐᒥ ᐃᓄᐃᑦ ᓄᓇᖃᑎᒌᖏᑦᑐᑦ ᐃᖕᒥᒃᑯᑕᐅᖅ ᐅᓂᑉᑳᖅᑐᐊᕐᑯᑎᖃᕐᒥᖕᒪᑕ ᑭᕕᐅᕐᒥᒃ. ᑖᒻᓇᓕ ᐅᓂᑉᑳᕐᓂᐊᕆᕋ ᓴᐅᓂᖅᑰᕐᒥᐅᑦ ᐅᓂᑉᑳᖅᑐᐊᕈᓯᖕᒐᓂᒃ ᒪᓕᖕᓂᐊᖅᑐᖅ. ᐃᐊ'ᓇᐃᑦᑐᖅ:

I'm going to tell a story about Kiviuq the way I used to hear it told by my mother, Helen Paunrngat. Please note, though, the story of Kiviuq has many variations in the Arctic. This version of the story is taken from the Hauniqtuurmiut. It goes like this:

ᑕᐃᒻᓇᒎᖅ ᑭᕕᐅᖅ ᖃᖕᒐᓴᕐᔪᐊᖅ ᐃᓅᓚᐅᖅᓯᒪᔫᓐᓂᖅ ᐊᐃᕋᖅᑑᒥ, ᕿᑭᖅᑕᕐᔫᑉ ᓵᖕᒐᓃᑦᑐᒥ. ᑭᕕᐅᖅ ᐊᖕᒐᔪᖅᑳᖅᑲᓚᐅᖅᑐᖅ, ᑕᐃᑉᓯᒪᓂᓗᒎᖅ ᐃᓄᐃᑦ ᐊᑖᖅᓯᒪᓕᕌᖕᒐᒥᒃ ᐱᙳᐊᑦᑐᐊᔪᓚᐅᕐᒪᑕ ᐋᑦᑕᐃᓕᔭᑦᑐᐊᖅᓘᑎᒃ ᕐᑯᕕᐊᓱᑦᑐᐊᔪᓚᐅᕐᒪᑕ ᐅᐱᕐᖓ'ᓈᒥ.

Kiviuq lived with his parents and family a very long time ago over in Airaqtuuq, just off Bibby Island. In those days, Inuit would celebrate the warm summer season by playing toss the ball.

ᑕᐃᒻᓇᔫᖅ ᓂᕕᐊᖅᓯᐊ’ᔪᐊᖅ ᐊᓈᓇᑦᑎᐊᒥᓃᑦᑐᖅ ᐱᙳᐊᓚᓂᒃᑳᖕᒐᑕ ᐊᓐᓄᕌᖕᒋᑦ ᐊᓚᒃᑐᖅᓃᓐᓇᐅᑉᓗᑎᒃ ᐊᐃᕙᖕᒪᑦ ᕿᐊᑉᓗᓂ. ᐋᑦᑕᐃᓚᔭᓚᕌᖕᒐᑕᔫᖅ ᐊᖑᑎᑦ ᐋᑦᑕᐃᓚᔭᖅᑐᑦ ᕿᑎᒃᓯᖅᑐᖦᖤᖅᒥᒡᓗ ᐊᓐᓄᕌᖕᒋᓐᓂᒃ ᐊᓚᒃᑐᐃᑦᑕᖅᑲᑦᑖᔪᖕᒪᔾᔪᒃ, ᐊᓚᒃᑐᖅᓃᓐᓇᐅᑉᓗᓂ ᐊᐃᕙᖕᒪᑦ. ᐋᓈᓇᑦᓯᐊᖕᒐᑕᔫᖅ ᑭᖦᖤᐃᔭᕋᓗᒃᖢᒍ ᐊᐃᔭᕌᖕᒐᑦ ᐊᓚᒃᑐᖅᓂᑯᑦ ᒥᖅᓱᖅᑲᑦᑖᖅᐸᖕᒪᒋᑦ. ᑭᖦᖤᐃᕈᑎᑯᓂᒐᓗᐊᕌᖕᒐᑕᔫᖅ ᐅᑎᖅᒥᔭᕌᖕᒐᑦ ᐋᑦᑕᐃᓚᔭᖅᑐᓄᑦ, ᑎᐊ’ᓇᑐᑦᓴᐃᓐᓇᖅ ᓱᓚ ᐱᖅᑲᑦᑖᖅᐸᖕᒪᔾᔪᒃ, ᐊᓚᒃᑑᖅᓃᓐᓇᐅᑉᓗᓂ ᕿᐊᒻᒫᖅᖢᓂ ᐊᐃᕙᖕᒪᑦ.

A young woman who lived with her grandmother was among those who played the game. But during the game, young men always teased her, ripping her clothes and sending her home with torn stitches. Her

grandmother faithfully mended her clothes tear after tear. But every time the young woman went back to the toss-the-ball game with mended clothes, the whole thing repeated itself all over again, and she would return home in torn clothes and crying.

ᐊᓈᓇᑦᓯᐊᖕᒐᒍᖅ ᐱᙵᒍᓕᑕᐃᓐᓇᕐᒥ, ᐋᑦᑕᐃᓕᔭᓯᒋᐊᑦᑐᐊᕐᒥᖕᒪᑕ ᓂᕕᐊᖅᓯᐊᖅ ᐅᖅᑲᐅᑎᓕᖅᐹ, ᓇᑦᓯᐅᑉ ᓂᐊᖁᐊᑕ ᐊᒥᐊᓂᒃ ᓇᔪᒃᓯᒪᔪᒥᒃ ᑐᓂᒻᒫᖅᑐᒍ ᐊᑭᒥᓂᑦ ᑎᒍᑉᓗᒍ, “ᐱᑦᓯᐊᖕᒋᑕᐅᕆᐊᑦᑐᐊᕐᓂᕐᒥᒍᕕᓇᐃ ᐅᐱᙵᒐᕐᓗᖕᒋᑦ ᐃᒫᓚᐅᕈᒫᖅᐳᑎᑦ ᑖᒻᓇ ᐊᑎᓗᒍ ᐳᐃᕝᔭᕐᓗᑎᑦ ᓇᑦᓯᐅᓯᖅᑐᓚᐅᕈᒫᖅᐳᑎᑦ.” ᓱᓇᐅᕝᕙ ᑕᒃᕙ ᐱᑦᑐᖅᑯᑎᒃᓵᓂᒃ ᑐᓐᓂᖅᓗᓂᐅᒃ ᓇᑦᓯᐅᑉ ᓂᐊᖁᐊᑕ ᐊᒥᐊᓂᒃ ᓇᔪᒃᓯᒪᔪᒥᒃ.

Finally, her grandmother became fed up with her behaviour. The grandmother handed the young woman the skin from a seal's head and said, "When the young men start to tease you, steal away into the water without being noticed and put this on. Then swim around in the water and imitate a seal." The grandmother knew using the sealskin head this way would let her granddaughter get back at her aggressors.

ᐊᓯᐃᓛᒎᖅ ᐋᑦᑕᐃᓕᔭ’ᑐᐊᓕᕐᒥᖕᒪᑕ ᐅᐱᕐᖕᒑ’ᓈᒥ ᓯᓚᑦᓯᐊᕐᔪᐊ’ᔪᐊᕐᒥ, ᑕᐃᒻᓇᓗᒎᖅ ᓂᕕᐊᖅᓯᐊ’ᑐᐊᖅ ᐱᓕᕆᐊᕆᔭᐅᒋᐊᕐᓂᕐᓗᖖᒋᒻᒥᒐᒥ, ᐅᐱᖖᒑᑦᓚᒃᖢᒋᖖᒎᖅ ᓇᑦᓯᐅᑉ ᓂᐊᖅᑯᐊᑕ ᐊᒥᐊ ᐊᑎᑉᓗᒍ ᐃᓛᖅᐳᖅ. ᐋᑦᑕᐃᓕᔭᖅᑐ’ᔪᐃᖖᒎᖅ ᓵᖕᒐᑎᒍᑦ ᑎᐊ’ᓇ ᐳᐃᕙᒃᖢᓂ ᐊᖅᑲᓚᐅᖅᐸᒃᖢᓂ ᓇᑦᓯᐅᓯᖅᑐ’ᔪᐊᓕᕐᒪᑦ.

The young woman returned to where the others were playing toss the ball. But as usual, she was again a target of abuse. She quickly stole away from their company and jumped in the water with the sealskin over her head. She then swam around in front of the people playing ball and imitated a seal by popping her head up and diving back into the water as seals would.

ᐋᑦᑕᐃᓕᔭᕐᑐ'ᔦᐃᖖᒎᖅ ᑕᑯᓇᓵᓚᐅᑯᓂᑦᑐᐊᕐᓯᓐᓇᕐᓗᑎᒃ ᐃᓚᖕᒐᓐᓂᒃ ᑕᑯᕋᐅᕐᑐᕐᑳᓪᓚᓱᖕᒐᔭᖕᒪᑦ ᓇᑦᓯ'ᔦᓂᕋᐃᑉᓗᓂ. ᐊᖑᑎᖖᒎᖅ ᐊᑉᑖᕐᑭᐊᓪᓚᒥᐊᕐᓗᑎᒃ ᐋᑦᑕᐃᓕᔭᓚᐅᕐᓯᒪᖖᒋᑦᑐᑎᑐᑦ ᖃᔭᕐᒥᖕᓄᑦ ᐊᕐᐸᓕᐅᔮᑎᕆᐊᓪᓚᑦᑐᐊᕐᐳᑦ, ᓵᒻᖓᕐᑎᐊᓪᓚᑦᑐᐊᓪᓚᕐᒥᒡᓗ.

The group was busy playing ball and did not notice the young woman for a while. Then one of them exclaimed that they had spotted a seal. The men suddenly dispersed everywhere as if a ball game had never occurred. They all ran to their qajait and in no time at all were out in the water.

ᓇᑦᓯ'ᓈᒻᖖᒎᖅ ᓴᓂᒐᔮᖕᒐᑎᒍᑦ ᐳᐃᕙᒃᓗᓂ ᓵᒻᖓᕐᑎᕈᑎᐅᔭᓕᕐᒪᒋᑦ, ᓵᒻᖓᕋᓗᐊᕐᑎᑦᓗᕆᖖᒎᖅ ᐸᔅᔭᕐᓗᑦᓯᐊᒥᐊᕐᒪᑦ, ᐊᕐᑯᓇᑦᓯᐊᒥᐊᓕᕐᓗᓂ. ᐅᐹᔭᕐᑐᖖᒎᖅ ᐊᐃᔮᕋᓚᓴᐅᒋᐊ'ᔦᐊᕋᓗᐊᕐᒪᑕ, ᓇᐅᒎᖅ ᐱᓐᓇᕈᓐᓇᐃᑐᕐᑲᒥᐊᕐᒪᑦ ᐊᖑᑎᕈᓈ'ᔦᐃᑦ ᖃᔭᐅᕙᒃᓗᑎᒃ ᓵᑉᑕᐅᓗᕐᑭᒥᐊᓯᑦᑐᐊᕐᐳᑦ.

The men began to hunt the little seal. But the young woman stealthily led them out to sea by popping her sealskin head up surprisingly close and then disappearing. No sooner had Kiviuq and the others reached the sea then a sudden storm came, and immediately the waters turned vicious. A lot of men capsized and were blown out to sea.

ᑭᕕᐅᖀᖅ ᓄᑲᖅᑲᓚᐅᖅᒪᑦ, ᓄᒃᑲᓂᓄ ᐊᒥᐊᒃᑯᑰᖅᑲᑦᑖᓕᓚᐅᖅᑰᒐᓗᐊᒃ, ᓄᓇᒨᖅ ᖃᒡᓕᒐᓗᐊᖅᑎᑦᑐᒍ ᒥᙳᖅᑐ'ᔪᐊᕋᒥ ᓄᑳ ᐳᓯᐊᑦᓚ'ᔪᐊᓕᖅᒪᑦ ᐊᖕᒐᔪᐊᑕ ᑭᕕᐅᑉ ᓇᔪᖅᑲᑦᑖᒐ'ᔪᐊᓇᓕᒫ ᑎᒍᒻᒥᑦᓖᑦᑐ ᐃᐳᓐᓂᑐᖅᑲᑦᑖᓕᖅᑰᒐᓗᐊᖅ ᓇᒻᓕᕆ'ᔪᐊᕋᒥᐅᒃ. ᓇᐅᒨᖅ ᐊᔪᖅᓇᖅᓯᖕᒪᑦ ᑕᒪᕐᒥᒎᖅ ᓵᕕᓯᓐᓇᓯᕆᐊᕋᒥᒃ ᓄᑳ ᕿᒪᕐᑯᒥᐊᖅᑕᓕᖅᒪᑦ, ᐊᖏᖅᓈᓴᒥᐊᓚᐅᑦᑐᐊᕋᓗᐊᖅᓱᒍᒎᖅ, ᕿᒪᕐᑯᓕᕐᒥᖕᒪᑦ, ᕿᒪᒍᐊᙱᖅᔪᐊᕋᓗᐊᖅᓱᒍ ᓴᑉᑯᒥᐊ'ᔪᐊᓕᕐᓂᖅᓱᓂᐅᒃ ᐊᔪᖅᓇᖅᓯᑦᑐᐊᕙᖕᒪᑦ.

For a long time, Kiviuq and his younger brother were the only survivors. They managed to come close to land, but suddenly the younger brother capsized from exhaustion. Kiviuq loved his younger brother dearly and he stayed with him for a long time, holding on to him with one hand and trying to paddle ashore. Eventually, though, the younger brother insisted on being left to die, because both looked like they might perish at sea. Kiviuq hesitated for a long time, but finally, against all his wishes, he let his younger brother go.

ᑭᕕᐅᖀᓇᒻᓇ ᐱᑦᑐᕐᑯᑎᕐᑲᓚᐅᕐᓂᕐᒪᑦ ᓵᕝᕋ'ᓈᒥᒃ, ᓵᕝᕋ'ᓈᖀᖅ ᕐᑲᔮᑕ ᐅᓯᐊᖓᓂ ᒥᙵᒐᕐᑲᑦᑖᕐᒪᑦ ᐳᓯᙵᑎᑕᐃᓐᓇᖅᖁᓂ ᓵᑉᑕᐅᖓᒪᑦ.

Now, Kiviuq apparently had a helping spirit in the form of a sandpiper. The little sandpiper landed on the tip of his qajaq and prevented him from capsizing while he drifted out into the stormy sea.

ᓄᓇᓯᓇᓵᑦᓯᐊᒥᐊᓚᐅᖅᓱᓂᒎᖅ ᓄᓇᓯᑦᑐᐊᑕᐃᓐᓇᕐᒪᑦ ᓄᓇ ᓴᓕᐊᖅᓱᒍ ᖃᔮᖅᑐᖅᑲᑦᑖᓕᕐᒪᑦ, ᑕᒃᐱᖕᓇᒎᖅ ᐃᓄᒃᓱ'ᓈᖅ ᑕᑯᓯᖕᒐᔭᖕᒪᒍ ᑐᖅᓲᖅᑐᐱ'ᔪᐊᖅ, “ᐅᕕᓗᖅᑭᐅᓯᐅᑉ ᑎᒍᓇᕚᑎᑦ, ᐅᕕᓗᖅᑭᐅᓯᐅᑉ ᐅᕕᓗᖅᑭᐅᓯᐅᑉ!"

After being out in the sea for a long time without any sight of land, Kiviuq finally made it near the shore. He then started to paddle along the shore until he spotted a little inuksuk. It called out to him, “Don't let the hungry shell get you! Don't let the hungry shell get you!”

ᐃᓱᒪᒋᖖᒋᐅᔭᒥᐊᖅᓱᒍᒎᖅ ᐊᐅᑦᑖᖁᐅᔭᒥᐊ'ᔪᐊᖁᒥ, ᐅᑯᒥᐊᑐᐃᓐᓇᐅᕙᓕᖅᓱᓂᒎᖅ ᐃᔪᐃᑦᓯᐊᒥᐊᓕᕐᒪᑦ ᑐᖅᓲᖅᑐᐱ'ᔪᐊᖅ, “ᐅᕕᓗᖅᑭᐅᓯᐅᑉ! ᐅᕕᓗᖅᑭᐅᓯᐅᑉ!"

Kiviuq ignored it and kept paddling along. But the little inuksuk called out all the more to the point of bending over, “Don’t let the hungry shell get you! Don’t let the hungry shell get you!”

ᐃᓗᖏᖅᑐᕐᓗᐊᕕᓕᕐᒪᖖᒎᖅ ᑭᖑᒻᒧᑦ ᕿᕕᐊᕐᒪᑦ ᑖᒻᓇᒎᖅ ᐅᕕᓗᑯᓗᒃ ᖃᔮᑕ ᑭᖑᓂᓗᐊᒐᔫᖕᒐᓂ ᑮᓯᒋᐊᒻᒥᔪᓗᐊᑯᓗᒃ ᑕᒃᑯᐊᓪᓚᓱᖕᒐᔭᖕᒪᒍ. ᐃᐴᑎᓂᒎᖅ ᖃᔭᕐᒥᓄᑦ ᐱᖅᐸᓪᓚᒃᑎᒐᔫᖕᒪᒍ ᖁᑭᕐᒥ ᑭᕕᒻᒫᑯᓗᓕᖅᑐᓂ.

Kiviuq noticed how intent the inuksuk was in getting his attention, so he turned around towards the back of his qajaq. There he saw a giant clam ready to take a bite out of his qajaq. Kiviuq suddenly struck his qajaq with his paddle. The loud noise killed the clam, and it sank into the water.

ᖃᔭᖅᑐᖅᑐᐃᓐᓇᐅᔭᒥᐊᕐᒪᖖᒎᖅ ᑕᒃᐱᖕᓇᑉᑕᐆᖅ ᓱᓇᑯᓗᑭᐊᖅ ᐸᒥᐅᕐᒥᓂᒃ ᖃᐃᖅᑐᒧᑦ ᓯᑕᔪᓗᐊᑯᓗᒃ. ᖃᔭᖅᑐᖖᒍᑕᕐᒥᒎᖅ ᑐᓚᒃᑐᓂ ᓯᓂᒃᑕᒥᐊᓯᒋᐊᕐᒪᑦ

ᒥᕐᖑᖅᑐᕋᒥ. ᑕᒪᓐᓇᒎᖅ ᒪᓂᖅ ᓯᓂᒃᑕᕋᕕᒋᓂᐊᒃᑲᓂ ᐅᔾᔨᕆᔭᕋᓗᐊᖑ ᐃᓄᕕᓂᖅᑕᖃᕐᒪᑦ, ᐃᓚᖏᒎᖅ ᐱᔭᐅᓹᕐᓂᑯ'ᓈᑦ ᐃᓚᖏᓗ ᓄᑕᐅᙱᓐᓂᖅᓴᑦ, ᐃᓐᓇᖅᑎᓯᒋᐊᖅᑎᓪᓗᒍᒎᖅ ᐅᖃᖅᐸᓪᓚᖕᒪᑦ, "ᓵᑦᑐᒐᕐᒥᒃ ᓴᖅᑲᕐᒥᐅᑦᓯᕐᓗᑎᑦ."

Kiviuq continued right along until he saw a weird-looking figure sharpening its tail upon a rock. Kiviuq was tired from paddling all day long, so he landed ashore to stay for the night. He chose an area to rest, but he was puzzled to see a number of human skeletons scattered around. As he was getting settled for the night, he heard someone say, "Place a flat stone over your chest."

ᑲᒪᖁᙱᑕᐅᕋᓗᐊᖅᓘᓂᒎᖅ ᓵᑦᑐᒐᖅᓯᐅᖅᓘᓂ ᓯᓂᓯᒋᐊᕋᒥ ᓴᖅᑲᕐᒥᐅᑦᓯᐅᑎᕇ. ᓱᓇᐅᕝᕙᒎᖅ ᓴᐅᓂᕕᓂᖅᑕᖃᓗᐊᑐᖕᑳᖅᐳᖅ ᓴᕕᖕᓂᒃ ᐸᒥᐅᓕᑯᓗᖕᓄᑦ ᐱᔭᐅᕝᕙᖕᓂᕐᒪᑕ. ᐃᓐᓇᖕᒐᓕᖅᑎᓪᓗᒍᒎᖅ ᑕᐃᒻᓇ ᐸᒥᐅᕐᒥᓂᒃ ᓯᓕᕐᔪᐊᖅᑕᓚᐅᖅᑐᖅ ᐅᔭᖏᕋᑕᖅᐳᖅ ᐃᓄᒃ ᓯᓂᓕᕋᓱᒋᒐᒥᐅᒃ.

He hesitated for a moment, but then he began walking the area looking for a piece of flat stone. When he found one, he placed it over his chest. Kiviuq again wondered why there were so many human skeletons around. They looked like they had been victims of a creature with a steel tail.

ᐅᔾᔭᖕᒋᑦᓯᖅᑐᖅᓱᓂᒎᖅ ᓯᓂᒃᓯᖅᑐᒥᐊ'ᔪᐊᓕᖅᒪᑦ ᓱᒋᐊᑦᑐᐊᖅᓂᐊᖅᒪᖕᒎᑦ ᐅᐃᑕᒐᔮᒃᓱᓂ ᑕᐅᑐᒃᓱᓂᐅᒃ.

When Kiviuq finally settled, the strange figure that had sharpened its tail earlier slowly appeared. It thought Kiviuq had fallen asleep. Kiviuq pretended not to notice him but watched to see what was about to happen by keeping his eyes open just a wee bit.

ᑭᕕᐅᕘᖅ ᐅᖅᓂ'ᔪᐊᖅᒥᐅᒃ ᓯᓂᒐᓱᒋᑉᓗᒍ ᐆᒪᑎᑭᓇᐊᖅᓱᒍ ᖄᖕᒐᓂᑦ ᐃᖕᒋᕝᕕᒋᖒ ᐸᒥᐅᖅᒧᓂᑦ ᑲᐱᒋᐊᒻᒫᖅᓱᒍ. ᐃᖕᒋᓇᔮᖁᐅᔭᓇᐊᖅᑑᒐᓗᐊᕘᖅ

ᐸᒥᐅᑯᓗᐊᑰᖅ ᓵᑦᑐᒃᑲᒧᑦ ᐅᔭᕋ’ᔪᐊᕐᒥ ᑐᕐᑯᓗᑲᕐᓗᖅᐳᖅ ᓯᑕᐃᐳᑎᒫᑯᓗᓚᖅᖢᓂ.

The strange creature then approached Kiviuq and slowly sat on his chest—intending to pierce the young man with his sharp tail. But as he gleefully let his weight down, his tail hit the flat stone. The creature fell dead and disappeared.

ᖃᐅᖕᒪᖖᑰᖅ ᖃᔭᖅᑐᓇᐊ’ᑐᐊᕐᒥᖕᒪᑦ ᑭᕕᐅᖅ ᐊᖕᒋᓪᕋᒥ ᓇᓛᓄᑦ, ᐊᐅᓪᓛᓚᖅᑲᒥᖖᒋ’ᓈᓪᓚᕐᒥᑰᖅ ᑕᑯᓯᖕᖓᔭᒃᑭᕗᖅ ᑎᒥ’ᓈᒥᓂ ᐃᓯᖅᑐᓗᐊᑯᓗᖕᒥᒃ. ᑐᓛᓪᓚᒃᖢᓂᑰᖅ ᑕᑯᓴᓇᐊᓂᓗᖕᖏᓐᒪᒍ, ᖃᕐᒪᐅᓐᓂᕐᒪᖖᑰᖅ ᑕᖅᑲᒧᖕᒐ ᕿᓛᓂᑦ ᐃᑦᓯᐊᕐᒪᑦ, ᑕᑲᓐᓇᑰᖅ ᐊᒪᐅᑕᓚᑯᓗᒃ ᐅᒃᑯᓯ’ᑐᐊᕐᒥᓄᑦ ᐃᒑᔪᓗᐊᑯᓗᒃ, ᐅᓗ’ᑐᐊᕐᒥᓂᒃ ᑎᒍᒥᓪᓗᓇᒃᓴᑦᑐᐊᓪᓚᕐᒥᓗ.

At daybreak, Kiviuq got in his qajaq for the long journey home. After a while, he spotted smoke just above him. He immediately landed his qajaq and curiously walked up to inspect what it was. He discovered the smoke came from a *qarmaq* (traditional sod house) and, looking in from above, he saw an *amautalik* (mythological ogress that steals children on the land) cooking something disgusting in her big cooking pot. She held a big *ulu* (crescent knife traditionally used by women) in her hand.

ᐃᔭᒃᑭᑕᔫᖅ ᖁᓕᒋᒃ ᑕᓗᐊᖅᓯᒪᒥᐊᖅᒪᓂᒃ ᖁᓖᕈᑎ'ᔪᐊᖕᒐᓂᒃ, ᑭᕕᐅᒻᖕᔫᖅ ᖃᓄᖅ ᐱᑦᑐᐊᖅᓂᐊᖅᒪᖕᒑᑦ ᕿᑦᓯᑦᑐᐊᖅᐹ. ᐃᔮᑕᔫᖅ ᑕᓗᐊᕈᑎ'ᔪᐊᖕᒐᔪᑦ ᕿᑦᓯᖅᒪᔪ ᐅᖅᑲᓱᖕᒐᔭᖕᒪᑦ, "ᐃᒃᑭᑦᕼᐃᖅ, ᐊᓱ ᐆᒪ ᑖᕋᖕᒐ."

The amautalik's eyes were totally covered with her floppy old eyelids. Curious to see what would happen, Kiviuq spat on her from above. His spit landed on one of her floppy eyelids and she said, "Ooo, that's cold! Perhaps this is casting a dark spell in my view."

ᐃᔨᒥᒎᖅ ᕐᑯᓛ ᑎᒡᒍᐊᓪᓚᒃᔪᒍ ᐅᓗ’ᔪᐊᕐᒥᓄᑦ ᐱᓛᓪᓚᒃᔪᒍ ᐅᑦᑯᓯᖕᒥᓄᑦ ᐆᒋᔾᔨᐅᑎᐊᓪᓚᑦᑐᐊᓪᓛᓪᓗ. ᐃᔮᑕᒎᖅ ᐃᓗᐊ ᕐᑭᑦᓯᕐᒥᖕᒪᒍᒎᖅ ᐅᕐᑲᑦᑐᐊᓇᕗᖅ, "ᐃᒃᑭᑭᓪᕼᐃᖅ, ᐊᓯ ᐆᒪ ᑖᕌᖕᒐ."

Then, she grabbed her eyelid and, with her big ulu, cut it off and dropped it into her big cooking pot to stew. Kiviuq then spat on her other eyelid and she said again, "Ooo, that's cold! Perhaps this is casting a dark spell in my view."

ᐃᖕᒥᓂᒎᖅ ᐱᓚᒃᖢᓂ ᐆᑎᔾᔨᕆᐊᕋᓗᐊᕐᒥᒐᒥ ᐃᓄᖕᒥᒃ ᕿᒃᓯᒥᒃᓯᐊᓪᓚᒃᑐ'ᑑᒐᒥ ᐊᒃᑎᕆᐊᕐᓂᕐᓗᖖᒋᒻᒪᑦ, ᑭᕕᐅᕉᖅ ᖃᔭᕐᒥᓄᑦ ᐊᖅᐸᓗᐊᕆᐊᑯᓗᖕᒪᑦ, ᐊᖑᓪᕌᖅᑎᓐᓇᒍᒎᖅ ᖃᔭᕐᒨᖅᖢᓂ, ᓵᒻᖕᒫᓪᓚᑦᑐᐊᓪᓚᕐᒥᓗ.

As she was about to cut another piece off of herself to throw in the stew, the amautalik caught a glimpse of Kiviuq and charged for the exit. Kiviuq ran for his qajaq. He reached his qajaq just before being caught, and then he pushed himself into the water out of her reach.

ᐊᒪᐅᑕᓕᐅᒻᖕᒎᖅ ᐊᖑᖖᒋᓐᓇᒥᐅᒃ ᐅᓗ'ᔪᐊᕐᒥᓄᑦ ᕿᓚᑉᓯᕆᐊᒻᒫᖅᖢᒍ ᐅᖅᑲᖅᖢᓂ, "ᓯᑯᐊᖅᑎᑦᐸᒋᑦ."

The amautalik, being slow to catch her prey, threw her big ulu in his direction and said, "I cast an ice spell on you."

ᐅᓗ'ᑐᐊᖕᒐᒎᖅ ᐃᒫᒍᑦ ᓴᓕᐅᒥᓕᕐᒪᑦ ᐃᒪᖅ ᓯᑯᐊᖅᑐ'ᑑᖕᒪᑦ, ᑭᕕᐅᒻᖕᒎᖅ ᐃᕗᑎᒥᓄᑦ ᓯᑯᐊᖅ ᑲᓕᒋᐊᓪᓛᓪᓗ ᐅᖃᕐᒪᑦᑕᐅᖅ ᖃᓅᒐᓗᐊᕿᐊᖅ ᐃᒪᕈᕐᒥᖕᒪᑦ ᐊᓂᒍᓕᕆᑉᓗᓂ, ᖃᔭᖅᑐᖅᑲᑦᑖᓕᕆᑉᓗᓂᓗ ᐊᖕᒋᕐᕋᐅᓂᓗᒃᖢᓂ.

Her big ulu skimmed along the water and it quickly forced the water to freeze over. But Kiviuq spoke a word against her spell and then touched the ice with his paddle, turning the ice back to water so he could continue his journey.

ᐅᑉᓗᓗᒃᑖ'ᓈᕉᖅ ᖃᔭᖅᑐᓚᐅᕆᑉᓗᓂ ᑭᕕᐅᖅ ᐃᓄᒃᓯᓱᖕᒐᔭᓕᕆᕗᕉᖅ ᐸᓂᒌᖕᒍᓐᓃᖕᓄᑦ ᐊᕐᓇᖅᑯᐊᒃᓵ'ᓈᒧᑦ ᓂᕕᐊᖅᓯᐊ'ᑐᐊᕐᒧᑦᓗ. ᑭᕕᐅᒻᖕᒎᖅ ᓂᕕᐊᖅᓯᐊ'ᑐᐊᖅ ᓄᓕᐊᖅᑖᕆᒐᒥᐅᒃ ᓇᒌᔭᒥᐊᓕᕐᒪᒋᒃ ᒪᖅᐃᖅᓱᒃᐸᒃᖢᓂ ᐊᐃᖅᕕᒋᑦᑕᐅᔭᓕᕐᒪᒋᒃ.

Kiviuq paddled the entire day until he came upon people—a little old lady and a young woman who was her daughter. Kiviuq took the young woman for his wife and remained with them for a time, hunting and returning to them as his home.

ᐊᕐᓇᖅᑯᐊᒃᓵ’ᓈᒻᖒᖅ ᐸᓂᓂ ᐅᐃᖏᕿᐊᖅᓱᒍ ᐃᓱᒪᑦᑕᖅᑐᑯᑑᓕᕐᓂᕋᒥ, ᓂᖓᐅᓂᒎᖅ ᑭᕕᐅᖅ ᒪᖅᑲᐃᓕᕐᒥᖕᒪᑦ ᐸᓂᓂᒎᖅ ᑯᒪᐃᕿᐊᓯᖓᔭᓕᕐᒪᒍ. ᓱᓇᐅᕝᕙᒎᖅ ᑯᒪᐃᖅᓯᖅᑐᑦᑖᑦᑐ ᓯᐅᑖᒍᑦ ᑲᐅᓗᒍ ᐃᒐᓚᐅᔫᕐᓗᒍ ᑐᕐᑯᑦᓱᐊᓕᕐᓂᕋᒥᐅᒃ. ᑯᒪᐃᓕᕋᒥᐅᒎᖅ ᐃᒐᓚᐅᔫᖅᓱᒍ ᑐᕐᑯ’ᑐᐊᕐᒪᒍ, ᓂᐊᖅᑯᐊᒎᖅ ᑕᒪᐅᓇ ᖅᑯᖏᓯᓂᐊᓂᑦ ᐱᑎᐊᖅᓱᒍ ᓇᔪᓱᖓᔭᓕᓇᕖ. ᓱᓇᐅᕝᕙᐅᓇ ᐃᖕᒥᓂᒃ ᐸᓂᑎᓯᖅᑐᓯᑎᐊᖅ ᐸᓂᖕᒥ ᓂᐊᖅᑯᐊᑕ ᐊᒥᐊᓂᒃ ᐊᑎᑐᓂ.

Now, the sly little old lady was secretly plotting in her mind to take away her daughter's husband. Sure enough, one day, while her son-in-law Kiviuq was away hunting, she offered to look for lice in her daughter's hair. As the old lady combed her daughter's hair, she stabbed her daughter in the ear and killed her. The old lady then skinned her daughter's head from the neck up. Her plan was to put the skin over her own head and pretend to be her daughter.

ᑭᕕᐅᕉᖅ ᑎᑭᓵᖅᑐᓕᕌᖓᑦ ᓄᓕᐊᖓᑕ ᓯᒡᔭᓇᖕᓂᖅᓯᐅᕈᑎᖏᖓᒍ ᓂᐅᖁᐃᕝᕕᑦᓯᐊᓇᒃᑐᑉ ᑭᒡᓕᖓᓄᑦ ᖃᔭᖅ ᐸᑎᒃᑎᓯᓐᓇᖅᖢᒍ ᐅᓯᖏᐊᖅᐸᖓᑦ. ᑭᕕᐅᕉᖅ ᒪᖃᐃᓚᐅᖅᖢᓂ ᑎᑭᓵᖅᑐᓕᕐᒪᑦ ᐊᕐᓇᖅᑯᐊᒃᓵ’ᓈᕉᖅ ᐸᓂᒋᓯᖅᑐᖅᖢᓂ ᑭᕕᐅᖅ ᑎᒫᓂᑦ ᑐᖅᖢᑖᓱᖕᒐᔭᓕᕐᒪᒍ ᓄᑐᕐᑦᑐᐊᓪᓚᕐᒥᒍ, “ᒫᔅᓴ ᒫᔅᓴ ᓯᒡᔭᓇᖕᓂᖅ! ᒫᔅᓴ ᒫᔅᓴ ᓯᒡᔭᓇᖕᓂᖅ!"

Normally when Kiviuq came home with his qajaq full of meat, his wife would find a deep spot in the water so he could pull his qajaq along the shoreline and toss his catch ashore. This time, when Kiviuq neared home after his hunt, the little old lady pretended to be her daughter and stood above Kiviuq, calling out and waving wildly, “Here, here! Over here! Here, here! Over here, a nice deep spot!”

ᑭᕕᐅᒻᖒᖅ ᖃᐅᔨᓪᓚᒃᓯᓐᓇ’ᑐᐊᕐᒥᐅᑉ ᓄᓕᐊᓇᙱᓐᓇᒥᐅᑉ ᑕᑉᐱᑯᖓ ᑐᖅᖢᒪᓕᖅᐹ, “ᑲᒥᓪᓚᕐᓗᑎᕐ! ᑲᒥᓪᓚᕐᓗᑎᕐ!”

Kiviuq noticed instantly that the woman was not his wife. So he called back to her, “Take off your boots! Take off your boots!”

ᑲᒥᑦᓚ’ᑐᐊᕐᒪᖖᒎᖅ, Hᐊᒻᒪᒎᖅ ᑳᓅᑎᓇᓐᓇᒃ ᕐᑭᕐᓇᓃᒃ, ᑐᒡᒐᓃᒃ ᐃᕙ’ᓈᖕᖑᔩᐱᑐᐃᓐᓈᒃ.

The old lady took off her boots, and guess what Kiviuq saw—pitiful, dark, skinny legs that looked like dry leaves.

ᑭᕙᐅᒻᖕᒎᖅ ᓄᓕᐊᓇᖖᒋᓐᓇᒥᐅᒃ ᕐᑲᐅᔨᒪ’ᑐᐊᑦᓚᕐᒥ ᓄᓕᐊᓇᔪᖅᑐᖅᑲᑦᑖᒥᐊ’ᔮᐊᓕᕐᒪᒍ ᐊᑦᕐᑳᒍᖖᒎᑎᑉᐳᒍ ᐊᒡᓛᑦ. ᕐᑭᒪᒍᐊᖅᕈᒍᒎᖅ ᐃᓯᒪᕙᓕᕐᒥ ᒪᕐᑲᐃᓕᕌᖕᒐᒥᒎᖅ ᑲᒻᖕᒋᖅᓯᖅᓯᖅᑐᕋᐳᒃᕈᓂ ᐳᐊᐳᐃᖅᓯᖅᓯᖅᑐᕋᐳᒃᕈᓂ ᐱᕙᓕᖅᐳᖅ ᓄᓇᒧᑦ ᕐᑭᒪᑐᓕᕙᒃᕈᓂ ᐊᐃᑭᐊᕐᒥᒍᒥ ᓇᒃᓴᒐᒃᓴᒥᓂᒃ. ᐊᐃᔮᕌᖕᒐᒥᒎᖅ ᐅᕐᑲᖅᐸᖕᒪᑦ, “ᐅᐸᓗᒥ ᑲᒻᖕᒋᖅᓯᕐᕋᕐᒥᒐᒪ.” ᐅᕝᕙᔫᕝᕙ, “ᐅᐸᓗᒥ ᐳᐊᐳᐃᖅᓯᕐᕋᕐᒥᒐᒪ.”

Kiviuq knew that this woman wasn’t his true wife. But he pretended to live with her as his wife for a full year. Eventually, though, he began to think about leaving. So he began to pretend to lose a boot or a mitt

whenever he was out on the land. Really, though, Kiviuq was storing them for the time when he would take them on his journey. Every time he came home, Kiviuq would say, "Clumsy me lost a boot again today!" Or, "Clumsy me lost my other mitt again today!"

ᑎᐊ'ᓇᒎᖅ ᐱᒐᔪᓗᐊᓕᕐᒪᑦ ᐲᖅᓯᖁᔪᓗᐊᓕᕐᒪᑦ ᐊᕐᓇᖅᑯᐊᒃᓵ'ᓈᖅ ᐃᓕᒪᑦᓴᒃᑲᒥ ᐅᕐᑲᓱᖕᒐᔭᖕᒪᑦ, "ᕐᑭᒪᒍᒪᕙᓕᖁᒥᖕᒐᕐᑳ ᐆᒪ ᑲᒻᖕᑎᖅᓯᖅᓯᖅᑐᖅᕈᓂᑐ, ᐳᐊᓗᐃᖅᓯᖅᓯᖅᑐᕐᕈᖅᐸᓚᖅᐸ?"

But the old lady became suspicious, noticing how often Kiviuq lost items, and so she said, "Perhaps someone is plotting to leave me when they are out losing boots and mitts."

ᑭᕕᐅᑮᖅ ᐅᕐᑲᖅᐸᒃᕈᓂ ᐅᔾᔮᖕᑎᑦᓯᖅᑐᖅᕈᓂ, "ᕐᑭᒪᓚᖖᑎᓐᓂᑉᑭᑦ ᐅᖕᒐᑎᕐᕈᖁᑉᑭᑦ."

Kiviuq would then sarcastically reply, "Oh, I would never dare leave you because I'm totally attracted to you."

ᐊᕐᓇᖅᑯᐊᒃᓵ'ᓈᕉᖅ ᑭᐅᓯᓐᓇᖅᐸᒃᕈᓂ, "ᕐᑭᒪᒍᒪᕙᓕᕐᓂᕈᖕᒪᐊᐃ ᓯᕗᕐᖕᑎᑦ ᐃᓗᕐᑭᐅᖅᑕᕐᑲᖅᐳᖅ."

The little old lady would simply reply, "I'll have you know that if you are plotting to leave me, many evil spells are before you."

"ᐊᓯᒎᖅ ᕐᑭᒪᓚᖖᑎᓐᓂᑉᑭᑦ ᐅᖕᒐᑎᕐᕈᖁᑉᑭᑦ."

Kiviuq would then answer again, "Oh, honestly, I will never leave you as I am totally attracted to you."

ᑭᕕᐅᒻᖕᒎᖅ ᕐᑭᒪᑐᓕᐊᓂ ᓈᒻᒪᒃᓯᓇᓱᑎᒐᒥᒥᑦ ᒪᕐᑲᐃᓯᑎᐊᕐᒥᒐᒥ ᐊᕐᓇᖅᑯᐊᒃᓵ'ᓈᖅ ᐅᕐᑲᐅᑎᓕᖅᐹ, "ᐅᖕᒐᕙᓕᐊ'ᑐᐊᕐᓂᐊᓕᖁᒪᐊᐃ ᑎᑭᓐᓇᓵ'ᑐᐊᕐᓂᐊᖅᐳᖕᒐ."

Finally, Kiviuq determined his collection of items was enough for the trip, and he told the little old lady before going hunting, "This time I am going on an extended hunting trip, so it will be a while before I get home."

ᐊᕐᓇᖅᑯᐊᒃᓵ'ᓈᕉᖅ ᐅᖅᑲᖅᓯᓐᓇᖅᕋᓂ, "ᓯᕗᕐᖏᓇᐃ ᐃᓗᕐᑭᐅᖅᑕᖅᑲᖅᐳᖅ."

The little old lady simply replied, "Be assured of evil spells before you."

ᑭᕕᐅᒻᒨᖅ ᐊᕐᓇᖅᑯᐊᒃᓵᑎᓇᓂᖅ ᕿᒪᒥᐊ'ᔪᐊᓕᕐᒪᒍ ᑎᐊ'ᓇ ᖃᔭᖅᑐᖅᑲᑦᑖᓕᖅᐸᒃᕋᓂ ᐃᒪᐅᓂᕐᓂ ᓄᓇᐅᓂᕐᓂᓗ ᐱᓱᖅᑲᑦᑖᓕᖅᐸᒃᕋᓂ. ᐅᖕᒐᕙ'ᓈᖅᓯᓐᓇᖅᑎᑦᓗᒍᒎᖅ ᐃᓗᕐᑭᐅᑎᑦ ᓯᕗᙵᓂ ᐊᓯᐃᑖ ᓵᖅᑭᑦᑕᓇᐊᓱᖕᒐᔭᓕᕐᒪᑕ. ᐃᓗᕐᑭᐅᑎᑦ ᐃᓚᖕᒐᑦ ᓯᕗᑦᓕᖅᐹᖅ ᑕᐃᓂᐊᙱᑦᑕᕋᓘᓐᓃᑦ ᑑᓵᔭᒃᓴᐅᖕᒋᒻᒪᑦ.

Kiviuq then left the despicable little old lady, taking extended paddling journeys over the waters and long treks over the land. But sure enough, having covered a considerable distance, the evil spells began to appear in front of him. I will refrain from telling about the first spell that appeared as it is too despicable for the listener's ear.

ᐱᓲᔭᖅᑲᑦᑖᖅᐸᒃᑲᒥᒎᖅ ᐊᐳᖅᓯᓱᖕᒐᔭᓕᓇᕗᖅ ᐅᒃᑯᓯ'ᑐᐊᕐᒥᒃ ᑎᖅᑎᑦᑐᓗᐊᒥᐊᑯᓗᖕᒥᒃ. ᐱᓯᒥᐊᕋᓗᐊᖄᖕᒐᖖᒎᖅ ᓯᕗᕐᖏᐅᐲᓐᓇᑦᓯᐊᒥᐊᓕᕐᒥᖕᒪᑦ ᖃᓄᖅ ᐱᑦᑐᐊᕐᓂᐊᓕᕐᒥᖕᒪᖕᒑᕐᒦ ᐃᖅᑲᖅᓴᖃᒥ ᐃᓯᒪᓱᖕᒐᔭᓕᖅᐳᖅ ᐅᒃᑯᓯᐅᑉ ᓯᓈᓄᑦ ᑐᑎᓚᐅᕐᓗᓂ ᐆᒥᑎᒍᑦ ᒪᐅᔭᕐᖄᑦᓚᒥᐊᑦᑐᐊᕐᓗᓂ ᐅᒃᑯᓯ'ᑑᑉ

ᐃᒡᓗᐊᓄᖅᓲᖅ ᑐᑎᓗᓂ. ᐊᓯᐃᓛᒎᖅ ᐃᓱᒪᒋᐊ'ᓈᓪᓚᕿᓗ ᐅᒃᑯᓯᐅᑉ ᓯᓈᓄᑦ ᑐᑎᓚᐅᖅᓱᓂ ᐆᒥᑎᒍᑦ ᒪᐅᔦᖀᓪᓚᒃᓱᓂ ᐊᑭᐊᓄᖅᓱᐅᑎᐊᓪᓚᑦᑐᐊᖅᐳᖅ, ᓱᑕᐃᕈᑎᒐᒥᓗᒎᖅ ᐅᒃᑯᓯᒃ ᓴᖅᑭᒃᑲᓐᓂᖏᑕᐃᓐᓇᓕᕆᑉᓗᓂ.

Kiviuq then took another long trek over the land until he came across a huge cooking pot boiling wildly. Every time he advanced a little, the pot would block his path. He pondered for a bit on what to do, and then he decided he would quickly jump up on the edge of the pot and spring over the cooking items until he stepped over the other edge of the pot. Before taking a second thought, he jumped suddenly and ran all the way across over the cooking items. The instant he crossed over the pot, it disappeared and never reappeared again.

ᐱᓲᔭᒥᐊ'ᑐᐊᓕᕐᒥᖕᒪᖖᒎᖅ ᐅᖕᒐᕙᖁᐊᕐᒥᑎᑦᓗᒍ ᑖᑉᑯᐊᒃᑕᐅᑰᖅ ᐊᒃᓴ'ᑐᐊᒃ ᐅᒋᐊᖅᑐᒥᐊ'ᑐᐊᒃ ᒥᒃᑭᐅᒥᐊᑦᑐᐊᖅᐳᑎᒃ. ᓂᒍᒐᒃᓴᐅᔪᖕᓇᐃᕐᒥᖕᒪᓂᒎᖅ ᐱᓱᒋᐊᖁᓗᐊᖀᖕᒐᑦ ᓯᕗᓂᕐᒥᐅᑕᓃᓐᓇᒥᐊᓕᕐᒐᒥᒋᒃ ᐃᓱᒪᓱᖕᒐᔭᓕᓴᕚᖅ ᐊᕙᑦᐸᓂᒃ ᐊᑉᓯᒪᓚᐅ'ᓈᖅᑐᖕᓂᒃ ᐊᑯᑦᑐᐊᓪᓚᕆᐊᑦᑐᐊᕈᐊᖅᐳᕆᒃ. ᐊᓯᐃᓛᒎᖅ ᑭᖕᒪᐅᑦᑐ'ᑐᐊᒃ ᐊᑉᓯᒪᓚᐅᑉᖃᖅᐸᖕᒪᓂᒃ, ᐊᑉᓯᒪᓚᐅ'ᓈᖅᑐᖕᓂᒎᖅ ᐊᓯᐃᓛᒃ ᐊᑯᑦᑐᕐᓱᕆᒃ ᐊᖅᐸᓗᐊᓇᐊᑯᓗᖕᒪᑦ, ᑮᔭᐅᑦᖀᕿᓂ ᐊᓂᒡᒍᐊᓪᓚᑦᑐᐊᕐᒥᖕᒪᕆᒃ ᓱᑕᖅᑲᓚᐅᖅᑐᕕᓂᖅᓯᒪᔾᔪᓐᓇᐃᓇᐳᓗᑎᒃ.

Kiviuq started off again on foot, and when he had gone a little ways, there suddenly appeared two angry brown bears viciously fighting in front of him. Again, there was no way of avoiding them because they kept blocking his path. So Kiviuq decided he would dash between the bears when they briefly stepped apart. But the bears hardly ever let go of each other. So when they finally separated for an instant, Kiviuq ran for it, and he again passed through and the bears disappeared as if they had never existed.

ᐊᐃᓱᐊ'ᑐᐊᕐᒥᒨᖅ ᐊᑕᐅᖅᑲ ᑭᕕᐅᖅ ᐱᓲᖅᑲᑦᑖᓕᕐᒥᖕᒪᑦ ᑭᖕᒍᓪᓕᖅᐸᖕᒍᒻᒫᓕᕐᓂᖅᑯᓂᒨᖅ ᐃᓗᕿᐅᑦ ᐊᐳᑦᑐᐊᓕᕆᓇᕚ ᑭᖖᒐ'ᑐᐊᒨᖅ ᑲᓲᑦᑐ'ᑐᐊᒃ, ᑲᓱᑦᑐᐊᖀᖕᒐᓂᒨᖅ ᐅᔭᕿ'ᑐᐃᑦ, ᐅᔭᕿᓲᒡᔭᕿᓗᒥᐊᑦᑑᒃ ᐱᒃᓯᒑᒥᐊᑦᑐᐊᓕᖅᐸᒃᓗᑎᒃ ᓇᒧᓗᒃᑖᖅ. ᓂᒍᒐᒃᓴᐅᔪᖕᓇᐃᕐᒥᖕᒪᖖᒨᖅ, ᐊᓂᒍᕐᓗᒍ ᑭᓯᐊᓂᐅᓕᕐᒥᖕᒪᑦ ᑭᕕᐅᕉᖅ ᐃᓱᒪᓱᖕᒐᔭᓕᕆᕗᖅ ᐊᑯᑦᑭᑦᓗᒋᒃ ᐊᖅᐸᓕᖅᑐᐊᓪᓚᕆᐊᑦᑐᐊᑭᐊᖅᑯᓂ.

With the urge to reach home, Kiviuq took another long trek across the land. But eventually one last evil spell appeared before him: two giant hills clashing at each other. When they banged each other, rocks and boulders flew everywhere. It was again difficult to avoid the obstacle and crucial to pass through it. Kiviuq decided to rush past the two clashing mountains.

ᑭᕕᐅᕉᕆᓪᓇ ᐊᑎᕆᖅᑲᓚᐅᖅᓯᒪᖕᒪᑦ ᐊᑯᕿᐅᔭᓕ'ᑐᐊᕐᒥᒃ, ᑕᑯᕿᓐᓂᑦᑐᐊᕙᓚᐅᕐᒥᖕᒪᑕ ᐊᑯᕿᐅᔭᓕ'ᑐᐃᑦ ᐊᖑᑎᑦ ᐊᑎᒐᐃ. ᑭᖖᒐ'ᑐᐊᒨᖅ ᐊᑯᑦᑐᖅᓯᒪᓚᐅ'ᓈᖅᑐᖕᓂ ᑭᕕᐅᖅ ᐊᖅᐸᓕᖅᑐᓗᐊᕆᐊᑯᓗᖕᒪᑦ ᐊᑯᑦᑭᔅᓗᒋᒃ. ᐊᐳᖅᑳᖅᑎᓐᓇᒋᒨᖅ ᐊᓂᒍᖅᑐᑯᓂᐅᒐᓗᐊᖅ, ᖀᔭᐅᑦᕿᔭᑦᓯᐊᒥᐊᕐᒪᖖᒨᖅ ᐊᑯᕿᐅᔭ'ᑐᐊᖕᒐ ᐊᓪᓛᑦ ᑭᓪᒋᑎᒐᒥ, ᐊᑯᐃᑐᐃᓐᓇᐅᒐᓗᐊᖅᑯᓂ ᐊᓂᒎᑎᑦᑐᐊᕐᓂᕆᓇᕙ ᐃᓗᕿᐅᑎᑯᓗᒃ.

Incidentally, Kiviuq was wearing a beautiful atigi with an extra-long back flap. When young men wore them in those days, they were a sight to see! Kiviuq waited until the two clashing mountains separated briefly and then ran as fast as he could between them. He got through, but he was almost crushed, and his extra-long back flap got caught and tore off. He did manage to pass the evil spell, but not until his back flap was torn off.

ᐃᓗᕿᐅᑎᑦ ᐊᓂᒍᖅᓯᒪᓕᕐᒪᑕ ᑭᕕᐅᖅ ᖃᔮᖅᑐᖅᑲᑦᑖᓕᕐᓂᕐᒥ ᐊᓯᐃᑖᓘᖅ ᑕᒃᐸᒐ ᓄᓇᐅᓕᖅᐳᖅ ᑐᐊᑦᑐᒪᔫᖑᒃᑉᓗᓂ. ᖃᖓᓕᓕᕐᒥᐅᓞᖅ ᐃᓕᑕᕆᕚ ᐊᐃᕐᖅᑑᖑᖓᒪᑦ. ᑎᑭᓵᖅᑐᓕᕐᖕᖓᒥ ᐊᕕᐅᕙᓚᐅᕐᓂᕐᒪᑦ ᐊᕕᐅᑦᑕᓕᖅᐳᕈᖅ.

Having passed all of the evil spells, Kiviuq again began his long journey home by qajaq. In time, he spotted land—a very thin outline on the horizon. When he came closer he recognized it to be Airaqtuuq and, as was his custom, Kiviuq let out a joyful howl like he had always done when he approached home after hunting.

ᑭᕕᐅᑉ ᐊᖓᔪᖅᑳᕆᒃ ᐊᑖᑖᓗ ᐊᓈᓈᓗ ᐊᓪᕌᒍᙱᑎᑉᓗᑎᒃ ᐊᒡᓛᑦ ᓴᓂᓕᓃ'ᓈᖅᓘᑎᒎᖅ ᖃᐃᖅᑐᑉ ᖄᖓᓂ ᐃᒃᓯᕙ'ᓈᖅᓘᑎᒃ ᐃᕐᓂᕐᒥᖕᓂᒃ ᓂᕆᐅᖅᑲᑦᑖᖅᑑᓐᓃᒃ ᑕᐅᓄᖕᓇ ᑕᕆᐅᑉ ᓇᑖᓄᑦ ᕿᓂᖅᑲᑦᑖᒥᐊᖅᓘᑎᒃ, ᐊᕕᐅᔦᒃᓴᒥᒡᓗ ᓈᓚᖅᑲᑦᑖᒥᐊᖅᑐᒃ.

Now, for a whole year Kiviuq's father and mother had sat side by side on a rocky surface, keeping watch on the horizon for their son's return. They had been constantly watching the horizon and listening for the joyful howl of a hunter.

ᑭᕕᐅᒻᖕᒨᖅ ᐊᕕᐅᖅᐸᓗᐊ ᑐᓴᖅᓴᕈᕐᒪᑦ ᐅᕐᑲᖅᑕᓕᖅᐳᒃ, "ᐄ, ᐄ, ᐃᒻᒪᓕᒨᖅ ᑭᕕᐅᑉ ᓂᐹ!"

When Kiviuq's joyful howl was heard faintly in the distance, the parents said, "Surely, yes surely, that is Kiviuq's joyful howl!"

ᐃᓄᐃᑦ ᖁᕕᐊᑦᓴᓗᐊᒧᑦ, ᖁᒡᓗᓗᐊᒧᑦᓘᖕᖏ ᓄᓯᓕᖕᓂᕋᒐᐅᕙᖕᒪᑕ ᑐᖅᑯᐊᑦᓚᒥᐊᖅᓱᑎᒃ, ᑭᕕᐅᒻᖕᒨᖅ ᐊᖓᔪᖅᑳᕆᒃ ᖁᕕᐊᑦᓴᓗᐊᒧᑦ ᓄᓯᓕᒃᓱᑎᒃ ᑐᕐᑯᓚᐅᖅᓯᒪᔪᒃ, ᐃᕐᓂᖓᒃ ᐊᐃᕙᖅᑑᒧᑦ ᑎᑭᓐᓇᒥ ᖃᑭᒐᓗᐊᖅᑎᑦᓗᒍᓗ. ᐊᖑᖅᑲᔭᕋᓗᐊᖅᓱᕆᒨᖅ ᑭᕕᐅᑉ ᐊᖓᔪᖅᑳᖕᓂ ᑐᕐᑯᑉᓗᑎᒡᓗ ᓄᓇᓕᓚᐅᖅᓯᒪᕗᖅ.

But it is known by Inuit that sudden excitement or sudden surprise can cause a person to succumb to heart attack and die suddenly. Kiviuq's parents were so overcome by excessive happiness that they succumbed to heart attacks, and both died at the very moment their son set foot on Airaqtuuq. Kiviuq almost made it to see his parents still alive, but they fell dead as he stepped ashore.

ᐅᖅᑲᐅᑎᔭᐅᕙᓚᐅᖅᐸᖕᒪᓕ ᐅᓂᑉᑳᒪᐅᒪᓂᒃᑳᖕᒪᑦ ᑭᕕᐅᖅ, ᓱᓕᒨᖅ ᐆᒪᖕᒪᑦ ᑭᓯᐊᓂᒨᖅ ᐃᓄᖕᓄᑦ ᑕᑯᔭᐅᓯᐊᔪᐃᑦᑑᓂᓚᐅᖅᑐᖅ ᑕᑕᕝᕗᓯᐊᖖᒋᕐᓱᓂ ᐃᑦᓴᖅᓂᑕᐅᓗᐊᓗᖕᒨᖅ ᓄᓇᑰᖅᑲᑎᕋᒥ ᐊᒃᓛᑦ ᐃᓕᑕᓇᔭᐅᓚᐃᖅᒪᑦ.

I used to be told soon after finishing Kiviuq's story that he is still alive, but that he refrains from being seen by people so as not to frighten them. He is so old now that earth has started to grow on him, and no one would recognize him anymore.

ᐃᓱᐊ
The end

ᐅᒃᑳᓚᔫᕐᓂᖅ ᑲᓪᓗᒡᓗ
LIGHTNING AND THUNDER

ᐅᓂᑉᑳᖅᑐᐊᕐᓂᐊᖅᑐᖓ ᐅᒃᑳᓚᔫᕐᓂᖅ ᑲᓪᓗᖕᓂᓪᓗ ᓇᑭᑦ ᐱᒋᐊᕐᓯᒋᔭᐅᕙᖕᒪᖔᑦ ᐃᓄᐃᑦ ᐅᒃᐱᕈᓱᖕᒋᑎᒍᑦ. ᑕᐃᑉᓱᒪᓂ ᐱᓇᓱᖕᓇᖅᑐᓄᑦ ᑳᖕᓇᖅᑐᕐᓗᖕᓄᑦ ᐊᓐᓂᐊᕐᓇᖅᑐᓄᓪᓗ ᐊᓪᓚᙳᖅᑎᑕᐅᕙᓚᐅᕐᒪᑦ ᐃᓅᓯᖅ, ᐃᓚᒌᑦ ᐃᓚᑯᙳᖅᔪᑎᒃ ᐃᓕᐊᕐᔫᓕᐊᓪᓚᒥᐊᖅᔪᑎᒡᓗ ᐱᕙᓪᓕᐅᕐᒪᑕ. ᑕᐃᒪ ᑖᓐᓇ ᐅᓂᑉᑳᖅᑐᐊᖅ ᑕᐃᑉᑯᓇᙵᑦ ᐱᓇᓱᖕᓇᖅᑐᕐᔪᐊᕕᓃᑦ ᐃᓚᖓᓐᓂᑦ ᐱᒋᐊᕐᓂᑯᕕᓂᐅᓐᓂᖅ ᐃᐊ'ᓇ ᐅᓂᑉᑳᒐᐅᑎᓪᓗᒍ ᑐᓵᕙᓚᐅᒐᕐ:

I am going to tell a story about the origin of lightning and thunder according to traditional beliefs of Inuit. Long ago there were periods of destitution because of famine or sickness. These forced drastic changes to life and loss of family often left orphans to abruptly fend for themselves. This story comes from such times. It goes like this:

ᑕᐃᑉᓯᒪᓂᑰᖅ ᑕᐃᑉᑯᐊᒃ ᐃᓕᐊᕐᔪ’ᓈᒃ ᓇᔾᒦᒃ ᓯᓚᑐᔪ’ᓈᖑᓛᒃ ᐊᐅᑦᓛᔾᔪᓄᑦ ᕿᒻᒪᑰᔫᓐᓃᒃ ᐃᒡᓗᕖᒃᑲᓄᑦ.

Long ago there were two orphans, a brother and a sister. The two were old enough to make their own judgments, and so one day they were left behind in an abandoned iglu as others moved on.

ᐅᓐᓄᖕᒪᖔᑰᖅ ᐃᒡᓗᕖᒃᑲᓄᑦ ᕿᒻᒪᑯᓯᐅᓗᓕᖅᐳᒃ ᓱᓇᐃᑦᑑᒐᒥᒃ, ᐊᕝᕙᒃᓴᕋᓗᖕᒥᖕᓂᒃ ᕿᐱᒃᓴᕋᓗᖕᒥᖕᓂᒃ ᕿᒻᒪᑯᖅᑲᑦᑐᐊᖏᒻᒪᖕᒌᑦ. ᐃᒡᓗᕖᒐᐃᖖᒎᖅ ᐃᑯᒪᖖᒋᓐᓇᒥᒃ ᑖᖅᑐ’ᑑᖕᒪᑕ ᑖᒻᓇ ᓇᔾᖓ ᐃᖕᓇᒃᓱᓂ ᓇᓂᕈᐊᕐᓂᓗᒃᑕᓕᖅᓱᓂ.

When night came, they went around to check the old igluit for any items left behind that they could use for things like placemats or bed covers. As the old igluit were dark without a lamp, the sister used a flint to make sparks to light their way.

ᐃᒡᓗᕕᒐᓗᒃᑖᖕᒨᖅ ᕿᓂᖅᓯᒪᓕᖅᑎᑦᑐᒋᑦ ᐃᓚᖓᓐᓂᑦ ᑭᖑᓪᓕᖅᐹᒥᑦ ᓇᒡᓖ'ᓈᑦᑐᐊᖅᐳᒃ ᒥᖅᑯᐃᑦᑐᕕᓂᕐᒥᒃ ᐸᓐᓇᖏᕐᒥᒃ. ᑎᒍᔭᕌᖓᒃᑯᒫᖅ ᐸᓂᕌᖅᐸᒍᑦᓯᐊᒥᐊᖅᑕᖅᑐᓂ. ᑖᒪᓇᒨᖅ ᐊᓂᐊ ᕿᕐᖓᒐᓱᖓᔭᓕᕐᒪᑦ ᐊᖓᔪᖅᑳᕕᓂᕐᒥᖕᓄᑦ ᐃᑲᔪᒐᐅᑦᑐᐊᕈᐊᖅᖢᓂ, ᑲᑦᑐᖕᖑᕈᐊᓕᖅᖢᓂ ᐊᒻᒪᒨᖅ ᓇᔭᓂ ᐅᒃᑳᓚᔮᖑᓕᕐᓗᓂ.

After going through each abandoned iglu, they came upon the last iglu and found an old animal skin without hair. Every time they picked it up, it made a deep, dry sound. The brother conjured the spirit of their parents and begged to be turned into thunder and his sister to be turned into a lightning flash.

ᑕᐃᒪᓕ ᐊᓯᐃᓛᒃ ᐊᓂᐊ ᕿᕐᖓᒐᒐ'ᑐᐊᕐᓂᕐᒪᑦ ᐅᒃᑳᓕᑦᑐᐊᕐᒪᖕᒨᖅ ᓇᔮ ᖄᖓᑦᑕᖅᖢᓂ ᐅᒃᑳᖕᖑᖅᖢᓂ ᐊᒻᒪᒨᖅ ᐊᓂᐊ ᖄᖓᑦᑕᖅᖢᓂᑉᑕᐅᖅ ᑲᑦᑑᒥᖅᐸᓪᓚᑦᑐᐊᓪᓚᕐᒥᒍ.

So it was that the brother's wish came to pass, when suddenly a bolt of lightning flashed. His sister was lifted off the ground and turned into lightning, while he was also lifted off the ground, and a loud rumble of thunder was heard.

ᑕᐃᒪ ᑲᑦᑐᓚᖀᖕᒐᑦ ᒥᖅᑯᐃᑦᑐᖅ ᐸᓂᖀᖅᐸᑐᑦᑐᐊᖀᖕᒐᑐᑦ ᐱᖅᐸᑐᑐᖕᒑᖅᐸᓚᖅᐳᖅ ᓇᔭᕇᒃ ᐊᓂᐊᑕ ᐱᖅᐸᑐᒃᑎᑦᓯᓂᐊ ᒥᖅᑯᐃᑦᑐᒥᒃ ᖃᖕᒐᑦᑕᐅᑎᓐᓂᑯᒥᓂᒃ, ᐊᒻᒪ ᐅᒃᑳᓚᔫᑦᑐᐊᕙᓯᑉᐳᓂ ᓇᔫ ᐃᖕᓇᐅᑎᒥᓂᒃ ᖃᖕᒐᑦᑕᐅᑎᓐᓂᑯᒥᓂᒃ ᑲᓯᑲᖅᑕᐅᑎᑦᓯᑉᐳᓂ ᐃᖕᓇᓚᖀᖕᒐᑦ.

That is why every time you hear thunder it sounds like a brittle dry skin—it's because the brother is shaking the skin that he took with him, and all that lightning is coming from the girl's flint stones as she hits them together, causing a flash of lightning.

ᑎᐊ'ᓇ ᑕᒪᓐᓇ ᐅᒃᑳᓚᔫᕐᓂᐅᑉ ᑲᑦᑐᒃᐸᑐᖕᓂᐅᑉᑐ ᐱᖅᐸᑐᒃᑕᕐᓂᖕᒐ ᐱᒋᐊᕐᓂᕋᒐᐅᑉᑐᓂ ᐅᓂᑉᑳᖅᑐᐊᒐᐅᑎᑦᑐᒍ ᑑᓴᕋᓚᐅᖅᐸᕋ.

That is how I heard the story being told of where thunder and lightning come from.

ᐃᓱᐊ
The end

ᑕᖅᑭᕐᓗ ᓯᕐᑭᓂᕐᓗ
MOON AND SUN

ᐅᓂᑉᑳᖅᑐᐊᕐᓂᐊᖅᑐᖓ ᐃᓄᐃᑦ ᐅᑉᐱᕈᓯᖕᒋᑎᒍᑦ ᓇᑭᑦ ᐱᒋᐊᖅᓯᒪᒻᒪᖕᒑᓃᑉ ᑕᖅᑭᕐᓗ ᓯᕐᑭᓂᕐᓗ. ᓱᓇᓗᑉᑖᑦ ᐱᒋᐊᕐᓂᖅᑲᖅᓘᑎᑉ ᑭᓯᐊᓂ ᓄᐃᑕᖕᒪᑕ ᐅᕝᓗᒥ, ᑐᓴᐅᒪᓐᓇᕐᒪᑦ ᖃᖕᒐᓴᕐᔪᐊᕉᖅ ᓯᑕᕐᔪᐊᖅ ᑖᖅᑐᕐᔪᐊᖕᒍᑕᐅᖅᓯᒪᖕᒪᑦ, ᐅᕝᕙᓕ ᖃᓄᖅ ᐅᕝᓗᒃᑯᑦ ᐅᓐᓄᐊᒃᑯᓪᓗ ᖃᐅᒪᔪᖅᓯᓐᓂᕐᒪᖕᒌᑦ, ᐃᐊ'ᓇ ᐅᓂᑉᑳᒐᐅᑎᓪᓗᒍ ᑐᓵᕙᑕᐅᒐᕐ.

I am going to tell you a story based on the traditional Inuit belief of where the moon and sun came from. It is said that a long time ago total darkness engulfed the earth. This story tells how light came to rule day and night.

ᖃᖕᒐᓴᕐᔪᐊᕉᖅ ᑕᐃᑉᑯᐊᒃ ᓇᔭᕇ'ᓈᒃ ᐊᖕᒐᔪᖅᑳᖕᒋᕈᑎᒐᒥᒃ ᕿᒻᒪᒎᓇᓪᓚᐊᕐᒥᔪᒃ, ᐱᓱᖅᑦᑖᓕᖅᑑᓐᓃᒃ ᐃᓄᒃᓴᓂᒃ ᐊᐳᖅᓵᖅᓘᑎᒃ. ᐱᓱᖅᑦᑖᖅᐸᒃᑲᒥᒎᖅ ᐊᓯᐃᓛᒃ ᑕᑯᓱᖕᒐᔪᖕᒪᓂᒃ ᑖᕐᓂᐅᑉ ᑭᓪᓕᖕᒐᓂ ᐃᒡᓗᑦ ᐅᒃᑳᖕᒋᓐᓂᒃ. ᒥᕐᖑᓱ'ᑐᐊᓕᕋᓗᐊᓪᓚᕐᒥᒎᖅ ᓄᖅᑲᖕᒐᓚᐅᖅᐸᒃᓗᑎᒃ ᖃᓪᓕᓕᖅᑦᑖᕋᒥᒃᑯ ᑎᑭᑦᑐᐊᑕᐃᓐᓇᕋᒥᒃ, ᐃᑯᒪᓚᐅᖕᒪᑕ ᐃᑎᖅᓘᑎᒃ ᐊᑭᒧᑦ ᓇᖕᒋᖅᓯᕚᓘᑎᒃ ᖃᐅᔨᑦᓯᓕᖅᐳᒃ.

A very long time ago, two pitiful young children, a brother and sister, were abandoned by their parents. They walked for a long time, hoping to find other people. Finally, one night, they saw lights from igluit flickering on the edge of darkness. They were tired and exhausted, but the children pressed on, stopping only to rest. At last, they neared the lights. The *qullit* (seal oil lamps) burned so brightly that their light drew the children towards them. Eventually, the brother and sister reached the entrance of an iglu and waited to see how the people inside would receive them.

ᖃᒡᒋ'ᐹᓂᖏᒪᙳᖅ ᒧᒥᑦᑐᐊᓪᓚᕐᒥᒃᑯ ᐱᙳᐊᕐᕕ'ᐹᓂᖑᒧᑦ ᐃᑎᖏᒪᓂᒃ ᓇᔅᒌ'ᓈᒃ, ᐃᑎᖅᑑᒎᖅ ᖃᐅᔾᔭᐅᒐᒥᒃ ᑎᑭᕗᒻᒥᑕᖅᑎᑕᐅᖅᑐᑎᒃ. ᖃᒡᒋᐊᔨᒪᔮᙳᖅ ᐊᖑᑎᕋᓗᐃᑦ ᐃᓅᓱᒃᑐᕋᓗᐃᑦ ᐊᕐᓇᑦ ᓂᕕᐊᖅᓯᐊᓪᓗ ᒧᒥᐊᓂᖕᒪᑕ ᐱᙳᐊᓯᒋᐊᖏᒪᑕ ᑖᑉᑯᐊᒃ ᑎᑭᕌᒃ ᐱᙳᐊᖃᑕᐅᒋᐊᕐᔫᒥᒻᒫᓚᖅᑯᑎᒃ.

The iglu the pitiful brother and sister entered was a large qaggiq, where drum dances and other activities were held. When the people inside noticed the brother and sister, they offered them food. In the qaggiq, older men and women, as well as young men and women, had been getting ready to play games after a drum dance.

ᖃᒥᕐᓗᒍᒎᖅ ᐱᙳᐊᑦᑐᐊᕙᓂᕐᒪᑕ, ᑯᓂᒃᓴᖅᑐᕋᕐᓗᑎᒃ ᑖᒪᓈᖅ ᑐᔪᕐᒥᐊ'ᓈᒃ ᐱᖃᑖ ᓂᕕᐊᖅᓯᐊᕐᔪᓂᖅᓴᖅ ᖃᐅᔨᓴᕈᐊᖅᓗᓂ ᐃᓱᒪᓱᖕᒋᔭᓂᕐᒪᑦ ᑭᓇ ᑯᓂᒐᔪᖕᓂᖅᓴᐅᖕᒪᖕᒌᕐᒥᐅᒃ. ᑲᑕᐅᒻᖕᒎᖅ ᓴᓂᐊᓂ ᓇᖕᒋᑦᓯᐊᓗᑲᐅᕐᒥ ᐃᒐᓗᐊᖅᓗᓂ ᑭᒃᓗᓂᑦ ᕿᙵᒐᓂ ᐸᐅᕐᑭᑎᓕᖅᐹ ᖃᐅᔨᓴᕈᑎᒋᓂᐊᕐᒥᐅᒃ.

The brother and sister soon joined everyone in the kissing game—a game where people would snuff out the *qulliq* (seal oil lamp) light and walk around and kiss each other in the dark. The young girl decided to find out who she was kissing the most. So she went to the cooking hearth and smeared her nose with black soot from a dead ember.

ᖃᒡᒋᒥᓯᐅᖅᑐᙵᒎᖅ ᓴᓐᒥᔭᓈᖕᒍᖕᒪᑕ ᐱᙳᐊᖅᑐ'ᑐᐃᑦ ᓂᕕᐊᖅᓯᐊᑉ ᐊᑭᒥ ᐊᕐᑯᒻᖕᒐᓚᐅᖅᑳᖅᓗᓂ ᓇᓂᕈᐊᓂ ᒪᓂᖅ ᐃᑭᑉᐹ, ᑕᒪᒃᑯᐊᓗ ᖃᒡᒋᐸᕐᖃᔪ'ᑐᐃᑦ ᐅᕐᓂᒃᐸᒃᓗᓂᒋᑦ ᑲᐃᕕᐅᔭᖅᓗᓂ ᑮᓇᐃ ᓇᓂᕈᐊᒻᒥᐤᓗᒋᑦ ᖃᐅᔨᓴᑕᖅᐸᐃ ᑭᓇ ᑯᓂᒐᔪᖕᓂᖅᓴᐅᓂᕐᒪᖕᒌᕐᒥᐅᒃ.

Then the girl lit her *maniq* (moss lamp) and went around looking at every face in the qaggiq and the adjoining igluit to find out who she had given the most kisses to.

ᖃᒡᒋᐸᖃᔪᙵᒋᙵᒨᖅ ᖃᐅᔨᓴᓗᒃᑖᓗᓂᖕᒪᑎᑦ ᐊᓂᐊᑕᑰᖅ ᕿᖕᒑ ᐸᐅᓕᓅᖕᒪᑦ ᑯᓂᒐᔫᖕᓂᖅᓴᐅᓐᓂᖁᒥᐅᒃ ᖃᐅᔨᒐᒥ, ᑲᖑᑦᓯᕐᓗᓂ ᑲᐃᕝᕕᓐᓂᓯᓂᑰᖅ ᓱᓐᓂᙵᒋᕐᓗᒍ ᖃᖕᒐᑦᑕᖅᔩᒥᖅᑕᒥᐊᓱᖕᒐᔭᖕᒪᑦ, ᖃᖕᒐᑦᑕᖅᒥᓗ ᑕᒃᐸᐅᖕᒐ ᓯᑕᒧᑦ ᖁᒻᒧᐊᓯᔾᔩᒥᒥᐊᖅᓗᓂ ᓇᓂᕈᐊᓂ ᒪᓂᖅ ᑎᒍᒥᐊᖅᑐᐃᓐᓇᖅᓗᒍ.

After examining each face, the girl realized her brother's nose was the only one darkened with soot. She knew this meant he was the only person she had been kissing during the game. She was so embarrassed that she began rushing from face to face around the qaggiq. Gradually, she began to float off the ground and rise into the sky above—all the while she held the maniq in her hand.

ᐊᓂᐊᑖᒍᖅ ᖃᐅᔨᒐᒥᐅᒃ ᓇᔭᓂ ᖃᖓᑦᑕᖅᑐᖅ, ᒪᓂᕆᒃᑕᐅᖅ ᓇᓂᕈᐊᕆᒃ ᐃᑭᑦᓯᐊᓪᓚᒃᑯᓂ ᒪᓕᒃᓴᖅᑯᓂᐅᒃ. ᑎᐊ'ᓇᑐᑦᑕᐅᕉᖅ ᖃᖓᑦᑕᕿᑕᒥᐊᕐᒪᑦ ᖁᒻᒧᐊᓯᔾᔩᒥᒻᒪᖅᑯᓂᑉᑕᐅᖅ ᓯᓚᒧᑦ ᖃᖓᑦᑕᖅᑯᓂ ᓇᔭᓂ ᒪᓕᒃᓴᖅᑯᒍ.

When the brother discovered his sister had floated up into the air, he also lit a lamp and gradually floated off the ground in the same way and went up into the sky to follow his sister.

ᓂᕕᐊᖅᓯᐊᕉᖅ ᑭᖑᒻᒧᑦ ᑕᑯᓴᕿᒥ ᐊᓂᓂᓗ ᑕᑯᒐᒥᐅᒃ ᐊᖑᔨᕆᓕᕐᓂᖅᑯᒍ, ᕿᕕᐊᕌᓪᓚᒃᑯᒍᒎᖅ ᓇᓂᕈᐊᖓ ᓱᐱᖕᒪᒍ ᐊᐅᒪᐃᓐᓇᕆᒃ ᐃᑯᒪᓚᐊᓪᓚᓱᖕᒐᔭᖕᒪᑦ, ᓇᓂᕈᐊᖓᓕ ᓂᕕᐊᖅᓯᐊᑉ ᓱᐱᙱᓐᓇᒥᓚ ᖃᐅᒪᑐᐃᓐᓇᖅᑯᓂ.

The young girl looked back and saw that her brother had almost caught up to her. So she turned to him and blew his flame out, leaving it no more than a soft, glowing, red cinder. But her flame still burned brightly because it had not been blown out.

ᑕᐃᒪᔫᖅ ᑕᐃᒪᙵᓂᑦ ᐱᕆᐊᖅᓱᒍ ᑖᑉᑯᐊᒃ ᖃᖓᑦᑕᕐᑕᒥᐊᕐᓂᑯᒃ ᓇᔭᕖ'ᓈᒃ ᖃᖓᑕᐃᓐᓇᓕᓚᐅᕐᒪᓂᒃ ᑖᒻᓇᔫᖅ ᓯᐱᔭᐅᓚᐅᖅᑐᖅ ᓇᓂᖁᐊᖓ ᐊᖑᑕᐅᓂᖅᓴᖅ ᖃᐅᒻᒪᖅᓱᕐᓂᖅᓴᐅᒐᒥ ᑕᖅᑭᙳᓚᐅᖅᓯᒪᕗᖅ, ᑖᒻᓇᓕ ᓇᔮ ᓇᓂᖁᐊᖓᓕ ᓯᐱᔭᐅᓯᒪᖕᕆᓐᓇᒥ ᖃᐅᒻᒪᑎᐅᖕᒪᑦ ᓯᕿᓂᙳᕐᓂᖅᓱᓂ.

The pitiful young brother and sister remained in the sky ever since. The brother, with his soft glowing light, became the moon, and the sister, with her lamp still brightly lit, became the sun.

ᑎᐊ'ᓇᓕ ᑕᐃᒪ ᐃᓄᐃᑦ ᐅᒃᐱᕈᓯᖃᕐᓂᖃᖅᓱᑎᒃ ᐅᓂᑉᑳᔪᕗᑦ ᑕᖅᑭᐅᑉ ᓯᕿᓂᐅᓪᓗ ᐱᕆᐊᕐᓂᕆᖕᓂᒃ.

This is the story Inuit believe and tell about the origin of the moon and sun.

ᐃᓱᐊ
The end

ᐊᕐᓇᖅ ᑕᖅᑭᕐᒧᑦ ᓄᓯᒐᐅᔪᕕᓂᖅ ᐃᒥᖅᑕᖅᑑᒐᓗᐊᖅ

A WOMAN PULLED BY MOON'S GRAVITY

ᐅᓂᑉᑳᖅᑐᐊᕐᓂᐊᖅᑐᖓ ᐃᓄᐃᑦ ᐅᒃᐱᕈᓯᖕᒋᑕ ᐃᓚᖕᒐᓐᓂᒃ ᑕᖅᑭᕐᒥᒃ ᐱᔾᔪᑎᓕᖕᒥᒃ. ᓱᓇᓗᒃᑖᑦ ᐱᒋᐊᕐᓂᖅᑲᖅᑐᑎᒃ ᑭᓯᐊᓂ ᓄᐃᑕᖕᒪᑕ ᐅᕝᓗᒥ, ᑐᓴᐅᒪᕗᖓ ᖃᖓᓴᕐᔪᐊᕉᖅ ᐱᓐᓂᑯᒥᒃ ᐅᕝᓗᒥ ᓯᓚ ᓄᐃᑕᔪᒥᒃ ᑕᖅᑭᕐᒥ ᐃᐊ'ᓇ ᐅᓂᑉᑳᒐᐅᑎᑦᑐᒍ ᑐᓵᕝᓚᐅᒐᕋ:

I am going to tell a story based on a traditional Inuit belief about the moon. Everything we see around us that exists today has its own beginning. I heard a story about something that happened a long time ago that explains what we can see on the moon today. The story is told like this:

ᖃᖓᓴᕐᔪᐊᖅ ᐃᓕᖅᑯᓯᖅ ᐅᕝᓗᒥ ᐃᓕᖅᑯᓯᐅᔪᑉ ᐊᔾᔨᒌᖖᒋᓚᐅᖅᑎᑦᑐᒍ, ᐅᑭᐅᒥ ᐊᐳᒻᒥᒃ ᐃᒡᓗᓕᐅᖅᑐᑎᒃ ᐃᒡᓗᕐᑲᔪᓚᐅᖅᑎᑦᑐᒋᑦ ᓱᓕ, ᐃᒥᕐᑲᔪᓚᐅᖅᐳᑦ ᑕᓯᕐᒥ ᓯᑯ ᑑᖅᑐᒍ, ᐊᖓᖅᑐᒍ. ᐃᒥᖅ ᑖᒻᓇ ᐃᒡᓗᑉ ᓯᓚᑖᓃᒻᒪᑦ, ᖃᑦᑕᓕᓴᖅᑐᑎᒃ ᐅᕐᓂᒃᑕᖅᑐᒍ ᐃᒥᖅᑕᖅᑕᔪᓚᐅᖅᐳᑦ.

A very long time ago, people lived differently than they do today. Inuit lived in igluit, and they often chiselled holes through the ice of nearby lakes to fetch water. People would then fill skin buckets with water from the holes.

ᑕᐃᒪᒎᖅ ᑕᐃᑉᓱᒪᓂᐅᔪᖅ ᖃᖕᒐᓴᕐᔪᐊᖅ ᐊᕐᓇᖅ ᐃᒪᐃᕈᑎᓐᓂᕋᒥᒃ ᐅᓐᓄᒃᑯᑦ ᑕᖅᑭᖅ ᐃᓗᐃᒃᑲᐅᕝᓗᓂ ᑕᖅᑭᕐᔪᐊᑦᑐᐊᖅᑎᑦᓗᒍ ᐃᒥᖅᑕᓚᖅᑑᓐᓂᖅ, ᖃᑦᑕᕐᒥᒃ ᒥᖅᑯᐃᑦᑐᒥᑦ ᖃᑦᑕᓚᐊᓇᓯᒪᔭᒥᒃ ᑎᒍᒥᐊᖅᓱᓂ.

One night, during those long-ago times, a woman decided to go fetch water under the bright light of a full moon. She carried a caribou-skin bucket in her hand.

ᐃᒥᖅᑕᓪᓚᕐᒥᒎᖅ ᓯᓚᑦᓯᐊᓗᒃᑲᐅᖕᒍᖕᒪᑦ, ᐊᓪᓚᑦᓯᐊᖅᓱᓂ ᑕᖅᑭᓇᒃᓯᓯᒪᑦᓯᐊᓗᒃᑲᐅᕐᒪᑦ ᑕᖅᑭᖅ ᖃᐅᒪᑦᓯᐊᓗᒃᑲᐅᖅᓱᓂ. ᖃᓗᐊᓂᒃᑲᒥᒎᖅ ᐊᐃᓯᕆᐊᖕᒍᓚᓗᐊᖅ ᑕᑯᓴᕐᒥ ᑕᖅᑭᕐᒧᑦ ᐊᓚᔪᐃᖅᓱᓂᐅᒃ, ᑕᐅᑐᐃᓐᓇᕈᐊᒥᐊᓚᖅᓱᒍ.

When the woman went outside, the weather was so peaceful and clear that it made the full moon's light extremely bright and attractive. After filling her skin bucket, the woman went to return home. But before she did, she turned her head towards the moon. She became so attracted to it that she could not turn away.

ᐃᔨᒋᖅᑲᑦᑖᒥᐊᓕᕐᒪᖖᒎᖅ ᑕᖅᑭᕐᒧᑦ ᖁᒻᒧᐊᓯᔾᔫᒥᒡᓗᓂ ᐊᒡᓛᑦ ᑕᖅᑭᐅᑉ ᓄᓯᖕᒪᒍ ᑕᖅᑭᕐᒧᐊᖅᕈᓂ. ᑕᐃᑉᑯᐊᒎᖅ ᐃᒥᖅᑕᒐᐅᔪᑦ ᐃᑎᕐᓇᓵᓗᐊᓕᕐᒪᑦ ᖁᓚᓕᕋᒥᒃ ᐃᑦᓯ’ᑐᐊᕐᒪᑕ, ᐃᒥᕐᒧᓕᐊᖅᕈᑎᒡᓗ ᕿᓂᓕᖅᕈᒍ. ᑐᑉᓯᒐᒥᑦᑯᒎᖅ ᐃᒥᕐᒥ ᖃᓗᐊᓂᓵᓕᓂᐅᒡᓗᓂ ᐊᐃᒋᐊᓕᓂᖃᕋᓗᐊᖅᕈᓂᓗ ᑕᒫᓂ ᐊᑯᓐᓂᕐᒥ ᑐᒪᐃᖅᓯᕐᒪᑦ, ᖃᐅᔨᓕᖅᐹᑦ ᑕᖅᑭᕐᒧᑦ ᕿᕕᐊᕋᒥᒃ ᐃᓕᑕᕆᒐᒥᔾᔪᒃ ᑕᖅᑭᒥᓱᐅᖅᑐᖅ ᖃᑦᑕᓕᔭᖅᑐᐃᓐᓇᖅᕈᓂ.

She stared at the moon for a very long time and, eventually, she was pulled straight into it. Others who had fetched water noticed the long delay in the woman's return, and they all went out to the water hole to search for her. They saw her tracks at the water hole, recent evidence of water being dipped into a bucket, and her tracks heading back home. But those tracks stopped halfway. They realized what had happened to the woman when they looked up at the moon and recognized her silhouette and the caribou-skin bucket that she still held in her hand.

ᑕᐃᒪ ᖃᖕᒐᒥᐊᖅ ᑕᖅᑭᕐᔪᐊᑦᑐᐊᓕᕐᒥᒃᐸᑦ ᑕᖅᑭᒧᑦ ᕿᓂᕈᕕᑦ ᑕᑯᓇᔭᖅᐸᑦ ᐊᕐᓇᖅ ᓯᓕ ᓇᖕᒋᖅᑐᖅ ᖃᑦᑕᓕᔭᖅᑐᓂ, ᑕᖅᑭᒧᑦ ᓄᓯᒐᐅᓐᓂᑯ ᐃᔨᒋᖅᑲᑦᑖᓗᐊᓕᕐᓂᕐᒪᑦ. ᓄᑕᕋᐅᒡᓗᑖ ᐅᖅᑲᐅᑎᔭᐅᒡᓚᐅᖅᐳᒍᑦ ᐃᔨᒋᖅᑲᑦᑖᖅᑕᐃᓕᑦᑕᕐᑯᔭᐅᒡᓗᑕ ᑕᖅᑭᒧᑦ, ᓱᔭᐅᓐᓇᕐᒪᑦ ᐃᔨᒋᖅᑲᑦᑖᓗᐊᓕᕌᓐᓂ.

So at night, when you look up at a bright full moon, you may see an outline of this woman standing with a bucket in her hand. She was pulled up to the moon for gazing at it for too long. This was something we were warned about as children—never gaze at the moon for too long, because there are consequences.

ᐃᓱᐊ
The end

ᐃᖕᓂᕐᔪᒃ

THE INGNIRJUK (SEA GHOST)

ᐊᒻᒪᔫᖅ ᑕᐃᒪᓇ ᐃᓄᒃ ᐃᖕᓂᕐᔪᖕᒥᑦ ᓇᑦᓯᖅᑕᐃᓂᒃ ᐊᖅᖄᒐᐅᑦᑕᖅᑲᑦᑖᖅᑐ’ᑐᐊᖅ, ᑕᒡᕙᔫᖅ ᑖᑉᑯᐊᒃ ᓄᓕᐊᕇᒃ ᐊᑖᒐᓂᖄᖅᑐᑎᒃ ᑳᐱᒃᓯᓐᓈᒃ.

This is a story about an ingnirjuk *(sea ghost) that stole seals from an Inuk and made it hard for a starving couple who had just arrived at the coast.*

ᑕᐃᒻᓇᔫᖅ ᐊᖑᑦ ᓇᑦᓯᖅᑕᒥᓂᒃ ᐅᓂᐊᖅᓱᓂ ᐊᐃᓕᕿᓗᐊᖀᖕᒐᑦ ᐃᖕᓂᕐᔫᒻᖕᔫᖅ ᒪᓕᐊᑦᓚᒃᓱᒍ ᐊᖅᖄᖅᑕᖅᑲᑦᑖᒥᐊᓕᕐᒪᒍ.

Every day, a man would go out hunting and return home pulling a seal behind him. But, every day, a sea ghost would chase the man to steal his catch.

ᐊᐅᓇᐊᓕᕐᒥᒐᒥᔫᖅ (ᓇᑦᓯᓕᐊᓕᕐᒥᒐᒥᔫᖅ) ᓇᑦᓯ’ᑐᐊᕐᒥᒐᒥ, ᐊᖅᖄᒐᐅᓂᐊᕐᒥᒐᒥ ᖃᐅᔨᒪ’ᑐᐊᕐᒥ, ᓇᑦᓯᖅᑕᓂᔫᖅ ᐅᓂᐊ’ᓈᖅᓱᒍ ᐊᐃ’ᑐᐊᓕᕐᒥᒐᒥ, ᑕᐃᑲᑯᓗᑏᓇᓛᒃ ᒪᓕᑦᑐᐊᓕᓇᕗᖅ ᐃᖕᓂᕐᔪᑯᓗᒃ.

One day, the man went out hunting, as usual, and caught a seal. But he knew the sea ghost would, once again, steal the seal from him.

Sure enough, the old ingnirjuk began following the man when he headed for home.

ᑕᒡᕙᓂᒨᖅ ᖃᐃᓕᕐᒪᑦ ᓇᑦᓯᖅᑕᕐᒥᓂ ᓄᖅᑲᖕᒐᒋᐊᒥᐊᓕᕐᒥ ᐊᖅᑳᕐᓂᐊᕐᒥᖕᒪᓂ ᓇᓗᙱ'ᑐᐊᕐᒥ. ᐃᓱᒪᓱᖕᒐᔪᓕᕐᒥᒨᖅ ᖃᓄᖅ ᐱᑦᑐᐊᕐᔭᕐᒪᖕᒋᑦ. ᖃᐃ'ᑐᐊᕐᒪᙵᖅ ᐄᓛᒃ, ᑲᒥᓂᒨᖅ ᓄᕗᐃᖒᓪᓚᒃᕈᒍ ᐅᑕᖅᑭᒥᐊᑦᑐᐊᓕᖅᕚ ᑎᐊ'ᓇ ᐃᑎᒃᑲᓂ ᓄᐃᖏᓗᑎᑦ.

Knowing the sea ghost was after him to steal his catch, the man stopped and sat down on top of the seal. Suddenly, an idea came to him. While the sea ghost continued to approach him, the man cut off the tips of his kamiik and sat down again on the seal with his toes exposed.

ᖃᒡᓚᒐᒥᒨᖅ ᓄᖅᑲᖅᕈᓂ ᐊᐱᕆᓱᖕᒐᔪᖕᒪᑦ, “ᓱᒥᒍᑯᐊ ᐃᑎᒃᑲᑎᑦ ᓂᕆᓱᖅᑐᑦ?”

When the sea ghost reached the man, it stopped. It had never seen toes before. The sea ghost was afraid, and so it asked the man, “What do your toes eat?”

“ᐃᓄᖕᓂᒃ.”

“People,” the man answered.

“ᐊᑏᒎᕋᐃ ᐊᖅᐸᓚᐅᕋᓗᐊᕐᓚᖕᒐ ᑎᒍᒻᒥᖅᑰᒃᑭᑦ.”

“Then hold on to them tightly while I run away!” the sea ghost said.

“ᐃᓛ ᐅᑯᐊ ᑎᒍᒻᒥᖅᑐᕋᓗᐊᓇᒃᑲ ᒪᓕᒍᒃᑳᑎᑦ.”

“That’s what I’m doing,” the man answered, “but they really want to go after you.”

ᐃᖕᓂᕐᔪᑯᓗᒎᖅ ᐊᖅᐸᑦᑐᐊᓕᕋᒥ ᑎᐊ’ᓇᒎᖅ ᑐᖅᓱᓚᑦᑐᐊᖅᐸᒃᓱᓂ,
“ᑎᒍᒻᒥᖅᑰᒃᑭᑦ! ᑎᒍᒻᒥᖅᑰᒃᑭᑦ! ᑎᒍᒻᒥᖅᑰᒃᑭᑦ! ᑎᒍᒻᒥᖅᑰᒃᑭᑦ!”

The old ingnirjuk started to run away as fast as it could, calling out as it ran, “Hold on to them! Hold on to them! Hold on to them!”

ᑕᐃᑯᖕᒐᒎᖅ ᐃᒃᑲᓪᕈᓄᑦ ᐊᖅᐸᑐᐃᓐᓇᖅᓱᓂ ᑕᓕᕐᓱᓂ.

The sea ghost ran and ran until it disappeared among the distant *ikkalrut* (pressure ridges in pack ice).

ᑕᒡᖤᒎᖅ ᑕᓕᒻᒪᑦ, ᐊᐃᓕᖅᓱᓂ ᓇᑦᓯᖅᑕᒥᓂᒃ ᐊᒡᒋᔾᔨᓕᑕᐃᓐᓇᖅᓱᓂ.
ᑖᓐᓇᒎᖅ ᓇᑦᓯᖅᑕᐃᑦ ᐊᒡᒋᑎᒋᐊᕋᓗᐊᕌᖕᒐᒋᑦ ᐋᑕᐅᖅᑲᑦᑖᒥᐊᖅᐸᒃᑲᒥ
(ᐊᖅᑳᓴᖅᑕᐅᖕᒋᓐᓇᖅᐸᒃᑲᒥ), ᖃᓄᑮᖅ ᐱᓗᓂ ᓇᑦᓯᓕᕋᔭᕐᒪᖕᒑᕐᒦ
ᐃᖅᑲᖅᓴᖅᑲᑦᑖᒥᐊᖅᐸᒃᑲᒥ, ᐊᓱᐃᓛᒎᖅ ᓇᑦᓯᖅᑕᒥᓂᒃ ᑎᑭᐅᔾᔨᑕᐃᓐᓇᕐᒪᑦ,
ᓄᓕᐊᖕᒐ ᐃᒐ’ᑐᐊᓕᕐᒪᑦ ᑕᒡᖤ ᓂᓇᓕᑕᐃᓐᓇᖅᓱᑎᒃ.

After the sea ghost disappeared, the man started again for home, pulling the seal behind him. For a long time, the old sea ghost had been snatching the man’s seal on his way home from hunting, and the man had long wondered how to stop the sea ghost and keep his catch. At last, he was able to bring a seal home for his wife to cook, and the couple ate for the first time in a very long while.

ᒪᖅᑲᐃᓕᖁᒥᒨᖅ ᑕᒃᐱᖕᓇ ᐃᖕᓂᖅᔪᐊᖕᒥᑦ ᖃᐃᕝᕕᐅᙱᑐᐃᑦᑐ'ᑐᐊᖅ ᓇᑦᓕᖂᖕᑕᒥᐅᒃ ᐃᒃᑲᑦᕈᖅ ᐅᐃᒪᐃᔭ'ᑐᐊᖅᐸᓕᖁᓗᐊᖁᒥᐅᒃ, ᐅᔭᙱᑎᑕᐃᓐᓇᓕᖅᒪᙱᒨᖅ ᑳᒍᖕᓇᐃᓕᖅᐳᒃ. ᑲᒥᓂᒨᖅ ᓄᕗᐃᒥᐊᖅᓱᒍ ᐃᖕᓂᖅᔪᐊᖕᒥᒃ ᑕᑕᕝᕗᒋᒥ (ᑲᑉᐱᐊᑦᓴᐃᒋᒥ).

After that, whenever the man went hunting, he would cautiously approach the area where he had last seen the old ingnirjuk. But the sea ghost never appeared again. So the couple's starvation ended, and all because the man had the ingenuity to cut off the tips of his kamiik and scare the daylights out of the ingnirjuk!

ᐃᓱᐊ
The end

ᓄᑕᖅᑲᑦ ᐊᒪᐅᑕᓕᖕᒧᑦ ᑎᒍᔭᐅᔪᑦ

CHILDREN ABDUCTED BY AN AMAUTALIK

ᐅᓂᑉᑳᖅᑐᐊᕐᓂᐊᖅᑐᖓ ᓄᑕᖅᑲᓂᒃ ᐊᒪᐅᑕᓕᖕᒧᑦ ᑎᒍᔭᐅᔪᓂᒃ ᐅᓐᓄᒃᑯᑦ ᓯᓚᒥ ᐱᙯᐊᖅᑎᓪᓗᒋᑦ. ᐅᓂᑉᑳᕐᓂᐊᖅᐸᕋ ᐅᓂᑉᑳᖅᑐᐊᖅᑎᓂᑦ ᐊᓯᖏᓐᓂᑦ ᑐᓴᑦᑕᕐᓂᑰᓂᑦ ᐊᐅᓚᔾᔨᓂᕋ ᐃᖅᑲᐅᒪᕐᓯᐊᕐᓂᓗᒃᓗᒍ. ᖃᐅᔨᒪᓂᐊᖅᐳᓯ ᐃᓄᐃᑦ ᓄᓇᖃᑎᒌᖏᑦᑐᑦ ᐃᒻᒥᒃᑯᑉᑕᐅᖅ ᐅᓂᑉᑳᖅᑐᐊᕐᑯᑎᖃᕐᒥᖕᒪᑕ, ᑖᒻᓇᓕ ᐅᓂᑉᑳᕐᓂᐊᒐᕋ ᓴᐅᓂᖅᑑᕐᒥᐅᓂᑦ ᐅᓂᑉᑲᒐᐅᑎᓪᓗᒍ ᑐᓴᑦᑕᕐᓂᑯᒐ ᐃᐊ’ᓇᐃᓕᐅᖅᑐᖅ:

I'm going to tell a story about an amautalik who abducted a group of children while they were playing late at night. I will tell it in the best way I remember it being told by other storytellers. Please note that there are many variations of this story, because many communities have their own unique version. This version of the story is one I've heard told by the Hauniqtuurmiut. It goes like this:

ᑕᐃᑉᓯᒪᓂ ᖁᕕᐊᒋᔭᐅᒡᒍᓚᐅᖅᒪᑦ ᐅᓐᓄᒃᑯᒥ ᓯᓚᒥ ᐱᙳᐊᕐᓂᖅ, ᐃᑎᕐᓇᖅᓯᒐᓗᐊᖅᑎᑦᓱᒍ ᓄᑕᖅᑲᑦ ᐊᓃᙳᓕᖅᓯᒪᙱᑦᓴᕌᖓᒥᒃ ᐃᑎᖅᑕᐃᓕᐅᔭᕙᓚᐅᖅᒪᑕ. ᑕᐃᒪᒎᖅ ᓄᑕᕋᐳᓈᑦᑐᐃᑦ ᐅᓐᓄᒃᑯᒥ ᓯᓚᒥ ᐱᙳᐊᖅᑐ'ᑑᖅᒪᑕ ᑕᖅᑭᕐᕙᐊ'ᕙᐊᕐᒥ. ᒪᑉᐳᖅᓂᒎᖅ ᐊᖓᔫᒃᑕᖅᐹᖅᑲᖅᓱᑎᒃ ᐃᒻᒪᖅᑲ ᒥᐊᓂᖅᓯᕗᐅᔫᖅᓂᒃ, ᐃᓅᓱᒃᑐᐊᕐᔪᖅᒥᒃ ᓂᕕᐊᖅᓯᐊᒥᒡᓗ.

Long ago, children loved to play outside late into the night. Even when it was time to go in, they would keep playing outside—especially if they weren't tired. It was on such a night as this that a group of children kept playing late outside under a crisp, bright moon. An older boy and a girl were also playing with them, perhaps to keep an eye on the younger ones.

ᐅᑭᐊᖑᖅᒪᙳᖅ ᐃᓄᐃᑦ ᐃᒡᓗᑖᓴᒥᖅᓂ ᐊᐃᓯᒪᔪ'ᑐᐃᑦ, ᓄᑕᖅᑲᑦ ᑕᐅᓇᓂ ᖁᐊᓴᒥ ᐊᖅᐸᓕᕋᑦᑐᐊᓪᓚᕐᒥᒡᓗ ᐱᙳᐊᑦᑐᐊᖅᑎᑦᓱᑎᑦ. ᐅᐱᙵᖅᓱᑎᙳᖅ ᐊᒪᐅᑕᓕᐅᑉ ᐱᙳᐊᖅᑐᓇᓯ'ᓈᑦ ᑎᑭᖀᕐᓂᕋᒥᑎᑦ ᑲᑎᖅᓱᖅᑎᓇᖅᓂᖅᓱᑎᑦ ᑎᒍᓱᖅᑲᔭᖅᒪᑎᑦ. ᐊᒪᐅᑕᓕᒎᖅ ᖃᒃᓱᖅᑲᐅᑕᐃᔾᓛᒃᓱᓂ ᓄᑕᖅᑲᖅ ᑲᑎᔅᓱᑎᑦ ᕿᓚᒃᓯᑦᑐᐊᓪᓚᐃᑕᓗ ᐃᓕᐅᓯᖅᑲᔭᓕᕐᒪᑦ, "ᐅᓗ'ᑐᐊᖅᓯᐅᑎᓚᑉᔫ ᐱᓚᒃᑐᕐᓚᑉᔫ, ᐅᓗ'ᑐᐊᖅᓯᐅᑎᓚᑉᔫ ᐱᓚᒃᑐᕐᓚᑉᔫ?"

It was early fall, and the adults were in their new igluit while their children were out running around and playing on the ice. But while the children were playing, an old amautalik snuck up on them and abducted them quickly and easily. The old amautalik untied her amauti strap and then tied them all up in a bunch, saying, "Shall I use my big, slicing ulu on you and cut you up? Shall I use my big, slicing ulu on you and cut you up?"

ᓄᑕᕋ'ᓈᙳᖅ ᑲᑉᐱᐊᓱ'ᑐᐊᓕᕐᒪᑕ, ᑖᑉᑯᐊᒃ ᐊᒡᓛᑦ ᐊᖓᔫᒃᑕᖅᐹᒃ ᐱᔭᐅᖅᑲᑕᐅᖅᒪᓂᒃ. ᖃᖓᓴᖅ ᐱᑦᑐᖁᑎᖅᑲᑦᑐᐊᕙᓚᐅᖅᒪᑕ, ᐱᑦᑐᖁᑎᓕᑎᓇᓂᐅᓐᓂᖅᒪᓂᒎᖅ ᑖᑉᑯᐊᒃ ᐊᖓᔫᒃᑖᒃ. ᐱᖅᑖᑕᒎᖅ ᐊᒪᐅᑕᓕᒃ ᐊᐱᕆᕚ; "ᓇᐅᒡᓕᒥ ᑕᐃᒪ ᐅᓗ'ᑐᐃᑦ?"

All the children were frightened, including the two older ones whom the amautalik had also caught. But long ago, people had guardian spirits. The older children knew this, so the older boy asked the old amautalik a question to stall for time: “Well then, where is your big, slicing ulu?”

ᐊᒪᐅᑕᓕᒎᖅ ᐅᓗ'ᑐᐊᕐᒥᓂᒃ ᐱᕆᐊᕋᓗᐊᕐᒥ ᐸᐃᒍᕐᓂᕋᒥᐅᒃ, ᑖᑉᑯᐊ ᓄᑕᖅᑲᑦ ᖃᒃᓱᖕᒐᐅᑎ'ᑐᐊᕐᒥᓄᑦ ᓂᒥᖅᑐᐊᓂ ᕿᒫᓪᓚᒃᓱᕆᑦ ᐅᓗ'ᑐᐊᒥᓂᒃ ᐊᐃᒃᓴᓇᐊᑦᑐᐊᖅᐸᖅ.

The old amautalik went to take out her ulu, but she discovered she had forgotten to bring it with her. So the amautalik left the children tied up in her long amauti strap while she went to get her knife.

ᐊᒪᐅᑕᓕᒎᖅ ᐅᓗ'ᑐᐊᒥᓂᒃ ᐊᐃᒃᓴᖅᑎᑦᓗᒍ ᖁᐸᓄᐊ'ᓈᑉ ᐊᒪᐅᓕᒑ'ᓈᑉ ᓄᑕᖅᑲᑦ ᕿᓚᒃᓱᖅᓯᒪᔪᑦ ᐅᕐᓂᓱᖕᒐᔭᖕᒪᕆᑦ ᐊᐱᖅᓱᓇᐊᒻᒫᖅᓱᓂ, “ᐃᒍᑉᑎᕐᓚᑉᓲ, ᐃᒍᑉᑎᕐᓚᑉᓲ?”

After the old amautalik had left, a little snow bunting suddenly appeared near the children and asked, “Shall I unbind you? Shall I unbind you all?”

ᓱᓇᐅᕝᕙᒎᕈᓇ ᓂᕕᐊᖅᓯᐊᑉ ᐱᑦᑐᖁᑎᒋᓐᓂᓖ. ᓄᑕᕋ'ᓈᖕᒎᖅ ᐊᖏᖅᓂᖅᓗᖕᖏᓪᓚᑕ ᑐᖅᓱᑖᓇᐊᐱᑦᑐᐊᓪᓚᖅᒥᒡᓗ, “ᐄ, ᐊᑏ ᐃᒍᑉᑎᖅᑎᒍᑦ, ᐃᒍᑉᑎᖅᑎᒍᑦ, ᐃᒍᑉᑎᖅᑏᒍᑦ!”

To the children’s surprise, the little bird was actually the guardian spirit of the eldest girl. Naturally, all the children agreed and excitedly called out, “Yes, yes! Unbind us all! Unbind us!”

ᐊᒪᐅᓕᒪ'ᓈᒻᖕᒎᖅ ᐃᒍᑉᑎᓕᖅᒪᒋᑦ ᓯᒡᒍ'ᓈᒥᓄᑦ ᖃᒃᓯᖕᒪᐅᑦ ᕿᑦᓚᐃᔭᖅᓗᒍ, ᓄᑕᕋ'ᓈᖕᒎᖅ ᕿᓚᐃᒪᐅ'ᓈᑦᑐᐊᕋᒥᒃ ᐊᐃᔮᕿᑦᓚᒥᐊᐱᑦᑐᐊᖅᓗᑎᒃ, ᖃᒃᓯᖕᒪᐅᑦ ᖁᐊᓴᒥ ᐊᒥᐊᒃᑰᓕᖅᓗᓂ. ᓄᑦᖃᖕᒎᖅ ᐊᐃᔮᓯᒪᓕᖅᑎᑦᓗᒋᑦ ᐊᒪᐅᑕᓕᒃ ᐅᑎᑦᑐᐊᑕᐃᓐᓇᕋᒥ, ᖃᒃᓯᖕᒪᐅᑕᐃᓐᓇᖅ ᑕᑯᒪᒥᐅᒃ ᐊᐱᕆᓱᖕᒪᔾᖕᒪᑦ, “ᖃᐅᒪᐅᓛᒃᑲ ᐃᑉᑯᐊ ᓇᐅᒃ?”

The little bird started to untie the children with its little beak. As soon as the knots were undone, the children ran home, leaving only the amauti strap behind on the ice. Long after the children were safely home, the amautalik returned to the abduction site. But she found only the amauti strap. She asked, “Where are all my *qaugaugait* (little children)?”

ᐊᒪᐅᓕᒫᓈᒻᖑᖅ ᖁᓛᓂ ᑎᖕᒥᕝᔪᓂ ᐅᖃᐅᑎᕚ, “ᖃᐅᒐᐅᒑᑎᑦ ᐊᖑᒋᐊᒃᑭᑦ, ᑎᐅᒃ.”

The little snow bunting was flying overhead and said to her, “Try to catch your qaugaugait now, *tweet*.”

ᐊᒪᐅᑕᓕᔫᖅ ᐅᖃᖅᑐᓂ, “ᑭᒍᑎᒪ ᐊᖁᖅᑲᓐᓄᑦ ᐃᓕᔪᑎᑦ ᑯᒃᑭᓕᐅᑎᓚᒋᑦ.”

The amautalik then replied, “Let me put you between my teeth and turn you into *kukki* (food particles between teeth).”

ᐊᒪᐅᓚᒐ'ᓈᕉᖅ ᑭᐅᕝᓱᓂ, “ᑭᒍᑎᕕᑦ ᐊᑯᖕᒐᓐᓄᑦ ᐃᓕᓗᖕᒐ ᑯᒃᑭᓕᐅᑎᖖᒐ, ᑎᐅᒃ.” ᑎᖕᒥᕝᓗᓂᓗ ᐊᒪᐅᑕᓚᒃ ᕿᒪᒃᐹ.”

The snow bunting replied, “Just try to put me between your teeth and turn me into kukki, *tweet.*” Then she flew away and left the old amautalik behind.

ᐃᓱᐊ
The end

ᐃᔨᖅᑲᒥᑦ ᑎᒍᔭᐅᔪᖅ

MAN SNATCHED BY IJIRAAK

ᑕᐃᑉᓱᐊᑉᑕᐅᕉᖅ ᓄᓕᐊᓃᒃ ᐃᕐᓂ'ᓈᖕᒐᑦᑐ ᐃᓄᐃᓚᖅᓯᐅᖅᑐ'ᓈᕐ. ᑕᐃᒪᓇᒎᖅ ᐊᖑᑦ ᒪᖅᑲᐃ'ᑐᐊᖅᐸᖕᒪᕐ, ᒪᖅᑲᐃᓕᕐᒥᒐᒥᒎᖅ ᖃᔭᖅᑐᖅᖁᓂ ᐸᖕᓂ'ᑐᐊᕐᒥᒃ ᑐᒃᑐᓱᖕᒐᔭᖕᒪᕐ. ᑐᒃᑐᑕᓇᒐᒥᐅᒎᖅ ᐋᒃᑐᓇᐊᖅᑐᓕᖅᐹ ᐅᕐᓂᒃᖁᒍ.

This is a story about a couple and their little boy who lived alone on the land. The man spent a good deal of time out hunting. One day, he was out hunting in his qajaq and killed a caribou bull. After he had killed the animal, the man got out of his qajaq and went to skin the caribou where it lay on the ground.

ᐋᒃᑐᓯᕆᐊᕋᓗᐊᕐᒪᒍᒎᖅ ᖄᖕᒐ ᑐᒃᑐᑉ ᐃᒪᕈᐊᑦᓚᒃᑕᖅᑐ'ᑑᓕᕐᒪᑦ ᓂᐸᓗᖖᕆ'ᑐᐊᖅᑎᑦᑐᒍ ᑎᐊ'ᓇ ᐊᓗᒃᐸᒃᖁᒍ. ᐋᒃᑐᓯᕆᐊᕋᓗᐊᖅᑎᑦᑐᒍᒎᖅ ᕿᒃᓯᒥᒃᓯᔅᓵᒥ ᓱᖕᒐᔭᒃᑲᒥ ᐃᓄ'ᑑᔮᖅᑐᒥᒃ. ᑕᑯᕐᓯᐊᓇᐊᕋᒥᐅᒎᖅ ᓯᓇᐅᕝᕙᒎᑭᓇ ᐃᔨᕋ'ᑐᐊᖅ ᐅᐱᖖᒐᖅᑎᕆᓕᕐᓂᑳ.

But as he made a slit to skin the animal, a puddle of water appeared on the caribou's belly from out of nowhere. This was surprising because it wasn't raining. But every time it appeared, the man simply slurped the water up. As he bent down again to skin the caribou, the man glimpsed what looked to be a person out of the corner of his eye. When the man took a closer look, he saw it was an *ijiraq* (large land spirit) who had crept up on him by surprise.

ᖃᔭ’ᓈᓂᒎᖅ ᓱᒃᔭᒥᓱᐅᕐᒪᑦ ᑕᑲᓄᖕᒐ ᐊᖅᐸᒋᐊᑦᑐᐊᖅᐳᖅ. ᑎᑭ’ᓈᓪᓚᕐᒥᓗᒎᖅ ᖃᔭᓂ ᓵᒻᒫᓪᓚᒃᓗᒍ ᐃᑎᓂᕐᒧᑦ ᕿᒪᒋᐊᕐᓗᐊᕐᒪᑦ, ᐃᔾᖅᑲᒎᖅ ᒪᑦᕈ’ᑐᐊᒃ ᐃᐱᖀᖀᑦᑕᒃᓗᑎᒃ ᖃᔮ ᐃᓱᒋᒃᑎᒃᑯᑦ ᑎᒍ’ᓈᑎᓇᓐᓂᖅᓗᒍ, ᖃᖕᒐᑦᑕᖅᑎᓇᖕᓂᖅᓗᒍ ᑎᒻᒨᑎᓕᖅᐹᒃ.

The man started to run towards his qajaq, which was pulled up to the shore. When he reached it, he shoved it into the water and paddled to try to escape. But *ijiraak* (two land spirits) waded in after him. With little effort, they grabbed both ends of the qajaq and lifted it out of the water with the man still inside. They then waded back to shore.

ᖃᑭᒐᒥᒎᖅ ᐊᖏᕋ’ᕘᒐᒥᒃ ᐱᓱᐊᓚ’ᑐᐊᕐᒪᓂᒃ, ᓄᓇᒧᓕᐅᑎᓕᕐᒥᑦᑯ, ᐅᔭᕐᓱᒡᑲ’ᕘᒻᖕᒎᖅ ᖄᖕᒐᓄᑦ ᖃᔭᓗᑖᖕᒐᓄᑦ ᐃᓕᕝᓗᒍ ᐅᕝᕙᖏᐊᖅᑐᓕᕐᒪᓂᒃ, ᐃᔾᖁ’ᑐᐃᖏᒎᖅ ᓇᑭᒥᐊᓗᒃᑖᖅ ᐅᔭᖏᐊᔭᒥᐊᓱᖕᒐᔭᓕᕐᒪᑕ ᐅᕝᕙᖏᐊᖅᑐᑦᑐᐊᓪᓚᕐᒥᒡᓗ.

The ijiraak were so tall that when they reached the shore, it took them no time at all to walk inland. The ijiraak soon came upon a

huge boulder and placed both the man and his qajaq on the boulder and started to whistle. As they did, more *ijirait* (large land spirits) appeared from every direction, returning the whistle call.

ᑕᐃᒪᒎᖅ ᑎᒍᔭᐅ'ᑐᐊᕐᒥ ᐃᔨᖅᑲᓂᑦ ᐊᒡᒋᑎ'ᑐᐊᕐᒪᔾᔪᒃ. ᓂᖅᑲᐃᓂᒎᖅ ᓂᖃᑦᑕᐃᓕᖅᑲᑦᑖᓕᕐᒥ ᒪᖅᑲᐃᑦᓯᕌᖓᒥ ᐱᑕᕐᒥᓂᒃ ᕿᔪᐊᓂ ᓂᖃᖏᒃᓱᓂ ᐊᐃᓯᐊ'ᑐᐊᕋᑐᐊᕐᒥ ᓄᓕᐊᕐᒥᓄᑦ ᐃᕐᓂᕐᒥᓄᑦᑐ. ᑎᐊ'ᓇᒎᖅ ᒪᖅᑲᐃ'ᑐᐊᖅᐸᒃᒥ, ᒪᖅᑲᐃᓕᕌᖓᒥᒎᖅ ᑐᐱᖅᑎᒃ ᐅᔭᖕᒋᑦᓯᕌᖓᒥᐅᒃ ᐅᕐᓂᒋᐊᕋᑐᐊᕌᖓᒍ ᑎᐊ'ᓇᒎᖅ ᒥᒃᓵ ᐃᒪ'ᑐᐊᕐᒥᑦ ᑕᒡᔭᕋᖅᕕᐅᒥᐊᑦᑐᐊᖅᓱᓂ ᐱᓱᕐᒪᑦ ᖅᑲᒡᓕ'ᓈᖅᐸᒃᑲᑐᐊᖅᓱᓂ.

The man was now in the ijirait's custody, and he went to live with them in their home. But while he was their captive, the man refrained from eating their food and only ate animals that he himself had captured, because he desperately longed to return to his wife and his little boy, whom he dearly loved. After a while, the ijirait let the man go out hunting by himself, and each time he would near his family's tent. But whenever he approached it, a giant wave would appear between him and the tent, preventing his return.

ᐊᐃᓂᓗᒋᐊᖅᐸᓚᐅᒐᓂᒃᑲᓗᐊᕋᒥᒨᖅ ᑎᐊ'ᓇ ᒪᖃᐃᑦᓯᖅᑐᖅᓱᓂ ᐱᓚᖕᒋᖅᑰᕋᒥ ᐃᓱᖅᑲᑦ ᐱᑕᐃᓂᒃ ᓂᕆᖅᑕᐅᒥᐊᖅᐸᓕᖅᓱᓂ. ᑎᐊ'ᓇᒨᖅ ᐅᖕᒐᒋᓕ'ᑐᐊᕋᒥᒥᑦ ᐱᖅᓯᐊᔪᔪ'ᑑᖕᒪᑕ ᒪᖃᐃᖅᑲᑕᐅᕙᓕᖅᓱᓂ ᐊᒡᓛᑦ ᐃᓱᖅᑲᓂ.

The man tried for a long time to return home, but he eventually gave up after realizing his attempts were useless. Soon after, the man began eating with the ijirait and accepting their food. In time, he even grew to appreciate their kindness, and he began accompanying them on their hunting trips.

ᒪᕐᑲᐃᕐᑲᑕᐅᓕᕐᒥᒐᒥᔫᖅ ᐸᖕᓂᑐᐊᕐᓂᒃ ᑐᒃᑐᖕᒪᑕ ᐃᔾᖅᑲᑦ ᑐᓐᓄᐃᔭᖅᑯᑎᖖᔫᖅ ᑐᒃᑐᑦ ᐱᕈᔾᐅᓱᖕᒐᔭᓕᕐᒪᑕ. ᓱᓇᐅᕝᕙᔫᖅ ᑐᒃᑐᑦ ᓂᕐᑲᐃᓂᒃ ᕿᓂᖅᓱᐅᓂᕋᐃᓱᕐᓂᕐᒪᑕ ᑐᒃᑐᑦᓴᕌᖕᒐᒥᒃ ᑐᓐᓄᐃᓂᒃ ᐃᖅᑲᑦᑕᒥᐊᔪᔪᑦ.

On one such hunting trip, the ijirait giants killed several caribou bulls. The man noticed that the ijirait first took all the fat off the animals before caching them. He discovered that ijirait considered caribou fat to be a gland, and therefore the fat was a taboo for them to eat. Every time the ijirait killed caribou, they threw the fat away.

ᐅᑭᐅᕐᒪᖖᔫᖅ ᒪᕐᑲᐃᑉᐸᓕᕋᒥ ᕿᔪᒃᓯᖅᑯᓂ ᐊᒪᖅᑯᓂᒃ ᕿᒻᒥᕐᑲᖅᑯᓂ, ᐃᔾᖅᑲᑦ ᐊᒪᖅᑯᓂᒃ ᕿᒻᒥᓕ'ᑑᓐᓂᕐᒪᑕ ᐊᒪᖅᑯᓂᒃ ᕿᒻᒥᕐᑲᕐᑲᑕᐅᓕᕐᒥ. ᒪᕐᑲᐃᓕᕌᖕᒐᒥᔫᖅ ᑕᐃᑉᑯᐊ ᐊᒪᖅᑯᑦ ᕿᒻᒥᓂ ᑎᓕᕝᓕᖅᐸᐃ ᐅᕝᕗᒍᒥᓄᑦ, ᓄᓕᐊᕐᒥᓂᒃ ᐃᕐᓂᕐᒥᓂᓪᓗ ᐊᐃᒃᓴᕐᑯᕝᓗᑎᑦ. ᐅᕐᑲᐅᑎᕝᕙᒃᓗᑎᑦ ᐅᓯᖖᒋᑦᓗᑎᔫᖅ ᕐᑲᐃᓐᓂᕈᒥᒃ ᒥᐊᓪᒍᑦᑐᐊᓇᓕᑦ, ᐅᓯᓐᓂᕈᒥᔫᖅ ᒥᐊᓪᒍᖕᒋᑦᓗᑎᒃ.

When winter came, the man started to hunt by dog team. But the man used wolves instead of dogs, since, to his surprise, wolves were what ijirait used to pull their sleds. On his hunting trips, he began again to try to reunite with his family. He instructed the wolves to go over to his camp and fetch his wife and son. He told the wolves that if they were coming back with an empty sled, to give a loud howling sound and, if they were carrying something on their sled, to approach silently.

ᑖᕝᔫᖅ ᐊᒪᖅᑯᑦ ᖃᒧᑕᐃᓐᓇᓕᔭᖅᓱᑎᒃ ᐊᐅᓪᓚᑐᐊᕐᒪᑕ, ᑕᐃᒪᓇᔫᖅ ᐃᕐᓂ'ᓈᖕᒐ ᓯᓚᒥ ᐱᖖᒍᐊᕐᑲᑦᑖᔪᖕᒪᑦ. ᐊᒪᕈ'ᑐᐃᖖᒍᖅ ᑎᑭᓐᓇᒥᒃ ᐅᓇᔮᖅᓱᒍ ᖃᒧᑎᖕᓄᑦ ᐃᑭᑎᓐᓂᓱᕐᑲᑦᑖᑦᑐᐊᓕᕋᓱᐊᕐᒪᔾᔪᒃ ᐃᑭᓱᐊᖖᒋᑦᑐᐱ'ᑑᖕᒪᑦ. ᐅᕝᓱᓱᒃᑖᕉᖅ ᓄᖑᔅᓱᒍ ᐃᑭᑎᓐᓂᐊᑦᑐᐊᕋᓱᐊᕐᒪᔾᔪᒃ ᐃᑭᖖᒋᑕᐃᓐᓇᕐᒪᑦ, ᐊᓯᐃᑖ ᒥᐊᓪᒍᑦᑐᐊᖅᓱᑎᒃ ᐅᑎᓯᑦᑐᐊᖅᐳᑦ.

When the wolves arrived near the wife and son's home, they came upon the young boy playing outside. The wolves began to caress the child gently to try to get him on the sled. But despite their effort, the boy refused to get on. The wolves spent the entire day trying to entice the child, but he refused to get on the sled. Eventually, the wolves headed back home, howling away.

ᑕᐃᒻᓇᒎᖅ ᐃᓅᓯᒃᑐᐊᕐᔪ’ᓈᖅ ᐋᓈᓇᒥᓄᑦ ᐅᓐᓂᖅᖑᓂ ᐊᒪᖅᑯᓂᑦ ᐃᑭᔾᐅᓂᓄᑕᐅᕐᓂᕋᖅᖑᓂ. ᐋᓈᓈᑕᒎᖅ ᐅᖅᑲᐅᑎᓯᓐᓇᖅᐹ ᐃᑭᑦᑕᐃᓕᑦᑕᕐᑯᖕᓄᒍ.

The child came in from playing outside, and he told his mother that wolves had tried to get him to sit on their sled. But his mother just warned him never to get on.

ᐊᒪᕈ’ᑐᐃᓐᖕᒎᖅ ᖃᐃᑦᑐᐊᓕᕐᒥᖕᒪᑕ ᖃᒧᑕᐃᓐᓈᖅᖑᑎᒃ ᑎᑭᒻᒪᑕ ᑎᐊ’ᓇ ᓱᓕ ᐅᓇᔫᖅᖑᒍ ᐃᑭᑎᓐᓂᐊᑦᑐᐊᓕᕋᓄᐊᕐᒥᖕᒪᔾᔪᒃ ᐅᕝᓄᓄᒃᑖ’ᓈᖅ, ᐅᖅᑲᐅᑎᔾᐅᓯᒪᒻᒫᓕᕋᒥᒎᖅ ᐋᓈᓇᒥᓂᑦ ᐃᑭᓐᖕᒋᑕᐃᓐᓇᕐᒪᑦ. ᓱᕐᑭᓐᓂᓐᖕᒋᑦᑐᐊᖅᓯᓐᓇᓕᕐᒥᖕᒪᓐᖕᒎᖅ ᐊᒪᕈ’ᑐᐃᑦ ᒥᐊᒡᒎᑦᑐᐊᖅᖑᑎᒃ ᐅᑎᖅᓯᓐᓇᓕᓇᕝᓄᑎᒃ.

A while later, the wolves approached the camp once again, pulling their empty sled behind them. When they arrived, the wolves tried again to caress and coax the child onto the sled. But it was even more difficult to entice the boy. All too soon, the sun was about to set, and the wolves headed home again with an empty sled, howling away.

ᑕᐃᒻᓇᒎᖅ ᐊᖑᑦ ᖁᕕᐊᓱᙱᑦᑐᐊᕋᓗᐊᕐᒥ ᐅᖓᑎᖕᒍᑎᒃ ᓄᓕᐊᓂ ᐃᕐᓂ’ᓈᓂᓗ, ᑕᐃᒪᒎᖅ ᐱᓚᙱᖅᑰᕐᒪᓂᒃ ᓄᓕᐊᖅᑖᕐᑯᔭᐅᖅᑲᑦᑖᖅᐸᓚᕋᒥ ᐃᔨᖅᑲᒥᒃ ᓄᓕᐊᖅᑖ’ᑐᐊᖅᓱᓐᓇᓕᖅᓱᓂ.

The man loved his wife and little son dearly. He was deeply discouraged and felt that they would never return to him. He realized his efforts were worthless, and he finally agreed to marry one of the ijirait, having been encouraged by them to do so for some time.

ᑕᐃᒪᒎᖅ ᐊᕕ’ᑐᐊᕐᒥᒐᒥᒃ, ᑕᐃᒻᓇᒎᖅ ᐊᕐᓇᒧᑦ ᑎᑭᓐᓇᒥ ᐅᓂᑉᑳᕐᕕᖕᒋᓕᕐᒪᒍ ᐊᕐᓇᖅ ᕿᐊᐱᑦᑐᐊᓕᕋᓗᐊᕐᒪᑦ ᑲᒪᓱᒃᑕᐃᓕᓚᐅᖅᓱᓐᓇᖅᑐᖅ ᐊᐃᔭᐅᓂᓗᒃᑕᓚᐅᕋᓗᐊᕐᒥᒃ ᐊᒪᖅᑯᓂᑦ.

Before marrying the ijiraq, the man sent a messenger to his wife's camp to give her his news. After the woman heard the story, she began to wail profusely, realizing that she had refused to return to her husband when he had sent for them.

ᓄᓕᐊᓴᓕᕐᒥᐅᒎᖅ ᓄᑕᕋ’ᓈᖅᑲᓕᖅᓱᑎᒡᓗ ᒪᖅᑲᐃ’ᑐᐊᖅᐸᒃᑲᒥ. ᒪᖅᑲᐃᓕᕐᒥᒐᒥᒎᖅ ᐃᓄᒃᓯᓱᖕᒐᔭᒃᑲᒥ ᐃᓕᑕᕐᓇᑯᓂ.

Shortly after his marriage, the man and his ijiraq wife had a child of their own. The man continued to go out on hunting trips, and during one of these trips, he met up with a fellow Inuk, who looked familiar.

ᑲᑎᒐᒥᐅᒎᖅ ᐊᐱᓴᕆᐊᑲ’ᓈᕐᒪᒍ ᓄᓕᐊᓂ ᐃᕐᓂᓂᓗ ᓇᐅᖑᖕᒪᖕᒫᓂᒃ. ᑕᐃᒪᐅᓂᕋᕐᒪᑎᒎᖅ ᕿᐊᑎᐊᒻᒫᖅᓱᓂ ᐅᕐᑲᓕᖅᐳᖅ ᐊᐃᓂᓗᒃᐸᓚᐅᕋᓗᐊᕐᒥᒎᖅ ᐊᖏᕐᒥ. ᐃᕐᓂᓂᓗᒎᖅ ᓄᓕᐊᓂᓗ ᖃᐃᕐᑯᖕᒍᑎᒃ ᐊᒪᖅᑯᑦ

ᐊᐃᒃᓱᖅᑎᑦᑕᓚᐅᖃᓗᐊᖃᒥᒋᑦ ᑲᒪᓱᖕᒋᑕᐃᓐᓇᖅᒪᑕ. ᐃᓯᖅᑲᒥᒎᖅ ᓄᓕᐊᖅᑲᓕᖅᓱᓂᓗ ᓄᑕᖃᖅᑲᓕᖃᒥᓕ, ᓄᓕᐊᖕᖓᑉᑕᐅᔫᖅ ᐅᐃᑖᒥᐊᓕᓇᓕ ᐅᖅᓂᓚᐃ'ᑐᐊᖅᒪᒍᒎᖅ.

The man's first question was to ask the stranger about the whereabouts of his wife and son. When he was told they were still around, he began to cry and said that he had tried desperately to come back home, but could not.

ᐃᓱᐊ
The end

ᐅᒃᐱ'ᑐᐊᕐᓗ ᓇᓄᕐᓗ ᑕᑯᕋᐅᓛᖅᑐᕋᐅᑦᑐᒃ
OWL AND POLAR BEAR TEASE EACH OTHER

ᐅᓂᑉᑳᖅᑐᐊᕐᓂᐊᖅᑐᖓ ᐅᒃᐱ'ᑐᐊᕐᒥᒡᓗ ᓇᓄᕐᒥᒡᓗ ᑕᑯᕋᐅᓛᖅᑐᕋᐅᑦᑐᖕᓂᒃ. ᐊᓈᓇᓚᐅᒻᓂᑦ Hᐊᓚᓐ ᐸᐅᕐᖓᒥᑦ ᑐᓵᑦᑕᕐᓂᑯᒻᓂᑦ ᐊᐅᓚᔾᔨᓂᕋ ᐅᓂᑉᑳᕐᓂᐊᖅᐸᕋ. ᖃᐅᔨᒪᓂᐊᖅᐳᔾ ᐅᑭᐅᖅᑕᖅᑐᒥ ᐃᓄᐃᑦ ᓄᓇᖃᕐᑎᒌᖕᒥᑦᑐᑦ ᐃᖕᒥᒃᑯᑦᑕᐅᖅ ᐅᓂᑉᑳᖅᑐᐊᕐᑯᑎᖃᕐᒥᖕᒪᑕ, ᑖᒻᓇᓕ ᐅᓂᑉᑳᕐᓂᐊᒐᕋ ᓴᐅᓂᖅᑑᕐᒥᐅᓂᑦ ᐅᓂᑉᑳᒐᐅᑎᑦᓱᒍ ᑐᓵᑦᑕᕐᓂᑯᒐ ᐃᐊ'ᓇᐃᓕᐅᖅᑐᖅ.

I'm going to tell you a story about how, long ago, the owl and the polar bear made fun of each other. I will tell it the same way I remember my mother, Helen Paurngat, telling it to me. Please note that there are many variations of this story because many communities have their own unique version. This version of the story is one I've heard told by the Hauniqtuurmiut.

ᑲᖕᒐᓴᐴᖅ ᓱᓇᒥᐊᑦ ᓂᕐᔪᑎᑦ ᐃᓄᐴᓪᒥᓯᒪᑦᑐᐊᔪᓚᐅᖅᑎᓪᓗᒋᑦ, ᑕᐃᒻᓇᑰᖅ ᓇᓄ’ᑐᐊᖅ ᓂᕿᒃᓴᖅᓯᐅᕆᓪᓗᓂᑉᑕᐅᖅ ᐅᓪᓗᓗᒃᑖᖅ ᐱᓱᒃᑑᓐᓂᖅ. ᒪᓂᖕᓂᒃᑯᖅᑎᓪᓗᒍᒎᖅ ᐅᒃᐱ’ᑑᑉ ᓂᐊᕐᑯᑉᑕᖕᒥᒃ ᒥᖖᒐᓪᓗᓂ ᐊᕕᖖᒐᒃᓴᓂᒃ ᐅᑕᖅᑭᓪᓗᓂ ᓇᖕᒋᐅᔭᖅᑐᑉ ᓴᑦᑐᑎᒋᓚᕐᒥᐅᒃ ᐊᐱᕆᕐᑕᓱᖕᒐᔭᖕᒪᒍ: “ᐱᓱᕐᑲᑦᑎᔮᕐᔪᐊᖅ ᐱᓱᕐᑲᑦᑎᔮᕐᓗᖅᐲᑦᕙ?”

A long time ago, a polar bear walked all day in search of food. It eventually came upon a smooth stretch of land where an owl was perched on a tiny mound, waiting for lemmings. The owl saw the bear and mocked it: “Is the slumpy walker taking his usual walk?”

ᓇᓄ’ᑑᒻᖕᒎᖅ ᐱᓱᒃᑐᐃᓐᓇᖅᖢᓂ ᐅᒃᐱ’ᑐᐊᖅ ᕿᕕᐊᖅᖢᒍ ᐊᐱᕆᕖᑉᑕᐅᖅ, “ᓱᕙ, ᓱᕙ ᓇᖕᒋᕐᑲᑦᓯᔮᕐᔪᐊᖅᕙ?”

The bear kept walking along at its usual pace, then turned around and asked the owl, “What’s that, forever-perched one?”

ᐅᒃᐱ’ᑐᐊᑰᖅ ᐅᕐᑲᒃᑲᓐᓂᓕᖅᖢᓂ, “ᐱᓱᕐᑲᑦᑎᔮᕐᔪᐊᖅ ᐱᓱᕐᑲᑦᑎᔮᕐᓗᖅᐲᑦ, ᐅᒃᐸᑎᓛᒃ ᖕᒪᒻᒥᖕᒐᔪᖕᓂᒃᕙ?”

The owl said again, “Is the slow walker taking his usual stroll, with his *mammingajuk* (droopy buttocks)?”

ᓇᓅ’ᑐᐊᖀᖅ ᑭᐅᒃᑲᓐᓂ’ᓈᖅᓯᓐᓇᑎᕗᖅ, “ᓇᖕᒋᖅᑲᑦᓯᔮᖅᔪᐊᖅ ᓇᖕᒋᖅᑲᑦᑎᔮᖅᑐᖅᐲᑦ, ᐃᓱᓚᒃ ᐊᒃᓴᓪᓛᔪᐃᑦᑑᖕᓂᒃ?”

The bear simply replied, “Forever-perched one, are you still perching there, with your *aksallajuittuk* (eyes that always stare in one direction)?”

ᐅᒃᐱ’ᑐᐊᖀᖅ ᑭᐅᒃᑲᓐᓂᖅᓱᓂ, “ᓱᓇ, ᓱᓇ ᐃᖅᑯᐃᓐᓈᖅ, ᐊᓇᐃᓐᓈᖅ?”

The owl answered, “What’s that, dirty buttocks full of manure?”

ᓇᓅ’ᑐᐊᖀᖅ ᐱᓯᒃᑐᐃᓐᓇᐅᔭᒥᐊᖅᓱᓂ ᐅᖅᑲᕋᑕ’ᓈᖅᓯᓐᓇᑎᕝᓱᓂ, “ᓱᓇ, ᓱᓇ ᐃᖅᑭᑦᑑᖅ?”

The polar bear kept walking and casually replied, “What’s that, *iqqituuq*[1] (one with no anus)?”

ᐅᒃᐱ’ᑐᐊᖀᖅ ᓂᖖᒐᒃᑲᒥ ᑎᖕᒋᒋᐊᒻᒫᖅᓱᓂ ᓇᓅ’ᑐᐊᖅᒧᑦ ᐅᖅᑲᓇᕗᖅ, “ᐊᖕᖑᓗᖕᒐ, ᐊᖕᖑᓗᖕᒐ.”

The owl took flight in anger and said to the bear, “Try and catch me! Try and catch me!”

ᓇᓄ'ᑐᐊᕌᖅ ᑎᖕᒋᓯᐃᑦᑑᒐᒥᓕ ᐅᒃᐱ'ᑐᐊᖅ ᒪᓕᒋᐊᒻᒫᖅᑐᓂᐅᒃ ᐅᖃᖅᐳᖅ,
"ᐅᑕᖅᑲᙵ, ᐅᑕᖅᑲᙵ."

But the bear couldn't fly, so it ran after the owl instead while crying,
"Wait for me! Wait for me!"

ᐅᒃᐱ'ᑐᐊᕌᖅ ᓇᓐᓄᒥᒃ ᓂᙵᐃᓵᓇᐅᔭᓕᖅᐳᖅ ᑎᖕᒋᓚᐅᖅᐸᒃᑐᓂ ᓯᕗᖅᖓᓄᑦ ᒥᑦᐸᒃᑐᓂ, ᐊᖑᓕᖀᖕᒐᒍ ᑎᖕᒋᕚᒃᑐᓂ.

The owl flew for a little while and then landed in front of the polar bear. But as soon as the bear was about to catch it, the owl spread its wings and flew away.

ᐃᓱᐊ
The end

1. ᐃᖅᑭᑦᑐᖅ ᐅᒃᐱᒍᒃᐱᒃ ᐃᑎᖅᑲᙱᑦᑐᖅ. ᐅᒃᐱ'ᑐᐃᙶᖅ ᐃᑎᖅᑲᙱᒻᒪᑕ ᑕᐃᒫᒃᑖᙶᖅ ᐊᓇᖏᔅᑐᑎᒃ ᒥᕐᐊᖅᑕᖅᓯᓇᔪᕗᑦ.

1. It is said owls have no anus because they regurgitate from their mouths.

ᐅᔾᕋᒍᖅᑐᑦ
THE PEOPLE WHO TURNED TO STONE

ᐊᒻᒪᑉᑕᐅᕉᖅ ᑕᐃᑉᑯᐊ ᓂᕕᐊᖅᓯᐊᑦ ᐱᖕᖓᓱᑦ ᕿᑎᒃᑐ'ᑐᐃᑦ ᓯᒡᔭᒥ ᐅᖕᖓᑎᙳᐊᖅᑐᑦ. ᑎᐊ'ᓇᐃᓚᐅᖅᑐᕋᐅᓱᖕᖓᔭᓚᕐᒪᑕᒎᖅ, "ᐱᖕᓇᓚ ᐅᐃᙳᐊᓇᓂᐊᖅᐸᕋ." ᓇᒃᑐᕋᓚ'ᑐᐊᕐᒥᒎᖅ ᐅᐃᙳᐊᕐᑲᕐᓂᐊᕐᓂᕋᖅᑐᖅ.

Long ago, three girls were happily playing house near the beach. As they were playing, the first girl said, "Hey, I'll pretend that thing up there will be my husband." The girl was referring to a big eagle.

"ᐅᓇᓚ ᐅᐃᙳᐊᓇᓂᐊᖅᐸᕋ." ᐅᔾᕋᖕᒥᒎᖅ ᐅᐃᙳᐊᕐᑲᓚᖅᑐᓂ.

"I'll pretend this thing down here is my husband," said the second girl. She was referring to a stone.

"ᑲᓐᓇᓚ ᐊᐃ ᐅᐃᙳᐊᓇᓂᐊᖅᐸᕋ." ᐊᕐᕕ'ᑐᐊᕐᒥᒃᓚᒎᖅ ᐅᐃᙳᐊᕐᑲᓚᖅᑐᓂ.

"Then that thing down there will be my pretend husband," said the last girl. She was referring to a huge whale.

ᑕᐃᒻᓇᒎᖅ ᐅᔭᕋᖕᒥᒃ
ᐅᐃᙳᐊᖃᕈᐊᖅᑐᖅ
ᐅᔭᕋᙳᖅᖢᓂ. ᓇᒃᑐᕋᓕᖕᒥᒎᖅ
ᐅᐃᙳᐊᖃᕈᐊᖅᑐᖅ ᓇᒃᑐᕋᓕᐅᑉ
ᑭᙵ'ᑐᐊᕐᒧᓕᐅᑎᖦᖢᓂᐅᒃ.
ᑕᐃᒻᓇᓗ ᐊᕐᕕ'ᑐᐊᕐᒥᒃ
ᐅᐃᙳᐊᖃᕈᐊᖅᑐᖅ ᐊᕐᕕ'ᑑᑉ
ᐊᒫᓪᓚᒃᖢᒍ ᕿᑭᖅᑕᒧᓕᐅᑎᖦᖢᒍ.

As soon as they had spoken out loud, the first girl was taken to a high cliff by the eagle, the second girl turned into stone, and the third girl was carried off by the whale to an offshore island.

ᑕᐃᒻᓇᒎᖅ ᓇᒃᑐᕋᓕᖕᒥᒃ ᐅᐃᙳᐊᓕᒃ ᐃᒻᓇ'ᑐᐊᕐᒥ ᐊᔪᖅᓯᓯᒪ'ᑐᐊᓕᕐᒪᑦ ᐊᖅᑲᓚᐃ'ᑐᐊᖅᖢᓂ ᖁᑦᓯ'ᑐᐊᕐᒥ. ᑕᐃᒻᓇᒎᖅ ᓇᒃᑐᕋᓕᒃ ᒪᖃᐃᑦᑐᐊᔪᖕᒪᑦ ᓄᕐᕋᕋᓗᒥᐊ'ᑐᐊᕐᓂᒃ ᑎᑭᐅ'ᔩᑦᑐᐊᖅᐸᒃᖢᓂ.

The girl who had pretended an eagle was her husband was left stranded high up on a cliff. She was not able to get down because of the extreme height. But the eagle would often go out hunting and bring home all sorts of animals, including caribou calves.

ᒪᖃᐃᑦᑕᑦᑐᐊᔪᖕᒪᙳᖅ ᐃᖅᑲᖅᓴᑦᑐᐊᖅᐸᓕᕋᒥ ᖃᓄᖅ ᐊᖅᑲᕋᔭᕐᒪᖔᕐᒦ, ᐅᐃᙳᐊᓂᒎᖅ ᒪᖃᐃᓕᕌᖓᑦ ᐊᕕᙵᖅᓯᐅᖅᑲᑦᑖᖅᐸᓕᖅᐳᖅ. ᐊᕕᙵᐃᙴᖅ ᐃᕙᓗᐃᓂᒃ ᑲᑎᖅᓯᐃᖦᖢᓂ ᐱᑦᕋᐃᖅᑲᑦᑖᖅᐸᓕᖅᖢᓂ. ᑕᐅᓄᖓᒎᖅ ᐃᒻᓇᕐᒧᑦ ᓂᖏᑎᑦᐸᒃᖢᒍ ᖃᐅᔨᓴᖅᐸᒃᖢᓂ ᑕᓴᒧᖓ ᐊᒃᑐᖅᑑᑦᓗᐊᓕᙱᒪᖔᑦ.

While the eagle was out hunting, the girl would try to think of ways to escape down the cliff. One day, while the eagle was out again on a long hunting trip, she began hunting for lemmings, collecting their little sinews, and braiding them. As the days went on, she continued her work, and at the end of each day she would extend the braid down the cliff to see if it could touch the bottom.

ᑕᐃᒪᒎᖅ ᓇᒃᑐᕋᓕᒃ ᑎᑭᑦᑐᐊᑕᐃᓐᓇᕐᒥᒐᒥ ᑕᒡᖓᖕᒐᒎᖅ ᓂᕕᐊᖅᓯᐊᒧᑦ ᐅᕐᑲᓱᖕᒐᔭᓕᕐᒪᑦ, "ᒪᕐᑲᐃᓕᕐᒥᒍᒪᐊᐃ ᑎᑭᓐᓇᓵ'ᑐᐊᕈᒫᓕᖅᐳᖕᒐ, ᓯᕐᑭᓂᐅᑉ ᓇᓛᓄᑦ ᐊᐅᓪᓚᕈᒫᓕᕐᒪ."

When the eagle returned, it said to the girl, "Please know that when I go hunting next, I won't be back for a long time, since I will be heading towards the sun."

ᑕᐃᒪᒎᖅ ᐊᐅᓪᓚ'ᑐᐊᕐᒥᖕᒪᑦ ᐱᑦᕋᐃᒋᐊᑦᑐᐊᓇᖓᖅ. ᐱᑦᕋᐃᓕᓂᕐᒥᒃ ᑯᐤᓗᐊᓗ ᑎᑭᐊᓗ ᓴᐅᓂᕐᒧᑦ ᐊᒡᓛᑦ ᑎᑭᔅᖢᑎᒃ ᐱᑦᕋᐃᕐᑲᑦᑖᖅᐸᖕᒪᑦ. ᓂᖕᒋᑎᓐᒥᖕᒪᒍᒎᖅ ᑕᓴᒧᖕᒐ ᓈᒻᒪᒃᓯᔫᔭᕐᒪᑦ ᕐᑲᐃᓐᓇᓂᒃ (ᕐᑲᔭᕐᓂᒃ) ᐅᑕᖅᑭᒥᐊᓕᖅᐳᖅ.

Of course, when it left, she went back to her braiding. She braided so much and so hard that she cut her thumb and index finger to the bone. Then she hung the braid over the cliff again, and it appeared to be the right length. So she began to wait for qajait to float by.

ᑎᓴᒪ'ᑐᐃᖖᒎᖅ ᐃᓛ ᕐᑲᐃᓐᓇᑦ (ᕐᑲᔭᐃᑦ) ᓴᑦᕈᑦᓴᖅᑐᖅᑐ'ᑐᐃᑦ. ᑕᒪᓐᓇᒎᖅ ᐱᑦᕋᓚᐅᒃᑲᒥ ᐃᓱᐊ ᐅᔭᕋᓱᒡᔪᖕᒧᑦ ᕐᑭᓗᐊᖅᖢᒍ ᐃᖕᒥᓂᒃ ᓂᖕᒋᑎᓯᒋᐊᓱᖕᒐᔭᖕᒪᑦ ᕐᑲᐃᓐᓇᑦ (ᕐᑲᔭᐃᑦ) ᓇᑦᑕᓇᐊᕐᒪᑕ.

At last, she saw qajait about to pass by. She tied one end of the braided sinew to a huge boulder and held on to the other end to let herself down, just as the qajait were passing by.

ᑲᑖᓕᕐᒥᒎᖅ ᑐᖅᖁᑖᓕᕐᒪᑦ,
ᑐᓴᒐᐅᒐᒥ ᐃᑭᑎᑕᐅᕝᓗᓂ
ᐊᐃᖅᑲᑕᐅ’ᑐᐊᓕᖅᖁᓂ.

As she was descending, she called out to the qajait. When the people on the qajait heard her, they helped her down so she could return home with them.

ᑕᐃᒻᓇᒎᖅ ᐊᕐᕕ’ᑐᐊᕐᒥᒃ ᐅᐃᙳᐊᓕᒃ
ᐊᕐᕕᐅᒻᖕᒎᖅ ᓴᐅᓂᑦᑐᐊᖕᒋᓐᓂᒃ
ᐃᒡᓗᕐᔪᐊᖅᑲᖅᖁᑎᒃ ᕿᑭᖅᑕᒥ
ᓄᓕᐊᓇ’ᑐᐊᓕᕐᒪᒍ.
ᐃᕐᓕᒋᕝᓗᓂᐅᒎᖅ ᖁᐃᔭᖅᑐᕐᓂᐊᓕᕌᖕᒐᑦ ᓯᓚᒧᑦ, ᑎᓗᒃᑑᙳᒎᖅ ᐊᒃᖁᓅᕐᒧᑦ
ᕿᓚᒃᖁᒍ ᖃᐅᔨᓴᕈᑎᖃᔪᖕᒪᑦ ᐊᒡᓛᑦ.

The girl whose pretend husband was a whale lived in a shelter on an island made from the whale's bones. She became the whale's wife. The whale was so possessive that whenever the girl went out to pee, she had to take a snow beater that was tied to a string. The whale held the other end of the string, to be able to tell where she was.

ᖁᐃᔭᖅᑐᓕᕐᒥᒐᒥᒎᖅ ᑖᒻᓇ ᑎᓗᒃᑑᑦ ᐅᖅᑲᐅᑎᓯᖕᒐᔭᓕᕐᒪᒍ,
“ᓄᕿᑦᑲᓗᐊᖅᐸᑎᓕᐊᐃ ᐱᑦᓯᓃᓴᑦᑐᐊᕐᓗᑎᑦ ᑲᒪᒋᒃᑕᐃᓕᑦᑐᐊᓇᖕᓇ.”

When she was out peeing again, the girl told the snow beater, “Next time he tugs on you, exert as much resistance as you possibly can.”

ᑕᐃ'ᓇᐃᓕᕐᓗᓂᓗᒎᖅ ᑕᑲᓐᓇᓗ ᖃᔭᐃᑦ ᐅᔭᖕᖏᑦᑐᐊᓪᓚᕆᒃ ᐱᖕᒪᑕ, ᑕᑲᓅᖕᒪᒎᖅ ᖃᐃᓐᓇᓅᑦ (ᖃᔭᕐᓅᑦ) ᐃᑭᑦᑐᐊᖅᐳᖅ.

Just as she said the words, qajait appeared, and she got on as their passenger.

ᐃᑭᒪᒥ, ᑕᐃᒪᓇᒎᖅ ᑎᓗᒃᑑᑦ ᐅᖃᐅᑎᔮ ᐱᑦᓯᓈᓴᖃᑦᑖᖅᑐᐱ'ᑑᖕᒪᑦ ᐊᕐᕕᐅᑉ ᓄᓯᔦᐃᕆᒥᐅᒃ ᓄᓕᐊᓇᓯᒋᕐᓗᓂᐅᒎᖅ ᓄᓯᓗᖃᕐᓗᓇᐊᑦᑐᐊᓪᓛᓪᓗ ᐅᖃᐅᑎᑦᑐᐊᖅᐹ, "ᒪᐃ, ᐊᓇᖅᑐᑯᓂ!"

After the girl left, the little snow beater put as much resistance on the string as it could for as long as it could. Eventually, the whale pulled on the string abruptly. The whale yelled at what it thought was its wife, "My, my, you sure take a long time shitting!"

ᓄᓯᒃᑲᒥᐅᒎᖅ ᑎᓗᒃᑑᑕᐃᓐᓇᑯᓘᖕᒪᑦ ᓂᖖᒐᒃᑲᒥ, ᐊᕐᕕ'ᑐᐊᖅ ᓴᐅᓂᕋᓗᖕᒥᓂᒃ ᐊ'ᑐᒥᐊᑦᑐᐊᖅᓗᓂ (ᐊᑎᐅᖅᑲᐃᕐᓗᓂ) ᐱᓕᕐᒪᑦ, ᖃᔭᐃᖖᒎᖅ ᐊᐃᕋᓚᓴᕐᓂᐊᑦᑐᐊᓕᕋᓗᐊᕐᒪᑕ ᑖᔅᓯᒥᖕᒪ ᐊᕐᕕᐅᑉ ᓄᓕᐊᖕᒪᓂᒃ ᐅᓯᓕᕋᒥᒃ.

When it realized it was just an old snow beater, the whale became furious and started putting its bones back on while the qajait were trying to escape with the girl.

ᐊᕐᕕ'ᑐᐊᕿᖅ ᖃᐃᓕᕋᒥ ᐱᐊᓚ'ᑐᐊᕐᒪᑦ, ᐊᖕᒍᑎᓕᕐᒪᖕᒎᖅ ᑖᐸᓯᒪ ᐊᕐᓇᐸ ᐊᓕᖅᑎᒋᒃ ᐃᒋᕐᔪᒋᒃ. ᐃᒋ'ᓈᑐᐊᕐᒪᑎᒋᒎᖅ ᐊᕐᕕ'ᑑᐸ ᐅᒋᐊᕐᑲᑦᑳᒥᐊᓘ'ᑐᐊᓇᓕᕐᒪᒋᑦ ᐅᖕᒐᓓᓇᖖᑐᑎᒃ.

When the whale had put all its bones on, it rushed into the water after them. Just as it was about to catch up to them, the men threw the girl's socks in the water. As soon as they were thrown in, the whale grabbed them and started to rip and tear at them, which gave the men more time to escape.

ᐅᒋᐊᓘᓂᒃᑲᒥᒎᖅ ᖃᐃᒋᐊᑦᑐᐊᕐᒥᖕᒪᑦ ᐱᐊᓚᔪ'ᑑᖕᒪᖕᒎᖅ ᐊᖕᒍᑎᐊᑦᓚᒃᐸᖕᒪᑦ ᐊᕐᓇᐸ ᐊᓐᓄᕌᖕᒋᓂᒃ ᐃᒋᑦᑎᖖᕕᒋᓓᒃᔪᒍ ᐊᐃᕋᓚᓴᕐᓂᐊ'ᑐᐊᓕᕐᒪᑕ.

After the whale had fought the socks for a while, it made another lunge for the qajait. Since it was so swift, the whale did not take long to catch up with them again. But the men kept throwing the girl's clothes into the water to buy them more time to reach home safely.

ᐅᒋᐊᕐᑲᑦᑳᑦᑐᐊᓘᓂᖕᒥᓘᒥᒎᖅ ᖃᐃᒋᐊᑦᑐᐊᕐᒥᖕᒪᑦ, ᐊᖕᒍᑎᑦᑐᐊᖅᓯᓐᓇᕐᒥᖕᒪᖕᒎᖅ ᐊᕐᓇᐅᐸ ᑲᕐᓕᒋᒃ ᐃᒋᕐᔪᓂᑎᒋᒃ. ᐅᒋᐊᕐᑲᑦᑳᒥᐊᓘ'ᑐᐊᓇᓕᕐᒪᒋᒎᖅ ᑎᑭᓕᕋᕈᐊᖅᑎᓪᓗᒋᓪᓗᒎᖅ ᖃᐃᒋᐊᓯᖕᒐᔭᖕᒥᖕᒪᑦ.

After another long fight with a piece of clothing, the whale made yet another charge towards the qajait, and the men decided to throw the girl's pants in the water. The whale struggled with the pants for a very long time. The people were about to reach land when the whale made one final charge for the qajait.

ᐱᐊᓚ’ᑐᐊᕐᒪᙳᖅ (ᐱᐊᓚᔪᐊᓘᖕᒪᙳᖅ) ᐊᙳᑎᑦᑫᔭᑦᑐᐊᖅᑎᑦᑐᒍᑐ ᖃᑭᕝᑐᑎᒃ. ᐊᙳᑎᖖᒋᑦᑐᕉᖅ ᑭᓯᐊᓂ ᑐᐊᖏᐅᓗᐊᒧᑦ ᓴᐅᓂᓂ, ᓴᑭᐊ’ᑐᐊᖕᓂ ᐳᐃᒍᕐᓂᑫᒥᒋᒃ.

It was so swift that the whale almost caught up to the people before they reached land. The only thing that prevented it from catching the group was that, in its rush to put its bones back on, it had forgotten to put on its shoulder blades.

ᑕᒡᕙᓚᒨᖅ ᐊᑦᖂᒍᙳᕐᒪᑦ, ᑕᐃᒻᓇᒎᖅ ᐊᕐᕕ’ᑐᐊᖅ ᓄᑕᐊᖕᒋᑕᕿ’ᑐᐊᕐᒥ ᓯᑕ, ᑕᒡᕗᖕᒐ ᑎᒻᒧᐊᑕᕐᓂᕐᒥᖕᒪᑦ, ᑕᐃᒻᓇᒎᖅ ᑐᖅᓱᑕᓯᖕᒐᔭᒃᐸᒃᐳᖅ ᐊᓈᓈ, “ᐸᓂᒃ, ᐊᕐᕕᕉᖅ ᓴᒻᓇ ᐳᔪᓃᓛ?”

The next year, the whale returned to where it had last seen the girl, because it was still yearning for her. As it swam along the shore, the girl's mother saw the whale and called out to her daughter, "Hey, daughter, that whale down there, is it free of dried blubber odour?"

“ᓈᒃᑲ, ᐳᔭᓂᑦᐳᖅ.”

“Oh no, it’s full of dried blubber odour!”

ᑎᐊ’ᓇᒨᖅ ᐱᖕᒪᑦ, ᑎᐊ’ᓇᒨᖅ ᐊᕐᕕᖅ ᐅᖃᓯᖕᒐᔭᖕᒪᑦ, “ᖃᓄᖅᑐᖅ ᐸᑭᑉᑯᐊ ᐅᔭᕋᒍᕐᓚᑦ.”

When the girl said this, the whale called out in revenge, “Oh, how I wish those creatures up on dry land would turn into stones!”

ᑕᐃᒪᒨᖅ ᐅᖄᓂ’ᓈᑐᐊᕐᒪᑦ ᑐᐱᖃᓗᐃᒨᖅ, ᕿᒻᒥᖃᓗᐃ ᓱᓇᒥᐊᖕᒋᑦ ᐅᔭᕋᖑᒥᐊᓱᖕᒐᔭᖕᒪᑕ. ᑕᐃᒻᓇᒨᖅ ᐳᔭᓂᓐᓂᖃᐃᓚᐅᖅᑐᖅ ᐅᔭᕋᒍᖅᐸᓪᓕᐊᓕᕐᒥ ᐃᓕᐅᓱᖕᒐᔭᓕᕐᒪᑦ. “ᐃᑎᒐᒃᑲ ᐅᔭᕋᒍᖅᐳᑦ, ᐊᒡᒐᒃᑲ ᐅᔭᕋᒍᖅᐳᑦ. ᑕᒡᕙ ᑕᒪᕐᒪ ᐅᔭᕋᒍᖅᐳᖕᒐ.”

As soon as it said this, all the people’s tents, dogs, and possessions started to turn to stone. The girl who had mocked the whale began

turning into stone too and, as she turned to stone, she said, "My feet have turned to stone, my hands have turned to stone, now all of me has turned to stone."

ᐅᔭᕋᖑᒥᐊᖅᑐ'ᑑᖕᒪᑕᓘᖅ ᑎᐊ'ᓇ ᕿᒻᒥᕋᓗᐃᑦ ᐊᖁᐱᓐᓂᓯᕋᓗᖕᒥᖕᓂᒃ ᐃᑐᐃᓐᓇᖅᓱᑎᒃ. ᑖᕙᓂᐊᒡᒑᙵᖅ ᑕᐃᒪ ᕿᒻᒥᑦ ᖁᑐᖕᒐᕕᓃ ᑎᒃᑯᓇᐅᖕᒪᑕᓘᖅ ᓇᖅᑯᑎᒃᓴᖅᓯᕝᕕᐅᕙᓚᐅᖅᓯᒪᕗᑦ ᓇᐱᑦᑕ'ᓈᖅᓱᑎᑦ.

The whale's words had turned everything at the camp into stone—even the dogs turned to stone where they sat tethered to the ground. To this day, there is a place where you can find the dog team's stone tether lines. The stone lines are straight and smooth, perfect for *natqut* (qulliq flame adjusters), and people break off pieces of the lines to use in stone lanterns.

ᐃᓱᐊ

The end

ᐃᒫᕋᓱᒡᔪᒃ

IIMAARASUGJUK, THE PEOPLE SWALLOWER

ᑕᐃᒪᓇᒎᖅ ᐃᓄᐊᒃᑳᓯ'ᑐᐊᖅ (ᐃᓄᐊᒃᑳᓯᐊᓗᒃ) ᐃᓚᒥᓂᒃ ᑳᒃᑐ'ᑑᒐᒥ. ᑳᒃᑐ'ᑑᒐᒥᒎᖅ ᐃᓚᓂ ᓄᖕᒍᓐᒪᑎᑦ ᓂᕆᕚᒃᓗᑎᑦ, ᑕᐃᒪᒎᖅ ᓄᓕᐊᓂ ᑕᐃᒪᑐᐊ'ᓈᖕᒍᓕᕐᒪᑦ ᕿᔪᒃᑕᕆᐊᕐᑯᑦᑐᐊᓕᖅᐹ, ᐸᓂᓂ ᓂᕆᓂᐊᓕᕐᒥᒐᒥᐅᒃ.

There is a story of a time when there was much starvation, and a man began slaughtering his relatives to feed himself. Over time, he killed and ate his relatives one by one. Eventually, his wife was the only one left alive, and so he asked her to go out and gather some firewood so he could cook up the daughter he had recently killed.

ᑕᐃᒪᔫᖅ ᐸᓂ'ᓈᓂ ᐃᒐᓂᐊᓕᕐᒥᒐᒥᐅᒃ, ᑕᐃᒻᓇ ᐊᕐᓇᖅ ᑕᐅᒐᓂ ᑳᒃᑭᒃᐸᓕᕐᒪᑦ ᐊᐱᕆᑦᑐᐊᕆᕚᔫᖅ, "ᓄᓕᐊᒃ, ᕿᐊᕖᑦ?"

When the wife returned from gathering firewood, she began to cook her daughter. But as she did, she sniffled and blew her nose. The old man had the nerve to ask, "My dear wife, are you weeping?"

"ᓈᒡᒐ."

"Oh, no," she answered.

"ᓱᕐᓕ ᑳᒃᑭᒃᐸᒃᐱᑦ?" ᑎᐊ'ᓇᔫᖅ ᐊᐱᕆᖕᒪᔪ.

"Then why all this sniffling and blowing your nose?" he asked.

"ᐃᓱᕐᓕᐅᖄ."

"Oh, my eyes are just burning from the smoke," she replied.

ᐸᓂᖕᒥᔫᖅ ᐊᒡᒐᐃ ᐊᒡᕿᓕᖄᒥᒃ ᑕᐅᔪᖕᒐ ᑎᖕᒐᐅᔮᑦ ᐃᑯᐊᓪᓚᖕᒪᑕ ᖃᒥᑦᑐᐊᖅᐸᒃᓱᓂ. ᑎᖕᒐᐅᔮᓂᔫᖅ ᖃᒥᑦᓯᔪ'ᑑᕙᓕᕐᒪᑦ ᑕᐃᒻᓇ ᐸᓂᐊᑕ ᐊᒡᒑ ᐊᒡᕿᖅᑐᖅ.

As the mother continued cooking, the girl's hands roasted in the fire, curled up into fists, grabbed hold of the burning moss, and smothered the flame.

ᑕᒡᕙᒎᖅ ᐸᓂ’ᓈᓂ ᓂᕆᐊᓂᖕᒥᒐᒥᐅᒃ ᕿᔪᒃᑕᕆᐊᕐᑯᑦᑐᐊᓕᕆᕚᒎᖅ ᓄᓕᐊᓂ. ᕿᔪᒃᑕᕆᐊᓕᖅᐳᕉᖅ ᐊᑎᒌᓂᕐᒥᒃ ᓇᒃᓴᖅᖑᓂ ᖃᖅᑲᒧᑦ ᕿᔪᒃᑕᕆᐊᓕᕐᒥ. ᑎᖕᒐᐅᔭᓂᒎᖅ ᐃᓗᑦᓕᖅᑐᐊᑦᓚᑯᓗᒃᓯᓐᓇᖅᖑᒍ ᐊᑎᒌᓂᖅ ᕿᒪᒃᖑᓂᐅᒃ ᐃᓅᓯᖅᑐᖅᖑᒍ.

After the man had eaten his daughter, he told his wife to gather more moss. She left, taking an old atigi with her to the hill above the igluit. When she reached the top of the hill, she quickly stuffed the old atigi with moss to make it look like a person and left it sitting there.

ᑕᐃᒪᒎᖅ ᖄᐃᕆᐊ’ᑐᐊᕐᓂᐊᕐᒪᑦ ᐃᒡᓗᑎᒃ ᑐᓄᕐᖑᑎᑦ ᑖᕗᖓ ᐊᖅᐸᓯᑦᑐᐊᖅᐳᖅ ᐃᓚᒥᓄᑦ.

The wife realized her husband would soon come after her, so she turned away from their iglu and started to run towards her relatives' camp.

ᑕᑲᓐᓇᑯᓗᔫᖅ ᐊᓂᑦᑐᐊᖅᐳᖅ. ᐊᓂᒐᒥᔫᖅ ᑕᑯ’ᓈᑐᐊᕋᒥᐅᒃ ᑕᒃᐱᖕᓇ ᖃᖅᑲᒥ ᐊᖅᑯᒻᖕᒐᔦᖅ, ᐱᓚᐅᓯᔭᑦᑐᐊᖅᖢᓂ, ᑕᒃᐱᑯᖕᒐ ᐅᕐᓂᓗᑲᕐᓗᓕᖅᐹ ᖅᑭᐱᖕᓂᔫᖅ ᐃᒻᒧᓯᖅᓯᒪᓇᓱᒃᖢᓂ.

Before long, her husband stepped outside. He was wrapped only in caribou covers, but he headed straight for the stuffed atigi that was resting on the top of the hill. The husband charged towards it with a knife in hand.

ᑕᒃᐱᖕᓇᔫᖅ ᑲᐱᑦᑐᐊᖅᐹ. ᑲᐱᑦᑐᐊᖅᓯᓐᓇᖅᖢᔪᔫᖅ ᐃᓅᖖᑎᒻᒪᑦ ᖅᑲᐅᔨᒐᒥᐅᒃ, ᑖᕙᒻᓇ ᓄᓕᐊᓂ ᐅᖕᒐᓯᒃᑐ’ᑑᓕᖅ ᑕᑯᒐᒥᐅᒃ ᐅᓪᓚᑦᑐᐊᓕᖅᐹ. ᐅᓪᓚᓕᕋᒥᐅᒃ ᐅᓯᖖᒐᔦᑯᓘᒐᒥ ᒪᓂᖅᑲᒧᑦ ᐊᖅᑯᕕᐊᓪᓚᑦᑐᐊᖅᐸᒃᖢᓂ ᖅᑭᐱᖕᓂᒃ ᐃᒻᒧᓯᖅᐸᒃᖢᓂ, ᐊᖅᐸᓐᓂᐊᑦᑐᐊᓕᖅᐳᖅ.

When he reached the atigi, the man stabbed it furiously. But he soon realized it was not a person. He then saw his wife running in the distance, and he started to chase after her. But because he was naked, he had to stop regularly and rewrap himself in his covers. The husband's need to constantly adjust the caribou covers slowed him down considerably.

ᓄᓕᐊᖕᒐᑕᒨᖅ ᕿᒪᒥᐊ'ᑐᐊᕐᒪᒍ ᐅᓯᖖᒐᔪᑯᓘᖕᒪᑦ, ᕿᒪᒃᓯ'ᑐᐊᕋᒥᒨᖅ ᐊᖅᐸᑦᑐᐊᓕᕆᕗᖅ ᑕᐃᒻᓇ ᐊᐃᑯᓗᒃᓗᓂ.

His wife got far ahead of him, and he was eventually forced to run home because of his nakedness.

ᐊᓂᒥᓄᖖᒨᖅ ᑎᑭᒻᒪᑦ ᐊᕐᓇᖅ, ᐊᓂᐊᑕᒨᖅ ᐊᐱᕆᓖᑦ, "ᓲᖅ ᑎᑭᐸᑦ?"

When the woman reached her brother's camp, the people there asked her, "Why did you come?"

"ᑳᒃᑐ'ᑑᓕᕋᑉᑕ ᐃᓖ ᐅᐃᒪ ᑐᕐᑯᑦᓗᖕᒐ ᓂᕆᓱᐊᒐ'ᑐᐊᕆᓕᕐᒪᖕᒐ ᕿᒪᒃᑐᖕᒐ."

"We were starving and my husband wanted to kill and eat me, so I ran away," she answered.

“ᖃᓄᕐᓕ ᐆᒪᕕᑦ?”

“Then tell us, what did you eat to survive?” they asked.

“ᑯᒪᖕᓂᑦ.”

“Lice,” she answered.

ᑖᒃᑲ ᑯᒪᖕᓂᑦ ᐆᒪᓂᕋᕐᒪᑦ, ᓇᓗᒃᑎᒎᖅ ᑲᐱᕝᓗᒍ ᑐᕐᑯᕐᓗᒍ ᖃᐅᔨᓴᑦᑐᐊᓕᕆᕚᑦ. ᑲᐱᖕᒪᒃᑯᒎᖅ ᑯᒪ'ᑐᐃᑦ ᑎᒡᔪᕐᒥᐊᓯᖕᖑᔪᓕᕐᒪᑕ, ᑕᒪᔾᔪᒎᖅ ᑎᒡᔪᖅᑐ'ᑑᖕᒪᑕ ᑭᒃᑐᕆᐊ'ᑑᓕᖅᐸᑦ.

The peopled doubted her claim, so they stabbed her to find out what she had been eating. When they did, mosquitoes flew out of her body. These mosquitoes are present to this day. Mosquitoes originated from the hoard of lice that took flight from the wife’s body.

ᑖᑉᓱᒎᖅ ᑕᐃᒻᓇᑯᓗᒃ ᑐᕐᑯᑕᐅᒐᓂᑦᑐᐊᖅᑎᑦᓗᒍ ᓂᖕᒐᐅᖕᒐᑦ ᑎᑭᓕᕐᒪᑦ ᐅᖃᐅᑎᑦᑐᐊᓕᖅᐹᑦ, “ᐄᒪᕋᓯᒡᔪᒃ ᐃᓄᖕᓂᒃ ᐃᓄᖕᓂᒃ.”

After she had died, her husband arrived at the camp. The people then said to him, “Iimaarasugjuk, you old scoundrel, you old people swallower! You are an evil Inuk eater.”

“ᑭᓇ ᐱᕙ, ᑭᓇ ᐱᕙ?”

“Says who? Says who?” the husband demanded.

“ᑕᐃᒪ ᓄᓕᐊᑦ ᐊᐅᓪᓚᕐᓂᖅ ᐸᕝᓚᓕᒐᖅ.”

“Your wife, Publaligaq, who escaped from you,” they replied.

“ᐅᓂᑉᑲᖅᑐᖅᑕ, ᐅᓂᑉᑲᖅᑐᖅᔪᒃᑕ!”

“Now, now! Speak up, speak up!” he demanded.

“ᐸᓂᖕᒥ ᐊᒡᒐᐃ ᐊᒡᒋᕋᒥᒋᑦ ᖅᑭᔪᒃᑐᓕᖅᒪᒍ ᑐᐸᕐᓴᖅᓗᙱᑦᑕᖅ.” ᑎᐊ’ᓇᒨᖅ ᐃᑕᐅᑕᖅᓱᒍ.

“When your daughter’s hands were being cooked, and the flame was being fed, you never even woke up, you old scoundrel,” they said to him in disgust.

ᑕᑕᒋᒨᖅ ᐊᓯᐃᑖ ᐃᓯᕕᑎᕐᓱᒋᒃ ᖅᑭᔪ’ᑐᐊᖅᒧᑦ ᖅᑭᓚᒃᓱᖅᓱᒋᒃ ᐱᓇᐃᔭᑦᑐᐊᓂᖅᐹᑦ. ᑖᒻᓇᒨᖅ ᖅᑭᔪ’ᑐᐊᖅ ᐱᓇᐃᖅᓯᒪᕝᕕ’ᑐᐊᓂ ᓇᐱᑯᓂᑦᑐᐊᖃᓗᐊᖅᐹ, ᑲᐱᔭᐅ’ᑐᐊᖃᒥ ᑐᖅᑯ’ᑐᐊᓂᖅᒪᑦ.

Then the people stretched out the husband’s arms and tied him to a long pole. He struggled to get loose and broke the pole in half. But his brothers-in-law wanted revenge, so they stabbed him and killed him.

ᐃᓱᐊ

The end

ᐊᕐᓇᖅ ᐊᒃᖤᒃᑐᖅ

THE WOMAN WHO KILLED AN AKŁAK

ᐊᒻᒪᑉᑕᐅᕘᖅ ᑕᐃᒻᓇ ᓯᑕ ᑳᒃᑑᓐᓃᖅᑕᐅᖅ, ᓄᓇᖅᑲᑎᓛᑦ ᑕᒪᕐᒥᒡᓗ ᑳ’ᑐᐊᖅᖢᑎᒃ ᐅᐃᓂᓗ.

There is another story about a group of people who were dying from starvation.

ᓄᓇᖅᑲᑎᒡᑖᒥᐊ’ᓈᖕᒋᔫᖅ ᐱᕐᓕᕚᖕᒐᑕ ᐅᐃᖕᒐᑕ ᓂᕆᑦᑕᒐ’ᑐᐊᕆᓕᕐᒪᒋᑦ.

There was a couple who was starving, just like their neighbours, but the husband decided to live off those people who had already died.

ᓄᓕᐊᓂᔫᖅ ᐅᕐᑲᐅᑎᓱᖕᒐᔭᓕᕐᒪᔪ ᕿᔫᒃᑕᓇᐊᓚᐅᕐᑯᖕᓗᔪ. ᕿᔫᒃᑕᓇᐊᓕᕐᒥᔫᖅ ᐅᕐᑲᑦᑐᐊᖅᐳᖅ, ᖃᓄᖅᑐᕘᖅ ᐊᐃᑦᑐᖅᑕᐅᓚᐅᕐᓕ ᓂᕐᔪᒥᒃ ᑲᑉᐱᐊᓱᒃᑐ’ᑑᒐᒥ ᓂᕿᒋᔭᐅᓯᐊᖕᒋᓐᓇᒥ ᐃᓅᓗᓂ. ᑖᒻᓇᔫᖅ ᐊᒃᖤ’ᑐᐊᖅ ᖃᐃᔪ’ᑐᐊᖅ.

One day, the husband told his wife, Inutquaq, to go gather a bit of moss for a fire. As she was on her way to gather the moss, the wife said aloud, “I’m begging, someone bring an animal to me, because I am terrified my husband will eat me.”

ᖃᐃᔦ’ᑐᐊᕉᖅ ᑕᑯᒪᒥᐅᒃ ᑎᓘᑎᒥᓇᖕᒎᖅ ᐳᐊᓗᓂ ᐃᓕᕆᐊᑦᓚᒃᓅᒍ ᑕᖅᑲᕗᖓ
ᐊᐃᑦᑕᑦᑐᐊᕐᒪᑦ ᒪᙳᓗᑲᕐᓗᕆᐊᑦᑐᐊᖅᐹ ᑕᑕᓗᒃᑖ’ᑐᐊᓂ. ᑖᕙᓂᒎᖅ
ᐃᐱᕐᓯᐊᕆᓚᕐᒪᒍ, ᐃᐱᖕᒪᑦ ᑐᕐᑯᔅᓅᓂᐅᒃ.

Suddenly, an *akłak* (grizzly bear) appeared. It came straight towards her. When she saw the bear, the wife took off one of her mitts and placed it at the tip of her *tiluut* (a stick or bone used to knock snow off). As the bear drew close, it opened its mouth to bite her, but the wife quickly drove the tiluut deep into the bear's mouth. She drove it in so hard that her hands reached into the animal's mouth too. She held the tiluut there until the bear died of suffocation.

ᐊᐃᒪᒥᒨᖅ ᐅᖅᑲᐅᑎᑦᑐᐊᓕᖅᐹ ᐅᐃᓂ, “ᐃᓐᓇᖕᒐᐅᖅ, ᐃᓐᓇᖕᒐᐅᖅ ᓂᕐᑭᒃᓴᓂᕐᕋᖅᐸᒋᑦ ᐱᔾᔪᑎᑦ ᐋᒐᔨᐊᓕᓇᑦ.”

The wife then returned to the iglu and said to her husband, “Hey, lazy one! Lazy one! I have killed an animal for you to eat. Dress up and go butcher it.”

ᐅᓯᖖᒐᔭᑯᔫᖕᒪᖖᒨᖅ ᓱᓕ ᐅᖅᑲᐅᑎᓕᓇᕖ, “ᐃᓐᓇᖕᒐᐅᖅ, ᐃᓐᓇᖕᒐᐅᖅ ᐊᓯᒨᖅ ᓂᕐᑭᒃᓴᓂᕐᕋᖅᐸᒋᑦ ᐱᔾᔪᑎᑦ ᐋᒐᔨᐊᓕᓇᑦ.”

But her lazy husband stayed in bed. So she said again, “Hey, lazy one! Lazy one! I have killed an animal for you to eat. Get dressed and go butcher it.”

ᑎᐊ’ᓇᐃᓕᕙᓕᖅᒪᒧᒨᖅ ᐊᓯ’ᑐᐊᖀᕿᓇ, “ᐃᓄᖅᑯᐊᖅ ᓴᓪᓗᓐᓂᖅᐸᑦ ᑲᐱᓗᒍ ᓂᓇᓂᐊᖅᐸᕋ.”

The wife kept insisting until, finally, her lazy husband remarked, “If Inutquaq lies, I’ll stab her and eat her.”

ᑎᐊ’ᓇᐃᓕᑦᑕᓕᖅᒪᒧᒨᖅ ᓄᓕᐊᖓᑕ, “ᐃᓐᓇᖕᒐᐅᖅ, ᐃᓐᓇᖕᒐᐅᖅ ᐊᓯᒨᖅ ᓂᕐᑭᒃᓴᓂᕐᕋᖅᐸᒋᑦ ᐱᔾᔪᑎᑦ ᐋᒐᔨᐊᓕᓇᑦ.”

But the wife again repeated, “Hey lazy one! Lazy one! I have killed an animal for you to eat. Get dressed and go butcher it.”

ᑎᐊ’ᓇᐃᓕᑦᑕᓕᖅᒪᒧᒨᖅ ᐊᑕᐅᖅᑲ ᖅᑭᔦᒃᑕᓇᐊᕐᕕᐊᓄᓕᐊᓕᖅᒪᑦ, ᓱᓇᐅᕝᕙᒨᕿᓇ ᐊᒃᕋ’ᑐᐊᕐᒥᒃ ᑐᖅᑯᑦᓯᓐᓂᕐᒥ ᑎᑑᑎᒥᓄᑦ ᑕᖅᑲᕗᖕᒐ ᑲᐅᑦᑐᐊᖅᓱᒍ ᐃᐱᑎᓐᓂᖅᒪᒍ. ᐃᐱᑎᓐᒪᒍ ᓂᕐᑭᒃᓴᓂ’ᑐᐊᕐᒥᐅᒃ ᐅᐃᓂ ᐊᓐᓇᓕᖅᓱᑎᒃ.

After much insistence, the husband finally walked to the spot where the wife had been gathering firewood and, sure enough, he saw that she had killed the bear by stabbing it deeply in its mouth with her tiluut and suffocating it. The wife had acquired food for her husband, and they regained their strength.

ᐃᓱᐊ

The end

ᑲᐅᒡᔭᒡᔪᒃ

KAUGJAGJUK

ᐃᓄᐃᑦ ᐅᓂᑉᑳᖅᑐᐊᖏᑦ ᐃᓗᓕᕐᑲᕐᒪᑕ ᐃᑦᑐᐊᖅᓴᐅᑎᒃᓴᓂᒃ ᑖᒻᓇ ᑲᐅᒡᔭᒡᔭᖕᒥᒃ ᐅᓂᑉᑳᖅᑐᐊᕈᓯᖅ ᐃᓱᒪᒋᓱᖅᐸᕋ ᐃᓕᐊᕐᔭᖕᓂᒃ ᐱᕐᓱᐊᖅᐸᒋᐊᕐᑲᕐᓂᕐᒥᒃ. ᑐᓵᕙᓚᐅᒐᕋ ᐊᓈᓇᓚᐅᕐᒪ ᕼᐊᓚᓐ ᐸᐅᕐᖓᐅᑉ ᐅᓂᑉᑳᖅᑐᐊᓕᒑᖓᒍ ᐃᒪᓐᓇ:

Inuit traditional stories often reflect principles meant to guide our behaviour. This story is one I heard told many times by my mother, Helen Paurngat. I believe it tells us that we should treat orphans with kindness. The story was told like this:

ᑕᐃᒻᓇᑉᑕᐅᕉᖅ ᐃᓕᐊᕐᔪ’ᓈᖅ ᐅᓂᕐᑳᖅᑐᐊᖅ ᑐᓵᕙᓚᐅᕐᒥᔭᕋ ᑲᐅᒡᔭᒡᔫᖅ. ᐃᑖᔭᓇᔭᐅᓗᐊᒧᑦ ᐃᒻᒪᕐᑳ ᑲᐅᒡᔭᒡᔭᖕᒥᒃ ᐊᑎᖅᑲᓯᕐᔩᒥᔭᕕᓂᖅ. ᐅᖅᓱᓂᒎᖅ ᐊᐃᕖᑦ ᐅᖅᓱᐃᓂᒃ, ᖁᓪᓕᐅᑉ ᐅᖅᓱᒃᓴᐃᓂᒃ ᑲᐅᒐᖅᓯᑎᑕᐅᕙᓚᐅᕐᓂᕐᒪᑦ. ᓇᖅᕿᒥᔭᐅᓗᐊᒧᑦ ᐊᑎᑦᓗᐊᕕᒥᙱᑕᖃᓗᐊᒥᓂᒃ ᐊᒡᒑᑦ ᐊᑎᖅᑲᓯᕐᔩᒥᔭᕕᓂᖅ ᑲᐅᒡᔭᒡᔭᐊᓗᖕᒥᒃ. ᐱᔾᔪᑳᓇᔭᐅᕝᓗᓂ ᑲᐅᒐᖅᓯᑎᑕᐅᖅᑲᑦᑖᖅᐸᓚᐅᕐᓂᕐᒪᑦ ᐅᖅᓱᓂᒃ.

There was a poor little orphan named Kaugjagjuk who was treated very badly by others. The little orphan was named Kaugjagjuk because people in winter would sometimes make him pound walrus fat to use in a qulliq. *Kaugjagjuk* means a person who pounds blubber.

ᑲᐅᒻᔭᒡᔪᒎᓇᒻᓇ ᐃᓅᓯᒃᑐᐊᕐᔪ'ᓈᖅ ᐊᖓᔪᖅᑳᖏᓱᑎᒐᒥ ᐃᓄᖕᓂᑦ, ᐃᒪᖄ ᐃᓚᒥᓂᑦ ᐱᓯᒪᔭᐅᓚᓚᐅᕐᓂᕐᒪᑦ ᐃᓛᔭᕆᔭᐅᓗᐊᒍᑦ ᐊᒡᓛᑦ ᑕᐅᒐᓂ ᕿᒻᒥᑦ ᓯᑎᒑᓐᓂ ᓯᓂᒃᑕᖅᑎᑕᐅᑦᑕᔪᔪᖅ. ᕿᒻᒥᓂ ᓯᑎᒐᕐᒥᖕᓂ ᐊᕐᑯᐱᔪᓂ ᐃᖅᑲᑕᐅᒥᐊᖅᖢᓂ ᕿᒻᒥᑦ ᐅᕐᑯᓱᑎᕆᓂᓗᒻᒦᖅᖢᓂᕆᑦ.

Kaugjagjuk went to stay with other people (perhaps his relatives) after his parents passed away. Those people abused him terribly—he was even forced to sleep with dogs in their den. He would lie down between the dogs to keep himself warm.

ᖃᖓᓴᖅ ᐃᓄᐃᑦ ᐅᒃᑯᓯᒃᓴᓂᒃ ᖁᑦᑕᒃᓂᒃ ᑕᐃᔭᐅᔪᓂᒃ ᐃᒡᓗᒥᖕᓂ ᖃᐅᒻᒪᖅᑯᑎᖅᑲᖅᐸᓚᐅᕐᒪᑕ ᐅᕐᑯᖅᓴᐅᑎᕆᒻᒫᖅᖢᒍ ᖁᓚᑉᓯᖅᖢᑎᒃ ᐃᒐᔾᔪᑎᖅᑲᖅᐸᓚᐅᖅᑎᑦᑐᕆᑦ, ᑲᐅᒡᔭᒡᔪᒎᖅ ᑎᒍᐊᖅᓯᒥᓂᑦ ᑲᐅᒐᖅᓯᖅᑯᔭᐅᓚᒌᖓᒐᒥ ᐅᖅᓱᓂᒃ ᕿᕿᔪᓂᒃ ᐃᒪᓐᓇᐃᓚᐅᒐᐅᕙᓚᐅᖅᑐᖅ: “ᑲᐅᒡᔭᒡᔪᐊᓗᒃ ᓇᐅᕆᒻᓇ, ᑲᐅᒐᖅᓯᔪᒃᓴᖅ, ᑲᐅᒐᖅᓯᔪᒃᓴᑐᐃᓈᓗᒃ?”

Anytime anyone wanted Kaugjagjuk to pound blubber, they would call him inside like this: “Where is Kaugjagjuk, the one who pounds walrus blubber? Where is that boy who is only good enough to pound walrus blubber?”

ᑲᐅᒡᔭᒡᔪᒃ ᐃᓖᔭᕐᓯᐊᖑᐱᒃᓯᓐᓇᖅ ᓂᕕᐊᕐᓯᐊᖕᓂᙵᕐᒃ ᒪᑦᑐᖕᓂᑦ ᑲᑕᖕᒥ ᐅᑕᖅᑭᔭᐅᕙᒃᑐᓂ ᐊᐃᕖᑦ ᑑᒎᖕᒋᓂᒃ ᑎᒍᒥᐊᖅᑐᖕᓂᑦ. ᑲᑕᖕᒥᔫᖅ ᐅᔭᖕᒋᑦᓴᕿᖕᒐᑦ ᖁᖕᒐᒃᑭᑕ ᐹᖕᒋᒃᑯᑦ ᑲᐅᕝᑐᒍ ᑲᐅᒐᖅᓯᕝᕕᒃᓴᖕᒐᓄᑦ ᐃᑎᖅᑎᑦᐸᒑᒃ ᐱᔮᓇᑐᐊᒧᑦ. ᑎᐊᑉᓇᔫᖅ ᐱᔭᐅᑦᑕᓕᓂᕐᒥᒃ ᖁᖕᒐᒋᒃ ᐊᒡᓛᑦ ᑕᓯᓐᓇᒥᒃ ᐹᖅᑯᖅᑐᓯᕝᑐᑎᒃ. ᑖᑉᑯᐊᔫᖅ ᓂᕕᐊᕐᓯᐊᒃ ᑲᑕᐅᑉ ᐊᕙᑖᓂ ᐃᒡᓘᕆᓕᑉᓈᖅᑐᑎᒃ ᐊᒡᓛᑦ ᐅᑕᖅᑭᐊᑕᔪᖕᒪᓂᒃ ᑑᒎᑉᔪᐊᖕᓂᒃ ᑎᒍᒥᐊᖅᑐᑎᒃ. ᑕᐃᒪᓐᓇᔫᖅ ᓱᕐᑐᒋᒃᑎᒍᑦ ᑲᐅᕝᑐᒍ ᑲᐅᒐᖅᓯᕕᒃᓴᖕᒐᓅᖅᑎᑦᐸᖕᒪᑦᑯ.

It was bad enough that Kaugjagjuk was treated so terribly, but there were also two girls who liked to add to his misery. The pair would wait to torment Kaugjagjuk by sitting on either side of the passageway into the iglu, holding walrus tusks in their hands. Anytime Kaugjagjuk came inside, they would poke the tusks inside his nostrils, lift him off the ground, and carry him to the spot where he pounded blubber. This was their way of abusing him even more, and the repeated abuse caused his nostrils to stretch until they were exceptionally wide.

ᑲᐅᒡᔭᒡᔫᖅ ᐃᓖᔭᖅᓯᐊᖑᓗᐊᒧᑦ ᓂᕆᑦᓯᐊᔪᐃᑦᑑᒐᒥ ᑳᓕᓂᕐᒧᑦ ᐃᒃᑮᓕᓂᕐᒧᑦᓗ ᐱᕈᖅᐸᑦᓕᐊᔪᖕᓇᐃᓚᐅᖅᑐᖅᓘᓐᓃᑦ. ᐊᐃᕚᓐᖑᖅ ᑲᐅ’ᑐᐊᖕᒋᓐᓂᒃ ᐊᐃᑦᑐᒐᐅᑦᑕᔪᖕᒪᑦ ᒥᒃᑭᐅᔭᖅᑲᑦᑖᖅᓱᒍ ᓂᕆᓯᖅᑐᖅ ᐊᕐᒍᖅᓯᒪᙱᑦᑐᒥᐊᒥᒃ ᐃᓗᐃᑦᑲᒥᐊᒥᒃ ᑲᐅᖕᒥᒃ ᐊᐃᑦᑐᒐᐅᕝᑲᒥ.

All this excessive abuse, the continual hunger, and the constant cold eventually stunted Kaugjagjuk's growth. The only food he was normally given was a piece of *kauk* (walrus skin). But when he was given a piece, it was never cut up—it was always a whole slab. He would have to munch on the tough skin for a long time, because it was difficult to chew.

ᓇᔮ ᐃᒻᓇ ᑲᐅᒡᔭᒡᔫᑉ ᐱᔭᐅᓯᒪᖅᑲᑕᐅᓐᓂᖁᒥ ᓴᕕᖁᔭ’ᓈᒥᒎᖅ ᑲᐅᒡᔭᒡᔫᑉ ᓂᕆᔾᔪᑎᒃᓵᓂᒃ ᓇᕝᕚᕈᑎᖕᒪᒍ ᐱᓚᐅᑎᒋᕝᓗᒍ ᓂᕆᔭᒥᓂᒃ ᓄᖒᑦᓯᑦᑕᓕᖅᓗᓂ ᐊᕐᒍᐃᔾᔪᑎᒋᑦᑕᓕᖅᒥᐅᒃ ᓂᕆᔭᒥᓂᒃ, ᐊᑐᐊᓂᒑᖓᒥᐅᒃ ᐃᔨᖅᐸᒃᓱᒍ ᓴᕕᖁᔭ’ᓈᖅ ᐱᓚᐅᑎᓂ. ᓄᖒᑦᓯᑦᑕᖅᒪᓐᖒᖅ ᕿᐸᒋᔭᐅᓕᖅᒥᒐᒥ ᑕᐃᒻᓇᒎᖅ ᑲᐅᒡᔭᒡᔫᑉ ᐱᓚᐅᑎᒋᑦᑕᓘ ᕿᓂᖅᓱᒍ ᓇᓂᒐᒥᔾᔪᒃ ᐊᖅᓵᒥᐊᕆᕝᓗᒍ. ᓂᕆᔾᔪᑎᒃᓴᐃᕈᑎᒐᒥ ᐊᐃᕙᐅᑉ ᑲᐅ’ᑐᐊᖕᒋᓂᒃ ᒥᒃᑭᒃᓗᓂ ᓂᕆᕙᓚᕆᕝᓗᓂ.

Kaugjagjuk had a sister who had been fostered by another family. One day, his sister found a piece of metal and brought it to Kaugjagjuk so he could use it to cut up his food. The piece of metal helped Kaugjagjuk finish his food more quickly, so he didn't waste time and energy chewing. When he was done eating, he would then hide the metal so no one would find it. But others soon noticed he was finishing his food faster than before.

They became very resentful towards him and searched him. When they discovered the piece of metal, they took it away. Once again, Kaugjagjuk had no tool to eat with, and so he went back to slowly chewing his food.

ᑲᐅᒡᔭᒡᔪᒋᒻᓇ ᐊᖓᔪᕐᑲᓚᐅᕐᓂᕐᒪᑦ ᐊᖓᒃᑯ’ᑐᐊᕐᒥᒎᖅ ᓄᓇᒥ ᐊᓯᐊᓂᑉᑕᐅᖅ ᐃᓐᓂᖅᓱᓂ, ᑎᐊ’ᓇᐃᑉᑯᐊ ᐃᓛᓐᓂ ᓄᓇᖅᑲᐅᒥᐊᖅᓱᑎᒃ ᖃᖓᓴᖅ ᐃᓅᕙᓚᐅᕐᒪᑕ ᓂᕐᑭᒃᓴᖅᑦᓯᐊᕐᓂᕐᒥ. ᐅᑭᐅᖑᑎᓪᓗᒍᒎᖅ ᐅᓐᓄᒃᑎᓪᓗᒍ ᕿᒻᒥᑦ ᓂᕝᔭᓪᓚᖑᑎᖕᒪᑕ, ᑭᕕᐅᖅ ᐊᑕᐅᕐᑳ ᕿᒻᒥᑦ ᓯᑎᒐᖕᒐᓐᓂ ᓯᑎᒐᖅᑲᑕᐅᒥᐊᖅᓱᓂ ᓯᓂᒃᐸᒃᑲᒥ, ᕿᓗᒻᖕᒫᓕᕌᖕᒐᑕ ᕿᒻᒥᑦ ᑎᓕᕙᒐᐃ, “ᑭᐱᖕᒫᒃ ᐊᓂᓚᐅᕐᒦᑦ. ᐊᑭᑎᕐᒫᒃ ᐊᓂᓚᐅᕐᒦᑦ, ᐊ’ᕙᕐᒫᒃ ᐊᓂᓚᐅᕐᒦᑦ.”

But Kaugjagjuk also had an older brother, a powerful shaman who lived in another area. (In the old days, it was normal practice to split people up into smaller groups. This helped everyone have better access to scarce food supplies.) One winter night, the dogs at Kaugjagjuk's camp started to bark. The young orphan was sleeping as he normally did with the dogs, and so he sent the ones beside him out to see why the others were barking. "My covers, go outside and check! Go outside, my pillows! Go outside, my bed mats, go outside!" he said.

ᓯᓇᐅᕝᕙ ᑭᕕᐅᑉ ᐊᖓᔪᒋᓐᓂᖅᓱᓂᐅᒃ, ᑎᑭᑦᑐᖅ. ᐊᖓᔪᐊᒎᑦ ᑎᑭᒃᑲᓗᐊᕐᒥ ᐃᓄᖕᓂ ᑐᔪᕐᒥᐊᖑᖖᒋᔅᓱᓂ ᐃᓪᓗᓕᐅᕆᐊᖅᓯᓐᓇᖅᓱᓂ, ᓯᓇᐅᕝᕙ ᑖᒻᓇ ᓄᒃᑲᓂ ᐱᕈᖅᓴᓂᐊᓕᕐᓂᕋᕐᒥᐅᒃ ᐃᓪᓗᓕᐊᒥᓂᓯᐅᖅᑲᑎᒋᓗᒍ.

Kaugjagjuk's older brother had arrived. His brother would not stay in other peoples' igluit. Instead, he started building his own. His plan was to take Kaugjagjuk to his own iglu and make his little brother stronger.

ᐊᒻᒪᒎᖅ ᑕᖅᑳᓂ ᓯᓚᒥ ᖃᑦᖃᒧᓕᐅᑎᕝᓗᒍ ᐱᒡᒍᒃᑎᓴᑦᑐᐊᖅᐸᓕᓇᕝᕓ ᐅᔭᕋᖕᓂᒃ ᒪᒃᐱᖅᓯᑎᑦᑕᖅᓱᒍ ᐲᓚᖅᑐᖅᑕᖅᓱᒍ ᐱᑦᓯᓃᓴᓕᕌᖓᑦ, ᒪᒃᐱᖅᓯᔭᕌᖓᑦ ᑭᓯᐊᓂ ᐊᓇᐅᑦᐸᒃᓱᒍ. ᐲᓚᖅᑐᖅᑕᓕᓵᕐᒪᒍᒎᖅ ᐊᓅᓅᑕ ᐱᓐᓂᑯᕕᓃ ᐱᒃᓯᓖᑦᓯᐊᒥᐊᖅᑕᖅᐳᑦ ᐊᒡᓕᔾᔫᔭᑎ’ᔭᐊᖕᒋᑦ ᐱᑦᓯᐊᖕᒋᓐᓂᑯᕕᓂ’ᔭᐃᑦ.

Soon, the older brother took Kaugjagjuk up the hill to build his strength. He made the young boy lift stones that had frozen to the ground, and he would whip Kaugjagjuk until he was able to lift a stone. When he first started whipping him, evil things Kaugjagjuk's mother had done started flying out of him. These evil things had stunted Kaugjagjuk's growth.

ᑕᐃᒪᒎᖅ ᓴᙱᒃᑎᓴᓕᕐᒥᒐᒥᐅᒃ ᐅᔭᕋᖕᓂᒎᖅ ᐊᖏᓕᕆᓪᓕᐊᕝᓗᒋᑦ ᒪᒃᐱᖅᓯᑎᑦᑕᕐᒪᒍ, ᐱᒋᐊᓵᕐᒪᙴᖅ ᒥᑭᔪᓂᒃ ᐱᑎᑦᑕᓚᐅᖅᓯᓐᓇᖅᓱᒍ, ᐊᓪᓕᕆᓪᓕᐊᕋᐅᔭᖅᓱᒋᑦ ᒪᒃᐱᖅᓯᑎᑦᑕᒑ ᐱᔨᐃᒻᒥᓕᕌᖕᒐᑦ ᐃᐱᕋᖅᑐᑦᓗᒃᑐ’ᓈᓕᖅᐸᒃᓱᒍ. ᑭᖑᓪᓕᖅᐹᒥᒎᖅ ᐅᔭᖅᑲᓂᒃ ᒪᖑᒃᓯᒪᔪᓂᒃ ᕐᑭᕐᑭᓪᕈᑎᓯᒪᔪᓂᒃ ᐊᓪᓛᑦ ᒪᒃᐱᖅᓯᔨᖅᓯᖕᒪᑦ ᑭᓯᐊᓂ ᐊᓄᐅᑦᐹ.

At first Kaugjagjuk's brother made him lift small stones, but gradually he began to lift larger ones. Kaugjagjuk was soon lifting very large stones that were sunk deep in the frozen ground.

ᑲᐅᒡᔭᒡᔫᒻᖕᒎᖅ ᐊᖓᔪᐊᑕ ᓄᒃᑲᓂ ᐱᔫᑦᑐᐊᕐᓯᕆᓕᕐᒥᐅᒃ ᐃᖕᒥᓂᒃ ᐊᑭᔫᑦᑐᐊᕐᓯᕆᓕᕐᒥᐅᒃ ᕿᒪᒍᒫᓕᕐᒥᒐᒥᐅᒃ ᐅᑲᐅᑎᔮ. "ᓇᓄᕐᓗ'ᔪᐊᕐᒥᒐᐃ ᑭᑎᑉᑎᖕᓂᑦ ᓯᒻᒥᐅᑎᓗᓂ ᑎᑭᑦᑐᖅᑲᕈᒫᖅᒪᑦ ᕿᒻᒥᑦ ᕿᓗᑦᑐᐊᕆᕐᓗᐊᖅᐸᑕ ᐊᓂᑦᑕᐃᓕᔫᒫᖅᐳᑎᑦ."

Finally, the older brother was satisfied that Kaugjagjuk's strength was sufficient, and that his younger brother would be able to defend himself. He then told Kaugjagjuk, "A big polar bear called a *nanurluk* will soon come. He will be so big he will block the eastern view. When this happens, even if the dogs are barking wildly, stay inside the den and don't go out."

ᖃᖓᓯᓐᓂᑉᑯᐊ ᑎᑭᑦᑐᖅᑲᕐᓗᒃᑳᖓᑦ ᖁᕙᐊᓯᒃᑯᑎᒃ ᕿᓚᐅᑎᖕᓂᑦ ᒧᒥᑦᑐᐊᔪᓚᐅᕐᒪᑕ. ᑲᐅᒡᔭᒡᔫᒻᖕᒎᖅ ᐊᖓᔪᐊᑕ ᑎᑭᐅᑖᑕ ᐅᓐᓂᖓᓂ ᒧᒥᓯᕆᐊᖅᑯᑎᒃ ᖃᒡᕆᖕᒪᑕ, ᐊᑕᐅᖄ ᑲᐅᒡᔭᒡᔫᑉ ᐊᖓᔪᐊ ᖃᒡᕆᖅᑲᑕᐅᕗᑐᓂ. ᑲᐅᒡᔭᒡᔪᓪᓕ ᖃᒡᕆᖅᑲᑕᐅᙱᑦᑐᖅᔫᓐᓃᑦ ᑖᑉᑯᐊᒡᓗ ᓂᕕᐊᖅᓯᐊ'ᑐᐊᒃ.

It happened that those at the camp had arranged to have a drum dance that night to mark the arrival of Kaugjagjuk's brother. You see, a long time ago, it was tradition for Inuit to hold a drum dance whenever visitors arrived from another camp. So when night came, the guests and Kaugjagjuk's older brother gathered together. Only Kaugjagjuk and the two girls who tormented him did not go to the celebration.

ᖃᒃᑎᒦᓕᖅᑎᑦᑐᑎᙵᒎᖅ ᐊᓱᐃᓛ ᑲᐅᒡᔭᒡᔭᒃ ᑭᓐᖑᒪᔭᐅᑦᑐᐊᓕᕆᒐᖅ ᑖᑉᑯᓇᙵᒐᑦ ᒧᒥᓯᑎᐊ'ᑐᐊᕐᓂᑦ, "ᑲᐅᒡᔭᒡᔮᐊᓗᒃ ᓇᐅᑎᒻᓇ, ᑲᐅᒪᖅᓯᔮᒃᓴᖅ. ᑲᐅᒪᖅᓯᔮᒃᓴᑐᐃᓐᓈᓗᒃ."

When the guests had all gathered at the drum dance, they began calling for Kaugjagjuk, "Where is Kaugjagjuk, the one who pounds walrus blubber? Where is that boy who is only good enough to pound walrus blubber?"

ᑲᐅᒡᔭᒡᔫᒻᖑᒎᖅ ᐊᖕᒪᔭᐊᖅ ᖃᒃᑎᔭᓂᓯᐅᖃᑕᐅ'ᔭᐊᕐᒥ ᐊᑕᐅᖅᑲ ᐅᖅᑲᖅᑐᓂ, "ᐅᕙᖕᒪᖕᒫᕐᐃ ᑲᐅᒪᖅᓯᔮᒃᓴᐅᓂᖅᓴᐅᖕᒫᖅᐸᖕᒪ ᑲᐅᒪᖅᓯᖕᒫᓚᐅᕐᓚᖕᒪ."

Kaugjagjuk's older brother, who of course was at the drum dance, said, "Allow me, as I am better able to pound seal blubber."

ᐊᓱᐃᓛ ᑕᐅᓄᖕᒪ ᐊᐃᕖ'ᑐᐃ ᐅᖅᓱᑦᑐᐊᖕᓂᐅᓄᑦ ᓵᒻᒪᖕᒪᖅᑐᓂ ᑲᐅᒪᖅᓯᓂᖅᓴᐅᑎᐊᓕᖅᐸᖅ, ᑲᐅᒪᖅᓯᐊᓂᒃᑲᒥᑐ ᑲᐅᒫᓂᓵᖅᑕᒥᓄᑦ ᐅᖅᓱ'ᑐᐊᕐᓄᑦ ᑕᒪᒃᑯᐊ ᖃᒃᑎᒥᓯᐅᖅᑐᑦ ᐃᐱᕐᖅᑐᓕᖅᑐᓂᑎᑦ ᐅᖅᓱᐃᓐᓇᓱᖅᑐᑎᑦ ᑮᓇᕐᑐᒥᐊᖕᑎᑎᒍᑦ ᓇᐅᒃᑯᒥᐊᖅ ᐃᐱᕐᖅᐸᒃᑐᓂᑎᑦ ᐱᐅᕐᑭᑎᑦᓯᐊᒥᐊᖅᑐᓂᑎᑦ.

So Kaugjagjuk's older brother walked towards the seal blubber pounding place and started pounding. When he was done, he grabbed the pounded blubber oil and started whipping people with it. He splashed it all over their faces and parts of their clothing, making a mess of them.

ᑕᐃᒪᓘᓇᓛ ᖃᒡᒋᑉᖃᑎᑦᑐᕆᑦ ᑲᐅᒡᔭᒡᔫᑉ ᐊᖓᔪᐊ ᑐᓴᐅᒪᔭᐅᒐᒥ ᐊᖓᒃᑯᔅᔫᖕᒪᑦ ᓴᙳᓐᓂᐊᒪᐅᑦᑐᐊᓕᓇᕗᖅ ᐊᖓᒃᑯᐊᖅᑭᖅᑯᔭᐅᕝᓗᓂ. "ᐊᑏᓘᖅ ᐊᖓᒃᑯ'ᔫᒪᕕᓐᖑᖅ ᑐᓴᐅᒪᒐᑉᑕ ᐊᖓᑦᑯᐊᖅᑭᓚᐅᓇᑦ ᐅᑉᐱᓕᖅᓂᐊᖃᑉᑕ."

Everyone at the drum dance had heard Kaugjagjuk's older brother was a strong shaman, and they pressed him to perform a shamanistic ritual. "We have heard you are a powerful shaman. Perform your shamanistic ritual for us so we will believe that you truly are a powerful shaman," they said.

ᑲᒪᓱᖕᓇᓵᓚᐅᖃᑐᐊᖅᓗᓂᒎᖅ ᑲᐅᒡᔭᒡᔫᑉ ᐊᖓᔪᐊ ᓴᙳᓐᓂᐊᒪᐅᒐᒥ ᐃᑦᓱᖅᑕᓕᖅᓗᓂ, ᐃᑎᖃᒥᓗᒎᖅ ᐅᖅᑲᖅᓗᓂ, "ᑕᑦᑭᒪ ᓯᓚᒥ ᐊᐃᕕ'ᑐᐊᖅ."

Kaugjagjuk's older brother resisted at first. But eventually, since people begged him so much, he stepped out of the iglu. When he came back in, he said, "There is a walrus sitting outside."

ᑖᑉᑯᐊᓗᒎᖅ ᖃᒡᒋᑉᖃᔪ'ᑐᐃᑦ ᐅᒃᐱᕈᓱᙱᓐᓂᑯᒧ ᒥᑕᐅᑎᒃᓴᒻᒫᖅᓗᑎᒃ ᐅᖅᑲᖅᓗᑎᒃ, "ᐊᑏ ᐃᒻᓇ ᐃᑎᑦᑐᐊᖅᓕ ᑕᑯᑦᑐᐊᖅᓂᐊᖃᑉᑎᒍᑦ, ᐊᐃᕕ'ᑐᐊᖅ."

People who were at the drum dance did not believe him and sarcastically replied, "Well then, bring it in so we can all see this big walrus."

ᑲᐅᒡᔭᒡᔪᒻᖕᒎᖅ ᐊᖓᔪᐊ ᐅᖅᑲᖅᑐᐊᖅᐳᖅ, "ᖃᓄᓇᓛᒃ ᐃᒥᖅ ᓯᕗᑦᓕᐅᓗᓂ ᐃᑎᖅᓂᐊᖅᒪᑦ ᐃᐱᓗᓯ ᑐᖅᑯᓯᓐᓇᓇᐊᖅᑲᖃᑉᓯ."

Kaugjagjuk's brother answered, "Well, you know, the water will come in before the walrus. If I do this, you could easily all drown and die."

ᑖᑉᑯᐊᒎᖅ ᐅᒃᐱᕈᓱᙱᒧᑦ ᓴᙳᓐᓂᐊᑐᐃᓐᓇᖅᓗᑎᒃ ᐅᖅᑲᖅᓗᑎᒃ ᐊᓪᓛᖅ, "ᐊᑏ ᐃᑎᑦᑐᐊᖅᓕ ᑕᑯᑦᑐᐊᖅᓂᐊᖃᑉᑎᒍᑦ ᐃᒫᑦᑐᐊᖅᓂᐊᖃᑉᑕ."

The people refused to believe him, and they begged, "Well then, bring it in so we can see it and all drown in the water."

ᑲᐅᒡᔭᒡᔫᒪᖕᔫᖅ ᐊᖕᒐᔪᐊᑕ ᐊᐃᕙ'ᑐᐊᖅ ᐃᑎᖅᑯᒥᐊ'ᑐᐊᓕᖅᒪᒍ
ᐊᐃᕙᖅᐸᓗᓯᑦᑐᐊᖅᐴᖅ ᐃᒪ'ᑐᐊᕐᓗᔫᖅ ᖃᒡᒋᐸ ᐃᓗᐊᓄᑦ ᑰᓯᑦᑐᐊᓪᓚᕆ.
ᐃᒡᓗᔫᖅ ᐃᒥᕐᒥᒃ ᑕᑕᕐᓱᓂ ᐊᐃᕙᕐᔫᓐᓃᑦ ᐃᑎᖅᑳᖅᑎᓐᓇᒍ ᓯᓕ, ᑕᐃᑉᑯᐊᓗ
ᖃᒡᒋᒦᑦᑐᑦ ᑕᑯᓯᐊᓚᐅᖅᑐᑦ ᐊᓂᓯᐃᕐᒥᒃ ᐃᕝᔪᕐᖅᓱᑎᒃ ᓄᖕᒍᑉᐳᑦ.

Kaugjagjuk's brother then allowed the walrus into the iglu. The sound of the walrus and the water poured into the iglu. The iglu was filled totally with water, and even before the walrus was inside, the people at the drum dance were trapped in water. They couldn't get out, and all of them drowned.

ᑕᐃᒪᔫᖅ ᖃᒡᒋᖅ ᐃᒥᕐᒥᒃ ᑕᑕᓐᓇᒥ ᕿᕿᓕᕐᒥ ᖁᒡᓗᐊᓗᖕᓂᖅᑲᓕᖅᓱᓂ
ᐊᒡᓛᑦ. ᑕᐃᑉᑯᐊ ᑲᐅᒡᔭᒡᔪᒡᓗ ᓂᕙᐊᖅᓯᐊᒡᓗ ᖃᒡᒋᒥᓯᐅᖅᑲᑕᐅᙱᓐᓇᒥᒃ
ᐆᒪᔪᑑᓕᖅᓱᑎᒃ.

The qaggiq was totally flooded with water. When it froze, it even started to crack. Kaugjagjuk and the girls had not been inside the drum dance iglu, so they were the only survivors.

ᐅᕝᓗᙳᖅ ᑕᓪᓕᒪᑦ ᐊᓂᒍᖅᑐᑦ ᑲᐅᒡᔭᒡᔫᒃ ᐊᖕᒐᔪᐊᑕ ᐃᕝᔪᕐᓚᐅᖅᑐᑦ
ᐆᒻᒪᖅᑎᒃᑲᓐᓂᖅᓱᓂᒋᑦ. ᐆᒻᒪᕐᒪᑕᔫᖅ ᑲᐅᒡᔭᒡᔫᒃ ᐊᖕᒐᔪᐊᑕ ᐅᖅᑲᐅᑎᕝᐃ
ᐅᕝᓗᓂᒃ ᑕᓪᓕᒪᓂᒃ ᐃᒦᖅᓯᒪᕝᓗᑎᒃ ᑐᑯᖕᒐᓚᐅᕐᓂᖅᓱᓂᒋᑦ. ᑖᒃᑯᐊᔫᖅ
ᑐᖅᑯᓚᐅᖅᑐᑦ ᐅᒃᐱᕈᓯᙱᑎᓕᓇᕝᓗᑎᒃ. ᑖᒃᑯᐊᔫᖅ ᓂᕙᐊᖅᓯᐊᒃ ᒪᑦᑎᒃ
ᖃᐅᔨᓚᐅᕐᒥᒃ ᐅᖃᕐᓗᐊᖅᐳᒃ, "ᑐᑯᖕᒐᑦᓗᐊᕙᓚᐅᖅᑐᓯ ᐅᕝᓗᓂᒃ ᑕᓪᓕᒪᓂᒃ.
ᓯᒃᑯᔾᔭᐅᓯᒪᑦᓗᐊᕙᓚᐅᖅᑐᓯ ᐃᒡᓗᓯ ᐊᒡᓛᑦ ᖁᕝᓗᐊᓗᖕᓂᖅᑲᓕᓚᐅᖅᑐᑦ
ᕿᕿᓗᐊᓘᑦ."

After five days had passed, Kaugjagjuk's brother brought all those that had drowned back to life. When they were alive again, Kaugjagjuk's brother told them that they had been dead in the water for five days. The people did not believe him, but the two girls who had witnessed it said, "Yes, it is true. You were all dead for five days. You were all frozen in the water! In fact, there were cracks in the ice where you were."

ᑖᒃᑯᐊᔫᖅ ᕿᕿᑦᕈ'ᔭᐅᓯᒪᓐᓂᑯᕙᓃᑦ ᐅᒃᐱᙱᑐᐃᓐᓇᖅᓱᑎᒃ.

But the people who had frozen in the water still refused to believe the story.

ᑕᐃᒪᒎᕆᓚᒃ ᑲᐅᒡᔭᒡᔫᑉ ᐊᖓᔪᐊ ᐅᖃᓚᐅᕐᒪᑦ ᓇᓄᕐᓗ’ᔪᐊᖅ ᑕᐅᓇᙵᑦ ᑭᑖ’ᓂᑦ ᐅᔭᖕᒋᑦᑐ’ᐊᕈᒫᕐᒪᑦ ᖃᖓᒍᙳᒍᕐᕋᓗᐊᖅᑎᑦᓗᒍᒎᖅ ᐊᓯᐃᓛ ᓇᓄᕐᓗ’ᔪᐊᖅ ᑎᑭᑦᑐ’ᔫᖕᒪᑦ ᐊᖑᑎ’ᔪᐃᑦ ᓇᓐᓂᕿᓯᑦᑐᐊᖅᐳᑦ. ᑲᐅᒡᔭᒡᔪᒎᖅ ᐊᖓᔪᒥᓂᑦ ᐅᖃᐅ’ᔭᐅᓚᐅᕐᓂᓂ ᒪᓕᒃᓗᒍ ᐊᓂᙵᑎᑕᐃᓐᓇᖅᓗᓂ.

A few more days passed, and then, one day, a big polar bear appeared. It was just as Kaugjagjuk's brother had said: the polar bear was so big that it blocked the eastern view. All the men in the camp tried to kill the bear. But Kaugjagjuk obeyed his brother's advice and stayed inside the dog den.

ᑲᐅᒡᔭᒡᔪᒎᖅ ᐅᐃᕆᓴᐅᑎᒋᔭᐅᓯᐊᖅᓗᓂ ᑭᓐᖒᒪᔭᐅᓯᑦᑐᐊᓄᕗᖅ, “ᑲᐅᒡᔭᒡᔪᐊᓗᒃ ᓇᐅᒥᒻᓇ ᐅᐃᕆᓴᐅᑎᒃᓴᖅ.”

People started calling for Kaugjagjuk, hoping to use him to bait the bear. They cried out, “Where is Kaugjagjuk so we can use him as bait?”

ᑲᐅᒡᔭᒡᔪᒎᖅ ᖃᐃᑯᔭᐅᒐᒥ ᐅᐃᕆᓴᐅᑎᒋᔭᐅᓯᐊᖅᓗᓂ ᓇᓐᓄᒧᑦ, ᐊᓯᐃᓛ ᓇᓐᓂᕿᔪ’ᔪᐊᕐᓄᓕᐊᓕᖅᐳᖅ ᐃᒻᖏᐅᔭᑦᑐᐊᑦᓚᕐᒥᓗ ᐃᒫᒃ, “ᑲᐅᒡᔭᒡᔪᐊᓗᒃ ᓇᐅᒥᒻᓈ ᐅᐃᕆᓴᐅᑎᒃᓴᖅ ᐅᐃᕆᓴᐅᑎᒃᓴᑐᐃᓈᓗᒃ ᔪᔪᕇ ᔪᔪᕆᐊᓗᒃ ᐱᕙᑦᓕᖅᑰ”ᔭᖕᒋᑦᑐᖓ ᐱᕙᑦᓕᖅᐳᖓ, ᐱᕙᑦᓕᖅᐹᑦᓕᖅᐳᖓ ᐅᐃᕆᓵᕐᓴᑕᕆᑦᔨ ᑲᔪᖕᒋᓵᓴᑕᕆᑦᔩ. ᔪᕐᔪᕇ ᔪᕐᔪᕆᐊᓗᒃ ᐱᕙᓕᖅᑰ’ᔭᖕᒋᑦᑐᖓ, ᐱᕙᑦᓕᖅᐹᑦᓕᖅᐳᖓ.”

When Kaugjagjuk heard this, he left the dog den and began walking towards the men trying to kill the bear. As he walked down, he sang, “Where, where, could Kaugjagjuk be? Where could the bait be? Where could the one who is only good for bait be? *Jurjurii jurjurialuk*. Am I not stronger, stronger? Stronger I've come to be! Bait, bait you be, jurjurii, jurjurialuk. Am I not stronger, stronger? Stronger I've come to be."

“ᐃᒡᓗᔪᐊᕌᓗᖕᓄᑦ ᐊᐃᕚᓴᓴᕌᖕᒪᑕ ᐊᖏᕐᕌᓴᓴᕌᖕᒪᑕ ᔪᕐᔪᕇ ᔪᕐᔪᕆᐊᓗᒃ ᐱᕙᓕᖅᑰ’ᔭᖕᒋᑦᑐᖓ ᐱᕙᑦᓕᖅᐳᖓ ᐱᕙᑦᓕᖅᐹᑦᓕᖅᐳᖓ.”

“When we all have entered a large iglu and everyone gone home. Jurjurii, jurjurialuk. Am I not stronger, stronger? Stronger I’ve come to be!”

“ᑲᐅᒡᔭᔪᐊᓗᒃ ᓇᐅᕆᒻᓇ ᐅᐃᕆᓴᐅᑎᒃᓴᖅ ᐅᐃᕆᓴᐅᑎᒃᓴᑐᐃᓐᓈᓗᒃ ᔪᕐᔪᕇ
ᔪᕐᔪᕆᐊᓗᒃ ᐱᕙᓪᓕᖅᑰ’ᔭᖕᕆᑦᑐᖓ ᐱᕙᓪᓕᖅᐳᖓ, ᐱᕙᓪᓕᖅᐹᓪᓕᖅᐳᖓ.”

“Where, where could Kaugjagjuk be? The enticer be? Good only for an enticer to be? Jurjurii jurjurialuk. Am I not stronger, stronger? Stronger I’ve come to be!”

“ᑲᐅᒡᔭᔪᐊᓗᒃ ᓇᐅᕆᒻᓇ ᐅᐃᕆᓴᐅᑎᒃᓴᖅ ᐅᐃᕆᓴᐅᑎᒃᓴᑐᐃᓐᓈᓗᒃ ᔪᕐᔪᕇ
ᔪᕐᔪᕆᐊᓗᒃ ᐱᕙᓕᖅᑰ’ᔭᖕᕆᑦᑐᖓ ᐱᕙᓪᓕᖅᐳᖓ ᐱᕚᓪᓕᖅᐹᓪᓕᖅᐳᖓ.”

“Where, where could Kaugjagjuk be? The enticer be? Good only for an enticer to be? Jurjurii jurjurialuk. Am I not stronger, stronger? Stronger I’ve come to be!”

“ᓱᓕᐊᖑᐊᓗᐊᖅᐲᒃ? ᔪᕐᔪᕇ, ᔪᕐᔪᕆᐊᓗᒃ ᐱᕙᓪᓕᖅᑰ’ᔭᖕᕆᑦᑐᖓ ᐱᕙᓪᓕᖅᐳᖓ
ᐱᕙᓪᓕᖅᐹᓪᓕᖅᐳᖓ.”

“Am I being treated so lowly? Here now, am I not stronger? Jurjurii jurjurialuk. Am I not stronger, stronger? Stronger I’ve come to be!”

ᑲᐅᒡᔭᒡᔫᒻᖒᖅ ᐊᓂᒐᒥ ᑕᒪᒃᑯᐊ ᐱᔮᓇᔨᕆᕙᓚᐅᒃᑲᓂ ᐊᖑᑎ’ᑐᐃᑦ
ᐃᒻᒋᐅᔭᒻᒫᖅᓗᓂ ᑎᒍᕝᓗᒋᑦ ᖃᖓᑦᑕᐅᑎᑎᓇᓐᓂᖅᓗᓂᒋᑦᓗᓂᒋᑦ
ᓇᓄᕐᓗ’ᔪᐊᕐᒧᑦ ᐃᖅᑲᑦᑕᐅᔭᓕᖅᓗᓂᒋᑦ. ᐃᒋᑦᓴᖀᖓᒥᑦ ᓇᓄᕐᓗ’ᔫᑉ ᓱᓕ
ᖃᖓᑕᑎᓪᓗᒋᑦ ᐊᑯᖅᐸᖅᓗᒋᑦ ᐅᕆᐊᖅᓗᒋᓪᓗ ᑐᑯᑦᑕᖅᓗᓂᒋᑦ.

When Kaugjagjuk reached the men, he grabbed those who had been cruel to him, lifted them off the ground, and threw them to the bear. The bear caught the men in mid-air, attacked them, and killed them.

ᐊᖑᑎᙵᔫᖅ ᓄᖑᒻᒪᑕ ᑲᐅᒡᔭᒡᔮᒻᖕᔫᖅ ᓇᓄ’ᔦᐊᖅ ᓯᕗᑦᓖᒥᑦᑯᑦ ᑎᒍᑎᓚᓐᓂᖅᓗᒍ ᖁᐊᓴᒧᑦ ᐃᐱᕋᐅ’ᔭᖅᓗᒍ ᑐᖁᑦᑭᕝᓗᓂᐅᒃ.

When all the men had been mauled to death by the bear, Kaugjagjuk then destroyed the bear by grabbing its front legs and bashing it to death on the ice.

ᐃᓱᐊ
The end

ᐃᒡᓗᖃᑎᒌᒃ
TWO MEN WHO SHARED A WIFE

ᑕᐃᑉᑯᐊᑉᑕᐅᕉᖅ ᐊᖑᑎᒃ ᐃᒡᓗᖃᑎᒌᒃ, ᑎᐊ'ᓇ ᐊᕐᓇᒥᒃ ᐊᑕᐅᓯᕐᒥᒃ ᓄᓕᐊᖅᑲᖅᓱᑎᒃ, ᓄᓖᕐᖑᓚᐅᑦᑕᓕᕐᒥᒎᖅ ᐱᑦᓯᐊᖏᑦᑕᖅᑐ'ᑑᓖᒃ.

This story is about two men who shared a wife and started fighting over her.

ᐊᑖᕐᒪᑕᒎᖅ ᑕᐃᒻᓇ ᓄᓕᐊᓕᑐᖅᑲᐅᓂᖅᓴᖅ ᓇᑦᓯᕐᒥᒃ ᑕᑯᖕᒪᑕ ᐊᐅᓚᐊᓕᖅᓱᓂ ᓄᓕᐊᓕᑐᖅᑲᐅᑉ ᓇᑦᓯᖅᑕᓚᖕᓱᓂᐅᒃ. ᓯᒡᔭᒥᒎᖅ ᐱᓚᓕᕐᒪᓂᒃ ᑎᐊ'ᓇᒎᖅ ᓇᑦᓯᖅ ᑲᐃᕖᓐᓇᑦᓯᐊᒥᐊᖅᓱᒍ ᐱᓚᖕᒪᓂᒃ, ᑲᐃᕕᑐᐃᓐᓇᖅᓱᒍ ᐱᓛᓂᒡᔩᒥᒋᓐᓇᓕᖅᓱᑎᒃ ᐊᒡᓛᑦ.

The two men and their wife had moved to the coast. When they arrived, the man who was the true husband saw a seal, went after it, and caught it. He brought it to the shore, and then both men started to butcher the animal. But the whole time, the pair made sure they stayed across from each other and moved around the seal to keep out of each other's reach.

ᐱᓛᓂᒃᑲᒥᒎᖅ ᑐᑉᐱᐅᑦᑐᐊᓕᕐᒥᖕᒪᓂᒃ, ᐊᓂᖅᑕᐃᒪᓪᓗᒎᖅ ᑐᐱᖅ ᓱᒃᑲᓇᒃᓴᑦᓯᐊᒥᐊᖅᓗᒍ ᑐᑉᐱᐅᑯᓂᒃᐳᒃ. ᑎᐊ’ᓇᒎᖅ ᑐᐱᖅ ᒪᓐᓇᐅᒥᖕᓗᒍ ᐱᖀᒥᐊᑦᑐᐊᓪᓛᓪᓗ ᑐᑉᐱᐅᕐᒪᓂᒃ.

After the butchering was finished, the two men went to put up the tent. But they were competing and showing off as they put it up. They made the tent so tight that it was completely smooth, and they used many extra stones to keep it weighted down.

ᑕᐃᒻᓇᒎᖅ ᐊᕐᓇᖅ ᐃᓕᒪᓱ’ᑐᐊᕋᒥ ᖃᓂᒑᔫᒧᑦ ᕿᔪᒃᑕᓇᐊᖅᓯᖅᑐᖅᓱᓂ ᖃᐅᔩᓴ’ᑐᐊᓕᕋᒥ, ᐊᓂᕙᓪᓕᐊᖕᒋᓱᖕᒑᔭᓕᕐᒪᓂᒎᖅ ᑐᐱᕐᒥᑦ ᑐᑉᐱᐅᑲᓂᒃᑲᓗᐊᕋᒥᒃ, ᓱᓇᐅᕝᕙ ᑳᐳᓯᒋᐊᖑᓐᓃᒃ.

Of course, the woman was deeply suspicious of this, and she pretended to collect moss near the tent so she could spy on her husbands.

ᑕᐃᒪᒎᖅ ᑕᖅᑲᕙᓂ ᑳᐳ’ᑐᐊᓕᕐᓂᕐᒪᓂᒃ ᑐᐱᖀᖅ ᓱᑲᖕᒐ’ᑐᐊᕋᓗᐊᕐᒪᑦ ᑎᐊ’ᓇ ᖃᓇᐅᕝᕗ ᑐᐱᐅᕝᕗ ᐃᑭᐊᖕᒐᒍᑦ ᐊᓂᒍᖅᑕᒥᐊᓕᕐᓂᖅᓱᑎᒃ ᐊᒃᓛᑦ ᕿᒫᔭᓗᐊᒧᑦ.

The woman saw that the tent was all set up, but her husbands didn’t come out. They had actually set up the tent to have a knife fight inside. The husbands soon began their fight, and the fighting was so aggressive that each man kept slipping between the tent pole and tent, trying to avoid each other’s knife stabs.

ᐊᕐᓇᖅ ᖃᓂ’ᓈᕋᒥ ᖃᐅᔩ’ᓈᑐᐊᕋᒥ ᐊᖅᐸᒋᐊᐱᑦᑐᐊᕋᓗᐊᕐᒪᑦ ᑐᐱᕐᒥᖕᓄᑦ, ᑐᐱᕐᒧᖖᒎᖅ ᑎᑭᓴᖅᑐᓕᕋᓗᐊᖅᑎᑦᓗᒍ ᑐᖅᓱᓚᖅᐸᑦᓚᓯᖕᒑᔭᖕᒪᑦ, “ᐊ”ᐋ!”

The woman ran down to the tent as soon as she sensed trouble. But when she reached the tent, she heard someone groan and holler, “Ouch!”

ᐃᑎᕐᒪᙱᒎᕐᒃ ᑖᒻᓇ ᐅᐃᑐᕐᑲᓇᙱᒋᓐᓂᕐᒃᓴᐅᔫ ᓇᑎᐅᑉ ᕿᕐᒃᑲᓂ ᐃᑦᑐᕐᒃ, ᓈᙱᒐ ᑲᐱᓯᒪᔪ’ᑐᐊᕐᒃ. ᐃᓪᕋᕕᓂᒎᕐᒃ ᐊᓃᕐᒃᑑ’ᑐᐃᑦ ᑲᑎᒋᐊᑦᑐᐊᕐᒃᐸᒃᖢᒋᑦ ᐊᑯᓐᓈᙱᒥᓄᑦ. ᑲᐱᔭᐅᔪᑮᕐᒃ ᑐᕐᑯ’ᑐᐊᕐᒪᑦ, ᑖᑉᑯᐊᒃ ᓄᓕᐊᑐᕐᑲᓃᒃ ᑲᑎ’ᑐᐊᓇᕗᒃ.

When she ran inside, she saw her second husband sitting in the middle of the floor. He had been stabbed in the stomach and was trying to hold his exposed intestines together with his hands. The woman’s second husband soon died, and the real husband and wife were together alone again.

ᐃᓱᐊ
The end

ᐃᓄᐃᑦ ᐅᒃᐱᕆᓴᕐᑲᐅᓯᕕᓂᖏᑦ
Inuit Beliefs

ᐃᓄᐃᑦ ᐅᒃᐱᕆᓴᖅᑲᐅᓯᕙᓂᖏᑦ
INUIT TRADITIONAL BELIEFS OF THE PAST

ᐃᑦᓴᖅ ᐃᓄᐃᑦ ᐃᓕᖅᑯᓯᑐᖅᑲᒥᖕᓂᒃ ᐊᑐᖅᑐᑎᒃ ᐃᓅᓚᐅᕐᒥᒃ ᐃᖕᒥᐊᓘᖕᒐᓪᓗᐊᕕᒃᑐᒥᒃ ᐅᒃᐱᕈᓯᖅᑲᓚᐅᖅᐳᑦ ᓯᕘᕆᓕᕐᓗᒍ ᒪᓕᔪᓴᒥᖕᓂᒃ, ᑐᑭᓗᐊᒍᑎᕆᕐᓗᒍᓗ ᐃᓅᓂᕐᒥᖕᓂ.

Long ago, when Inuit still practiced their traditional ways, they followed their own unique belief system, which they held in fearful reverence, and it guided them in life.

ᐅᒃᐱᕆᓴᖅᑲᐅᓯᖅ ᒪᓕᒃᓗᒍ ᓯᓇᒥᐊᓂᒃ ᐱᑦᑕᐃᓕᓴᖅᑲᕈᔫᓴᖅᐸᓚᐅᖅᐳᑦ, ᐱᑦᑕᐃᓕᓴᐅᔪᒥᒃ ᐱᒍᒥᒃ ᓯᕘᕆᓴᒃᓴᖅᑲᖅᑎᑕᐅᕐᓗᑎᒃ ᐃᓅᓯᕐᒧᑦ ᖁᕙᐊᓇᐃᑦᑐᒥᒃ ᐱᑎᑕᐅᔪᖅᑲᕈᖕᓇᖅᓂᖅᒥᒃ ᓂᑉᑕᖕᖏᑦᑐᒥᑦ.

In accordance with their beliefs, they avoided doing certain things, and they tried to heed these admonitions carefully, fearing that if they broke the rules an unseen force would lead them to an unhappy life.

ᐅᒃᐱᕆᓴᐅᖅᑲᐅᓯᑐᖅᑲᐃᑦ ᓇᐅᒃᑯᓗᒃᑖᖅ ᐊᑕᓂᖅᑲᓚᐅᖅᐳᑦ, ᓯᓕᕆᓂᒃᑯᑦ, ᓂᖅᑭᑎᒍᑦ, ᐃᒥᒃᑯᑦ, ᐃᓅᖅᑲᑎᒌᒍᓯᒃᑯᑦ ᐊᓯᖕᒋᑎᒍᑦᓗ.

This traditional belief system was linked to every area of life, affecting how they worked, how food was harvested and used, how water was used, how relationships were formed and maintained—it affected all areas of life.

ᓱᓇᐅᖕᒪᖕᒑᑖ ᑕᐃᑦᑕᐅᓴᒥᐊᓚᐅᕐᓗᑎᑦ ᐃᓚᐃᓐᓇᕋᓗᐊᖕᒋᑦ ᒪᑯᐊᖑᕙᓚᐅᖅᐳᑦ.

In this book, I have written down some of these beliefs that were taught, learned, and practised.

ᐃᓕᐊᕐᔪᓕᕆᑦᓯᐊᕐᓂᖅ
SHOWING KINDNESS TO ORPHANS

ᐃᓕᐊᕐᔫᓂᕋᓚᐅᕙᒃᐳᑦ ᓄᑕᕋ'ᓈᑦ ᐊᖓᔪᖅᑳᖏᕈᑎᓐᓂᑯ'ᓈᑦ, ᐱᑦᓯᐊᖏᑕᐅᔪ'ᓈᑦ ᐃᓚᒐᓗᐊᒥᖕᓂᑦ ᓵᓚᑯᒥᐅᔪᒥᐊᓇᓱ'ᓈᑦ, ᐱᑎᑕᐅᑦᑕᐃᓕᕋᓗᒃᔪᑎᒃ ᓱᓇᒥᐊᓂᒃ ᐃᓱᒪᖅᓱᖅᑎᑕᐅᙱᑦᑎᐊᒥᐊᖅᑐᑦ, ᐃᓕᐊᕐᔫᖏᑦᑐᑦ ᐱᑦᓯᐊᒐᐅᔪᓪᓕ ᐱᕙᒃᑕᖏᓐᓂᒃ ᑐᓯᑎᑕᐅᔪ'ᓈᑦ.

Orphans are children who have suffered the loss of their parents. Orphans were often mistreated even by their extended families, and were denied many things and freedoms that were enjoyed by others. Orphans were children who had lost parental love, care, and protection, for which they strongly yearned.

ᑕᐃᒪᓐᓇᐃᑦᑐ'ᓈᓂᒃ ᐱᑦᓯᐊᕐᑯᔭᐅᕙᓚᐅᖅᐳᒍᑦ ᐃᑲᔪᖅᑎᒃᓴᐃᕈᑎᓯᒪᔪ'ᓈᓂᒃ ᐃᔨ'ᓈᖏᑦ ᓇᒧᒥᐊᖅ ᕿᕕᐊᖃᖅᓗᑎᒃ ᓇᐅᑦᓯᖅᑐᑦᑐᓇᒃᓴᖅᑐ'ᓈᑦ.

We were told to show kindness to orphans who had no one to help or defend them, whose eyes were always in search of protection.

ᓲᖅᓗ ᐅᓂᑉᑳᖅᑐᐊᖅᑕᖅᑲᕐᒪᑦ ᑲᐅᒡᔭᒡᔪᖕᒥ ᐊᒥᓱᓂᑦ ᑐᓴᐅᒪᔭᐅᔪᒥᒃ. ᑲᐅᒡᔭᒡᔫᕆᓐᓇ ᐃᓕᐊᕐᔪ'ᓈᖑᓚᐅᖅᓯᒪᓐᓂᕐᒥᖕᒪᑦ, ᐅᓂᑉᑳᖅᑐᐊᖑᓂᕋᓚᐅᕙᒃᒎᒐᓗᐊᖅ, ᑭᓯᐊᓂ ᐱᒻᒪᕆᐅᓯᓐᓇᕆᐊᖅᑲᒻᒫᕐᒥᔪᖅ.

There is a traditional story of Kaugjagjuk that many people have heard or know of. It is said that Kaugjagjuk was also a little orphan. People claim it to be just a story, but it can also be an actual true story.

ᐱᔹᖑᔭᐅᔪᐊᒧᑦ ᐃᓕᐊᖅᔮᖕᒪᑦ ᑐᖅᓱᖕᒥᐊᒡᓛᖖᔫᖅ ᕿᒻᒥᑦ ᓱᑎᓛᓐᓂ ᓱᑎᓚᖅᑲᖅᑲᑕᐅᕝᓱᓂ ᓱᓐᑎᑕᐅᕙᓚᐅᖅᑐᖅ. ᕿᒻᒥᓐ ᐊᓪᓕᐊᖅᑲᖅᑐᓂ ᐅᕝᕙᔫᕝᕙ ᐊᓪᓕᓂᖅᑲᖅᑐᓂ ᐊᒻᒪ ᕿᐱᖅᑲᖅᑐᓂ ᕿᒻᒥᓐ.

Kaugjagjuk was mistreated so badly as an orphan that he slept in a dog cave in the outer porch. He slept among the dogs, who served as his bedding and covering.

ᐱᔹᖑᔭᐅᔪᐊᒧᑦ ᐅᖅᓱᓐ, ᖁᓪᓕᐅᑉ ᐅᖅᓱᒃᓴᐃᓐ ᐊᐃᕖᑦ ᐅᖅᓱᖕᒋᓐ ᕿᖅᑭᔮᓐ ᑲᐅᓚᖅᓯᑎᑕᐅᕙᓚᐅᖅᓯᒪᔭᕕᓂᖅ. ᑕᐃᒪᔫᖅ ᑲᐅᒡᔭᒡᔭᖕᒥᒃ ᐊᑎᖅᑲᓕᕈᑎᒋᓐᓂᖅᐹ, ᐊᐃᕖᑦ ᐅᖅᓱ’ᔭᐊᖕᒋᓐᓂᒃ ᑲᐅᓚᖅᓯᑎᑕᐅᑦᑕᔭᓚᒥ. ᐃᒻᒪᖅᑳ ᑭᓇᒥᑭᐊᖅ ᐊᑎᓪᓗᐊᕕᖅᑲᓚᐅᖅᓯᒪᔩᓚᓗᐊᖅ, ᐊᑦᓯᕋᐅᓯᐊᖅᒥᓐ ᐊᑦᓯᓚᐅᒻᒫᒥᐊᖅᓂᖅᒪᑦ ᑲᐅᒡᔭᒡᔭᖕᒥᒃ, ᐊᐃᕖᑦ ᐅᖅᓱᐃᓐ ᕿᖅᑭᔮᓐ ᑲᐅᓚᖅᓯᑎᑕᐅᕙᖕᓂᓂ ᐱᔾᔭᑎᒋᔅᓱᒍ, ᕿᐸᒋᔭᐅᔪᐊᒧᑦ ᑲᐅᒡᔭᒡᔭᖕᒥᒃ ᐊᒡᓛᑦ ᐊᑦᓯᓚᐅᓐᓂᖅᒪᑦ.

He was treated as a slave and was often given the chore of rendering frozen chunks of walrus blubber by pounding them with a mallet into oil for the lamps. This is how he became known as Kaugjagjuk, "the pounder," because he was always pounding on frozen walrus blubber. He probably had his own real name, but he was further demeaned and dehumanized by being given the name of Kaugjagjuk. He was so disdained that others simply called him by the given nickname to mock him.

ᑭᓯᐊᓂ ᐊᖑᔮᖅᑲᓚᐅᖅᓂᖅᒪᑦ ᓄᓇᓕᖕᒥᑉᑕᐅᖅ ᐊᓯᐊᓂ ᓄᓇᖅᑲᖅᑐᓐ. ᐊᖑᔮᐊᑕᔫᖅ ᑎᑭᓐᓇᒥ, ᐃᒻᒪᖅᑳ ᐊᖑᓪᑯᕋᔫᓐᓂᖅᒥᒐᒥ, ᐃᓄᖕᓄᑦ ᑕᖕᓖᖕᒋᔅᓱᓂ, ᐃᓐᒥᒍᑦ ᐃᒡᓗ’ᓇᖅᑲᖅᑐᓂ ᓄᒃᑲᓂ ᖃᐃᖅᑯᕙᒃᓱᖕᒍ ᐱᒡᒍᒃᑎᓴᓕᖅᓂᓛ. ᑕᐃᒪᔫᖅ ᐅᓐᓄᒃᑳᖕᒐᑦ ᖃᐃᖅᑯᕙᒃᓱᒍ ᐃᐱᕋᐅᑦᑕᒧᑦ ᐃᐱᕋᖅᑐᖅᑕᒐ’ᔭᐊᓇᓕᓛ. ᐃᐱᕋᖅᑐᓕᕌᖕᒐᒍᔫᖅ ᐊᓐᓄᕌᖕᒋᓂᑦ ᐊᖑᔮᖅᑳᖕᒋᑕ ᐱᓐᓂᑯ’ᔭᐊᖕᒋ ᐱᑦᓯᐊᖕᒋᑦᑕᖅᓂᑯ’ᔭᐊᖕᒋᑦ ᐱᒃᓯᒐᖅᑕᖅᑐ’ᔫᕙᒃᑐᑦ.

It turns out that he had an older brother who lived in a distant inland camp. This older brother arrived one day, but he didn't move in as a guest to any of the people's igluit. Probably because he was a shaman, he built his own iglu. He would invite his younger brother over and started training him to strengthen him. At night, Kaugjagjuk would come over, and his older brother would lash him with a dog-whip. With every lash of the whip, the evil that his parents had left him seemed to come out of his shirt.

ᐊᒻᒪᔫᖅ ᖃᑦᖃᔫᖅᑲᑎᒋᓪᓗᒍ ᖃᑦᖃᒥ ᐃᐱᖏᖅᑐᑦᑐᐊᓕᖅᐸᒃᑭᓪᓗᒍ ᐅᔭᖅᑲᓂᒃ ᒪᓂᖅᑲᒧᑦ ᕿᕿᑦᕈᑎᓯᒪᔪᓂᒃ ᒪᒃᐱᖅᓯᓯᖅᓴᑎᑦᑕᖅᓗᒍ. ᐅᔭᖁᒡᔪᐊ'ᔪᐊᕐᓂᔫᖅ ᒪᓂᖅᑲᒧᑦ ᕿᕿᑦᕈᑎᓯᒪᔪᓂᒃ ᐊᒡᓛᑦ ᒪᒃᐱᖅᓯᓯᖅᓯᖕᒪᑦ ᑭᓯᐊᓂ ᐱᑕᕋᐊᕋᔪᖕᓂᓵᖅᓗᒍ.

Then his older brother took Kaugjagjuk up to a small hill and began to whip him some more and made him pry out stones frozen solid into the ground. When Kaugjagjuk was able to pry boulders from the frozen ground, the older brother finally stopped whipping him.

ᑕᐃᒪᔫᖅ ᐊᓱᐃᓛ, ᐱᐊᓂᒃᑲᒥᐅᒃ ᐊᐅᑦᓚᕈᒫᓕᖁᒥ ᐊᖑᑎᑉ ᓄᒃᑲᓂ ᐅᖅᑲᐅᑎᓕᖅᐹ ᓇᓄᖅᓱ'ᔪᐊᖕᓂᔫᖅ ᑎᑭᑦᑐᖅᑲᕈᒫᖅᒪᑦ ᐱᑕᕋᐊᕋᔫᒪᖅᐸᒃ. ᖃᑯᖓᒍᓈᖅᓯᓐᓇᖅᑎᑦᓗᒍ ᓇᓄᖅᓱ'ᔪᐊᔫᖅ ᑎᑭᑦᑐ'ᔫᒃᒪᓂᒃ ᐃᒡᓗᓄᑦ.

When the older brother had completed the boy's training and was ready to leave, he told his younger brother that two huge, evil polar bears would arrive to the camp and that he was to handle them. Not long after, two huge, evil polar bears walked into their igluit encampment.

ᐊᖑᑎᖕᖑᔫᖅ ᑐᖅᓗᑖᓯᑦᑐᐊᖅᐳᑦ, "ᑲᐅᒡᔭᒡᔪᐊᓗᒃ ᓇᐅᒥᒻᓇ, ᐅᐃᕆᓴᐅᑎᒃᓴᖅ, ᐅᐃᕆᓴᐅᑎᒃᓴᑐᐃᓐᓈᓗᒃ" ᑲᐅᒡᔭᒡᔪᒃ ᑭᖕᖑᒪᓕᖅᐹᑦ ᐊᓐᓂᕐᓇᖕᖏᑦᑑᑎᒋᓯᐊᒧᑦ, ᓇᓄᖅᓱᖕᓄᑦ ᐃᒋᑉᐸᒡᓗᒍ ᐅᐃᕆᓴᐅᑎᒋᓯᐊᒧᑦ ᒥᑕᐅᑎᒋᓗᒍ.

Some men saw the bears and called out, "Where is the great Kaugjagjuk, the one to bait the bears!" They wanted Kaugjagjuk because he was considered dispensable. They wanted to throw him at the evil bears to bait and enrage them.

ᑲᐅᒡᔭᒡᔫᖅ ᑐᓴ’ᓈᑐᐊᕐᒥ ᐊᖑᑎ’ᔪᐃᑦ ᓇᓐᓂᓯᔪ’ᔪᐃᑦ ᐅᕐᓂᓕᖅᐸᐃ ᐃᒻᖕᒋᐅᔭᑦᑐᐊᓪᓚᕐᒥᒎ, “ᑲᐅᒡᔭᒡᔪᐊᓗᒃ ᓇᐅᒋᒻᓈ, ᐅᐃᕆᓴᐅᑎᒃᓴᖅ, ᐅᐃᕆᓴᐅᑎᒃᓴᑐᐃᓐᓈᓗᒃ. ᐅᐃᕆᓵᔅᓚᓕᕆᑉᔨ, ᑲᔪᖕᒋᖅᓵᔅᓚᓕᕆᑉᔫ, ᔪᕐᔪᕇ, ᔪᕐᔪᕆᐊᓗᒃ ᐱᕙᓪᓕᕐᑰ’ᔭᖕᒋᑦᑐᖕᒐ. ᐱᕙᓪᓕᖅᐳᖕᒐ. ᐱᕙᓪᓕᖅᐹᓪᓕᖅᐳᖕᒐ.” ᐃᒻᖕᒋᓕᖅᑐᕈᓇ ᐃᓕᐊᕐᔪᕐᓚᒥᐊ’ᓈᒍᖖᒋᓕᕐᒥ, ᐃᖕᒥᓂᒃ ᓴᐳᑎᑦᑕᖅᑑᑦᓗᐊᓕᕐᒥ.

As soon as Kaugjagjuk heard the men calling out for him, he began walking towards them, singing his pihiq: “Where is that great Kaugjagjuk, the one to bait the bears, use him as a bait now. Jurjurii, jurjurialuk, I consider myself more able now, I'm truly more able now.” He sang thusly because he was no longer just an ordinary, mistreated orphan; he was now able to defend himself.

ᑲᐅᒡᔭᒡᔮᒻᖕᔫᖅ ᓇᓐᓂᓯᔪ’ᔪᐊᕐᓅᕐᒥ, ᐊᖑᑎ’ᔪᐃᑦ ᑎᒍᕋᒃᓱᒥᑦ ᓇᓄᕐᓗ’ᔪᐊᖕᓄᑦ ᐃᖅᑲᑦᑕᐅᔭᓕᕐᒪᕆᑦ, ᓱᓕᔫᖅ ᖃᖕᒐᑕᑎᓪᓗᕆᑦ ᐊᑯᒐᐅᔭᕌᖕᒐᒥᒃ ᓇᓄᕐᓗᖕᓄᑦ ᐱᔭᐅᕙᒃᓗᑎᒃ. ᐊᖑᑎ’ᔪᐃᓐᔫᖅ ᐱᔭᖅᑕᖅᑎᕆᕙᓚᐅᒃᑲᓂ ᓄᖑᒻᒪᑕ, ᑲᐅᒡᔭᒡᔮᒻᖕᔫᖅ ᓇᓄᕐᓗ’ᔪᐊᒃ ᓱᕗᓪᓖᕆᒃᑯᑦ ᑎᒍᑎᓯᓂᖅᓗᕆᒃ ᑲᐃᕝᔭᐅᑎᓚᐅ’ᓈᖅᑳᖅᓗᖕᕆᒃ ᒪᓂᖅᑲᒧᑦ ᐃᕆᔅᓗᖕᕆᒃ ᑕᒪᕐᒥᒃ ᑐᕐᑯᔅᓗᓂᕆᒃ.

When Kaugjagjuk reached the men who were harassing the bears, he started flinging them at the bears. The bears would catch them mid-air and kill them. When all the men who were his tormentors were gone, he grabbed the bears by their front paws, swung them around and around, and smashed them to the ground and killed both of them.

ᑖᒻᓇ ᐅᓂᑉᑳᖅᑐᐊᖅ ᐃᓚᖅᑲᖅᑲᓐᓂᖅᑑᒐᓗᐊᖅ ᓱᓕ, ᑭᓯᐊᓂ ᑐᑭᓯᕆᐊᕈᑕᐅᖁᕝᓗᒍ ᐃᓚᖓ ᐅᓂᑉᑳᖅᐸᖅ, ᐃᓕᐊᕐᔪᖕᓂᒃ ᑲᒪᑦᓯᐊᖅᐸᕆᐊᖅᑲᖅᓂᖏᑦ ᐃᓱᒪᕆᔭᐅᑦᓯᐊᖅᑯᖅᓗᒍ.

There is still a lot more to this story, but I want to highlight part of the story to bring understanding to why it is important to consider caring for orphans.

ᑭᑐᒥᐊᕐ, ᐅᕙᑉᑎᖕᓂᑦ ᐊᔪᕐᓂᖅᓴᐅᓯᕆᔭᕗᕐ, ᓱᐃᓐᓇᕐᓘᓯᕆᔭᕗᑦ ᐊᓪᓛᑦ ᐱᕐᓯᐊᖅᐸᕆᐊᕐᑲᕋᑉᑎᒍ, ᐅᕙᑉᑎᖕᓂᑦ ᐊᓪᓛᑦ ᐊᔪᙱᓐᓂᖅᓴᐅᓕᕐᓗᑎᒃ ᒪᑭᑦᑑᑦᓗᐊᕐᒪᑕ, ᐅᕙᒍᑦ ᐊᓪᓛᑦ ᐃᑲᔪᖅᑎᒋᖕᒎᕈᖕᓇᖅᓯᓗᑎᒍ. ᑕᐃᒪ ᑕᒪᓐᓇ ᐱᒻᓗᒍ ᐊᖕᒐᔪᖅᑳᕋᑕ. ᐊᔪᕐᑭᖅᑐᖅᐸᓚᐅᖅᐹᑎᒍᑦ ᐃᓕᓴᐊᕐᔪᖕᓂᒃ ᐃᓄᒡᓗᕆᔭᐅᔪᓂᒃ ᐱᕐᓯᐊᖅᐸᕐᑯᓪᓗᑕ, ᐃᑲᔪᖅᐸᕐᑯᓪᓗᑕᓗ. ᑕᒪᓐᓇ ᐊᐅᓚᔾᔭᒃᓴᑦᑎᐊᕙᒻᒪᓇᐊᓘᕗᖅ.

We must always show kindness to people who we consider to be less fortunate than us, because they can rise up to become more powerful than us, and we ourselves may require their help someday. That is why our parents taught us to show kindness to orphans and to those who are shunned by others. We are to offer them kindness and help. This is a precious thing to build our memories on.

ᑖᒻᓇᓕ ᐅᓂᑉᑳᖅᑐᐊᒥᐊᖑᒐᓗᐊᖅ, ᑐᑭᓯᓐᓇᕈᑕᐅᔪᖅ ᐊᕐᕕ'ᔪᐊᖅ ᐳᔭᓂᓐᓂᕋᒐᐅᒐᒥ ᐊᑭᔪᕕᓂᖅ, ᐃᓄᖕᓂᒃ ᐃᓕᔫᕐᓂᒃᑐᖅ ᐅᕐᑲᖅᖢᓂ, “ᕐᑲᓄᖅᑐᖅ ᐸᑭᑉᑯᐊ ᐅᔭᕋᒍᑦᓗᕐᓕᑦ” ᐊᓯᐃᓛ ᐃᓄᐃᑦ ᐅᔭᕋᖑᕐᑯᔭᐃ ᓯᓇᓗᒃᑖᖕᒋᑦ, ᕐᑭᒻᒥᕋᓗᒥᐊᖕᒋ ᐱᕐᑯᑎᕋᓗᒥᐊᖕᒋᑦ ᐅᔭᕋᒍᖅᖢᑎᒃ ᓄᖑᓚᐅ'ᔪᐊᖅᓯᒪᓂᖅᐳᑦ.

Here is just another story that contains a lesson in it. It is a story of a big whale that fought back when others said he stank like old dried-up blubber fat. He fought back and put an evil spell on the people: “May you all turn into stones.” So it was that not only people, but all their possessions—their dogs and belongings—were all turned into stones.

ᐃᕐᓕᒃᑕᐃᓕᓂᖅ ᓂᕿᓂᒃ
AVOID BEING STINGY ABOUT FOOD

ᐊᖕᒐᔪᖅᑳᑉᑎᖕᓂᑦ ᐱᕈᖅᓴᔭᐅᓂᑉᑎᖕᓂ ᐅᖃᐅᔾᔪᒐᐅᑦᑎᐊᖅᐸᓚᐅᖅᐳᒍᑦ ᓂᕿᓂᒃ ᐃᕐᓕᒃᐸᖁᔭᐅᙱᔅᓱᑕ, ᓂᕿᒥᒎᖅ ᐃᕐᓕᒍᔾᔭᐅᓂᖅ ᐃᓕᕋᓇᑦᑎᐊᒥᐊᕐᒪᑦ. ᐊᖕᒐᔪᖅᑳᑉᑎᖕᓂᑦ, ᑖᑉᑯᓇᙵᑦ ᐊᑖᑕᑉᑎᖕᓂᒃ ᐊᓈᓇᑉᑎᖕᓂᓪᓗ, ᓴᓇᔭᐅᕙᓚᐅᕋᑉᑕ ᐅᖃᐅᔾᔪᖅᑕᐅᕙᒌᖅᓱᑕ ᐊᔪᙱᓕᕈᑉᑕ, ᐱᔪᖕᓇᖅᓯᒍᑉᑕ ᐅᕙᑉᑎᖕᓂᒃ, ᐃᓅᓯᖃᐅᓯᒃᓴᕆᓂᐊᖅᑕᑉᑎᖕᓂᒃ ᐅᕙᑉᑎᖕᓂᒃ ᒥᐊᓂᕆᓗᑕ, ᐃᓅᖃᑎᒋᔭᑉᑎᖕᓂᒡᓗ ᓇᐅᑦᓯᖅᑐᑦᓯᐊᕐᓗᑕ, ᐊᔪᓕᕌᖕᒐᑦ ᐃᑲᔪᕆᐊᕈᖕᓇᕐᓗᑕ ᐱᔫᑦᓗᐊᕐᓂᕗᑦ ᒪᓕᒡᓗᒍ.

We grew up raised by our parents who told us that we should always be generous about sharing food, because being denied food to eat is a scary thing.

ᑕᐃᑉᓱᒪᓂ ᓄᓇᒥᐅᑕᐅᕝᓗᑕ ᐃᓅᓯᑎᓚᐅᖅᑕᕗᑦ ᐅᕝᓗᒥᑐᑦ ᐊᔪᖅᓴᓗᐊᙱᔅᓱᑕ ᐃᓅᕙᒃᑲᑉᑕᑐᑦ ᐃᙱᑦᓚᕆᓚᐅᕐᒪᑦ, ᓂᖃᐃᑐᕆᐊᕐᕕᒃᓴᖃᕋᓂᓗ, ᐊᔪᖅᓴᖅᑐᓕᕆᔨᑕᖃᕋᓂᓗ ᐃᓅᓐᓇᓚᐅᕐᒪᑦ ᐅᕙᑉᑎᖕᓂᒃ ᑭᓯᐊᓂ ᒥᐊᓂᕆᓗᑕ, ᐱᑕᖃᕐᓂᕐᓄᑦ ᐊᐅᓪᓛᖅᑕᕐᓗᑕ ᐃᓛᓐᓂ ᐅᖕᒐᕙᓕᐊᕐᓱᓂ ᑭᓯᐊᓂ ᐱᓐᓇᖅᓯᓚᐅᖅᐸᒃᓱᓂ ᓂᕐᔪᑎᑦ ᐊᑐᐃᓐᓇᐅᖕᒋᓐᓇᖅᐸᙱᒻᒪᑕ ᖃᓂᑦᑐᒥ, ᑭᓯᐊᓂ ᐅᕐᓂᒡᓗᒋᑦ ᕿᓂᕐᓗᒋᑦᓗ ᐱᔭᕆᐊᖃᕋᒥᒃ.

Our fathers and mothers taught us, preparing us for what we should do when we became able to do things on our own, advising us how to look after ourselves, and to care for other people. We would be able to assist others who are experiencing problems and hardships according to our learned abilities.

ᑕᒪᓐᓇ ᐱᕝᓗᒍ ᐃᓄᐃᑦ ᒥᐊᓂᕆᑐᕋᐅᑦᑎᐊᒻᒪᕆᐊᓗᒐᓯᒃᓱᑎᒃ ᑭᓯᐊᓂ ᐊᔪᖅᓴᕐᓇᖅᑐᓂᒃ ᐊᓂᒎᑎᔪᖕᓇᖅᐸᓚᐅᖅᐳᑦ ᐊᒃᓯᕈᖅᓱᑎᒃ ᐃᑲᔪᖅᑎᒌᑦᑎᐊᖅᓱᑎᓪᓗ. ᐃᑲᔪᖅᑎᒌᑦᑎᐊᕐᓂᖅ ᐊᔪᖅᓴᖅᑐᓂᓪᓗ ᑲᒪᑦᓯᐊᔪᓂᖅ ᐊᔪᙱᓐᓂᐅᑉ ᐃᓚᒋᖅᑲᑕᐅᖕᒪᒍ ᐱᕕᒌᓐᓇᕆᐊᖅᑲᖅᐸᕗᑦ. ᐅᖅᑲᒻᒫᔪᓚᐅᖅᒪᑕ ᐊᔪᙱᓐᓂᕉᖅ ᐃᒡᓗᕙᖅᑖᖅᐅᓴᒥᐊᔪᖕᒪᑦ ᐃᑲᔪᕈᖕᓇᖀᖕᒐᑉᑕ ᐃᑲᔪᒥᐊᖅᐸᒋᐊᖅᑲᖅᑐᒍᑦ, ᐊᔪᖅᓴᕐᓂᖅᓴᐅᓕᕐᓂᑭᑉᑕᓕ ᐃᓯᒪᒋᔭᒃᓴᖅᑲᑭᒫᕐᑯᕝᓗᑕ.

In the old days, we had less than what we have today. For instance, things that we take for granted today were certainly not available then. For example, there were no social services, and we had to rely on ourselves to survive. We had to travel to areas where animals were abundant, and often had to travel a great distance when animals were not readily available close by; we had to go after them and search them out.

ᑕᒪᓐᓇ ᐱᕝᓗᒍ ᐃᓄᐃᑦ ᒥᐊᓂᕆᑐᕋᐅᑦᑎᐊᒻᒪᕆᐊᓗᒐᓯᒃᓱᑎᒃ ᑭᓯᐊᓂ ᐊᔪᖅᓴᕐᓇᖅᑐᓂᒃ ᐊᓂᒎᑎᔪᖕᓇᖅᐸᓚᐅᖅᐳᑦ ᐊᒃᓯᕈᖅᓱᑎᒃ ᐃᑲᔪᖅᑎᒌᑦᑎᐊᖅᓱᑎᓪᓗ. ᐃᑲᔪᖅᑎᒌᑦᑎᐊᕐᓂᖅ ᐊᔪᖅᓴᖅᑐᓂᓪᓗ ᑲᒪᑦᓯᐊᔪᓂᖅ ᐊᔪᙱᓐᓂᐅᑉ ᐃᓚᒋᖅᑲᑕᐅᖕᒪᒍ ᐱᕕᒌᓐᓇᕆᐊᖅᑲᖅᐸᕗᑦ. ᐅᖅᑲᒻᒫᔪᓚᐅᖅᒪᑕ ᐊᔪᙱᓐᓂᕉᖅ ᐃᒡᓗᕙᖅᑖᖅᐅᓴᒥᐊᔪᖕᒪᑦ ᐃᑲᔪᕈᖕᓇᖀᖕᒐᑉᑕ ᐃᑲᔪᒥᐊᖅᐸᒋᐊᖅᑲᖅᑐᒍᑦ, ᐊᔪᖅᓴᕐᓂᖅᓴᐅᓕᕐᓂᑭᑉᑕᓕ ᐃᓯᒪᒋᔭᒃᓴᖅᑲᑭᒫᕐᑯᕝᓗᑕ.

For this reason, Inuit had to really look after each other in order to pass through hard times; they had to work very hard and support each other. Helping those in need is part of being a good citizen, and we must always treasure it. Inuit used to say that good fortune usually passes on from one place to another, and that we should always be helpful whenever we are able to, so when it's our turn needing help others will think of us because of what we did for them.

ᐃᓕᒃᑕᕐᓂᒃᑕᐃᓕᓂᖅ ᓂᕐᔪᑎᑦ ᐊᒥᖏᓐᓂᒃ
AVOID SCORCHING ANIMAL SKINS

ᓂᕐᔪᑎᑉ ᒥᖅᑯᓕᐅᑉ ᐊᒥᖓᑕ ᒥᖅᑯᖏᓂᒃ ᐊᒥᖓᓂᓪᓘᓐᓃ ᐃᓕᒃᑕᕐᓂᒃᑕᐃᓕᓐᓂᓚᐅᖅᐳᑦ ᐆᑕᖅᑎᕐᓯᑦᑕᐃᓕᓐᓂᓚᐅᖅᐳᑦ, ᐃᑯᐊᓚᔪᒧᑦᑐ ᐃᓕᓯᑦᑕᐃᓕᕐᓗᑎᒃ ᐊᖑᓯᐃᓕᓱᐊᙱᔅᖢᑎᒃ, ᑎᓇᒐᓂᐊᔪᐃᓕᓱᐊᙱᔅᖢᑎᓪᓘᓐᓃ, ᐅᕝᕙᓘᓐᓃ ᖃᑯᒍᓴᖅ ᐊᑭᕝᕕᐅᓯᐊᙱᔅᖢᑎᒃ ᐱᓇᓱᖕᓇᕐᓂᕐᒧᑦ ᑲᐸᐊᓇᕐᓂᕐᒧᑦᓘᓐᓃ ᐱᔭᐅᓂᒃᑯᑦ.

It was forbidden for a person to burn off animal hair or throw animal skins into fire lest they become poor hunters, poor fox trappers, or experience no return for their efforts, and otherwise put themselves in great peril.

ᐃᓄᐃᑦ ᐅᓂᑉᑳᖅᑐᐊᕐᑯᑎᖅᑲᕐᒪᑕ ᐊᒥᓲᓂᒃ ᑐᑭᓯᐊᒃᑲᓐᓂᕈᑎᓂᒃ ᒫᓇ ᐃᔾᑉᑎᖕᓄᑦ ᑕᐅᑐᙱᖏᑕᑉᑎᖕᓂᒃ ᐊᑐᖅᓯᒪᙱᖏᑕᑉᑎᖕᓂᓪᓘᓐᓃ ᓱᓕ, ᑕᐃᒪᓕ ᐅᓂᑉᑳᖅᑐᐃᑦ ᐃᓚᖓᓐᓂ ᐃᒪᓇ ᐅᓂᑉᑳᖅᓯᒪᔪᖅᑳᖅᑐᖅ:

Inuit have many traditional stories that can help us understand things that are not visible to the naked eye, or teach us of situations and circumstances we have not yet experienced. There is one story that goes something like this:

ᑕᐃᒪᓐᓇᒎᖅ ᐊᖑᑦ ᓄᓵᖅᓯᖅᑐᖅ, ᓄᓕᐊᖓ ᐊᐅᓪᓚᕐᓂᕐᒪᑦ ᐅᓐᓄᐊᒥ. ᐊᖑᑎᒪᒎᖅ ᑐᕝᕙᖅᖢᒍ ᒪᓕᖅᑲᑦᑖᓕᓘ ᐅᓐᓄᐊᕉᑎᕐᓗᓂ ᐊᓪᓛᑦ ᐊᑕᐅᖅ ᐱᓯᒃᑐᐊᖅᖢᓂ. ᑐᕝᕙᖅᑲᑦᑖᕐᒪᒍᒎᖅ ᑕᑦᕿᑦᓯᐊᒥᐊᕐᒪᑦ ᑐᒪᐃᒎᖅ ᓯ’ᔭᑦ ᓇᓵᖕᓄᑦ ᑐᕌᕐᒪᑕ ᑐᒥᖏᒎᖅ ᐃᓪᓗᕆᔪᖕᓃᖅᖢᑎᒃ, ᑐᒥᐊᑕ ᐱᖅᑳ ᐃᓅᑉ ᑐᒥᕆᓪᓗᓂᐅᒃ, ᑐᒥᐊᑕᓕ ᐃᓪᓗᐊ ᑎᓇᒐᓂᐊᑉ ᑐᒥᕆᓪᓗᓂᐅᒃ.

Once there was a man who lost his wife. She had run away during the night. The man found her tracks and followed them on foot all day and into the night. Deep into the night he followed her tracks under the bright moonlight. The tracks headed towards a warren. As he got closer to the dens, the woman's tracks inexplicably changed. One was still a track of a human foot, but the other foot became a fox's track.

ᓯ’ᔭᓄᓕᓐᒪᖖᒎᖅ ᓂᕐᔪᑎᑦ ᐊᔾᔨᒌᙱᑦᑐᑦ ᐊᓂᕙᒃᓱᑎᒃ ᐱᕐᑯᑦᑕᕋᓗᐊᕐᒪᑕ, ᐱᔪᒪᙱᓗᒃᑖᖅᓱᓂᑎᑦ. ᐊᓂᔪᕐᑲᕐᒥᖕᒪᖖᒎᖅ ᐅᕐᑲᐅᑎᔭᐅᓕᖅᓱᓂ ᐃᑎᕐᓗᓂ ᐱᕐᑯᔭᐅᓕᖅᓱᓂ, ᑭᖕᒍᒻᒧᖖᒎᖅ ᓵᖖᒐᐃᓐᓇᕐᓗᓂ ᐃᑎᖅᑎᕐᓗᓂ. ᐃᑎᖅᑎᓕᕋᒥᒎᖅ ᓯᕗᒻᒧᑦ ᓵᑎᐊᒐᔮᓚᐅᕐᒪᑦ ᓯ’ᔭᐅᒻᖕᒎᖅ ᐹᖕᒐ ᓂᑳᒃᑯᕕᑦᑕᐊᑦᑎᐊᒥᐊᓇᐊᕐᒪᑦ ᑭᖕᒍᒻᒧᑦ ᓵᑦᓯᐊᒃᑲᓐᓂᖅᓱᓂ ᐃᑎᖅᓱᓂ ᓂᕐᔪᑎᑦ ᓯ’ᔭᐃᓄᑦ.

When he came up to the warren, different kinds of creatures came out of their dens to offer themselves as his partner, but he refused all of them. By and by, one came out and told him to come into its den, saying that he was to crawl in backwards as he entered. As he entered the den, he turned to see where he was going only for an instant, but the tunnel immediately started to shrink, so he turned away and was able to enter the den.

ᓱᓇᐅᕝᒍᖅ ᓯ'ᔭᓃᑦᑐᖅᑲᖅᓂᖅᑯᓂᑉᑕᐅᖅ ᐊᕕᖕᒐ'ᓈᖕᓂᒃ. ᐊᖑᒻᒥᒎᖅ ᐃᓕᑕᖅᓯᒪᒥᒃ ᐊᕕᙵ'ᓈᖅ ᐃᕕ'ᓈᒥᒃ ᑎᒍᒥᐊᖅᑯᓂ ᑳᐳᑎᒃᓴᒥᓂᒃ, ᐊᖑᒻᒥᒃ ᐅᖅᑕᖅᑐᒻᒫᖅᑯᓂ ᐅᖅᑲᑕᖅᐳᖅ. "ᐆ, ᑕᒡᕙ ᑖᒻᓇ ᐆᑕᖅᑎᒐ, ᐃᖅᑯᔨᒐ". ᐊᕕᙵᓈᒎᑦ ᑮᓇᖃᓗ'ᓈᒥᒃ ᐃᖅᑯᖕᒐᓗᖅᑭᔪ'ᓈᒃ, ᓱᓇᐅᕝᕙ ᑖᐸᓯᒪ ᐊᖑᑎᑉ ᐅᒃᑳᒍᑦ ᐃᓕᕝᓗᒥᒃ ᐆᑕᖅᑎᑦᑕᖅᓂᑯᕕᓂᒥᒃ.

He discovered that there were a couple of little lemmings in the den. One of them recognized the man and started wagging a blade of grass at him and said, "Oh, here is the man who burned and tortured me, and twisted my looks." The lemming's face was all crooked from having been tortured by the man.

ᑕᐃᒪᓕ ᐊᓯᐃᓖ, ᐊᖕᒐᔪᖅᑳᑉᑕ ᐅᖅᑲᐅᑎᕙᓚᐅᖅᐹᑎᒍᑦ ᓱᓇᒥᐊᓂᒃ ᐆᒪᔪᓂᒃ ᓂᖅᔪᑎᓂᒃ ᑎᖕᒥᖃᔭᒃᑐᓂᒡᒎᓐᓃᑦ ᓂᕕᐅᕙᖃᓗᖕᓂᒃ, ᐹᒻᖑᖅᑐᓂᒡᒎᓐᓃᑦ ᒪᓂᖅᑲᒥ ᐱᑦᓯᐊᖅᐸᖅᑯᓚᐅᖅᐹᑎᒍᑦ ᐱᔭᕆᑦᑕᐃᓕᓗᒋᑦ, ᒥᐊᓂᕆᖅᑎᐊᖕᒫᖅᓗᒋᑦᓕ ᐱᖅᑯᕝᓗᑕ ᐊᔪᖅᑭᖅᑐᖅᐸᓚᐅᖅᐹᑎᒍᑦ.

Our parents used to tell us to treat all living things, like birds, insects, crawling things on the ground, and other animals, with care and respect: to not mistreat them, but to be concerned for their well-being.

ᑕᒪᓐᓇ ᓱᓕᒻᒪᕆᒃᑐᖅ, ᓱᓇᓗᒃᑖᑦ ᓄᓇᒥ ᐆᒪᔪᑦ ᒥᐊᓂᖅᓯᔨᑲᖅᒪᑕ, ᓇᐅᑦᓯᖅᑐᖅᑎᖅᑲᖅᓗᑎᓪᓗ, ᑕᒪᓐᓇ ᐱᕝᓗᒍ ᐅᕙᑉᑎᖕᓂᒃ ᒥᐊᓂᕆᒃᑲᑉᑕᑐᑦ, ᐊᕙᑎᑉᑎᖕᓂᑦᑐᑦᑕᐅᖅ ᒥᐊᓂᕆᑦᑎᐊᕆᐊᖅᑲᖅᐸᕗᑦ ᓱᒥᒃ ᐃᓕᒪᓯᙱᑦᓗᑕ ᐃᓅᑦᓯᐊᖃᐅᔭᕈᐊᕈᑉᑕ.

This is true, as every living thing on the land has a guardian watching over it, just as we watch out for ourselves. We must also be mindful of everything around us if we want to live peacefully without the constant fear that something bad will happen to us.

ᐃᓕᓰᓪᕈᑦ
EVIL SPELLS

ᖃᖓᓴᒃᑲᓐᓂᖅ ᐃᓄᐃᑦ ᐃᓕᖅᑯᓯᑐᖃᒻᒪᕆᖕᒥᖕᓂᒃ ᐃᓅᓯᖅᑲᑕᐅᖅᑎᓪᓗᒋᑦ ᑐᓴᐅᒪᓇᖅᐳᖅ ᐃᓚᖕᒋᑦ ᐃᓕᓰᓪᕈᑎᖃᖅᓂᖁᐅᕙᓚᐅᖅᒪᑕ, ᓂᑉᑕᖕᒋᑦᑐᒃᑯᑦ ᐱᓂᖅᓗᒃᑎᑦᓯᔾᔪᑎᓂᒃ. ᖃᐅᔨᒪᓗᐊᙱᑦᑕᕋᓗᐊᒃᑲ, ᑭᓯᐊᓂ ᐱᒻᒪᕆᐅᑕᐅᖅᓯᒪᓂᖕᒋᑦ ᐅᒃᐱᕆᔭᒃᑲ.

Long ago, when Inuit still lived their traditional lifestyle, it is said that some of them could cast evil spells secretly on people and cause bad situations and circumstances for them. I do not have full knowledge of this subject, but I believe what I have heard to be true.

ᐃᓕᓰᓪᕈᑎᑦ ᑐᒃᓯᐅᑎᑎᑐᑦ ᓲᖅᓗ ᐃᓯᒪᒋᓲᖅᑕᒃᑲ, ᓴᓇᓯᒪᕙᖕᒪᑕ ᐅᖅᑲᐅᓯᖅᑕᓕᐅᖅᓯᒪᕙᓗᑎᒃ ᐅᖅᑲᐅᓯᑐᐃᓐᓇᐅᖕᒋᑦᑐᑦ ᓱᑎᑦᓯᓱᖅᑐᑦ ᐊᑐᒐᐅᕙᓗᑎᒃ, ᐃᓅᑉ ᐃᓕᖅᑯᓯᓇᓇᔭᑕᐅᙱᑦᑕᖓᓂᒃ ᓱᑎᑦᓯᓱᖅᑐᑦ, ᖃᓄᐃᓕᑎᑦᓯᓱᖅᑐᑦ ᐱᑦᓴᐅᖕᒋᓐᓂᖅᒧᑦ ᐃᓕᖕᒐᓕᖅᑎᑦᓯᓱᖅᑐᑦ.

I tend to regard evil spells as being similar to prayers, because they are also designed in such a way with words that can cause something to happen by reciting them. Evil spells can cause something unexpected to happen to a person, causing them to fall into something evil.

ᐃᒻᒪᖄ ᑐᑭᓯᓐᓇᖅᓯᕚᓪᓕᖅᓴᖅᒥᔪᖅ ᐃᓕᓰᓪᕈᑦ ᖃᓄᖅ ᐊᑐᖅᑕᐅᕙᖕᓂᖅᒪᖔᑦ ᑐᓴᒐᔮᖕᒥᓗᑕ ᐅᓂᑉᑳᖅᑐᐊᒥᑦ ᐱᔭᒥᒃ. ᐊᒥᓱᓂᖅ ᑐᓴᐅᒪᔭᐅᔪᒃᓴᐅᒐᖅ ᐃᓄᐃᑦ ᐅᓂᑉᑳᖅᑐᐊᖕᒐᑦ ᖃᖓᓂᑕᖅᓯᐊᖅ, ᐊᓈᓇᑕᐅᖅᒪ ᐸᐅᖅᖓ'ᓈᑉ ᐅᓂᑉᑳᕋᔪᓚᐅᒎ, ᐊᖅᕕ'ᔫᑉ ᐅᔭᖅᒍᖅᑎᑦᓯᓂᖓ ᐃᓄᖕᓂᒃ, ᐱᖅᑯᑎᓂᒃ, ᕿᒻᒥᓂᒃ ᓱᓇᓗᒃᑖᓂᓪᓗ ᐃᓕᓰᒐᐅᔪᑉ ᐊᒃᑐᐊᔭᖕᒋᓐᓂᒃ. ᐃᒪᓐᓇᐃᑦᑐᖅ ᐅᓂᑉᑳᖅᑐᐊᑉ ᐃᓚᖓ:

Perhaps evil spells and how they were used can be explained by listening to something from a story. Many Inuit have probably heard of this old story that my late mother, Paurnga'naaq (my dear little Paurngat), often told. It's a story of a narwhal that turned people, their possessions, their dogs, and everything into stones by reciting an evil spell on them. This is how the story goes:

ᐃᒪᓐᓇᐃᑦᑐᖅ ᐅᓂᑉᑳᖅᑐᐊᑉ ᐃᓚᖓ, ᑕᐃᑉᑯᐊᒎᖅ ᓂᕕᐊᖅᓯᐊᑦ ᓯᓚᒥ ᐱᙳᐊᖅᑐᑦ ᐅᐃᙳᐊᖅᑲᖅᑐᖅᓱᑎᒃ, ᐃᓚᖓᑦ ᐅᔭᖓᒥᒃ, ᐃᓚᖓᑦ ᓇᒃᑐᕋᓚᖕᒥᒃ ᐊᒻᒪ ᐃᓚᖓᑦ ᐊᕐᕕᕝᕙᐊᕐᒥᒃ ᐃᒫᓃᑦᑐᒥᒃ. ᐅᔭᖅᑲᒥᒎᖅ ᐅᐃᙳᐊᖅᑲᖅᑐᖅ ᐅᔭᖁᖅᓱᓂ, ᐊᒻᒪ ᓇᒃᑐᕋᓚᖕᒥᒃ ᐅᐃᙳᐊᖅᑲᖅᑐᖅ ᓇᒃᑐᕋᓚᐅᑉ ᑭᙵᕝᕙᐊᕐᒧᑦ ᑭᖕᒋᒃᑐᒧᑦ ᓇᒃᓴᖅᓱᓂᐅᒃ. ᐊᕐᕕᕝᕙᐊᕐᒥᒎᖅ ᐅᐃᙳᐊᖅᑲᖅᑐᖅ, ᐊᕐᕕᕝᕚᑉ ᕿᑭᖅᑕᒧᑦ ᐊᒡᒋᑎᖕᓗᓂᐅᒃ, ᓴᐅᓂᕝᕙᐊᖏᓂᒃ ᐃᒡᓗᖅᑲᓚᖅᓱᑎᒃ.

One day, three young maidens were playing outside, and they decided to choose pretend husbands for themselves. One of them chose a stone, another a bald eagle, and the third, a huge narwhal that was swimming in the water nearby. The one who had chosen the stone herself turned into a stone. The one who had chosen the bald eagle was plucked up by an eagle and taken up to a high cliff. The one who had chosen the narwhal rode off on the back of the narwhal and was taken to an island that was the home of the whale. Their dwelling was made from the bones of a whale.

ᑕᐃᒻᓇᒎᖅ ᓂᕕᐊᖅᓯᐊᑦ ᐃᓚᖓᑦ ᐅᔭᖅᑲᒥᒃ ᐅᐃᙳᐊᕐᑲᓚᐅᖅᑐᖅ ᐅᔭᖁᓚᐅᕝᕙᐊᕐᒪᑦ, ᑖᒻᓇᓗ ᓇᒃᑐᕋᓚᖕᒥᒃ ᐅᐃᖑᐊᓕᒃ ᐊᕕᙵᐃᑦ ᐃᕆᓗᐃᓂᒃ ᐱᑦᖃᖅᑲᑦᑖᖅᓱᓂ ᐊᑦᖅᑲᒍᑎᒃᓴᓚᐅᖑᓚᐅᖃᒥ, ᖅᑲᐃᓐᓇᑦ (ᖅᑲᔭᐃᑦ) ᓴᑦᕈᓚᕐᒪᑕ ᐃᖕᒥᓂᒃ ᓂᖏᑎᒃᓱᓂ ᐃᑭᔭᐅᖕᓗᓂ. ᑕᐃᒻᓇᒎᖅ ᐊᕐᕕᕝᕙᐊᕐᒥᒃ ᐅᐃᙳᐊᓕᒃ ᐊᖑᑎᓂᑦ ᖅᑲᔭᖅᑐᖅᑐᓂᑦ ᐃᑭᔭᐅᖕᓗᓂ ᓴᑐᒐᐅᖕᒪᑦ.

The one who had chosen the stone for her pretend husband turned into stone permanently. The one who had chosen the eagle for her pretend husband, in a bid to escape, started braiding a thong from lemming skins to climb down the cliff. As a group of qajait passed by, she jumped the last length of the rope into the water and got on one of the qajait. Meanwhile, the girl who had pretended to be married to a whale was retrieved and picked up by the men of her camp on their qajait.

ᐊᕐᕕ’ᔦᐊᕉᖅ ᖃᐅᕚᒥ ᖃᔭᖅᑐᖅᑐᑦ ᒪᓕᒃᑯᑎᑦ ᓴᑐᖅᓯᔭᖅᑐᕐᓂᑐᓕᖁᑐᐊᕐᒪᑦ, ᐊᖕᖑᑎᖕᒋᑕᐃᓐᓇᖁᒥ ᓄᓇᓕᐅᔦᓄᑦ ᐅᖃᓕᖅᐳᖅ ᓂᖕᖓᒃᑲᒥ, "ᖃᓄᖅᑐᖅ ᐸᑭᑉᑯᐊ ᐅᔭᖁᑦᑐᕐᑕᖁ!"

When the whale discovered what had happened to his "bride," he immediately went after the qajait in an attempt to get her back. He couldn't catch up. He was enraged and cursed the people of the camp: "May you all become stones!"

ᑕᐃᒪᑰᖅ ᐊᕐᕕ’ᔦᑉ ᓄᓇᓕ ᐃᓕᑰᑦᕈᓯᕐᒪᑎᑦ ᓯᓇᑐᒃᑖᕐᓯᐊᒥᖕᒋᑦ ᐅᔭᖁᖖᑐᓚᐅᖅᓯᒪᕗᑦ, ᐃᓄᐃᑦ, ᕿᒻᒥᖁᑐᖕᒋᑦ ᐱᕐᑯᑕᐃᑐ.

Because the whale cast a spell on them, they and everything they owned all turned into stone—the people, their dogs, and their personal possessions turned into stone.

ᖃᖕᒐᓴᕉᖅ ᐊᒡᓛᑦ ᐃᓄᐃᑦ ᕿᒻᒥᑦ ᕿᑐᕐᖕᒐᕕᓂᖁᑐᖕᒋᓐᓂᒃ ᑕᑦᕐᑯᑎᒃᓴᖅᓯᕙᓕᓚᐅᖅᑐᑦ, ᐅᔭᖁᖁᐅᔭ’ᓈᑎᐊᑐᒃᑯᕝᖑᖕᒪᑕᑰᖅ ᓇᐱ’ᓈᖅᑯᑎᑦ ᑕᑦᕐᑯᑎᒃᓴᖅᓯᕙᓕᓚᐅᖅᑐᑦ.

In fact, a long time ago Inuit used to go to that place and collect lengths of stone that were apparently once dog leashes, to use them for fixing the flames of their qullit. They were nice, long, slender pieces of stone. People would snap them in half and use as them as *taqqut* (wick trimmers) for their qullit.

ᐃᑦᓗᐃᔭᐅᑦ ᑏᕐᓗᒃ
TREATING SNOW BLINDNESS

ᖃᖕᒐᓴᖅ ᑏᕐᓗᐃᑦ ᓯᖅᑳᓚᑦ ᐃᑦᓗᐃᔭᐅᑕᐅᓂᓗᔪᓚᐅᖅᐳᑦ ᐃᔨᖕᓄᑦ ᐃᓕᓯᒪᒥᐊᖅᓱᑎᑦ. ᐅᐱᕐᖓᒃᓴᒥ ᐅᕝᓗᖅᑐᓯᔭᕌᖓᑦ, ᓯᕿᓐᓂᖅᑕᑦᑖᒡᒍᓂᖅᓴᐅᓕᖅᓱᓂ ᐊᐳᑦᓗ ᖃᑯᑦᓯᐊᓯᒥᐊᖅᓱᓂ ᐃᒡᒐᖅᓯᒪᙱᔅᓱᓂ ᕿᖕᒐᕐᓇᑦᓯᐊᒥᐊᓕᔪᖕᒪᑦ. ᐃᒡᒐᐃᑦᑑᖅᑲᑦᑖᕐᓗᓂ ᐊᓃᖅᑐᓂ ᐃᑦᓗᖕᓇᓯᓯᕐᒪᑦ, ᐅᐃᑕᓯᐊᕐᓇᕈᖕᓇᐃᖅᓗᓂ, ᐊᒻᒪᓗ ᐃᔩᒃ ᖁᕝᕕᐅᑦᓯᐊᒥᐊᖅᑕᖅᓱᑎᒃ ᐊᐅᐸᓗᒃᓯᕝᓗᑎᒡᓗ, ᑎᐊᑦᓇᐃᓕᓐᓇᖅᓯᓯᕐᒪᑦ ᐅᐱᕐᖓᒃᓴᒥ.

Long ago, they used to apply wet, loose tea leaves directly from a cup on the eyelids to try to treat snow blindness. In the springtime, when days become longer, the sun shines longer on the pure white snow, and this can be very hard on the eyes.

ᐊᓕᒃᑯᓂᒃ ᑖᖅᑐᓂᒃ ᐃᒪᓛᓕᖕᓂᒃ ᐃᒡᒐᖃᔪᓯᖅᑳᖅᑎᓐᓇᒥᑦ, ᐃᓄᐃᑦ ᐃᒡᒐᖃᔪᓚᐅᖅᐳᑦ ᓇᒡᔪᕐᓂᒃ ᓴᓂᒧᑦ ᐊᖕᒪᕋᐅᔭᖅᓯᒪᔪ’ᓈᓂᒃ ᐃᑦᓗᓕᓅᒃᑯᑎᓂᒃ.

You need to wear sunglasses in this brightness; otherwise if you're out there with no sunglasses, you may suffer snow blindness, and you may not be able to keep your eyes open. You begin to uncontrollably shed tears, and your eyes turn bleary red in the brightness of the springtime.

ᐃᔨᕗᑦ ᑲᒪᒋᑦᓯᐊᖅᐸᕆᐊᖃᒃᑲᕗᑦ ᐃᑦᓗᖕᓇᖅᓯᔭᕌᖓᑦ ᐃᒡᒐᖅᓯᒪᕕᒡᓗᑕ ᐃᑦᓗᓕᓅᒃᑯᑎᓂᒃ.

Before sunglasses with dark lenses became available to us, Inuit used to wear snow goggles made of caribou antler with very narrow eye slits designed to cut the glare to avoid snow blindness. We must take good care of our eyes in the springtime by wearing sunglasses to avoid snow blindness.

ᐃᒋᑦᓯᓂᖅ ᑲᒥᖕᒥᒃ
THROWING A PAIR OF KAMIIK

ᐅᓇᑕᖅᑐᖅᑲᑦᑐᐊᖅᑎᓪᓗᒍᒎᖅ ᐊᕐᓇᖅᑯᐊᒃᓵ’ᓈᖅ ᓴᐳᔾᔨᓂᓗᓯᒋᐊᖅ ᐊᖖᒍᑎᓚᐃᖅᒥ ᓱᓗᕿᑐᖅᐅᖖᒋᓚᐅᕐᓂᒋᖕᓂ, ᐃᒡᓗᐊᓂᒃ ᑲᒥᑦᑖᑦᑕᒃᑰᓂ ᑲᒥᖕᒥ ᐃᒡᓗᐊ ᐊᑯᖖᒐᖕᖏᑦ ᐃᒋᒥᐊᕐᒪᒍ ᓴᐳᔾᔨᓚᐅᖅᓯᒪᕗᖅ, ᐅᓇᑕᓚᐅᖅᑑᒐᓗᐊᒃ ᓴᑉᑯᑐᕐᐅᔅᓱᑎᒃ ᐅᒡᒍᐊᕐᓇᖅᑐᒥᒃ ᐱᔪᕐᑲᓚᐅᖅᑎᓐᓇᒍ.

Once upon a time, a little old lady tried to intervene in a fight between two men. Realizing that she would not be able to get there in time before they got into real trouble, she took one of her kamiik and flung it between them to stop them. The men, fortunately, let each other go before anything happened that would cause them sorrow.

ᖃᖓᓴᖅ ᐃᓐᓇ’ᕗᐃᑦ, ᐅᑐᖅᑲᐃᑦ ᐊᕐᓇᖅᑯᐊᒃᓵᑦᓗ ᐅᐱᒋᔭᐅᕐᕗᐊᑦᓯᐊᒥᐊᓚᐅᖅᓯᒪᖕᒪᑕ ᓯᓚᑐᓂᖕᒋᑦ, ᖃᓄᖅᓗᒃ ᐱᑎᑦᓯᓂᖕᒋᑦ ᓈᑦᑕᓇᒃᓴᒐᐅᕙᓚᐅᖅᐸᑦ, ᖃᐅᔨᒪᔭᐅᒻᒪᒍᑎᒃ ᐱᑦᓴᐅᓂᕐᒧᑦ ᓯᕗᓪᓕᖅᑎᐅᖕᒪᑕ, ᐊᑉᑯᑎᑦᓴᐅᓂᐅᓇᔭᖅᑐᒃᑯᑦ, ᐃᓅᓯᑦᑕᐅᓂᐅᓇᔭᖅᑐᒃᑯᑦᓗ ᑕᓯᐅᖅᑎᐅᖕᒪᑕ.

Long ago, Elders—old men and old women—were deeply respected for their wisdom. Whatever they advised was done right away, because people knew the advice was for their own good. The Elders were leaders for their wisdom, for knowing which route was best to take, and for what was for the greater good.

ᐃᖅᑲᓪᓚᐊᕐᓂᐊᑦ ᐊᖅᑯᑦᓱᐃᑦᑐᑦ
ONE MUST NEVER SAY THEY'RE GOING FISHING TOMORROW

ᐃᖅᑲᓪᓚᐊᕐᓂᐊᑦ ᖃᖓᓴᖅ ᐊᖅᑯᓐᓂᐊᕐᓂᖃᖅᑕᐃᓕᓱᓚᐅᖅᑐᑦ ᐃᖅᑲᓗᒃᓱᐃᓕᓱᐊᙱᔅᔪᑎᒎᖅ. ᑕᒪᓐᓇ ᐃᓄᐃᑦ ᐅᒃᐱᕆᔭᖅᑲᐅᓯᑐᖅᑲᖓᑦ ᒪᓕᒐᐅᖃᐅᔾᒥᐊᓚᐅᖅᑐᖅ ᐃᒻᒪᖄ ᐃᓱᒪᕐᓗᑎᒃ ᐃᖅᑲᓗᒃ ᑐᓴᐅᒫᑕᕈᒥ ᐃᖅᑲᓪᓚᐊᕈᒫᖅᑐᒥᒃ ᖃᖅᖁᖅᓴᒥᒃ ᑰᓯᓱᐊᓚᙱᓐᓇᓱᕆᕐᓗᒍ.

Long ago, people who planned to go fishing avoided saying they were leaving tomorrow to go out and fish. They avoided speaking outright of their plans so they would not have a hard time catching fish. This was a traditional belief of Inuit. Perhaps it is based on the thinking that fish might not want to bite at a fisherman's hook because they already knew he was out there to catch them.

ᑭᓯᐊᓂ ᖃᖓᓴᖅ ᐃᖅᑲᓗᐃᑦ ᐃᓅᓂᓗᙴᑕᐅᕙᓚᐅᖅᒥᖕᒪᑕ, ᑐᒃᑐᖅᑲᑦᓯᐊᖕᒋᑦᓴᖐᖕᒐᑦ ᓂᖅᑲᐃᓪᓕᐅᓕᖐᖕᒐᒥᒡᓗ ᐊᓐᓇᖕᓂᓗᒋᐊᖅᐸᓚᐅᖅᒥᖕᒪᑕ ᐃᖅᑲᓗᖕᓄᑦ, ᑕᓯᖅᓂᓗ ᐃᖅᑲᓗᖅᑲᖅᓂᖅᓂ ᓄᓇᖅᑲᖁᓚᐅᖅᑐᑦ ᐊᐅᓚᓴᖅᕕᑦᓯᐊᑎᒃᑐᓂ.

In any case, long ago, fish were also the main source of food to keep Inuit from starving when caribou were scarce. That is why Inuit generally chose lakes with fish that were easy to catch with the hook-and-line method.

ᐅᕝᓗᒥᐅᓕᖅᑐᖅ ᐅᖅᑲᐅᓯᑐᖅᑲᐃᑦ ᑕᐃᒎᓰᑦ ᐃᓚᖕᒋᑦ ᐊᑐᕙᐃᑦᑑᓕᖃᑉᑎᒥᒃ, ᐊᑕᐅᖅ ᐊᑐᙱᓪᓖᓕᖃᑉᑎᒥᒃ, ᓲᖅᓗ ᐃᓄᒃ ᐅᖅᑲᖅᐸᑦ "ᖃᐅᒪᓂᖅᓯᐅᑎᐊᓚᐅᖅᓂᐊᖃᒪ," ᖃᖓᓴᐅᒃᐸᑦ ᑐᑭᓯᓇᔭᖅᐸᑦ ᐃᖅᑲᓪᓚᐊᖅᓂᐊᖅᓂᖃᖅᒪᑦ. ᐃᒻᒪᖄ "ᖃᐅᒪᓂᖅᒥᒃ" ᑕᐃᔭᐅᓚᖅᑭᔾᔪᑎᒋᕙᖕᒐ ᐊᒡᓗᐊᖅ ᐊᖕᒪᖐᖕᒐᑦ ᐊᖕᒪᖅᓂᖕᒐ ᐃᒪᖅᒥᒃ ᖃᐅᒻᒪᐃᙵᖕᒪᑦ ᓯᑯᑉ ᐊᑖᓂ. ᑕᐃᒪᓕ ᐃᖅᑲᓗᐃᑦ ᖃᐅᒪᓂᖅᑐᑦ ᓄᔭᐃᓯᓕᖐᖕᒐᑦ ᖃᖅᔭᖅᓴᖅᑕᖅᑲᒻᒫᖅᓗᓂ ᐃᖅᑲᓗᓚᒃᔭᑕᐅᒃᑲᓂᔭᓇᓱᕆᓗᒍ ᐃᓱᒪᓇᖅᐳᖅ.

Today, we are no longer using some of the old sayings, because we are no longer living in an age when they were used originally. For example, people used to say, *Qaumaniqsiurialaurniarama* (I am going to go and cast light under a hole). In the old days, we took for granted that the person saying that meant that they were going fishing through the ice.

ᐃᖁᖕᒪᔪᖕᒫ
"I HAVE A LOPSIDED FACE"

ᖃᖓᓯᖅ ᐃᒡᓗᒥᑦ ᑖᖅᑎᓪᓗᒍ ᐊᒃᑎᓕᖅᖕᒪᒥᒃ ᐃᒪᓐᓇᐃᓕᐅᔪᓚᐅᖅᐳᑦ, "ᐃᖁᖕᒪᔪᖕᒫ, ᐃᖁᖕᒪᔪᖕᒪ. ᐃᖁᖕᒪᔪᖕᒫ, ᐃᖁᖕᒪᔪᖕᒪ" ᓯᓇᒧᑦ ᑲᐱᐊᓇᖅᑐᒧᑦ ᑑᖅᖕᒪᖅᑕᖕᒧᑦ ᐸᐃᔮᒧᓪᓘᕙ ᐱᔮᓯᐊᙵᕆᒧᑦ, ᑮᓇᖅᒥᖕᓂᒃ ᐃᖁᒻᒥᖕᓂᒃᑯᑎᒃ ᐊᒃᑎᙵᐊᖅᐸᓚᐅᖅᑐᑦ ᖄᓕᖅᑕᓇᖅᓂᖅᓴᐅᓯᐊᒧᑦ.

Long ago, whenever Inuit came out of their igluit at night, they would call out, "I have a lopsided face! I have a lopsided face!" to protect themselves from being captured by *paijaa* (evil snow spirits). They would twitch their mouth downwards to one side to make a funny face as they stepped out, and try to display a scarier face than whatever bogeyman was waiting out there.

ᖃᖓᓯᖅ ᓄᑕᖄᕆᓪᓗᑕ ᑖᖅᓂᖅᒥᒃ ᑲᐱᐊᖅᑕᐅᕆᓪᓗᑕ ᓯᓕ ᑕᒪᓐᓇ ᐅᒃᐱᓇᕙᓚᐅᖅᓯᒪᔭᕗᑦ ᓯᓕᔫᓇᓯᕆᕙᓪᓗᒍᓗ ᐃᓯᒪᕙᒃᑲᑕ ᑲᐱᐊᓯᙳᕆᑉᐹᑦᓚᕈᑎᕆᕙᓚᐅᒃᑲᕗᑦ ᑖᖅᑎᓪᓗᒍ ᐊᒃᑎᓕᖅᖕᒪᑉᑕ. ᑖᖅᓯᔭᖅᖕᒪᑦ ᐊᑕᐅᖅᑲ ᓯᓇᒥᐊᑦ ᓂᑉᑕᔪᖕᓇᐃᖅᑯᑎᒃ, ᖁᑳᖅᓯᕆᓪᓗᑎᒡᓗ, ᓂᑉᑕᖅᓚᒃᑲᓗᐊᖅᑯᑎᒡᓗ ᐃᓕᑕᖅᓇᕐᓯᐊᕈᖕᓇᐃᖅᐸᖕᒪᑕ, ᐅᐊᔫᔭᓕᖅᑯᑎᒃ ᐊᒡᓛᑦ ᐃᓛᓐᓂ.

In the old days, when we were children and easily scared, we used to be terrified of stepping out into the dark. We so believed the saying to be true that we felt emboldened to step out into darkness simply by displaying a more scary face. And for what it's worth, of course in the dark everything is nearly invisible and hard to make out, and sometimes shadow phantoms seemingly move about in one's diminished vision.

ᐃᖅᑲᓗᖕᒥᒃ ᐊᓐᓇᐃᓂᖅ
THE FISH THAT GOT AWAY: FISHING BELIEFS

ᐃᖅᑲᓗᒃ ᐊᒧᖅᑲᔭᖅᓯᓐᓇᕐᓗᓂ ᐊᓐᓇᒃᐸᑦ ᐅᑎᖅᑳᓴᒪᐅᓇᔭᖅᐳᖅ ᐃᒪᓐᓇᐃᓕᐅᕐᓗᓂ, "ᖅᑲᖅᑲᖅᑲᖅᑳ" ᐅᕝᕙᓘᕝᕙ "ᖅᑲᖅᑲᖅᑲᖅᑳᖅ." (ᖅᑲᖅᓴᐅᖅᐸᓗᒃᑐᑦ ᓲᕐᓗ). ᐃᓚᖏᓗ "ᖅᑭᕙᑦᑐᐃᑦᑐᖕᒪᑖ, ᖅᑭᕙᑦᑕᐃᑖᓐᓇᑖ, ᖅᑳᖅᑲ, ᖅᑲᖅᑳ, ᖅᑲᖅᑳ, ᖅᑲᖅᑳ." ᐅᕝᕙᓘᓐᓃᑦ "ᑮᓗᒎ, ᑮᓗᒎ."

When a fish flopped and got away just before you pulled it out of the fishing hole, you would try to recover it by saying, "*qaq-qa-qaq-qaa*" or "*qa-qa-qa-qaa*" (making a noise like the loon). Some people would say, "I don't give up easily: *qaa, qaa, qaa, qaa*," or they'd say, "Take the bite, take the bite" repeatedly.

ᑕᐃᑉᓯᒪᓂ ᐅᑭᐅᒥ ᓯᑯᖃᓕᖅᑐᒥ ᐊᐳᑎᖃᓕᖅᑎᑦᑐᒍᓗ ᐃᖃᑦᓕᐊᕐᓂᖅ ᖁᕕᐊᓇᕕᒡᔪᐊᖅᐸᓚᐅᖅᓯᒪᔪᖅ ᐊᒡᓗᐊᖅᑐᕐᕕᖕᓄᑦ (ᐊᒡᓗᐊᖃᕐᕕᖕᓄᑦ) ᐱᓲᔭᖅᔪᓂ ᐃᖃᑦᓕᐊᓕᖅᑐᓂ. ᖃᕐᔪᖅᓴᑦ ᑕᐃᒎᓯᕋᓘᔭᖕᒋᑦ ᑐᓵᑦᑑᖅᐸᒃᐸᒃᑲ ᓯᑕ, ᓲᕐᓗ ᒪᑯᐊ:

- ᖃᕐᔪᖅᓴᖅ: ᓴᕕᐅᓂᖓ ᓂᐅᖓᔪᖅ ᑲᑭᓯᔾᔪᑎᖓ
- ᒥᑭᒃᓱᒍᑦ: ᓴᕕᐅᓂᖓᓄᑦ ᐃᓕᓯᒪᔪᖅ ᐃᖃᓘᑉ ᐊᕿᐊᒍᖓ ᓇᓕᐊᖅ
- ᑎᑉᔭᖅ: ᖃᕐᔪᖅᓴᐅᑉ ᐅᖁᒪᐃᑐᑕᖓ ᑑᒑᖅ ᐅᕝᕙᓘᕝᕙ ᓇᒡᔪᒃ
- ᒪᓇᖅ: ᐃᖃᓘᑉ ᐸᐱᕈᐊ ᓴᐅᓂᕐᒥᒃ ᓴᓐᓂᕈᐊᒃᓴᒥᒃ ᐃᑦᓕᓕᓯᒪᔪᖅ
- ᐃᐱᐅᑕᖅ: ᖃᕐᔪᖅᓴᐅᑉ ᐃᐱᐅᑖ ᐃᕙᓗ ᐱᑦᖃᖅᓯᒪᔪᖅ
- ᐊᐅᓚᔾᔪᑦ: ᖃᕐᔪᖅᓴᐅᑉ ᐃᐱᐅᑕᖓᑕᓗ ᑎᒍᒻᒥᕕᖓ ᕿᔪᒃ ᐅᕝᕙᓗ ᐊᓯᐊ

As children, we had lots of fun going down to the frozen lake to the fishing holes in the season when there was still snow on the ground. Thinking of this, it reminds me of various traditional Inuktut terms I used to hear being used to describe traditional fishing equipment:

- *qarjuqsaq*: a length of stiff metal rod bent and fabricated in a way to hook and ensnare a fish by the mouth
- *mikiksugut:* bait; fish viscera placed on the hook as bait to attract prey fish
- *tipjaq:* the weight of a hook, usually made of a bulb of walrus tusk or caribou antler anchored on the hook
- *manaq:* a straight bone hook and line placed in the fish tail
- *ipiutaq*: thin fishing line made of continuously braided caribou sinew
- *aulajjut*: a hook-and-line handle, made of a piece of wood or something else

ᒪᓇᐅᓂᕋᐃᓯᓚᐅᖅᐳᑦ ᓴᓇᓯᒪᔪᒥᒃ ᐃᖃᓘᑉ ᐸᐱᕈᐊᓂᒃ, ᐅᕝᕙᓘᕝᕙ ᖃᕐᔪᖅᓴᒥᒃ ᐊᒡᓗᐊᕐᒧᑦ ᐃᒫᖅᓯᒪᓗᒍ ᐅᑕᖅᑭᑦᑎᓯᓂᖅ ᑮᔭᐅᑦᓯᐊᓇᓗᒍ ᐅᕝᕙᓗ ᐄᔭᐅᑦᓯᐊᓇᕝᓗᒍ.

Manaq is usually hung down the ice hole or fishing hole; it is designed to wait for fish to nibble on it and swallow it, and to be reeled in.

ᐃᓄᒃᓯᓚᐅᑎᔭᐅᓂᖅ
A STONE MARKER

ᐃᓄᒃ ᓴᒡᓗᑐᓗᐊᖅᐸᑦ ᐃᓄᒃᓱᒃᑎᑐᑦ ᒪᓂᖅᑲᒥ ᐃᓯᒪᕆᔭᐅᓇᔭᖅᐳᖅ, ᐃᓄᒃᓯᓚᐅᑎᔭᐅᔪᑦ ᓴᖅᑮᔭᑦᓯᐊᓚᕐᓗᓂ ᖃᑦᖃᒥ ᓴᒡᓗᑐᓂ'ᔪᐊᖕᒐ ᑭᑐᒃᑖᓂᑦ ᑕᐅᑐᒐᐅᓚᕐᓗᓂ.

When a person is a habitual liar, he is thought of as a stone marker on the land. He is like placing a stone marker on the land so everyone knows he is a habitual liar.

ᐃᓄᐃᑦ ᐊᑕᐅᖅᑳᐸᑕᐅᖅ ᓴᒡᓗᕐᑯᐹᓯᐃᑦᑑᓚᐅᕐᒪᑕ, ᖃᐅᔨᒪᕙᓗᑎᒃ ᓴᒡᓗᓂᖅ ᓈᒻᒪᖕᖏᒻᒪᑦ ᐊᒻᒪᓗ ᐱᕋᓪᓚᒍᑕᐅᔪᖕᓇᖅᓗᓂ ᐱᑦᓯᐊᖕᖏᓚᕈᑕᐅᓗᓂᓘᓐᓃᑦ. ᓴᒡᓗᑐᐃᓐᓂᖅ, ᒥᒃᓱᖃᖅᑐᓚᓂᕐᓗ ᐃᓅᓯᓇᓂᓗᕐᑯᔭᐅᕙᓗᓂ ᐅᖃᐅᔾᔪᐃᑦᔪᑕᐅᕙᓚᐅᖅᐳᖅ ᐊᖕᒐᔪᖅᑳᐸᑎᖕᓂᑦ ᐃᓄᑐᖃᓇᔭᐸᑎᖕᓂᓪᓗ.

Inuit did not like being told lies, knowing that lying is wrong and can cause a lot of trouble or upset good relationships. Our parents encouraged us to live in honesty and be truthful in our family and among other people.

ᐃᓱᒪᓂᕐᓗᖕᓂᖅ
HARBOURING EVIL THOUGHTS

ᐱᑦᓯᐊᖅᓯᖅᑐᑦᓚᕐᒥᓗ ᓱᐃᓐᓇᕐᒧᑦ ᐱᑦᓯᐊᕐᓇᖏᑦᑐᒧᑦᓘᕝᕙ ᐱᔭᐅᑎᑦᓯᓂᓗᖕᓂᖅ ᐊᓯᒥᓂᒃ. ᐱᐅᖏᑦᑐᒥᒃ ᐃᖅᑲᖅᓴᐅᑎᕐᑲᕐᓗᓂ ᐃᓱᒪᑦᑎᐊᖕᒋᓐᓂᖅ ᐱᐅᖏᑦᑐᒨᖅᑎᑦᑎᓇᓱᐊᕐᓗᓂ.

We were taught never to think evil things about other people. This could be anything from feigning kindness with an intent to harm another person or harbouring evil thoughts in order to put another person in harm's way.

ᐃᓱᒪᑦᑕᐅᖕᒋᑦᑐᓂᒃ ᐃᖅᑲᖅᓴᐅᑎᕐᑲᕐᑯᔭᐅᕙᓚᐅᖏᓚᒍᑦ ᐊᓯᑉᑎᖕᖑᓂᑦ. ᐊᒻᒪᓗ ᐅᕐᑲᐅᔾᔪᖅᑕᐅᕙᓚᐅᖅᑐᒍᑦ ᖄᐅᔨᔭᐅᔪᖕᓇᐃᓚᖏᓐᓇᑉᑕᒎᖅ ᐱᑦᓯᐊᕐᓂᓗᐃᓐᓇᕐᑯᕙᓗᑕ ᐃᑲᔪᖅᑐᒐᐅᕙᓗᑕ, ᐃᓱᒪᓂᕐᓗᒃᑕᐃᓕᓗᑕ, ᐃᓱᒪᓂᕐᓘᑎᑉᑕᒎᖅ ᐅᓇᑕᕐᓂᖅᓴᐅᓕᕈᖕᓇᕐᒪᑎᒍᑦ.

Our parents used to encourage us to always do good, since we would always be found out, and never to think evil thoughts about other people. Our evil thoughts about others could turn on us instead.

ᑕᒪᓐᓇ ᐱᕝᓗᒍ ᐱᑦᓯᐊᕐᓇᖅᑐᒥ ᐃᓅᓯᐊᕈᑉᑕ, ᐱᑦᓯᐊᕐᓂᒡᓗᑕ ᐊᓯᑉᑎᖕᓂᒃ ᑭᓯᐊᓂ ᐃᓅᓯᐊᕈᖕᓇᖅᐳᒍᑦ.

So if we wish to live peacefully, we must treat others kindly.

ᐃᑦᓱᖅᑕᕐᓂᖅ
STEPPING OUT TO CHECK THE WEATHER

ᑐᐸᒃᑳᖓᒪᑦ ᐅᕝᓛᒃᑯᑦ ᐃᑦᓱᕐᑯᔭᐅᕙᓚᐅᖅᐳᑦ ᓯᓚᒨᖅ ᐃᓄᖅᑲᕐᒪᑦ ᐊᒻᒪᒨᖅ ᐃᓅᖅᑲᑦᑖᕈᐊᕈᐸᑦ ᓯᓚᐅᑉ ᐃᓄᐊ ᐅᐱᒋᔪᒍ.

Every morning when we got up from sleep, we were encouraged to step outside and observe the weather and greet the day, because it was said that nature is a spirit. If we want to live a long, successful life, we must show respect to that unseen force outside.

ᑕᐃᑉᓱᒪᓂ ᐃᓅᓯᑐᖅᑲᓪᓚᑦᑖᕚᑦ ᐊᑐᓚᐅᕐᐸᑎᒍ ᓯᓂᖅᑲᑦᑖᕐᑯᔭᐅᓱᐃᑦᑐᓚᐅᖅᐳᒍᑦ, ᐊᒻᒪ ᑐᐸ’ᓈᑐᐊᕌᖓᒪᑦ ᒪᑭᓪᓚᒃᓯᓐᓇᕐᓗᑕ ᐃᑦᓱᕐᓗᑕᓗ ᓯᓚ ᖃᐅᔨᓴᕐᓗᒍ ᖃᓄᐃᒻᒪᖔᑦ, ᓇᑭᑦ ᐊᓄᓂᖅᑲᕐᒪᖔ] ᒐᑦ ᖃᓄᐃᓕᖓᓂᐊᖅᑑᔭᕐᒪᖔᓪᓗ ᖃᐅᔨᓴᖅᓗᑎᒍ.

Back when we were living our own culture, we were always encouraged not to sleep in. As soon as we awoke, we were told to get up, go out, check the weather, check which way the wind was coming from, and try to determine what the day would be like.

ᑕᒪᓐᓇ ᑕᐃᒪᐃᑎᑕᐅᓂᖅ ᐃᓕᓐᓂᐊᕐᓂᕐᕙᖑᓚᐅᖅᐳᖅ ᓯᓚᐅᑉ ᐃᓕᖅᑯᓯᖓᓂᒃ ᓇᐅᑦᓯᖅᑐᕙᓴᓂᕐᒥᒃ. ᖃᖓᓴᖅ ᐃᓐᓇᐃᑦ ᓯᓚᐅᑉ ᖃᓄᐃᓕᖓᓂᖓᓂᒃ ᑕᑯᐃᓐᓇᖅᓗᑎᒃ ᖃᐅᔨᒪᕙᓚᐅᖅᐳᑦ ᐃᓕᖅᑯᓯᕆᓂᐊᕈᓇᖅᑕᖓᓂᒃ ᐅᕝᓗᓂ ᖃᐃᕙᓂ.

This kind of upbringing is a very wonderful lesson in itself, as it helps you to learn weather patterns. Long ago, Inuit could check the weather and know what the weather would be like that day and in the following days.

ᓱᓚᒥᒃ ᓇᐅᑦᓯᖅᑐᕆᓂᖅ ᐱᐅᔪᒻᒪᕆᐊᓘᒐᖅ.

The ability to observe the weather is a wonderful thing.

ᐅᑦᕐᑯᑦ
A SPELL THAT CAUSES ONE TO RETURN

ᐊᐅᓪᓚᕆᐊᓚᐅᖅᑑᒐᓗᐊᒥᒃ ᐅᑎᖅᑎᑦᓯᓐᓂᐅᑦ. ᓱᓐᓂᐅᑎᕋᓗᖕᓂᒃ, ᓱᑎᑦᓯᓐᓂᐅᑎᕋᓗᖕᓂᒃ ᖃᖕᒐᓴᖅ ᐃᓄᐃᑦ ᐃᓚᖏᑦ ᐱᖃᕐᓂᕋᒐᐅᓪᓚᐅᕐᒪᑕ, ᐱᒋᔭᐅᓪᓚᐅᕐᓂᕆᒍᖅᑕᐅᖅ ᐅᑦᕐᑯᑦ, ᐅᕝᕙᓘᕝᕙ ᐅᑎᖅᑎᑦᓯᓐᓂᐅᑦ.

Some Inuit had the ability to use their words to cause certain things to happen. One of the spells they could use was to help people return home.

ᓱᑎᑦᓯᓐᓂᐅᑎᑦ ᑕᐃᒨᓯᕐᓂᒃ ᓴᓇᓯᒪᔪᓂᒃ ᐊᑐᖅᑕᐅᖃᑦᑕᕈᓐᓇᖅᑐᓂᒃ ᐱᑎᑦᓯᔪᒧᑦ ᐱᑕᖃᖅᑕᔪᖕᒪᑦ, ᑭᓯᐊᓂ ᖃᐅᔨᒪᙱᑦᑐᖓ ᐅᑦᕐᑯᑦ ᕿᓐᖓᒐᐅᑎᖃᕋᓗᐊᕐᒪᖕᒫᑦ ᐅᑎᖅᑎᑦᓯᓂᐊᖅᑑᑉ ᐊᑐᐊᒐᒃᓵᓂᒃ.

Inuit used to have special sayings to recite that could cause something to happen, but I do not have the words of the spell that causes a person to return back.

ᐃᓕᔭᑦ
OLD PERSONAL BELONGINGS IN GRAVES

ᐃᓗᕕᖅᓃᑦᑐᑦ ᐱᖁᑎᕕᓃᑦ ᑎᒍᖁᔭᐅᓯᐃᑦᑐᑦ ᑎᒍᓯᕙᖅ ᖃᐅᔨᔭᐅᙱᒃᑲᓗᐊᖅᑐᓂ ᑭᓇᒥᐊᒧᑦ ᓱᓗᖅᑭᓕᖅᓯᓐᓇᓄᐊᖅᑲᖅᒪᑦ, ᐊᓐᓂᐊᓕᕐᓗᓂᓘᓐᓃᑦ ᐅᕝᕙᓘᓐᓃᑦ ᐊᓯᐊᓂ ᓱᓂᖅᑲᓕᖅᓗᓂ ᐃᓅᓯᕐᒥᓂ. ᐱᓐᓂᑯᓂ ᐅᑎᖅᑎᑦᐸᒍ ᑭᓯᐊᓂ ᓱᕙᖕᓇᐃᕿᔭᖅᑐᓂ.

Old personal items in burial sites are not to be taken. A person might take something from the grave without it being known, but something might begin to happen to him later on in life. He would have to return the thing he took from the grave in order to get well again.

ᐅᑐᖅᑲᓕᓇᑦᓯᐊᕐᓂᖅ
TREATING ELDERS KINDLY

ᐅᑐᖅᑲᓂᒃ ᐊᕐᓇᖅᑯᐊᒃᓵᕋᓗᖕᓂᒃ ᐃᑲᑦᓯᓇᒃᓴᖅᑯᔭᐅᕙᓚᐅᖅᐳᑦ ᐃᓅᓯᖅᑲᑦᓯᐊᖅᑯᔭᐅᕐᓗᑎᒃ ᐊᒻᒪ ᐃᓅᖅᑲᑦᑖᑦᓯᐊᖅᑯᔭᐅᕐᓗᑎᒃ. ᓄᑕᕋᐅᑕᐅᕋᑦᑕ ᐅᐱᒍᓱᒋᐊᖅᑲᕙᓚᐅᖅᐳᒍᑦ ᐅᑐᖅᑲᓂᒃ ᐊᒻᒪ ᐊᕐᓇᖅᑯᐊᒃᓵᓂᒃ. ᐊᒻᒪᓗ ᑭᐅᒪᖕᒫᖅᑯᔭᐅᓯᐃᑦᑑᓚᐅᓇᒐᒍᑦ ᐅᑐᖅᑲᓂᒃ ᐊᕐᓇᖅᑯᐊᒃᓵᓂᓪᓗ ᓯᕝᕖᑎᑕᐅᓇᒐᒧᖕᒨᖅ.

We were taught to be considerate of old women and old men and to be helpful to them so that we in turn have happy and successful lives.

When we were children, we were told to respect old women and old men. We were not to talk back at old men and old women; otherwise our hip joints would get dislocated.

ᑕᒪᓐᓇ ᓯᕝᕚᑎᑕᐅᓂᖅ ᓯᕘᕋᓴᐅᑎᒥᐊᖑᓚᐅᕐᒪᖕᒫᑦ ᐱᒻᒪᕆᐅᓚᐅᕐᓂᕐᒪᖕᒫᑦᓗ ᖃᐅᔾᒪᒻᒪᕆᙱᑦᑕᕋᓗᐊᕋ, ᑭᓯᐊᓂ ᐅᒃᐱᕆᔭᕋ ᖃᖏᓴᒃᑲᓐᓂᖅ ᑕᐃᒪᐃᑉᐸᓚᐅᕋᓱᒋᕝᓗᒍ, ᐱᓐᓂᑰᓐᓂᕋᒥ ᑭᓯᐊᓂ ᑐᓴᐅᒪᓐᓇᕐᒪᑦ.

I am not sure whether or not this idea of causing dislocated hip joints was to put fear into people, but I believe it to have happened a long time ago. The story is told because it could have actually happened long ago, and was passed down through the generations.

ᐃᓛ, ᐅᑐᖅᑲᐃᑦ ᐊᕐᓇᖅᑯᐊᒃᓵᑦᓗ ᐅᐱᕆᔭᐅᕙᕆᐊᓖᑦ ᓯᓚᑐᓂᕐᔪᐊᕐᒥᒃ ᐃᓅᓯᕐᒥᓗ ᐊᑐᖅᓯᒪᕐᔪᐊᕐᓂᑯᒥᖕᓂᒃ ᓇᔪᖅᑎᖅᑲᕐᒪᑕ, ᖃᐅᔨᓚᐅᖅᓯᒪᙱᑦᑕᑉᑎᖕᓂᒃ ᐃᓚᐃᑎᒍᑦ ᖃᐅᔨᓯᒪᔪᖅᑲᕐᒪᑕ, ᓯᕗᓂᕐᒥᓗ ᖃᓄᐃᓕᖓᓂᐊᖅᑰᖅᑐᓂᒃ ᐃᓕᓯᒪᔭᖅᑲᖅᓘᑎᒃ.

Certainly, old women and old men ought to be respected, because they have gained and hold much wisdom and knowledge. They have gone through a lot of experiences that none of us probably have ever experienced. They also know what the future might hold.

ᐅᓯᖖᒐᓗᓂ ᐊᓂᑦᑕᐃᓕᓂᖅ
AVOID GOING OUT NAKED

ᐃᓅᓯᕐᒥᒃ ᐅᐱᒍᓱᑦᑎᐊᕐᓗᑕ ᐱᕈᖅᓴᓂᑉᑎᖕᓂ ᓴᓇᔭᐅᖕᒍᔭᖅᐸᓚᐅᖅᐳᒍᑦ, ᓯᓚᒥᓗ ᐃᒡᓗᑉ ᑐᐱᐅᕝᓘᓐᓃᑦ ᓯᓚᑖᓂ ᐃᓕᖅᑯᓯᐅᔪᓇᐊᓕᖕᓂᒃ ᐃᓕᓐᓂᐊᖅᑎᑕᐅᖕᒍᔭᖅᐸᓚᐅᖅᐳᒍᑦ.

As we grew up, we were taught to respect life and were shown how to conduct ourselves properly outdoors, indoors, and even in tents. We were patiently taught to behave in life.

ᐱᔮᓇᓗᑕ ᐊᓐᓄᕋᐃᑦᑑᓗᑕ, ᓲᕐᓗ ᐅᓯᖖᒐᓗᑕ ᐊᓂᕐᑯᔭᐅᕙᓚᐅᖖᒋᓚᒍᑦ, ᐅᓯᖖᒐᓗᑕᑰᖅ ᐊᓂᒍᑉᑕ ᓯᓚᓗᓕᑐᐃᓐᓇᓇᐊᕐᑲᕐᒪᑦ, ᓯᓚᑰᖅ ᐅᓯᖖᒑᕐᕕᐅᖖᒋᒻᒪᑦ.

We were told never to walk around outdoors naked or without our clothes on; otherwise the weather would turn bad. They told us the outdoors was not a place to be exposed or naked.

ᐱᔮᓇᖖᒋᑦᓗᓂ, ᐱᔭᓇᐊᓕᒻᒪᓇᖕᒥᒡᓗ ᐱᓕᕆᓂᐊᕐᓗᓂ ᓲᕐᑯᑕᐅᖖᒋᑦᑑᓗᒐᓗᐊᖅ, ᓲᕐᓗ ᓯᓚᒥ ᐃᒫᓂ ᐱᖖᒍᐊᕐᓂᐊᕐᓗᓂ ᓇᓗᒑᕐᓗᓂᓘᓐᓃᑦ.

If we were doing it with good purpose, or doing something that was necessary, there was no harm, like playing in the water or swimming in water.

ᐅᕕᖖᒋᐊᖅᑐᖅᑕᐃᓕᓂᖅ ᐊᖅᓴᓕᔮᒥᒃ
AVOID WHISTLING AT THE NORTHERN LIGHTS

ᐊᖅᓴᕐᓂᖅ ᐅᕕᖖᒋᐊᖅᑐᕐᑯᔭᐅᓱᐃᑦᑐᖅ ᖃᓪᓕᕙᓪᓕᐊᓱᕐᒪᑦ ᐅᕕᖖᒋᐊᖅᑐᖅᑐᒍ, ᑎᑭᑦᑯᒥᑐ ᓂᐊᖅᑯᐃᕐᓂᒃᓯᓐᓇᓇᐊᖅᑲᖅᑐᓂ ᐊᖅᓴᖖᒍᐊᖅᑲᓕᕐᑐᓂᑐ ᓂᐊᖅᑯᒥᒃ. ᖃᓪᓕᑐᐊᕌᖕᒐᑦᑐᒎᖅ ᐃᑎᓇᐊᕐᓂᕐᒥᒃ ᕐᑯᒃᓴᑦᑕᐃᕝᑐᓂ ᑎᒍᓯᓱᕐᒪᑦ. ᑕᐃᒪᓐᓇ ᐅᖅᑲᐅᑎᔭᐅᕈᔫᔭᖅᐸᓚᐅᖅᐳᒍᑦ ᐊᖕᒐᔪᖅᑳᑉᑎᖕᓂᑦ ᓄᑕᕋᐅᕝᑐᑕ.

We were told to avoid whistling at the northern lights, because if you whistle they will get closer, and the northern lights could cut your head off and play with it like a soccer ball. If they descend too closely, you could freeze and become scared to go back indoors, and the lights could take you. These are things our parents used to tell us as children.

ᑭᓯᐊᓂ ᐊᖅᓴᓕᔮᕐᓂᖅ ᑕᑯᕋᓐᓂᖅᑐᖅ ᓯᓚ ᐊᓪᓚᕐᔭᐊᖅᑎᓪᓗᒍ ᓄᐃᑕᓱᕐᒪᑦ ᓯᓚᒥ ᖃᓪᓕᐅᒥᔮᖅᑐᓂ.

But northern lights are beautiful to watch when the weather is crystal clear and they become visible outdoors, becoming more intense and swaying back and forth.

ᐊᐅᓪᓚᕐᓂᖅ
RUNNING AWAY

ᕿᕕᐊᓂᐅᑉ ᐊᔾᔨᖅᑲᔭᕋᓗᐊᖕᒐ, ᑭᓯᐊᓂᓕ ᑐᑭᓕᒃ ᕐᑯᕕᐊᓱᖖᒋᓗᐊᒧᑦ ᑐᕿᒐᖅᑲᖖᒋᒥᐊᖅᑐᓂ ᐊᐅᓪᓚᕐᓂᖅ ᑕᒻᒪᓇᐊᒥᐊᖅᑐᓂ. ᐊᐅᓪᓚᕐᓂᑐᕐᑯᔭᐅᓱᐃᑦᑑᓚᐅᕐᒥᔪᑦᑕᐅᖅ ᖃᖕᒐᓴᖅ.

This one is about a distressed person running away with no direction at all, running away to get lost and perish. Long ago we were told to avoid doing it.

ᐊᐅᓚᓴᖅᑕᐃᓕᓂᖅ ᑖᖅᓯᑎᑦᑐᒍ
AVOID JIGGING FOR FISH IN THE DARK

ᐅᓐᓄᐊᒃᑯᑦ ᑖᖅᓯᑎᑦᑐᒍ
ᐊᐅᓚᓴᕐᓇᕈᖕᓇᐃᖅᑎᑦᑐᒍ
ᐊᐅᓚᓴᕐᑯᔭᐅᓱᐃᑦᑑᓚᐅᖅᑐᑦ
ᑭᕝᒐᓗᖕᒧᖖᒎᖅ ᑮᔾᔭᐅᓇᕗᖅ.

Nighttime, when it is dark, is not a time to jig for fish. We were told not to cast a fishing hook in a hole in the dark lest we snag a *kivgaluk* (an evil fish that bites a hook).

ᐊᐸᐱᔭᕐᓂᖅ
WINTER THUNDER

ᐅᑭᐅᒥ ᓄᓇᒥ ᐊᐸᐱᔭᓕᕌᖕᒐᑦ ᐱᖅᐸᓗᕐᑭᒥᐊᑦᑐᐊᓪᓚᕐᒥᓗ ᐅᒃᑳᓕᔮᓗᕐᑭᒥᐊᑦᑐᐊᔪᖕᒪᑦ ᑲᑦᑑᒃᑐᑐᑦ, ᑭᓯᐊᓂᒎᖅ ᓴᓂᕙᒐᔮᓗᓂ ᐱᔭᕆᐊᓕᒃ. ᓴᓂᕙᒐᔮᒥᐊᖅᑐᓂᒎᖅ ᑕᒡᕙᓂᓪᓚᕆᐅᙱᑦᑐᖅ ᐃᒡᓗᑖᖅᑐᓂ ᓱᕋᐃᔪᔪᖅ. ᐊᒪᒎᖅ ᕐᑯᒻᓂᕐᒧᑦ ᓯᕐᒥᖅᓯᒻᒥᒃ ᓇᓅᑉ ᐊᒥᐊᓂᒃ ᕐᑭᒡᒋᑦᓯᔪᓂ ᐱᔪᖕᓇᐃᔪᕝᑐᓂ.

When thunder happens inland during winter, you can hear it and see lightning like you see in a thunderstorm. When this happens, the advice was to move away a bit from your location. When you move away a bit and build another iglu in another location, the thunder usually stops. Another way to deal with a winter thunderstorm was to put a piece of polar bear skin that is used to glaze ice over the runners of the *qamutiik* (sled) in a crack in the ice, and the lightning or flashing incident would stop.

ᖃᖕᒐᓴᖅ ᐊᑉᓯᔭᕐᓂᕐᒧᑦ ᐱᓗᕐᑭᔭᐅᔪᖅᑲᕐᔩᒥᓱᓚᐅᖅᑐᖅ, ᑲᑉᐱᐊᓯᔭᐅᕝᓗᓂᓗ ᐱᕙᓚᐅᖅᑐᖅ ᐃᑯᒪᔪᓂᒃ ᐊᒃᓛᖖᒨᖅ ᓱᐱᓯᑦᑕᔪᖕᒪᑦ.

Long ago, when some Inuit experienced this phenomenon, they were afraid of it, because it could even blow out your lights.

ᐊᑭᔾᔪᕐᓗᒃᑕᕈᕕᑦ
WHEN YOUR PILLOWS ARE TOO LOW

ᐳᒃᑭᑦᑐᒐᔫᓂᒃ ᐊᑭᑎᕐᑲᖅᑕᕈᕕᑦ, ᐊᐅᓇᐊᓕᖀᖕᒐᕕᑦ ᓇᑦᓯᓕᐊᓕᖀᖕᒐᕕᑦ ᑕᑯᔭᐅᓪᓚᒃᓯᓐᓇᖅᑕᕿᔭᖅᐳᑎᑦ ᕐᑲᒡᓕᖅᑳᖅᑎᓐᓇᒡᓗ ᐊᖅᑲᐃᑦᑕᕐᓗᑎᑦ ᑕᑯᔭᐅᔭᖀᖕᒐᕕᑦ.

If you slept on low pillows and went out seal hunting after, the seals might spot you right away even before you could get close enough, and they would dive under the ice through their holes if they saw you.

ᑕᒪᔾᔭ ᖃᖕᒐᓴᖅ ᐅᒃᐱᓇᔭ ᐅᔪᑦ ᐃᓚᒋᕙᓚᐅᕐᒥᔭᖕᒐᑦ. ᓂᕐᔪᑕᐃᓐᓇᕐᓄᑦ ᐃᓅᒡᒍᑎᒃᓴᖅᓯᐅᔪᒻᒧᑎᒃ ᓱᓕ ᐱᑦᑕᐃᓕᔭᕐᑲᕐᓗᒃᒍᑎᒃ ᐃᓕᖅᑯᓯᕐᑲᕐᓘᔭᖅᐸᓚᐅᕐᒪᑕ, ᒪᓕᑦᓯᐊᕐᓂᓗᐃᓐᓇᖅᒍᕆᑦᓗ ᐃᓅᓇᓯᐊᖅᐸᓚᐅᕐᒪᑕ.

This is another part of beliefs Inuit had long ago. They lived and survived only by hunting animals. They had certain rules they had to observe and had to abstain from doing certain things. They tried their best to follow all the rules set out for them.

ᖁᐸᓄᐊᖅ ᐃᑎᖅᐸᑦ
WHEN A BIRD ENTERS A DWELLING

ᐃᓄᐃᑦ ᐅᑉᐱᕈᓯᖏᑎᒍᑦ ᖁᐸᓄᐊᕐᒥᒃ ᑐᐱᕐᒧᑦ ᐃᑎᖅᑐᖃᖅᐸᑦ ᐊᓂᑎᑕᐅᑎᐊᙱᓪᓗᓂ ᑐᖁᑕᐅᖁᔨᕙᓚᐅᖅᐳᑦ, ᓯᓚᒥᐅᑕᐅᖕᒪᑦ ᐃᒡᓗᑉ ᐃᓗᐊᓂᕐᒥᐅᑕᐅᙱᒻᒪᑦ ᑲᑉᐱᐊᒋᔭᐅᖕᒪᑦ ᓱᓇᒥᑦᑭᐊᖅ ᐃᒻᒪᖄ ᐱᑎᑕᐅᓇᓱᒋᕝᓗᒍ.

According to Inuit traditional custom, if a bird enters a tent, they should be prevented from escaping and should be dispatched. This is because it is a wild animal that belongs outside and does not belong indoors. If a bird flew inside, they were afraid of it, thinking that it was sent in by something evil to bring harm.

ᐃᖅᑯᔾᔨᓯᓐᓇᓇᐊᖅᑲᕐᒪᑦ ᐃᓗᖅᑭᐅᒻᒥᒃ ᓱᐃᓐᓇᕐᒥᒃ ᓱᓗᖅᑭᓐᓇᖅᑐᒥᒃ.

It could easily be bringing in something evil that could cause misfortune.

ᐊᑦᓚᔭᖕᓇᕐᓂᖅ
VITAL SIGNS

ᑐᖁᓚᓯᓐᓂᖅᑬᖕᒐᒥᒃ ᐃᓕᖅᑯᓯᓕᙱᑕᒥᒃᑯᑦ ᐃᓅᓂᖅ, ᓵᖅᓗ, ᖁᕕᐊᓱᓗᐊᖅᑐᖅ, ᐃᑲᑦᓱᓕᒃᑐᖅ, ᖃᓄᖅᑬᓗᒡᓘᕝᕙ ᒪᓗᖕᓈᖅᑭᔭᖅ ᐃᓅᓯᖕᒐ.

It is believed that when people are nearing death, they begin to show signs that should not be ignored. For example, a sudden change in the person's attitude, like becoming unusually happy or helpful, or if they start doing things they normally wouldn't. These are signs Inuit would watch for.

ᐊᓇᒐᐅᓂᖅ ᑐᓗᒐ'ᑐᐊᕐᒧᑦ
WHEN A RAVEN POOPS

ᐃᓄᒃ ᑐᓗᒃᑲᑉ ᐊᓇᖅᐸᒍ ᐅᑦᕐᑯᓯᒐᐅᓂᕋᒐᐅᓇᔭᖅᐳᖅ (ᐅᑎᕈᐊᓕᕋᔭᖅᐳᖅ), ᐊᐅᓪᓚᓇᐊᓚᐅᕋᓗᐊᕐᓗᓂ ᐅᑎᒥᐊᓕᕐᓗᓂ ᐊᖕᒋᓪᕋᒥᓄᑦ.

If a raven poops on a person, that person should abandon a planned trip (one should feel compelled to head back home).

ᐊᕕᐅᔨᓂᖅ
RINGING IN THE EAR

ᓯᐅᑎᒃ ᕐᑯᕐᑯᐊᖅᐸᓪᓚᒐᐅᔭᕐᓂᖕᒐ ᓱᔪᖅᑲᓯᒋᐊᖅᑐᒥᒃ ᖅᑲᐅᔨᔾᔪᑕᐅᕙᓚᐅᓇᕗᖅ.

If you heard a long buzzing sound in your ear, it was considered a sign that something unusual was about to happen.

ᓱᖖᑭᐅᓯᒥᐊᑦᓚᕐᒥ ᐃᓖᓐᓂ ᓯᐅᑎᒃᑯᑦ ᓯᕙᓂᖅᐸᑦᓚᖃᐅᔭᖅᑰᔭᖅᑐᒥ ᑐᓴᖅᑕᔪᒐᑉᑕ, ᐃᓄᐃᑦ ᐃᓚᖏᑕ ᓇᓗᓇᐃᒃᑯᑕᕆᓂᖃᔪᓚᐅᕐᒥᔫᑦ ᑕᒪᓐᓇ ᐅᖅᑲᖅᖢᑎᒃ ᓲᕐᓗ ᐃᒪᓐᓇ, "ᓯᐅᑎᒐ ᐊᕕᐅᔨᑦᑐᐊᕐᒥᖕᒪᑦ ᑕᐃᒪ ᓱᔪᖅᑲᑦᑎᐊᖕᒋᑦᑐᒥᒃ ᖁᕕᐊᓇᐃᑦᑐᒥᓂᒃ ᓘᕝᕙ ᑐᓴᕐᓂᐊᓕᕆᕗᒍᑦ."

Sometimes, we might hear a long ringing sound in our ear. Some Inuit used to take it as a sign; they might say, "Oh, I hear that long ringing sound in my ear again." It was a sign that we may hear of unpleasant news or that something very sad was about to happen.

ᐊᒡᓚᕐᓂᖅ
TABOOS

ᐱᑦᑕᐃᓕᔭᕐᑲᕐᓂᖅ ᓱᓇᒥᐊᓂᒃ, ᓂᕆᑦᑕᐃᓕᓗᓂ, ᓱᓇᒥᐊᒥᒃ ᐱᓕᕆᐊᖅᑕᐃᓕᓗᓂ.

There were Inuit customs of forbidding certain foods and activities at certain times. These taboos could be imposed on a person regarding:

- ᓂᕿᑎᒍᑦ
- ᐃᒪᒃᑯᑦ
- ᐃᓕᖅᑯᓯᒃᑯᑦ
- ᓄᓇᑎᒍᑦ
- ᓴᐅᓂᖅᑎᒍᑦ
- ᓂᕐᔪᑎᑦ ᓱᓈᖏᑎᒍᑦ

- food
- water
- traditional customs
- use of land
- our skeleton
- bones and other parts of animals

ᐊᒥᓲᓚᐅᖅᐳᑦ ᐊᒃᓕᕐᓃᑦ.

There were many obligatory taboos.

ᐊᒥᖦᖁᑦ ᑐᒃᑐᑦ
CARIBOU HERD

ᐊᒥᖦᖁᑦ ᑐᒃᑐᑦ ᓯᓚᖦᓯᐊᕐᓗᖕᓂᖁᒐᐅᓯᓚᐅᖅᑐᑦ, ᓲᕐᓗᔫᖅ ᐊᐅᔭᒥ ᐊᕐᕕᐊᒥ ᐊᒥᖦᓇᖅᑐ'ᔫᒃᒪᑦ, ᒪᕐᑲᐃᑎᖦᓗᒋᑦ ᓂᐸᓗᓕᖦᑎᐊᒥᐊᕐᒪᑦ ᕿᕐᖁᖅᑐᕐᑲᓚᐅᖅᓯᒪᔪᖅ ᐊᒻᒪ ᕿᕐᖁᖅᑲᔭᖅᑐᕐᑲᖅᓘᓂ (ᕿᕐᖁᑲᓴᒃᑐᕐᑲᖅᓘᓂ).

It was believed that as a caribou herd approached, it usually brought bad weather. As an example of this belief, during one summer in Arviat a herd of caribou passed through, and while hunters were out hunting, heavy rains came and one of the hunters died of exposure and another just barely made it.

ᐊᔪᖃᖅᓯᑦᑕᐃᓕᓂᖅ ᖃᖅᓴᐅᓂᒃ
IMITATING THE CALL OF THE LOON

ᖃᖅᓴᐅᑦ ᕿᐊᖅᐸᓗᒃᑑᔭᖅᓗᑎᒃ ᓂᕐᔮᖅᑐᑦ ᐊᔪᖃᖅᓯᖁᔭᐅᓯᐃᑦᑐᑦ ᕿᐊᙵᐃᓐᓇᓕᕐᓇᕐᒪᖕᒎᖅ ᓯᖕᒋᔪᐃᕐᓗᓂ.

It was forbidden to imitate the call of the loon, as they make the sound of a wailing person. People who imitate the sounds of a loon may end up not being able to stop crying.

ᐊᓗᐹᕐᓂᖅ ᐃᔨᖕᓂᒃ
LICKING THE EYES

ᓄᑕᖅ ᐃᓪᓗᒃᐸᑦ ᐅᐱᕐᖓᒃᓵᒥ ᐃᔨᒋᒃ ᐊᓗᐹᖅᑕᐅᓇᔭᖅᐳᒃ ᐃᓪᓗᒍᑖ ᐲᔭᕐᓂᓗᒃᓗᒍ, ᓄᑕᕋᐅᕐᓗᑕ ᐃᔨᕗᑦ ᐊᓗᐹᖅᑕᐅᕙᓚᐅᖅᑐᑦ ᐅᐱᕐᖓᒃᓴᒥ.

If a child got snow blindness in the springtime, the parents would lick the eyes to make the snow blindness go away. When we were children, in the springtime our parents often licked our eyes to prevent us from getting snow blindness.

ᐊᓐᓂᐊᖅᑐᑦ
SICK PEOPLE

ᐊᓐᓂᐊᖅᑐᑦ ᐅᐊᓂᓗᒥᐊᕐᑯᔭᐅᓯᓚᐅᖅᐳᑦ ᐊᓐᓂᐊᕈᖕᓇᐃᑲᕐᑯᔭᐅᕐᓗᑎᒃ.

Sick people were encouraged to keep active so they could get better sooner.

ᐊᖅᓴᕐᓂᕐᒧᑦ ᑯᑭᒌᖅᐸᓗᒃᑎᑦᓯᓂᖅ
USING FINGERNAILS ON THE NORTHERN LIGHTS

ᐊᒻᒪᐃᑦ ᓄᕗᖕᓂᑦ ᐃᕐᑭᕝᓗᓂᑦ ᑯᑮᓐᓇᐃ ᐊᒃᑐᐊᕝᓗᓂᑦ ᑯᑭᒌᖅᐸᓗᒃᑎᑦᓯᓯᓚᐅᖅᐸᑦ ᐊᖅᓴᕐᓂᕐᒥᒃ ᐅᖕᒐᕙᖅᑎᑦᑎᓇᓱᒃᓗᑎᒃ.

People believed that if they rubbed their fingernails together, the sound would make northern lights go away.

ᐊᖅᓴᕐᓂᕐᒥᒃ ᕐᑯᐃᕙᕖᑖᕐᓂᖅ
USING PHRASES ON THE NORTHERN LIGHTS

ᐅᖕᒐᕙᕐᑯᓯᓚᒌᖕᒐᒥᒃ ᐊᖅᓴᕐᓂᕐᒥᒃ “ᕐᑯᐃᕙᕖᑖᔪᓚᐅᖅᑐᑦ” ᕐᑭᒫᕐᑯᓯᕝᓗᑎᒃ ᐊᖅᓴᕐᓂᕐᒥᒃ.

When people wished the northern lights to go farther away, they would call out, “I piss on you,” to try to drive away the northern lights.

ᐱᑦᑐᕐᑯᑦ
MAGIC SPIRIT HELPERS

ᓱᓇᒥᐊᖅ ᐱᒡᒍᕐᑯᑎᒋᔭᐅᓂᓗᒃᑐᖅ, ᐱᕐᑯᓪᓘᓐᓃᑦ ᓂᕐᔪᑎᖏᓘᖏᕙ ᓱᓈᕐᓗᐊ ᒥᐊᓂᖅᓯᔾᔨᒋᓂᓗᒑ ᐱᐅᙱᑦᑐᒧᑦ ᐱᑦᓯᐊᕐᓇᙱᑦᑐᒧᑦᑐ ᑲᓚᒍᐅᕐᑯᓇᓂ.

Inuit used talismans and amulets as their helpers. These could be made from anything, from something one owned to an animal part, and it would protect you from being touched by something evil.

ᐳᑐᒍᖅ ᑎᑭᖄᖅᓯᔪᖅ
SUDDEN PAIN ON THE BIG TOE

ᐳᑐᒎᑉ ᐊᓐᓂᓪᓚᒃᑎᕐᓂᖓ ᑎᑭᑦᑐᖅᑲᓯᒋᐊᕐᒪᑦ, "ᐊ'ᐊᐸᐹ, ᐳᑐᒍᖅ ᑎᑭᖄᖅᓯᑯᓂ" ᑎᑭᑦᑐᖅᑲᓪᓗᐊᕚᒻᒫᑦᑐᐊᕙᓚᐅᕐᒪᑦ ᕐᑯᕕᐊᓇᖅᐸᓚᐅᖅᓯᒪᕙᖅ.

When someone felt a sudden pain on the tip of the big toe, they would call out, "Oooh, ouch, my big toe is hurting, someone is arriving soon." And sure enough, some visitor would arrive. It used to be a happy occasion when this happened.

ᑎᑎᕋᐅᔭᖅᑕᐃᓕᓂᖅ ᐃᒐᓛᒃᑯᑦ
AVOID DRAWING ON AN ICE WINDOW

ᐃᒡᓗᑉ ᐃᒐᓛᖓᒍᑦ ᓯᑯᒃᑯᑦ ᑎᑎᕋᐅᔭᖅᑕᐃᓕᓯᓚᐅᖅᑐᑦ, ᑕᒫᙵᒐᒥᐊᖅ ᓱᓇᑕᐃᑦᑐᒥᑦ ᐊᒃᑭᕕᐅᑦᑐᐊᕋᕗᖅ.

We were told not to draw or scrawl anything on the ice window of an iglu, or else something unseen, something unknown, would send us a message back.

ᑎᑦᓕᒥᓯᐊᖅ
SOMETHING GOOD IS ABOUT TO HAPPEN

ᐅᖅᑯᕐᒥᐅᑦ ᓂᕆᐅᔮᕈᓯᖕᒐᑦ, ᖃᓂᕐᒥ ᓯᓈᒍᑦ ᐅᖏᑦᑕᐅᒥᒃᐸᑦ, ᐃᓚᖏᑐᖑᖅ ᓴᓂᕐᕕᒍᑦ ᐊᓂᐅᒥᒃᐸᑦ.

Northern Quebec Inuit had a way of telling that something good was about to happen. If one had a sudden itch on the lips or a sudden pain in one's side, that would be taken as sign that something good was about to happen.

ᑎᑎᒍᓱᖕᓂᖅ
AVOIDING SOMETHING

ᖁᐃᓇᒋᔭᖅᑲᖅᓂᖅ, ᓱᑦᑕᐃᓕᓂᖅ ᓱᓇᖅᑐᒍᑦ ᑲᓕᒪᐅᕙᒪᓇᓂ.

Don't avoid doing something because it creeps you out.

ᑎᒃᓕᒋᔭᕐᓃᓴᐅᑦ
PROTECTION AGAINST THEFT

ᑎᒃᓕᒋᔭᐅᔾᔭᓂᒃᑯᑦ, ᐃᑎᓇᓕᐅᑦ ᐊᑐᒐᐅᒃᐸᑦ ᑎᒃᓕᒃᑐᒍᑦ ᖃᓄᐃᓕᖕᓇᖅᑐᖅ.

There was protection from having someone steal from you; it was a magical saying that could cause misfortune for the thief.

ᑎᒡᓚᖕᓂᖅ
STEALING

ᑎᒡᓚᕐᑯᔨᓱᐃᑦᑐᑦ ᑎᒡᓚᒃᑐᓂ ᑯᑮᕐᓇᕐᒪᑦ.

We were told not to steal, because if we did, we might lose a fingernail.

ᑎᒥᒃ ᑯᕕᖅᑐᖅᑕᐃᓚᓂᖅ
AVOID SPILLING TEA

ᖃᖕᒐᓴᖅ ᐅᒃᐱᕈᓯᕆᔭᐅᓚᐅᕐᒥᔪᖅ ᓴᕐᕙᖅᑰᕐᒥᐅᓂᑦ ᑏᒥᒃ ᓇᑎᕐᒧᑦ ᑯᕕᖅᑐᖅᑕᐃᓚᓂᖅ. ᓇᑎᕐᒧᖖᒨᖅ ᑯᕕᖅᑐᖅᐸᑦ ᑎᓇᒐᓂᐊᔪᐃᓚᓇᕗᖅ.

An old belief by *Sarvaqtuurmiut* Inuit was to avoid spilling tea on the floor. If you spilled tea on the floor, you would have a hard time catching foxes.

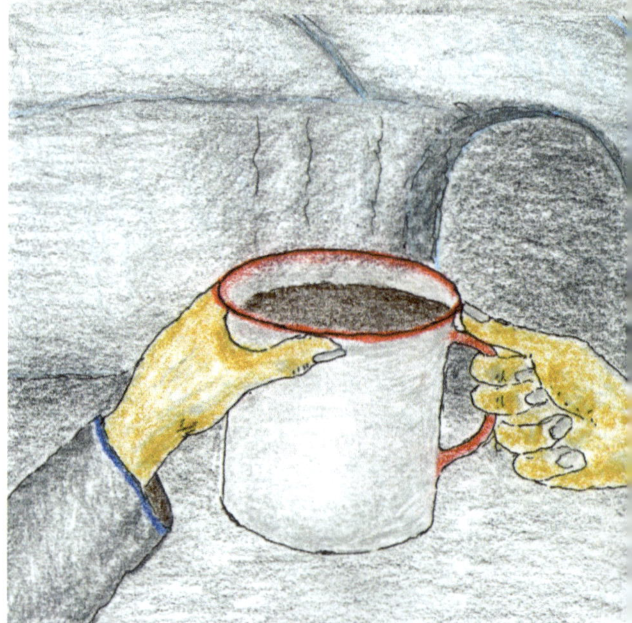

ᑐᓂᓪᓚᕐᓂᖅ
OFFERING A TOKEN GIFT

ᐱᕐᑯᒻᒥᒃ ᓱᓇᒥᐊ'ᓈᒥᒃ ᑐᓂᓯᓂᖅ ᒪᓂᖅᑲᒧᑦ ᐊᒡᔭᖅᓗᒍ ᐱᑦᓯᐊᕐᓇᖅᑐᒥᒃ ᐱᕝᕕᐅᔪᒪᒧᑦ.

Inuit would offer a gift of any item to the land. People would

bring these gifts and leave them on the ground in hopes that good times would come to them.

ᐃᓛᓐᓂ ᐊᓐᓂᐊᕐᓃᑦ ᓱᓇᐅᖕᒪᖕᒫᑖ ᖃᐅᔨᒪᓐᓇᔪᐃᑦᑐᓚᐅᖑᖕᒪᑕ, ᓄᕙᖕᓂᖃᓗ'ᓈᖑᙱᑦᑐᑦ, ᓈᕐᓗᖕᓂᖃᓗ'ᓈᖑᙱᑦᑐᑦ ᐅᕝᕙᓘᕝᕙ ᐊᓐᓂᐊᕐᓂᒥᐊ'ᓈᖑᙱᑦᑐᑦ, ᐊᑯᓂᓗᐊᖅ ᐊᓐᓂᐊᓕᖄᖕᒐᒥᒃ ᓱᓇᒥᐊ'ᓈᓂᒃ ᐱᕐᑯᑎᓐᓇᓇᔭᒥᖕᓂᒃ ᑐᓂᑦᓴᐅᑎᖃᔪᓴᐅᖅᐳᑦ ᒪᒥᑎᑕᐅᓯᐊᖅᓱᑎᒃ ᐊᓐᓂᐊᕈᑎᒋᔭᒥᖕᓂᑦ.

Sometimes it was hard to determine the kind of ailments people were having if it wasn't an ordinary common cold or stomach flu or any other common ailment. If sickness persisted for a length of time, the people would offer a small item that they owned in order to be healed from the sickness they were suffering from.

ᐊᓐᓂᐊᖅᑐᖅ ᐱᕐᑯᑎᒥᓂᒃ ᓱᓇᒥᐊᒥᒃ ᑎᒍᒐᕐᒥᒃ ᒪᓂᖅᑲᒧᑦ ᐊᒡᔭᖅᓯᑎᑦᓯᓇᔭᖅᐳᖅ ᖃᐅᔾᒪᓐᓇᖕᒋᒋᐊᖅᑐᒧᑦ ᐊᑭᓚᐅᑎᒋᓂᓗᒃᓲᒍ ᓂᑉᑕᖕᒋᑦᑐᒧᑦ ᐱᔪᖕᓇᕐᓂᓚᖕᒧᑦ ᒪᓂᒨᑦᑎᑎᒋᓗᒍ ᐊᓐᓂᐊᕈᑎᒋᖅᑲᑦᑖᓚ ᐃᓄᖕᒥᑦ ᐲᕐᓗᓂ ᑎᒍᒐᕐᒧᑦ ᐃᑕᔭᐅᔪᒧᑦ ᓄᒃᑎᖕᒫᕐᑯᓗᒍ.

A sick person could delegate someone to offer an item he owned and ask them to leave it as a token to be healed somewhere on the land where no one would find it. It was offered to an unseen force that had the power to accept the gift and the power to transfer the ailment onto the item that was placed on the ground.

ᑐᓂᑦᑕᐅᑎᖏᓃᑦ ᒪᓂᖅᑲᒦᑦᑐᑦ ᑎᒍᕐᑯᔭᐅᓯᐃᑦᑑᕗᑦ ᑕᐃᑉᓯᒪ ᑐᓂᑦᑕᖅᑐᖏᓂᐅᑉ ᐊᓐᓂᐊᕈᑎᖏᓂᖕᒐᓂᒃ ᑐᕝᕕᐅᖅᑯᓇᑕ, ᐊᓐᓂᐊᕈᑎᒋᖕᒐᑕᕐᓗᒍ ᑐᖅᑯᑎᒋᖕᒐᑕᕐᓗᒍᓘᕝᕙ ᐱᕐᑯᔨᓇᑎᒃ.

No one was to collect this item from the ground or pick it up, or else the old sickness would transfer to the one picking it up. They did not want anyone to pick it up so they wouldn't get sick instead or even die from it.

ᑐᓂᓪᓚᕐᕕᒃ
OFFERING PLACES

ᐱᕐᑯᒻᒥᒃ ᓯᓇᒥᐊᒥᒃ ᐃᓕᓯᑦᑕᕐᕕᒃ, ᑐᓂᓯᔭᖅᑐᕐᕕᒃ.

There were places to leave gift offerings. You would bring something and leave it there as a gift.

ᐱᑕᖃᕐᔫᒥᑦᑕᔪᕆᕗᖅ ᓇᓂᒥᐊᖅ ᓄᓇᒥᕋᓗᒃ, ᓲᕐᓗ ᓇᖕᒐᕆᔭᐅᔪᓂᒃ ᐅᐱᕆᔭᐅᔪᓂᓪᓘᕝᕙ ᐅᔭᕋᖕᓂᒃ, ᐅᔭᕋᓯᒡᔪᖕᓂᒃ, ᖁᐱᓐᓂᑯᓂᒃ, ᖃᐃᖅᑐᒥ ᐃᓗᓕᐅᒪᓂᕐᓂ, ᐃᓅᒃᓯᓕᐊᖑᕝᓗᑎᓪᓘᕝᕙ ᑐᓂᓪᓚᕐᕕᒃᓴᓕᐊᖑᓐᓂᑯᑦ.

Once in a while someone might find something unusual somewhere on the land. It could be a piece of intriguing stone, a boulder, a split rock, a cave on the side of a rock hill, or stone markers that were put up as an offering place.

ᑎᐊᑦᓇᑐᑦᑕᐅᖅ ᓂᑉᑕᖕᒋᑦᑐᑉ ᐱᔪᖕᓇᕐᓂᖕᒐ ᓯᕗᕋᕆᕝᓗᒍ ᑕᒪᒃᑯᐊ ᓯᓚᓇᕝᕖᑦ ᐋᖅᑭᒃᑕᐅᓐᓂᑯᑦ, ᓲᕐᓗ ᓄᓇᒧᑦ ᑎᑭᑕᒥᓄᑦ ᓴᐃᒪᕝᕕᐅᓯᐊᕐᓗᓂ, ᓯᓗᕿᓐᓇᖅᑐᒧᑦ ᑎᑭᑕᐅᔪᒪᓇᓂ, ᓯᓇᒥᐊ'ᓈᒥᒃ ᐃᓕᓯᓇᔭᖅᐳᖅ ᒪᓂᒎᑦᑎᑎᕆᓗᓂᐅᒃ, ᐊᑭᓕᐅᑎᕆᓂᓗᒡᓗᓂᐅᒃ ᐱᑦᓯᐊᕐᓇᖅᑐᒦᑎᑕᐅᓯᐊᖅᓗᓂ.

All of these different places were set up out of fear of that unseen force. The people wanted to experience peace and kindness from the land they had recently moved into. They did not want misfortune to fall upon them, so they would offer a small gift to the land to be at peace. Their gift was like a payment to be at peace with nature.

ᑐᓂᓪᓚᐅᑎᕕᓃᑦᑕᐅᖅ ᑕᒪᒃᑯᐊ ᑎᒍᔭᐅᑦᑕᐃᓕᓯᓇᕗᑦ, ᑎᒍᓯᔪᖅ ᓯᓐᓇᖅᑐᒧᑦ ᑲᑉᐱᐊᓇᖅᑐᒧᑦ ᓘᓐᓃᑦ ᑎᑭᐅᑎᕐᑯᓇᒍ.

These offering items were not to be taken; otherwise the person would fall into misfortune or danger.

ᑐᒃᑯᖅᓴᕐᓂᖅ
BEING GENEROUS

ᓂᕿᓄᑦ ᑐᒃᑯᖅᓴᕐᑯᐹᒡᒍᓚᐅᖅᐳᑦ, ᐊᓪᓛᑦ ᓂᕿ ᒥᑭᔪᑯᓘᓗᐊᖅᐸᑦ ᒥᓂᑦᓯᑦᑕᐃᓂᕋᓚᐅᖅᐳᑦ, ᑕᒧᐊᒃᓴᐅᑦᑐᐊᓱᖕᒐᖅᐸᑦ ᐊᐃᑦᑐᕐᓂᑐᔪᓚᐅᖅᐳᑦ ᒥᑭᑦᑐᒥᐊ'ᓈᒥᒍᓐᓃᑦ ᐊᔪᖅᓴᕐᓇᖅᑐᕐᑲᖅᑎᓪᓗᒍ.

People were encouraged to be generous about food. In fact, even if they only had a small amount of food, they were told to make sure they shared with everybody, even if the offering was only big enough to be put in the mouth to chew. People always made sure they had enough food to give away, even if it was very small in times of need and scarcity.

ᑐᑦᑯᔪᕐᑲᕌᖕᒐᑦ
WHEN SOMEONE SLEEPS OVER

ᓄᑕᕋᖅ ᐊᖏᓪᕋᓇᖖᒋᑕᒥᓂ ᓯᓂᒃᑕᖅᐸᑦ (ᑐᑦᑯᒃᐸᑦ) ᓯᓂᒃᑕᕐᑯᔭᐅᖖᒋᓪᓚᕐᒥ, ᐅᕐᑲᔪᓚᐅᖅᐳᑦ ᐊᓈᓈᑕᒎᖅ ᐳᑐᒍ'ᔪᐊᖕᒐᑕ ᐊᐃᓯᓐᓇᓇᐊᕐᑲᕐᒪᒍ ᐊᒪᖅᑯᓂᒃ ᕿᒻᒥᕐᑲᕐᓗᓂ.

When a child sleeps over at another person's home without permission from parents, people would say that the big toe of the distraught mother would follow the child and bring them back. The big toe would come and fetch the child on its dog team of wolves.

ᑕᑯᓯᐊᕐᓂᕋᖅᑕᐃᓕᓂᖅ ᐃᖅᓱᓇᖅᑐᒥᒃ
NEVER WISH TO SEE A FEARFUL THING

ᓂᕐᔪᑎᓂᒃ ᐃᖅᓱᓇᖅᑐᓂᒃ
ᑕᑯᓯᐊᕐᓂᕋᒥᐊᑦᑐᐊᓴᐊᕐᑲᖕᒋᑦᑐᖅ
ᑕᑯᓯᐊᓗᐊᒐ'ᔪᐊᕐᒥᓄᑦ
ᐱᔭᐅᓯᓐᓇᓴᐊᕐᑲᕐᒪᑦ.

People must never wish to see fearsome animals; otherwise that same fearsome animal might attack and kill them.

ᑕᒃᐲᓕᓂᖅ
GETTING POOR VISION

ᐊᖕᒍᑎᓂᒃ ᐊᕐᓇᓂᓪᓘᓐᓃᑦ
ᑕᑯᔨᖕᓂᒃᑕᕐᓂᖅ
ᑕᒃᐲᓕᐊᓚᓐᓇᖅᑐᖅ.

Casting eyes on the private parts of men or women can deteriorate your vision very quickly.

ᑕᓗᑦᓯᕐᓂᖅ
PUTTING UP A BLIND

ᐊᒡᔪᓕᕐᕕᐅᑉ (ᑎᓯᒻᐸ)
ᑕᖅᑭᖕᒐᓂᒃ ᑕᖅᑭᓂᒑᖕᒐᑦ,
ᐊᑖᑕᒐ ᑰᒐᖅ, ᐊᖕᒐᔪᒪ
ᐃᔅᓱᐊᕐᓂᐅᑉ ᖃᐅᔨᕙᓚᐅᕐᓂᓂᒑ
“ᑖᓗᑦᓯᔪᓚᐅᕐᒪᖖᒎᖅ”

ᐃᒃᑭᓐᓂᑯ'ᓈᒥᒃ ᐃᖃ'ᓈᒥᒡᓘᖅᑯ ᓯᑯᑉ ᐃᒪᓛᑉ ᐃᒡᖤᕐᓇᐅᔭᖕᒐᓄᑦ ᓇᑉᐸᖅᓯᕙᓚᐅᕐᓂᕐᒪᑦ. ᓱᑦᑐᕐᑯᑕᐅᖕᒪᖕᒫᑦ ᐊᐱᕆᓱᕐᓂ ᐅᔾᔨᕆᕙᓚᐅᕐᓂᓛ.

During the month of December, my brother Isluarniq watched my father Kuugaq putting a blind on the iglu ice window. The material my father used was a matchstick or a small leaf, and he would stick it up on the ice window. My brother never asked why he did it or what the purpose was.

ᑕᒋᐅᒃᑐᕈᒥ
WHEN SOMEONE SNEEZED

ᑭᓇᒥᐊᖅ ᑕᒋᐅᒃᑐᕈᒥ "ᐅᕙᖕᓛ ᖃᐃᑦ"-ᓚᓇᔭᖅᐳᖅ ᑕᕐᓂᕐᒥᓄᑦ, ᐊᓂᕐᓂᕐᒥᓄᑦ ᕿᒪᒪᒐᐅᓱᐊᖖᒋᒧᑦ, ᐅᖅᑯᓘᖅᑯ ᐊᓯᒋᒃᐸᒍ, ᐊᑎᖓ ᐊᖑᖅᑐᕐᑐᒍ ᖅᑲᐃᕙᖅᓴᕋᔭᖅᐹ ᓲᕐᑐ ᐊᐸᑎᒥᒃ ᐊᑎᖅᑲᖅᓂᖅᐸᑦ ᐃᐊᓪᓇ ᐅᖅᑲᕋᔭᖅᐳᖅ, "ᐊᐸᑏ ᖃᐃᑦ."

Anytime someone sneezed they used to say, "Come back, myself," to their soul. They did not want their breath of life to leave them. Or they would call out the name of the person they were named after. For example, if he was named after Apati, he would say, "Come back, Apati."

ᑯᒪᖅᑭᓐᓂᖅ
GETTING BUGGED

ᐊᒡᖤᖅᑳᕋᓂ (ᐊᖕᒋᖤᖅᑳᕋᓂ) ᐊᒃᑐᒥᒃ ᐊᕐᓂᓇᑦᑕᐃᖤᓂᖅ ᐊᒡᖤᓯᐃᕐᓇᕐᒪᓐᒎᖅ ᓄᑕᕋᐅᓗᐊᕐᓗᓂ ᓯᖤ ᐊᕐᓇᒥᒃ ᐃᓐᓇᐅᖤᖅᑐᒥᒃ ᐱᖅᑲᑎᖅᑲᖅᓂᖅ.

No person was allowed to sleep with a woman before he was old enough. Otherwise, if he did, he would get bugged, and his growth would abort; he would not get any bigger.

ᑰᖕᒪᓕᕐᓂᖅ
GETTING INWARD FEET

ᓄᑕᕋᓛᖅ ᐊᒪᐅᖕᑎᓐᓇᓗᐊᖅᑕᕈᒥ ᓂᐅᓈᑎᒃ ᑰᖕᒪᓕᕐᓂᐊᒃ.

If a baby was in an *amautik* (baby pouch) all the time, their feet would start pointing inward.

ᑲᕕᓯᖅᑐᖅᑕᐃᓕᓂᖅ
AVOID EATING THE PERICARDIAL SAC

ᑐᒃᑐᑉ ᐆᒻᒪᑎᖕᒪᑕ ᐋᖕᒪᓂᒃ ᓂᕿᑦᑕᐃᓕᓯᖅᑐᑦ ᐊᓇᔪᐃᕐᓇᕐᒪᑕᒎᖅ ᐊᓕᒃᑐᖅᓯᓇᕐᓯᐊᒥᐊᕐᒥᒃ ᐃᓇᓗᐊᑦ ᐃᓗᐊᓂ ᐊᔪᖅᓯᓯᓐᓇᑎᐊᖅᑲᕐᒪᑕ.

Inuit were advised to avoid eating a caribou pericardial sac because it could disrupt bowel movement. The sac is very hard to tear apart, and it can get stuck in your intestines.

ᕿᕐᙵᒪᕐᓂᖅ
ASKING TO BE GIVEN SOMETHING

ᑐᓂᔭᐅᓯᐊᕐᓗᓂ ᕿᓄᓂᖅ, ᐱᑎᑕᐅᔪᒪᓂᖅ ᓱᓇᒥᐊᒥᒃ ᐱᓂᖅ ᐊᔪᒃᑲᒥᓂᒃ ᓲᕐᓗ ᑐᒃᓯᐊᖅᑐᑐᑦ.

Inuit avoided asking to be given something that one cannot get. It is similar to praying for something.

ᕿᐊᙶᐊᖅᑕᐃᓕᓂᖅ
AVOID PRETENDING TO CRY

ᓄᑖᖅᑲᑦ ᕿᐊᙶᐊᕐᑯᔭᐅᓯᐃᑦᑐᓚᐅᑦ ᐊᓈᓇᐃᕋᕚᙶᖅ.

As children we were discouraged from pretending to cry; otherwise we might lose our mother.

ᓱᖖᒋᑦᓚᑉᑕ ᕿᐊᖖᒍᐊᕐᑯᔭᐅᓯᐃᑦᑑᓚᐅᖅᐳᒍᑦ
ᐊᓈᓇᐃᑦᓗᐊᕕᒃᓯᓐᓇᓂᐊᕐᑲᕋᑉᑕᒎᖅ ᕿᐊᖖᒍᐊᖅᑕᕈᑉᑕ.
ᐊᓈᓇᐃᕈᐊᕐᓇᐃ’ᑐᐊᕐᒪᑦ ᓇᒡᓕᒋᔮᑐᐊᑉᑎᖕᓂ ᕿᐊᖕᒍᑲᓲᖕᓇᐃᑉᐸᓚᐅᖅᑐᖅ.

We used to be told to never pretend to cry when there was nothing wrong with us. If we pretended to cry, we could lose our mother, who is the only person to love us. So we dared not pretend to cry.

ᕿᐊᑦᑕᐃᓕᓂᖅ ᓯᓚᒥ
AVOID CRYING OUTSIDE

ᓯᓚᒥ ᕿᐊᑦᑕᓕᓯᓚᐅᖅᑐᑦ, ᓯᓚᒥᒎᖅ ᕿᐊᑦᑕᖅᑐᓂ ᑕᒃᐲᓕᑲᖕᓇᖅᑐ’ᓈᖕᒍᖕᒪᑦ.

We were asked never to cry outside; if we cried outside we would get poor vision very soon.

ᕿᓕᖅᓯᓈᑦ
GLANDS

ᕿᓕᖅᓯᓈᑦ
ᓂᕆᑦᑕᐃᓕᕐᑯᔭᐅᕙᓚᐅᖅᑐᑦ
ᑭᑐᒥᐊᓄᑦ ᓈᕐᓗᖕᓇᑦᓯᐊᒥᐊᕐᒪᑕᒎᖅ.

We were often told not to eat the *qiliqsinat* (glands) of animals because they can cause a terrible bellyache.

ᕿᓗᔪᔪᖅ ᓄᓇ
THE LAND BARKS

ᓄᓇᒨᖅ ᐅᕐᓂᒐᐅᓇᓵᓗᐊᓕᕌᖕᒐᒥ ᕿᓗᔪᖕᒪᑦ ᐅᕐᓂᒐᔪᕆᐊᓕᒃ ᑐᓂᓪᓚ’ᓈᕐᓗᒍᓗ ᓱᓇᒥᐊ’ᓈᒥᒃ.

If you’ve been away from your land for a long time, when you return to it, it will bark. So you must visit the land frequently and offer it a small gift.

ᕿᕕᑦᑕᐃᓕᓂᖅ
NEVER GIVE UP

ᐃᓄᐃᑦ ᕿᕕᓚᔪ’ᓈᑦ ᖁᕕᐊᒋᔭᐅᓯᐃᑦᑑᖕᒪᑕ ᕿᕕᑦᑕᐃᓕᕐᖁᔨᒡᒍᓚᐅᖅᐳᑦ.

Inuit have never been impressed with people who give up too easily, so we’ve always encouraged others to be strong and to persevere.

ᕿᕕᑦᑐᐃᑦᑐᖕᒐᓕ ᕿᕕᑦᑕᐃᓖᓪᓕ
“I WILL NEVER GIVE UP”

ᐊᓐᓇᐃᒍᒥ ᐃᖃᓗᖕᒥᒃ ᖃᐃᕙᖅᑲᓴᐅᑎᙱᒍᐊ’ᓈᖅ ᕿᕕᙱᑦᑐᓂ ᑮᓯᒃᑲᓐᓂᕐᖁᕝᓗᒍ ᓲᕐᓗ ᐃᒪᓐᓇ: “ᕿᕕᑦᑐᐃᑦᑐᖕᒐᓖ, ᕿᕕᑦᑕᐃᓖᓪᓖ, ᖄ,ᖄ.ᖄ,ᖄ.”

If someone lost a fish he had caught, there was a little saying that could coax the fish to come back and bite again very soon. It went something like this: “I will never give up, so be like me and don’t give up, qaa, qaa, qaa, qaa.”

ᖁᖅᑕᖅᑐᖅ
WETTING SKIN

ᐅᑭᐊᓖᑦ ᑐᒃᑐᑦ ᐊᒥᖏᑦᑕ ᐃᓚᖏᑦ ᐊᒡᒐᕆᔭᐅᓯᐊᔪᐃᑦᑐᑦ ᖁᖅᑕᖄᖕᒪᑕ, ᐸᓂᖁᓗᐊᖅᖢᓂ ᐊᒥᖅ ᒥᖅᑯᖏᑦ ᐃᖕᒥᖕᓂᒥᐊᖅ ᒥᑦᓯᓕᖅᑕᔪᔪᑦ (ᑭᓂᑦᑕᔪᔪᑦ).

Some fall-season caribou skins tend to get wet easily, so people didn't use them for bedding. Even when they are dry, the fur tends to condensate the humid air easily on its own.

ᖁᔭᓴᐃᓂᖅ
MAKING ANOTHER PERSON THANKFUL

ᐃᓄᐃᑦ ᖃᑯᑎᒃᑯᑦ ᖁᔭᓴᐃᓯᓚᐅᖅᐳᑦ ᓱᓇᒥᐊᒥᒃ ᐃᓅᑉ ᖁᕕᐊᕆᔪᓇᖅᑕᖕᒪᓂᒃ ᐊᐃᑦᑐᖅᖢᑎᒃ ᐳᐃᒍᐊᓪᓚᖕᓇᕈᓇᐃᕆᐊᖅᑐᒥᒃ, ᓲᖅᓗ ᖃᖕᒪᔅᐅᒃᐸᑦ ᐸᖕᓂ'ᔫᑉ ᑐᓐᓄᕈᔅᖢ'ᔪᐊᖕᒪᓂᒃ.

Inuit had a custom of giving something that would be really appreciated by the recipient—something that was really hard to forget. For example, if it was in the old days, a nice, big, thick piece of caribou fat would be a real prize.

ᒥᓕᖅᑖᖅᓂᖅ
GETTING FRECKLES

ᕿᒻᒥᖅ ᓂᓕᖅᐸᑦ ᐃᒡᓚᖅᑕᐃᓕᓂᖅ ᒥᓕᖅᑖᕋᕗᖅ ᐅᕝᕙᓘᕝᕙ ᓄᖕᓂᖅᑖᕋᕗᑦ, ᑕᐃᒃᑯᐊ ᕿᓯᐅᒃ ᐃᑭᐊᖕᒪᓂ ᕿᖅᓂᖅᓂ'ᓈᑦ ᒥᓕᐅᓂᕋᒪᐅᔪᑦ ᓄᖕᓂᐅᓂᕋᒪᐅᔪᑦᖢᓘᕝᕙ.

People were told not to laugh at or make fun of a pooping dog, or else they would get freckles. *Miliit* or *nungniit* are little brown blotches on the skin.

ᒪᑉᐸᑐᖅᑕᐃᓕᓂᖅ
AVOID EATING MAPPA

ᐊᖑᑎᑦ ᑐᒃᑐᑉ ᒪᑉᐸᖓᓂᒃ ᓂᕆᑦᑕᐃᓕᓱᖅᑐᖅ ᑎᒃᓴᓱᐃᕈᐊᖖᕆᔅᓗᑎᒃ ᓂᕆᔪᓂᒎᖅ ᑎᓴᒃᓕᔪᐃᖅᓇᖅᒪᑕ.

Men were to avoid eating the *mappa* (visceral membrane) of a caribou, because it could cause erectile dysfunction if they ate it.

ᒪᑭᑎᕆᑦᑕᖅᓂᖅ
PUTTING THINGS UPRIGHT

ᓱᓇᒥᐊᓂᒃ ᐃᓗᓕᖓᓂᒃ ᑕᑯᔭᖄᖓᑉᐸᑕ, ᐱᑐᖅᕿᖅᓗᖓᓂᒡᓗ ᐃᓐᓇᖓᒐᔪᓂᒃ ᒪᑭᑦᓯᑦᑕᖅᑯᔭᐅᕙᓚᐅᖅᐳᒍᑦ ᐃᔅᓗᖅᑫᐅᓴᕈᑎᒋᓪᓗᒍ ᑎᒍᒃᑲᓂᒃ ᐊᒻᒪᓖᑦ ᐱᑦᓯᐊᕙᖅᓂᒃᑯᑦ.

Every time we noticed things that had been knocked over, we were advised to put them back upright so we would enjoy a long, healthy life. We were even told to treat our possessions with great care.

ᖁᓚᒃᓯᒃᑯᑦ ᒪᓕᒍᓐᓇᖅᓂᖅ
ABILITY TO FOLLOW

ᓱᒃᑲᐅᔪᓐᓂᐅᑦ ᐃᕆᓇᓕᐅᑦ, ᒪᓕᒃᒍᓐᓂᐅᑦ ᖁᓚᒃᓯᖅᑐᓂᒃ ᐊᖖᒍᑎᑦᑕᔪᓗᓂ.

There were magical spells that enabled a person to follow and catch up with another dog team quickly.

ᐃᓗᐊᓕᖅᑎᑦᓯᔪᓐᓇᖅᓂᖅ
ABILITY TO HEAL

ᐊᓂᐊᖅᓂᖅᒥᒃ ᒪᒥᑦᓯᓐᓂᐅᑦ ᐃᕆᓇᓕᐅᑦ, ᓱᔪᖕᓇᐃᑦᑎᑦᓯᔾᔪᑦ.

There were magical spells to heal ailments or sickness.

ᓂᕆᐅᔮᕐᓂᖅ
BEING HOPEFUL SOMETHING GOOD IS ABOUT TO HAPPEN

ᐱᑦᓯᐊᕐᒥᒃ ᐱᔪᕐᑲᕐᓂᐊᒥᒃ ᓇᔪᓇᐃᒃᑯᑕᖅ, ᐱᓚᐅᖅᓯᒪᙱᑕᕐᓂᒃ ᐱᒐᔪᐃᑦᑐᒥᒡᔫᓐᓃᑦ ᐱᔪᕐᑲᕐᓂᒃᑯᑦ ᓇᔪᓇᐃᒃᑯᑕᖅ ᓱᔪᕐᑲᕐᓂᐊᓕᕐᒥᔪᒥᒃ ᓂᕆᐅᕆᓚᐅᙱᑕᕐᓂᒃ ᐱᐅᔪᒥᒃ.

When you sense something good is about to happen, it usually comes to you in a dream. The happy result usually begins to happen almost the same day.

ᓂᕆᐅᔮᕐᓂᕋᔪᔪᑦ ᐅᔾᔨᕐᓇᖅᑐᒥᒃ ᓯᓐᓇᒃᑐᖅᑑᑎᒃ ᐊᒻᒪ ᓯᓐᓇᒃᑐᕐᓂᖓᑕ ᐅᓪᓗᑉ ᐃᓚᖕᒐᓂ ᓱᓇᒥᐊᒥᒃ ᐱᐅᔪᒥᒃ ᕿᒍᐊᓇᖅᑐᒥᒃ ᐱᔪᕐᑲᖅᑐᓂ. ᓲᕐᓗ ᓅᓇᒦᐅᑕᐅᕙᓚᐅᖅᑐᑦ ᑕᓯᕐᔫᑉ ᕿᙵᑯᐊᓃᑦᑐᑦ ᓯᓐᓇᒃᑑᒪᕆᔭᕋ ᐳᐃᒍᔪᐃᕋᑉᑯ ᐃᓪᓚᖅᑐᖓ ᐊᓪᓛᑦ ᑐᑉᑲᒪ, ᑕᐃᒪ ᐃᓄᒃ ᑕᓯᕐᔫᑉ ᕿᙵᐊᒍᑦ ᑐᓯᐊᑦᑖᓪᓗᓂ ᖃᐃᓐᓂᕈᒪᓗᒍ ᑐᐱᑉᑎᖕᓄᑦ, ᓄᖅᑲᓚᐅᖅᐸᒃᑐᓂ ᑭᖑᒧᑦ ᕿᓂᓕᖅᐸᒃᑐᓂ. ᑐᑉᑲᑉᑕ ᐅᔾᔨᕆᒐᑉᑯ ᐃᓪᓚᓕᖅᐸᒃᑐᖓ ᐅᓂᑉᑳᕆᓚᐅᖅᓯᒪᔭᕋ ᐅᓪᓚᒃᑯᑦ ᑐᑉᑲᑉᑕ.

This was a sign that something nice would happen; that a rare event was coming to pass; that something nice you were not expecting was coming.

ᑐᐸᖅᑲᒥᖕᒋᒐᔮᓕᖅᑎᑦᓗᑕ ᑐᒃᑐᒥᒃ ᐊᑕᐅᓯ'ᓈᒥᒃ ᑐᓯᐊᑦᑐᐱ'ᔪᐊᕐᒥ ᖃᐃᕋᐅᔭᖅᑐᒥᒃ ᑐᐱᑉᑎᖕᓄᑦ ᑕᑯᓚᑉᑕ ᐅᕐᑲᕋᒪ ᓯᓐᓇᒃᑐᓇᓚᐅᖅᑕᑉᑐᑦ ᐱᓯᖕᓂᕋᖅᓗᒍ ᐅᖃᐅᑎᔭᐅᓚᐅᖅᓯᒪᕗᖓ ᓂᕆᐅᔮᕐᓂᕋᖅᑕᐅᓪᓗᖓ.

For example, when we used to live inland, we were living around the west end of Tasirjuaq Lake, and I had a dream that I could not forget. In fact, I was laughing when I woke from the dream. I dreamed of a person coming towards our tent from the west of the lake with a very funny limp. The person in my dream would occasionally stop and look back. When we awoke that morning, I was laughing as I told my dream. After we were up for a while, we saw one lone caribou coming slowly towards our tent with a funny limp. When we saw it, I said it was walking exactly like I had seen in my dream. Then they told me it's like a vision in my dream, about something good about to happen.

ᓂᑕᕐᓂᖅ
WHEN YOU POOP

ᑭᓇᒥᐊᖅ ᓂᑕᕈᒥ "ᒧᕌᖅ," ᓚᓇᔭᖅᐳᖅ ᑎᕆᒐᓂᖅᐸᓗᖖᒍᐊᖅᑐᖅ, ᑎᕆᒐᓂᐊᒥᒃ ᑎᕆᒐᓂᐊᖅᓯᐅᑎᒥᓄᑦ ᓇᒃᑲᕐᑯᔨᕝᓗᓂ.

When anyone poops, he would say, "*Muraaq*," imitating a fox's call, in order to get a fox to fall into his trapline.

ᓂᒻᔪᒍᑎᑦ
MAGICAL FRINGES

ᐊᖕᒐᑦᑯᑦ ᑕᑉᓯᐊᓄᑦ ᓂᕕᖖᒐᖅᑎᕐᓂᑯᑦ ᓱᓇᒥᐊᑦ ᐱᑦᑐᑯᑎᑦ.

Magical fringes were items that were tied up in the shaman's belt by other people for a good wish.

ᓄᑕᕋᒃᓴᓛᑦ
PREGNANT WOMEN

ᐃᑦᓱᖅᑕᕐᑯᔭᐅᓯᓚᐅᖅᑐᑦ ᐊᒻᒪ ᑭᖑᐱᐊᖅᑐᕐᓗᑎᒃ ᐃᑎᖅᑎᖅᑕᐃᓐᕐᑯᔭᐅᕝᓗᑎᒃ ᑭᖑᒻᒧᑦ ᓵᖖᒐᕙᒥᒃ ᓄᑕᖅᑭᓇᕗᖅ.

Pregnant women were encouraged to go outside as soon as they woke up and were prohibited from crawling backwards as they entered the iglu. This was to ensure that when they went into labour, the child would not come out with their feet first.

ᓂᕕᐊᖅᓵᕐᕚᓗᓂ ᑭᓗᒻᒧᑦ ᓵᖖᒐᒐᕙᑦᑐᐊᕈᒥ ᖁᒻᒧᑦ ᓵᖖᒐᕙᐃᓐᓇᕐᓂᒃ ᓄᑕᕋᖅᑖᖅᑕᕋᔭᖅ.

Girls were not allowed to lie on the bed with their head against the back of the iglu; otherwise, when they were in labour, their child would come out with their feet first.

ᐊᖑᑎ’ᓈᖑᓂᐊᖀᖕᒪᑕ ᓄᑕᖃᒃᓴᓖᑦ ᓈᖕᒋᑦ ᓄᕝᕙᓇᑦᑎᐊᒥᐊᔪᔪᑦ
ᐊᕐᓇ’ᓈᖑᓂᐊᖀᖕᒪᑕ ᓈᓗᒃᑖᖕᒪ ᖃᑦᓯᔪᔪᖅ ᓄᕝᕙᕐᓗᒃᓗᓂ.

If the baby was a little boy, the lump on the mother’s belly would be pointy.

ᐊᕐᓇ’ᓈᖑᔾᔭᖀᖕᒪᑕᔫᖅ ᒥᓇᐊᙵᑦᑕᙵᒪᐃᓐᓇᔪᔪᑦ ᒥᓇᐊᙵᒪᐃᓐᓇᖅᑕᖅᓗᑎᒃᓗ
ᒥᑭᓂᖕᒋᓐᓂ.

If the baby was a little girl, the lump on the mother’s belly would be even.

ᐊᖑᑎ’ᓈᖑᔾᔭᖀᖕᒪᑕ ᓂᓇᑦᑕᒥᐊ’ᑐᐊᓪᓚᕐᒥᒃ ᔫᕐᐳᓪᓕᖅᑕᔪᐃᑦᑐᑦ ᓄᑕᖃᒃᓴᐅᓂᖕᒋᓂ.

If the child was a little boy, the mother would not feel burning in her food sack while she was pregnant.

ᓄᑕᖃᖅᑖᒪᓂᓵᑦ ᐆᓯᒪᔪᐃᓐᓇᕐᓂᒃ ᓂᓇᕐᑯᔭᐅᓗᐊᖅᑑᔭᔪᓚᐅᖅᑐᑦ.

It seemed like women with newborn babies were only fed cooked food.

ᐃᒥᕋᖅᑐᒡᔪᐊᖅᑕᕐᑯᔭᐅᕙᓚᐅᖅᑐᑦ ᐃᒻᒧᕐᑲᑦᓯᐊᕐᑯᒧᑦ ᓄᑕᕋᓛᖕᒐ ᐱᕈᑦᓯᐊᕐᓂᐊᕐᒪᑦ.

A mother was encouraged to drink lots of fluids so she would produce lots of milk.

ᐅᒃᑯᓲᑦ ᓯᓇᐃᓂᒃ ᐃᑉᐸᖅᑕᕌᖕᒐᑕ, ᐃᒥᕋᖅᑑᑎᓂᒡᓗ ᓴᓗᒪᖅᓴᐃᑦᑕᕌᖕᒐᑕ ᐃᓂᕐᑯᓇᖅᑐ'ᓈᓂᒃ ᓄᑕᕋᖅᑖᔪᓚᐅᖅᑐᑦ.

When pregnant ladies had a habit of cleaning around the cooking pots and ladles, it was said that they would have quiet little babies that didn't whine.

ᐊᕐᓇ'ᓈᑦ ᐃᓗᑐᖅᑕᕐᑯᔭᐅᓯᐃᑦᑐᓚᐅᑦ (ᐊᐳᑎᑉ ᐃᒡᓗᑉ ᐃᒐᓛᖕᒐᑕ ᓯᑯᑉ "ᐃᓗᖕᒐᓂᒃ" ᐸᑐᖕᓂᑯᒥᒃ) ᓈᕐᓗᑦᓯᐊᒥᐊᕋᕗᕉᖅ ᓄᑕᖅᑭᓂᓗᓕᕈᒥ.

Young women were not allowed to eat frost (frost that was on an ice window); otherwise they would experience a lot of bellyaches when they were in labour.

ᑭᑉᑲᖅᑕᐃᓕᓯᓚᐅᖅᑐᑦ ᐊᕐᓇᑦ ᓄᑕᖅᑖᓵᑦ (ᓴᐅᓂᓕᒃᑐᖅᑕᐃᓕᔪᑦ) ᓄᑕᕋᓛᑉ ᐱᕈᖅᓴᓂᖕᒐᓂ ᑕᖅᑭᓂ ᐊᕐᕕᓂᓕᖕᓂ.

Women who had just had babies were not allowed to eat meat with the bone in while the baby was growing up for a period of six months.

ᐊᕐᓇᐃᑦ ᓄᑕᕋᓛᒥᒃ ᐊᒫᒪᒃᑎᑦᓯᔪᑦ ᐃᒥᕋᖅᑐᕐᑯᔭᐅᒡᒍᓚᐅᖅᐳᑦ ᐃᒥᕋᕉᖅ ᐃᒻᒧᑦᓯᐊᕆᖕᓇᕐᒪᑦ.

Women with suckling babies were encouraged to drink lots of broth in order to have good milk, so the baby would grow up strong and healthy.

ᓄᕙᒃᑐᓂ ᐃᒥᖅᑕᕐᓂᖅ
DRINKING WATER WHILE HAVING A COLD

ᓄᕙᒃᑐᑦ ᐃᒥᕐᒥᒃ ᐃᒥᖅᑕᐃᓕᓯᓚᐅᖅᐳᑦ ᓄᕙᓕᒪᒋᓐᓇᕐᓂᐊᕋᓱᒋᕝᓗᑎᒃ. ᖃᖕᒐᓴᖅ ᓄᕙᓕᖄᖕᒐᑉᑕ ᐃᒥᖅᑕᐃᓕᕙᓚᐅᖅᐳᒍᑦ ᓄᕙᓕᒃᑲᓐᓂᖁᔭᐅᓇᑕ.

People who suffered a cold abstained from drinking water, believing that it would worsen their cold. In the past, we sometimes abstained from drinking water to avoid getting a cold.

ᓇᑉᐸᐃᑦᑕᕐᓂᖅ
PUTTING UP A SMALL STICK

ᑕᖅᕿᖅ ᓄᑖᖅ ᑎᑭᑦᓴᖄᖕᒐ ᐱᖅᑯᓯᖅᑕᖅᑲᓚᐅᖅᐳᖅ ᓇᑉᐸᐃᑦᑕᕐᓂᕐᒥᒃ ᕿᔪ'ᓈᒥᒃ ᓂᕐᔪᑎᑦ ᓇᓪᓕᐊᖕᓂᒥᐊᖅ ᐱᑕᖅᑕᕈᐊᖅᓱᑎᒃ.

When a new moon arrived, it was customary to erect a short piece of stick so that one could get any kind of animal that was out there.

ᓇᖅᑭᖅᓱᕐᓂᖅ
MAKING A CONFESSION

ᐱᑦᓯᐊᙱᓐᓂᑯᐃᔭᕐᓂᖅ. ᐱᑦᓯᐊᖕᒋᓐᓂᑯᒧᑦ ᑲᙳᓇᖅᑐᒥᒃ ᑭᓇᒥᐊᖅ ᐊᓐᓂᐊᕈᑎᖃᕈᒥ ᐊᙱᐊᓇᖅᑲᑦᑖᒃᑲᒥᓂᒃ ᓴᖅᑭᑎᒥᐊᖅᑐᒍ ᐅᖅᑲᖅᑯᔭᐅᕙᓚᐅᖅᐳᖅ ᐋᖅᑭᖕᓂᐊᕐᒪᑦ. ᐃᓗᒥᐅᑕᓇᔪᓐᓇᐃᕐᓗᒍ ᐱᑦᓯᐊᖕᒋᓐᓂᑯᓂ ᐃᓅᑦᓯᐊᕋᐅᔭᖅᑲᑕᐅᓕᕐᓂᐊᕐᒪᑦ.

Confessing and renouncing evil things you had done could help heal you. If someone was sick because of a shameful thing he had done, that was hard to heal. They were encouraged to be brave and confess their wrongdoing in order to get healed. If the penitent could expunge the thing that was within himself, he would be healed and be able to live a long, peaceful life.

ᓇᓚᕐᑕᐃᓕᓂᖅ ᑭᓗᒻᒧᑦ ᓵᙵᓗᓂ
AVOID LYING ON A BED WITH YOUR HEAD AGAINST THE BACK WALL

ᑭᓗᒻᒧᑦ ᓵᙵᓗᑎᒃ ᓂᕐᕿᓚᐅᔭᖅᑕᐃᓕᕙᓚᐅᖅᐳᑦ ᐃᒡᓕᕐᒥ ᒪᒃᑯᒃᑐᑦ, ᑲᖕᒍᑦᓯᑖᒐᐅᕙᓚᐅᖅᓱᑎᒡᓗ ᐃᒡᔪᖕᒥᖕᓂᒃ ᐅᕐᑯᒪᐃᒃᓴᓗᐊᒧᑦ ᓇᓚᓂᖅᑕᐅᕝᓗᑎᒃ. ᑕᒪᒃᑯᐊ ᓯᕘᕐᓴᐅᑎᕐᓘᔭᐃᑦ ᑲᖑᓇᖅᑐᑦ ᓘᕝᕙ ᐊᑐᒐᐅᕙᓚᐅᖅᐳᑦ ᐃᓅᕐᒥᒃ ᐱᑦᓗᓇᒃᑑᕐᑯᔨᓂᕐᒧᑦ ᐃᑦᕐᑯᒪᑦᑎᐊᕐᓗᓂ ᓇᓚᓗᕐᑭᐅᔭᖅᓯᓐᓇᙱᑦᓗᓂ ᐊᓐᓂᐊᙱᒃᑯᒥ.

Young people were told to avoid lying on the bed with their heads facing the back wall. People would say things that made the offending party feel shameful, like, “Are your balls getting too heavy so that you have to lie in bed like that?” Embarrassment and shaming were used in these cases so that the child would learn to be alert and not just lay around doing nothing if they were not sick.

ᓱᖅᑯᓕᒪᓂᖅ
BULGING KNEECAP

ᖃᖓᓴᖅ ᐊᓕᐅᖅᑐᖃᔪᓚᐅᕐᒪᑦ ᐃᓄᒐᕈᑦᓕᐅᓂᕋᖅᑕᐅᔪᓂᒃ (ᐃᓄᒐᔮᐱ'ᔪᐊᕐᓂᒃ) ᐸᔮᕐᓂᒃᓱᑎᒎᖅ ᑐᖁᑦᓯᓯᖅᑐᓂᒃ, ᓲᖅᑯᓕᓂᓕᖕᓂᒎᖅ ᐊᑦᑕᖅᑖᓕᖕᓂᒃ (ᖃᕐᓕᓕᖕᓂᒃ) ᑲᑉᐱᐊᒋᔭᖃᕐᒪᑕ ᓲᖅᑯᓕᓂᖃᕐᓂᓕᔪᓚᐅᖅᐳᑦ ᑲᑉᐱᐊᒋᔭᐅᓯᐊᒧᑦ ᐃᓄᒐᕈᑦᓕᖕᓄᑦ.

Long ago there were little people that Inuit called *inugaru'niit.* They were reputed to fight people to kill them. It is said that they were normally scared of people with pants that showed bulging kneecaps. We used to try to have bulging kneecaps in our pants so these little people would be afraid to attack us.

ᓯᖖᒍᑦ
MAGIC SPELL THAT PUT A PERSON TO SLEEP

ᓯᓂᓕᖅᑎᑦᓯᔾᔪᑦ ᐃᕆᓇᓕᐅᑎᒃᑯᑦ. ᖃᓄᑐᐃᓐᓇᖅ ᓯᑎᑦᓯᔾᔪᑎᓂᒃ ᐃᓄᐃᑦ ᐃᕆᓇᓕᐅᑎᖃᔪᓚᐅᕐᒪᑕ ᐱᑕᖃᖅᐸᓚᐅᕐᓂᕆᕗᖅ ᓯᖖᒍᒻᒥᒃ, ᓯᓃᓐᓇᑭᐊᓕᖅᑎᑦᑎᔪᑦ.

In the past, people had magic that could put people to sleep. Inuit had different kinds of magic spells, and putting people to sleep was one of them. People under the spell would not want to wake up.

ᓯᓂᖃᑦᑖᖅᑕᐃᓕᓂᖅ
AVOID SLEEPING TOO LONG

ᓯᓂᖃᑦᑖᖅᑕᐃᓕᓯᓚᐅᖅᐳᑦ ᐊᒧᓂᐊᒐᐅᓯᐊᖖᒋᔅᓱᑎᒃ ᐃᒡᓕᕐᒥᑦ ᐊᒻᒪ ᐱᑕᒃᓴᕋᓗᐊᒥᓂᒃ ᑭᖑᕋᐃᖅᑯᓇᒍ ᓯᓂᒃᓯᓐᓇᑦᑐᐊᖅᑎᑦᓗᒍ. ᖃᖓᓴᖅ ᑖᖅᑎᑦᓗᒍᐊᒡᓛᑦ ᓯᓕ ᑐᐸᔪᓚᐅᖅᑐᑦ ᐃᑦᓯᖅᑕᐅᔭᖅᓗᑎᒡᓗ ᓯᓕ ᖃᐅᒻᒪᖅᓴᓕᖖᒋᒻᒪᖔᑦ ᓇᐅᑦᓯᖅᑐᖅᓗᑎᒃ.

Inuit tried to avoid oversleeping lest someone came and pulled them out of bed forcibly. People also avoided oversleeping to avoid going out too late when the animals had already gone through the area while they were sleeping. Long ago, Inuit would get out of bed while it was still dark, long before dawn, and they would prepare and wait for daylight.

ᓯᓐᓇᒃᑐᕐᓂᖅ
DREAMING

ᐊᔾᔨᐅᖕᒋᑦᑐᒥᒃ ᓯᓐᓇᒃᑑᒪᓂᖅ ᐃᓅᓯᕐᒥᒃ ᐊᑐᓕᓪᓗᐊᕕᖕᓂᐊᖅᑐᒥᒃ. ᐃᓄᐃᑦ ᐃᓚᖏᑦ ᓯᓐᓇᒃᑐᕐᓂᕐᒥᒃᑎᒍᑦ ᖃᐅᔨᑎᑕᐅᕙᓚᐅᖅᑐᑦ.

Inuit believed that dreams could be used to interpret and predict things that were going to happen in their lives. Some Inuit were able to find out things through their dreams.

ᓯᕗᓂᕐᓗᐊᓂᖅ
WHEN YOUR FUTURE IS NOT GOING RIGHT

ᐱᑦᓯᐊᓕᖓᐃᕐᓂᖅ, ᓱᓕᓇᒐᓗᐊᕐᓗᓂᔫᕝᕙ ᐱᓂᕐᓗᐊᓪᓚᒥᐊᕐᓂᖅ, ᓇᑯᐊᓕᕈᑎᓯᐃᕐᓂᖅ ᐱᑦᓴᐅᖕᒋᑦᑐᒧᑦ ᑎᑭᑕᐅᓕᕐᓂᕐᒥ, ᓯᕗᓂᓇᓂᐊᓖ ᐱᐅᖕᒋᑦᑐᖅᑕᖃᐃᓐᓇᖅᑐᖅ.

Sometimes things seem to go all wrong. It was believed that experiencing a hard time was due to an evil force that had come upon you. Everything you did seemed to have something wrong with it.

ᓱᐅᖅᑲᒥᒃ ᐃᒫᓄᑦ ᐃᒋᑦᓯᑦᑕᐃᓕᓂᖅ
AVOID THROWING SAND IN THE WATER

ᐃᒫᓄᑦ ᐃᖅᑲᑦᑕᖅᑕᖅᐸᑦ ᓂᐸᓗᓕᖁᔭᖅ. ᓱᐅᖁᒥᒃ ᐃᒫᓄᑦ ᐃᖅᑲᑦᑕᖅᑕᐃᓕᕙᓚᐅᖅᐳᒍᑦ ᐃᖅᑲᑦᑕᖅᑕᕐᓂᕉᖅ ᓂᐸᓗᓕᕐᓇᖅᒪᑦ.

If someone threw sand in the water, it might start raining. So we tried never to throw sand in the water because we heard it could cause rain.

ᓱᐱᓯᓂᖅ ᐃᔨᖕᓂᒃ
BLOWING IN THE EYES

ᑭᓇᒥᐊᖅ ᐃᔾᔨᑉᐸᑦ
ᐃᔨᖓ ᐊᐅᐸᑉᐹᖅᑎᑦᑐᒍ
ᓯᖕᑐᐊᖀᑦᓚᕆᐊᖅᓗᒍ ᐃᔾᔨᓯᒪᐅᑎᖓ
ᓱᐱᔾᐅᓂᓗᔪᓚᐅᖅᐳᖅ.

If a person got something in their eye, someone else would keep the eye open with their fingers and blow at it in order to rid the eye of the splinter.

ᓴᑭᐊᒃᑐᖅᑕᐃᓕᓂᖅ
AVOID EATING CARIBOU BRISKET

ᑐᒃᑐᑉ ᓴᑭᐊᖓᓂᒃ ᐊᖑᑎᑦ
ᓂᕿᑦᑕᐃᓕᕈᓚᐅᖅᐳᑦ ᓂᕿᒃᐸᙳᖅ
ᓄᓕᐊᓯᐊ ᓴᑭᐊᑦᓗᓕᖁᕗᖅ.
ᐊᖑᑎᑦ ᓴᑭᐊᖅᑐᖅᑕᐃᓕᓯᓚᐅᖅᑐᑦ,
ᓴᑭᐊᒃᑐᖅᐸᑕᒎᖅ ᓄᓕᐊᖓ
ᓴᑭᐊᑦᓗᓕᖁᔭᕐᒪᑦ. ᓴᑭᐊᑦ
ᓂᕐᑭᑦᓯᐊᕙᐅᖕᒪᑕ
ᑐᓐᓄᕐᑲᕋᓘᔭᖅᓗᑎᒡᓗ
ᐃᒃᓚᖕᓇᖅᓯᐊᕐᒪᑕ ᐊᕐᓇᓄᑦ
ᓂᕿᔭᒃᓴᐅᑎᑕᐅᕙᕐᒪᑕ ᐊᖑᑎᑦ
ᓴᑭᐊᒃᑐᖅᑕᐃᓕᓯᓚᐅᖅᑐᑦ.

Inuit men were prohibited from eating a cut of the caribou brisket, believing that if they ate it, their female partner would have a sore pectoral muscle. The brisket cut is a very appetizing food with a bit of fat on the meat. The meat was reserved exclusively for women, so men tried not to eat it.

ᓯᕿᓂᐅᑉ ᕿᓚᐅᑖ
A RING AROUND THE SUN WILL MAKE YOU EAT ALL THE TIME

ᓯᕿᓂᐅᒻᒨᖅ ᕿᓚᐅᑖᑕ ᖃᖓᑦᑕᖏᓐᓂᖓᓂ ᐊᒡᓗᐊᕐᒥᖕᓂ ᐃᖃᓗᒃᑐᖅᑕᐃᓕᕙᓚᐅᖅᑐᑦ. ᐃᖃᓗᒃᑯᒥ ᓯᕿᓂᐅᑉ ᕿᓚᐅᑖ ᖃᖓᑦᑕᖅᑳᖅᑎᓐᓇᒍ ᓂᕆᑦᑕᐃᓕᓇᔭᖅᑐᖅ ᐃᖃᓗᒃᑕᒥᓂᒃ ᐊᒡᓗᐊᕐᒥᓂᓯᐅᕐᓗᓂ ᑳᒃᑲᓗᐊᕈᒥᓘᓐᓃᑦ ᖃᖓᑦᑕᖅᓱᓚᐅᕐᓗᓂ ᑭᓯᐊᓂ ᓂᕆᒋᐊᕋᔭᖅ. ᖃᖓᑦᑕᖅᑳᖅᑎᓐᓇᒍᒨᖅ ᓂᕆᔪᑦ ᑲᐃᔪᐃᔪᖕᒪᑕ, ᓂᕆᙵᐃᓐᓇᒥᐊᕈᐊᓕᖅᓘᑎᒃ.

Long ago, Inuit avoided eating fish near the fishing hole if there were sun dogs around the sun. So if a fisher caught a fish and they were hungry, they would have to wait until the sun dogs disappeared. People who ate before the allotted time ended up wanting to eat all the time, never feeling full.

ᐃᓚᕇᒍᓯᖅ
FORMS OF RELATIONSHIPS

ᐊᑦᓯᖅᑐᐃᓂᖅ ᑐᑭᖏᓗ:

What different names mean:

ᐃᕐᓂᖅ: ᓄᑕᕋ ᐊᖑᑕᐅᒃᐸᒃ

Irniik (my son): If the child was a boy

ᓄᑕᕋᖅ: ᓄᑕᕋᓐᓇᓇᔾ ᐊᖑᑦ ᐊᕐᓇᕐᓘᓐᓃᑦ

Panik (daughter): If the child was a girl

ᐸᓂᒃ: ᓄᑕᕋᖅ ᐊᕐᓇᐅᕐᐸᑦ

Nutaraq (child): Someone's favourite child, either a boy or a girl

ᐸᓂᕐᑯᑎᒐ: ᓄᑕᕋᖅ ᐊᕐᓇᐅᒃᐸᑦ ᐸᓂᓐᓇᖑᒥᐅᒃ ᑕᐃᒪᓐᓇ ᑐᖅᓱᕋᕋᔭᖅᐹ

Paniqutiga (my little daughter): If the child was a much loved girl

ᐊᑦᓯᐊᖅ: ᓄᑕᕋᖅ ᐊᖖᒐᔪᖅᑳᓚᐅᖖᒐᓂᒃ ᐊᑎᓕᒃ, ᐊᓈᓇᓚᐅᖖᒐᓂᒃ
ᐊᑖᑕᓚᐅᖖᒐᓂᓪᓘᓐᓃᑦ

Atsiaq: A child named after one of their parents

ᐃᔨᕐᑯᑎᒐ: ᓄᑕᕋᖅ ᓇᒡᓕᒋᔮ ᐃᔨᒋᒃᑕ ᖃᓄᐃᓐᓂᒋᒃ ᐱᐅᓗᒋᒃ

Ijiqutiga (my little eyes): A much-loved child with beautiful eyes

ᐅᓗᐊᕐᑯᑎᒐ: ᓄᑕᕋᖅ ᓇᒡᓕᒋᔮ ᐅᓗᐊᒋᒃᑕ ᖃᓄᐃᓐᓂᒋᒃ ᐱᐅᓗᒋᒃ

Uluaqutiga (my little cheek): A much-loved child with beautiful cheeks

ᐃᓄᒃᑎᑐᑦ ᐅᖃᐅᓯᑦ ᑐᑭᖏᑦ
GLOSSARY OF INUKTITUT WORDS

The pronunciation guides in this book are intended to support non-Inuktitut speakers in their reading of Inuktitut words. These pronunciations are not exact representations of how the words are pronounced by Inuktitut speakers. For more resources on how to pronounce Inuktitut words, visit inhabitmedia.com/inuitnipingit.

WORD	PRONUNCIATION	DEFINITION
Aggaittuq	ahg-GAH-eet-took	name
Airaqtuuq	ah-ee-rahk-TOOK	place name
akłak	ahk-LAHK	grizzly bear
aksallajuittuk	ahk-sahl-lah-YOO-EET-took	eyes that always stare in one direction
Aliqtiksaq	ah-LEEK-teek-SAHK	name
amautalik	ah-MAH-oo-tah-leek	mythological ogress that steals children on the land
amauti	ah-MAH-oo-tee	woman's parka with a pouch for carrying a child
amautik	ah-MAH-oo-teek	baby pouch
anginniq	ah-NGEEN-neek	becoming alive again after he was dead
Arviat	AHR-vee-aht	place name
atigi	ah-TEE-gee	coat or parka
atsiaq	AHT-see-ak	a child named after one of their parents
aulajjut	ah-oo-LAH-joot	a fishing hook and line handle, made of a piece of wood or something else
Hauniqtuurmiut	hah-oon-EEK-toor-mee-oot	the people who live in big bone place
iglu	EEG-loo	snow house
igluit	EEG-loo-eet	snow houses
Iimaarasugjuk	ee-mah-rah-SOOG-JOOK	name
ijiqutiga	ee-yee-koo-TEE-gah	my little eyes

ijiraak	ee-yee-RAHK	large land spirits (dual)
ijirait	ee-yee-RAH-eet	large land spirits (plural)
ijiraq	ee-yee-RAHK	large land spirit (singular)
ikajuqatigiingniq	ee-kah-yoo-KAH-tee-geen-gneek	working together
ikkalrut	eek-kahl-ROOT	pressure ridges in pack ice
ingnirjuk	EENG-neer-jook	sea ghost
inugaru'niit	ee-noo-gah-ROO-neet	little people
Inuit Qaujimajatuqangit	ee-noo-EET kah-oo-yee-mah-YAH-too-kah-ngeet	traditional Inuit knowledge
inuksuk	ee-NOOK-sook	stone marker used to aid hunters and indicate direction
Inutquaq	ee-noot-KOO-ahk	name
ipiutaq	ee-pee-oo-TAHK	thin fishing line made of continuously braided caribou sinew
iqqittuuq	ee-KEET-TOOK	one with no anus
irniik	eer-NEEK	my son
Isluarniq	ee-sloo-AHR-neek	name
jurjurii, jurjurialuk	yoor-yoor-EE, yoor-yoor-ee-AH-look	chant
kamiik	kah-MEEK	two skin boots
kaugjagjuk	kah-OOG-jahg-jook	a person who pounds blubber
kauk	kah-OOK	walrus skin
kivgaluk	KEEV-gah-look	an evil fish that bites a hook
Kiviuq	kee-vee-OOK	name
kukki	KOOK-kee	food particles between teeth
Kuugaq	KOO-gahk	name
mammingajuk	mahm-mee-NGAH-yook	droopy buttocks
manaq	mah-NAHK	straight bone hook and line placed in a fish tail
maniq	mah-NEEK	moss lamp
mappa	MAP-pah	visceral membrane

mikiksugut	mee-KEEK-soo-goot	bait; fish viscera placed on the hook as bait to attract prey fish
miliit	mee-LEET	freckles or little brown blotches on the skin
nanurluk	nah-NOOR-look	giant polar bear
natqut	naht-KOOT	qulliq flame adjusters
Nigvik	NEEG-veek	name
nungniit	noo-NG-neet	freckles or little brown blotches on the skin
nutaraq	noo-tah-RAHK	child
paijaa	pay-YAH	evil snow spirits
pana	PAH-nah	snow knife
panik	PAH-neek	daughter
paniqutiga	pah-NEEK-oo-tee-gah	my little daughter
Paurnga'naaq	pawr-NGAH-nahk	my dear little Paurngat
Paurngat	pow-RNGAT	name (meaning "blue berries")
pihiq	pee-HIQ	song
pijitsirarniq	pee-yeet-see-RAH-neek	a life of service
piliriqatigiingniq	pee-lee-REE-kah-tee-geen-gneek	working together
Publaligaq	poo-blah-lee-GAHK	name
qaggiq	KAHG-gik	a large iglu made for celebration purposes; also the name of the celebrations held in this iglu
qajait	KAH-yah-eet	kayaks
qajaq	KAH-yahk	kayak
qaliujaaqpait	kah-lee-oo-YAHK-pah-eet	roman orthography
qallunaat	kah-LOO-naht	white people
qamutiik	KAH-moo-teek	sled
qamutiit	KAH-moo-teet	sleds
qanniujaaqpait	kahn-nee-oo-YAHK-pah-eet	syllabics

qarjuqsaq	KAHR-jook-sahk	a piece of metal bent inward to hook fish in the mouth
qarmaq	KAHR-mahk	traditional sod house
qaugaugait	KAH-oog-ah-oog-AIT	little children
qaumaniqsiurialaurniarama	KOW-mah-neek-see-oo-ree-ah-lah-oor-nee-ah-rah-mah	I am going to go and cast light under a hole
qiliqsinat	KEE-lerk-see-naht	glands
Qisarua'naaq	KEE-sah-roo-ah-NAHK	name
Quinaksaut	koo-ee-NAHK-sah-oot	name
qulliq	KOO-leek	seal oil lamp
qullit	KOO-leet	seal oil lamps
Qurviujat	koor-vee-oo-ee-AHT	place name
samungaa	sah-moo-NGAH-ah	way down there
Sarvaqtuurmiut	sahr-VAHK-toor-mee-oot	people from Sarvaqtuuq
savgut	sahv-GOOT	snow depth tester
taqqut	tahk-KOOT	wick trimmers
Tasirjuaq	tah-seer-joo-AHK	place name
taunimiik	tah-oo-nee-MEEK	oh, a human scent in the air
tiluut	tee-LOOT	a stick or bone used to knock snow off
tipjaq	teep-YAHK	the weight of a hook, usually made of a bulb of walrus tusk or caribou antler anchored on the hook
ulu	OO-loo	crescent knife traditionally used by women
uluaqutiga	oo-loo-ah-KOO-tee-gah	my little cheek
Utuni	oo-too-NEE	name

ᑭᓇᐅᓂᖓ
BIOGRAPHY

ᒫᑯᓯ ᑲᓗᐊᖅ ᓈᓚᒃᐸᓚᐅᖅᑕᖏᓐᓂᒃ ᐊᓈᓇᖓᑕ ᐃᓐᓇᐃᑦᑐ ᐊᕐᕕᐊᕐᒥ ᐅᓂᒃᑳᖅᑐᐊᖏᓐᓂᒃ ᑎᑎᕋᖅᑲᑦᑕᖅᓯᒪᔪᖅ, ᑕᐃᒪᙵᓂᑦ 1970 ᐊᕐᕌᒍᖏᓐᓂ. ᖃᑦᑐᓈᑎᑑᓕᖅᑎᒃᐸᓚᐅᖅᑕᖏᑦ ᑎᑎᖅᑐᒐᖅᑐᓂᒋᑦᑐ, ᓴᖅᑭᑎᑦᑎᕙᒃᑐᓂ ᖁᕕᐊᒋᔭᐅᔪᓂᒃ ᓱᕈᓯᕐᓄᑦ ᐃᓐᓇᕐᓄᑦᑐ. ᑖᒃᑯᐊ ᐅᓂᒃᑳᓕᐊᓇᕙᓚᐅᖅᑕᖏᑦ ᐊᓯᖏᑦ ᐱᓕᕆᐊᕆᓯᒪᔭᖏᑦ ᒪᐃᔭᐅᓯᒪᔪᖅ ᐊᕐᕕᐊᓄᑦ, ᑲᑎᒪᔨᐅᖃᑦᑕᖅᓯᒪᓪᓗᓂᓗ ᐊᒥᓱᒐᓚᖕᓄᑦ ᐅᑭᐅᖅᑕᖅᑐᒥ, ᐱᕙᑦᓚᐊᔪᓂᒃ ᑎᑎᕋᖅᑲᑦᑕᖅᓯᒪᔪᖅ ᐋᖅᑭᒃᓯᐃᔨᐅᓯᒪᔪᕐᓗ, ᐊᒻᒪᓗ ᐃᖅᑲᓇᐃᔭᖅᑲᑦᑕᖅᓯᒪᒋᑐᖅ ᒐᕙᒪᑐᖅᑲᒃᑯᓐᓄᑦ. ᒫᑯᓯ ᐃᖅᑲᐅᒪᔭᐅᕙᒃᐳᖅ ᐃᓚᓕᐅᑎᑦᑎᐊᖅᓯᒪᓚᐅᕐᓂᖓᓄᑦ ᓄᓇᓕᖏᓐᓄᑦ, ᐊᒻᒪᓗ ᑐᓴᐅᒪᔭᐅᓕᖅᑎᑦᑎᔨᐅᓚᐅᖅᐳᖅ ᑐᑭᓯᓂᕐᒥᒃ ᐃᓄᐃᑦ ᐱᖅᑯᓯᖏᓐᓂᒃ ᓄᓇᕐᔪᐊᓕᒫᒧᑦ.

Mark Kalluak collected stories from his mother and other Elders around Arviat, Nunavut, starting in the 1970s. He translated and illustrated them himself, creating works that have been enjoyed by young and old alike. Along with preserving traditional Inuit stories, Mark served as mayor of Arviat, as board member for various organizations in the North, was a journalist and newspaper editor, and held federal positions. He is remembered as an integral part of his community, and for spreading Inuit culture throughout the world.

Inhabit Media Inc.
Iqaluit • Toronto